STAR TREK

365

THE ORIGINAL SERIES

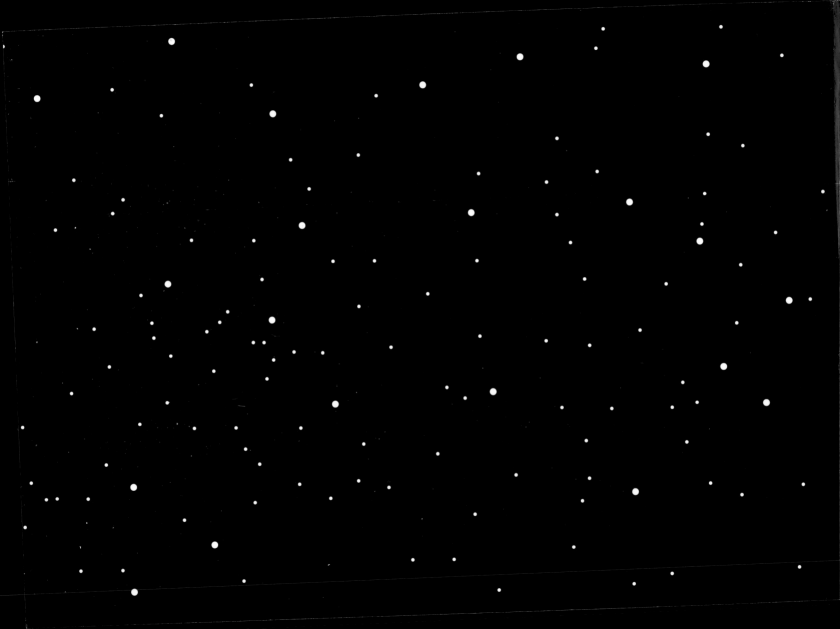

STAR TREK 365

THE ORIGINAL SERIES

BY PAULA M. BLOCK WITH TERRY J. ERDMANN

ABRAMS, NY

Star Trek did not spring full-grown from the mind of Gene Roddenberry as Athena did from the brow of Zeus. That's a myth, and I can say so because I was there. *Star Trek* was born and grew over a five-year period, with Gene at the core of it all and with the input of a number of people. You're wondering about five years, when *Star Trek* was on for only three? Well, follow along with me here.

In 1963, I had been in the MGM script-typing pool after serving as Samuel A. Peeples's secretary on a movie he wrote. When it didn't go, he moved on, and I stayed. One day, I noticed an ad on the job board for a production secretary on a series called *The Lieutenant*. I had been Sam's production secretary on three series at Revue (now Universal)—*Overland Trail*, *The Tall Man*, and *Frontier Circus*. I applied for *The Lieutenant* and landed it. Working for Del Reisman, the associate producer, put me in daily contact with producer/creator Gene Roddenberry. He learned I had written and sold three stories, two scripts, and a rewrite for television, and that my goal was to become a full-time writer.

In the spring of 1964, Gene's series about a young Marine Corps second lieutenant (played by Gary Lockwood) was just ending its first and only season. During that time, we had seen President John F. Kennedy assassinated—and his accused assassin murdered—on television. We had a new president and one foot in a war in Southeast Asia that would become the Vietnam conflict, and a series about a young Marine officer in that environment was kind of dicey in the network's mind.

One day in April, while we were waiting for final word on pickup or cancellation of *The Lieutenant*, Gene called me into his office and

handed me a small sheaf of typed pages. "Tell me what you think of that," he said.

It was about eleven pages. The title page read "Star Trek." It was an outline for a proposed one-hour series set in space, featuring the adventures of the spaceship *S.S. Yorktown*, captained by Robert April. The pages were sketchy but delineated several key characters and the general thrust of the show. At the time, a science fiction series with continuing characters was not a popular idea. The sci-fi shows then on the air were anthologies—*The Twilight Zone* and *The Outer Limits*—which did very well with new stories and new characters every week. But, to my mind, there was something very powerful in Gene's proposal and in those characters.

The next day, I went into his office and gave the pages back. "Who's going to play Mister Spock?" Gene slid a photo across his desk. It was of Leonard Nimoy, who had done a guest-starring role on *The Lieutenant*—and who had been the guest star in the first story I sold to television, on *The Tall Man*. And they say there are no coincidences in life. . . .

The story is well known that MGM and Arena Productions, its television arm under Norman Felton, had a first-look agreement with Roddenberry—and they turned *Star Trek* down. *The Lieutenant* was canceled, our office was packed up, and Gene started the rounds trying to interest someone in this science fiction project of his. It's also well known that Oscar Katz and Herb Solow of Desilu Studios decided to bank on *Star Trek*, and that after CBS turned it down, NBC ordered a pilot episode.

There were a lot of details to expand from those initial few pages

ION

while on the way to an hour-long pilot episode. Gene decided first that he would change the name of the ship to the "U.S.S. Enterprise." The dictionary definition of "enterprise" is "willingness to engage in risky or daring action." That certainly was in line with the adventures Star Trek proposed to undertake.

Another change was the captain's name. The more he thought about it, the more Gene was convinced that "Robert April" was too soft for the man he envisioned. He decided a short, hard-sounding name was in order. Enter Captain Christopher Pike.

While Gene wrote the script for "The Cage," Walter "Matt" Jefferies was assigned the job of coming up with the design of the Enterprise. Matt Jefferies not only had been a B-17 bomber copilot in World War II, he was also a private pilot and an aviation artist.

Gene contacted Sam Peeples, who had an extensive collection of science fiction magazines going back to the 1930s. Gene borrowed a number of issues that had interesting spaceship cover designs, handed them to Matt, and invited him to come up with "something else." Gene was clear he didn't want a standard upright-tube rocket ship, and Matt agreed. The Enterprise would be born in space and would never set down on a planet. Matt toiled over a series of renderings, and then Gene went down to the art department to look at them. Gene would point out pieces of the suggested designs, saying, "I like that," or "No on that." Then Matt would go back to the drawing board and start again. Eventually, the now-famous saucer-and-three-nacelles shape satisfied Gene, and the U.S.S. Enterprise was born. Matt gave her the number NCC-1701, the "NCC" being a combination of civilian and military aircraft numbers that was completely original.

Change continued to work its way in. Mister Spock originally was described as being a Martian with red skin. That, and his pointed ears, would set him apart visually from the rest of the cast. Gene and Fred Phillips, who applied the required red makeup on Leonard Nimoy for a screen test, were horrified to realize that, while it didn't look too bad in color (in which Star Trek would be broadcast), on a standard black-and-white set of the day, Leonard looked like an escapee from a minstrel show. Fred did some other trials, and Leonard's base makeup became what was then called "Chinese Yellow." Other makeup details started to be refined—pointed sideburns on all male crew members; Spock's ears individually molded by Fred Phillips.

Eventually, the pilot was fully cast and shot on the Desilu Culver lot, then edited, scored, dubbed, and presented to NBC early in 1965.

They thought it was "too cerebral."

But they requested another pilot. This was unheard of in NBC history.

After Gene thought about it, he commissioned Sam Peeples to write the second pilot. When the script came in, more changes followed.

Jeffrey Hunter and his then-wife, Dusty Bartlett, came in to confer with Gene about his Captain Pike character and the new script. Dusty did most of the talking. Gene told me that she and Jeff demanded certain conditions for the new pilot to which he could not in good conscience agree. Jeff Hunter was out.

Gene changed the captain's name to James Kirk and began casting a new lead. He found him in William Shatner, who had a brilliant history as a young leading man and the charm and physicality that would become Kirk's trademarks. Other characters were changed or dropped—including Number One, the female executive officer played by Majel Barrett—and new personalities made their appearance on the bridge. Notably, Mister Spock stayed, relatively unchanged and stalwart. Gene decreed that Spock must not smile; he had done so in "The Cage," and Gene felt it broke character.

One more thing was added: the opening narrative (absent in "The Cage") with its classic phrase, "to boldly go where no man has gone before." Gene revised it into its final form, but it originated with Sam Peeples.

"Where No Man Has Gone Before" was shot in the summer of 1965. *Voyage to the Bottom of the Sea* had debuted the previous fall, and by the time *Star Trek* (version 2) was presented to NBC, *Lost in Space* was also on the air. Both were pulling respectable ratings, proving that serialized science fiction was a viable venture. *Star Trek*'s second pilot was accepted by NBC, and we were given the order for the first season, with shooting to begin the following June.

Gene began bringing in writers early in 1966, calling on a number of prominent science fiction writers then working in the industry. Harlan Ellison, Richard Matheson, George Clayton Johnson, Robert Bloch, and Theodore Sturgeon were among the writers given assignments on *Star Trek*.

As we neared the commencement of shooting, more cast changes were made. George Takei and James Doohan, who had other roles in "Where No Man Has Gone Before," respectively became Helmsman Lieutenant Sulu and Chief Engineering Officer Lieutenant Commander Montgomery Scott. DeForest Kelley, whom Gene had known for a long time, was cast as Chief Medical Officer Leonard "Bones" McCoy. He was only ten years older than Bill Shatner (and Leonard Nimoy, for that matter), and Gene felt the character would be a better fit with Kirk and Spock—more of a partner instead of an older father figure. And Nichelle Nichols (who had guest starred on The *Lieutenant*) began her role as Lieutenant Uhura.

Although the civil rights movement had made significant advances

Gene was informed that certain stations in the South had notified NBC they would not carry *Star Trek* because of Nichelle Nichols's continuing role. Gene gave the American middle-finger salute known around the world as "flipping the bird" and said, "Too bad. They lose." OK, I cleaned that up for readers here, but Gene was right. Nichelle gained fans and supporters with her grace, beauty, and talent, and *Star Trek* was the better for it.

We probably had five or six shows in the can, with Kirk giving his name as "James T. [later explained in the animated series episode 'Bem' as 'Tiberius'] Kirk," before Bob Justman, our associate producer, suddenly remembered that the tombstone on which Gary Mitchell had carved Kirk's name in "Where No Man" read something else. He was right: The name there was "James R. Kirk"! Gene took in that information with a shrug and a grin: "Gary was a mere human, after all. *He made a mistake!*"

Every show evolves as it shoots. At its base, this comes from the scripts and is amplified by the actors as they grow into their characters. Kirk's strong and adventurous captain was balanced by Spock's calm, thoughtful logic and McCoy's passion and emotion. We soon discovered that a caustic give-and-take between Spock and McCoy (played brilliantly by Nimoy and Kelley, respectively) led to this kind of exchange becoming a fun moment in many scripts. After thirteen episodes, we lost Yeoman Rand (Grace Lee Whitney) and gained Nurse Christine Chapel (Majel Barrett). Personal characteristics, abilities, and the family of our characters began to be revealed. Who knew Uhura could sing, or Spock could play the Vulcan harp, or Kirk had a brother and a nephew, or Sulu harbored a talent for swordplay?

One of the key changes came when Gene L. Coon was hired as producer at the end of the first thirteen episodes, while Roddenberry moved up to executive producer. There is no doubt Gene Coon's polished writing and sense of humor gave more tone to the evolving stories. John D. F. Black and Steve Carabatsos served one after the other as story editors during the spring, summer, and fall of 1966. And in late autumn, after I had written two scripts and done a heavy rewrite on another, Gene moved me into the story editor's position. He said, "You've been on this show since the beginning. You know it as well as I do." At twenty-seven, I was the youngest story editor in town and one of the few female writers on a series staff.

As the end of the 1966-67 season approached, we were aware that *Star Trek*'s future might not be in the stars—or on NBC. While Gene did tap into the science fiction network by asking for support from some of the established genre writers who had contributed to the show, the larger response came from uncounted *Star Trek* fans. (They were uncounted because they weren't "Nielsen families" and so weren't reflected in the official ratings.)

We had always had a strong mail response. The first week on air drew a bag of fan mail. The second week, three bags arrived. And it kept growing and growing, until Desilu turned the avalanche of mail over to a professional firm to handle the responses. We did get the more interesting letters in the office, but even we didn't realize how large the fan base really was. The fans heard about a possible cancellation and overwhelmed NBC with mail. Ultimately, NBC gave us a renewal.

As we prepared to begin the second season, I sat down with each of the actors for a personal chat: "You've been living in the skin of this character for a year. Tell me what you know about him or her." Not surprisingly, these dedicated, intelligent people had evolved character nuances for their roles and, occasionally, background histories. William Shatner had given a lot of thought to it and gave Gene a long treatise on Captain James T. Kirk. I asked DeForest Kelley if Doctor McCoy had any family—a son, perhaps? Blue eyes sparkling, he told me he felt McCoy had a broken marriage and a daughter. In the show's bible, I named her "Joanna," but I never got to use that.

One last character was added to the cast. Gene had been impressed by the impact that the Beatles had on America (and the world) and created Ensign Pavel Chekov, the Russian navigator who had "that haircut"—played by Walter Koenig, who had to grow into the hair. He was a talented young actor and a great addition to the crew.

In early 1968, in the middle of the second season, Bjo Trimble, a well-known figure in fandom, heard that *Star Trek* might not be renewed, and she began organizing a drive to let NBC know that "the fen" were not happy. The network began to directly receive massive amounts of protest mail. But the real capper was a march on NBC by fans. On March 31, 1968, President Lyndon Johnson made the startling announcement in a speech on NBC that he would not seek or accept a nomination for the upcoming presidential election. This was followed by an on-air announcement that *Star Trek* would return in the fall. In other words, "You can stop writing the letters now!" We had our third season.

And the beat went on (as they used to say). *Star Trek*'s characters evolved—partly from Gene Roddenberry, partly from Gene Coon and later John Meredyth Lucas, partly from me, partly from our writers, and partly from our actors. It was not one mind, but many—a creation by people who lived and loved the show. More than forty years later, audiences still watch and enjoy *Star Trek*—the original series and its many iterations. Quite an accomplishment for a show that almost didn't make it.

—D. C. Fontana

Dorothy "D. C." Fontana served as writer and story editor for many beloved episodes of *Star Trek: The Original Series*, after having worked on the show's development as Gene Roddenberry's personal assistant. She was also instrumental in the development of *Star Trek: The Next Generation* and has written many scripts for other television series. She currently lives in Los Angeles, where she teaches screenwriting at the American Film Institute.

PREFACE

A confession: I am a geek, both by nature and by profession.

Nature came first. I've always had a fascination with things that set me apart from "the cool crowd." When the Beatles broke in America, I was going through a James Bond phase. All the other girls talked constantly about the Fab Four. No one wanted to talk about *Goldfinger*. So I was a cultural outcast—which was fine considering I'd never much liked those girls anyway. (I did, by the way, come to adore the Beatles, particularly George, but that's a different story.)

I was in high school when *Star Trek* debuted. My family didn't have a color TV, but the *Enterprise* crew's weekly adventures hooked me from day one. I'd always liked *The Twilight Zone* and *The Outer Limits*, but those were anthology shows, with wildly varying premises and without continuing characters. *Star Trek*, on the other hand, was episodic fare, an intelligent science fiction series that invited me to zip through the stars every week with a group of familiar characters. And what characters! Yes, the ship was impressive, the gizmos were fabulous, and the aliens—most of them, anyway—were fascinating. But I must admit that I really watched it for Kirk's swagger, Spock's cool, and McCoy's palpable humanity. I loved the byplay among them, which bespoke friendships that went beyond words. It inspired me to write *Star Trek* stories—stories that I couldn't show anyone because, well, they were geeky stories.

Flash-forward to college and the fateful day I saw a small ad in the campus newspaper announcing the formation of a *Star Trek* fan club. Intrigued, I went to the first meeting and found myself in a room full of people who shared my passion and who were familiar with every aspect of *The Original Series*. And on that day, my life changed.

The student who'd placed the ad was Lori Chapek (later Lori Chapek-Carleton). You could call Lori my "entry-level drug" to fandom. Lori talked about fanzines—amateur publications filled with fan-written *Star Trek* stories—and said the club would publish one. (In fact, Lori and her T'Kuhtian Press would go on to publish *dozens* of issues of a fanzine called *Warped Space*.) She talked about conventions and said she'd like to throw one right on the campus! Somehow, Lori made *that* happen, too. In fact, MediaWest*Con is still held every year in Lansing, Michigan—and Lori and her husband, cartoonist Gordon Carleton, still run it, more than three and a half decades later.

Those years in active fandom were extraordinarily fun. I traveled to conventions all over the country. I contributed to lots of fanzines and made a ton of friends. Eventually, realizing that one has to earn a living in the real world, I *gaffiated* (a geeky verb derived from the acronym "Getting Away From Fandom") and pursued a career in publishing. Ironically, that career would bring me *back* to *Star Trek* years later. The licensing department at Paramount Pictures needed someone with a professional publishing background who also knew a lot about *Star Trek*—and I was lucky enough to be in the right place at the right time. That's when the "geek by profession" portion of my life kicked in. For the next two decades, I oversaw the studio's *Star Trek* publishing program. And I won't deny it—it was cool.

Star Trek still means a great deal to me. I have the deepest admiration for the men and women who worked in front of the cameras and behind the scenes, making the show the iconic marvel that it was and still is. And I can't tell you how happy I am that Dorothy "D. C." Fontana agreed to write the introduction to this book; she's been a hero of mine since I first read her name in the series' credits.

Star Trek 365 is a celebration of The Original Series. My hope is that this book will evoke in you a bit of the same excitement that colors my personal Star Trek memories. Then you'll understand why so many people, geeks and non-geeks alike, were drawn to the program decades ago, and why so many people lined up at theaters in May 2009 when the newest Star Trek movie opened. My collaborator in this effort is my husband, Terry J. Erdmann, author of numerous behind-the-scenes books on film and television. He, too, is a geek, although his primary infatuation is with rock 'n' roll rather than science fiction. Terry has been entrenched in the entertainment industry longer than I have, but for this particular book, my geek credentials trumped his, so I got to sit in the captain's chair.

Live long, prosper, and set course one more time for the Final Frontier.

—Paula M. Block

BEFORE *STAR TREK* WAS *STAR TREK*

In April 1964, former Air Force pilot and Los Angeles police officer Gene Roddenberry approached Herb Solow, the head of Desilu Studios' television department, with a concept for a science fiction series. Roddenberry was no rookie when it came to showbiz. He'd already sold a number of scripts to producers, including episodes of *Highway Patrol* and *Have Gun Will Travel*. He'd also created and produced a well-received but short-lived series called *The Lieutenant*, starring Gary Lockwood (who would appear in the *Star Trek* episode "Where No Man Has Gone Before") in the title role, and Robert Vaughn (soon to be cast as the lead in *The Man from U.N.C.L.E.*). Solow liked what he heard and offered Roddenberry a script development deal.

Roddenberry's original pitch, which included character and set descriptions, began:

Star Trek *is a* Wagon Train *concept—built around characters who travel to worlds "similar" to our own, and meet the action-adventure-drama which becomes our stories. Their transportation is the cruiser* S.S. Yorktown, *performing a well-defined and long-range Exploration-Science-Security mission which helps create our format.*

The time is "Somewhere in the future." It could be 1995 or maybe even 2995. In other words, close enough to our own time for our continuing characters to be fully identifiable as people like us, but far enough into the future for galaxy travel to be thoroughly established (happily eliminating the need to encumber our stories with tiresome scientific explanation).

Several studios, including CBS (which produced Desilu's *The Lucy Show*), passed on *Star Trek*, but ultimately NBC stepped up and bought the project—modified in the details but not in the basic concept (for example, the *S.S. Yorktown* became the *U.S.S. Enterprise*).

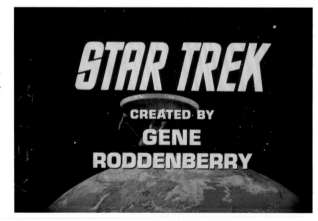

Gene Roddenberry's original pitch for *Star Trek* included descriptions of five main characters:

Robert M. April—The 'skipper,' about thirty-four . . . a space age Captain Horatio Hornblower, lean and capable both mentally and physically . . . a colorfully complex personality . . . capable of action and decision which can verge on the heroic—and at the same time lives a continual battle with self-doubt and loneliness of command.

By the time the show went to pilot, April had been rechristened "Christopher Pike," although other details remained the same. And, in fact, much of the above also fits the persona of the captain who would replace Pike when the show finally hit the airwaves, James T. Kirk. One big difference: James Kirk would never admit to feelings of "self-doubt," nor would he dwell on "the loneliness of command." The *Enterprise* would be the only permanent fixture in his life, a demanding mistress who left no time for loneliness.

The Executive Officer—Never referred to as anything but "Number One," this officer is female. Almost mysteriously female, in fact—slim and dark in a Nile Valley way . . . An extraordinarily efficient officer . . .

Number One appeared in "The Cage," but she didn't survive beyond that doomed pilot. Twenty-three years later, in *Star Trek: The Next Generation*, Roddenberry would refer to the (male) first officer of that show's *Enterprise* as "Number One."

Ship's Doctor—Phillip Boyce, an unlikely space traveler. At the age of fifty-one, he's worldly, humorously cynical. . . . Captain April's only real confidant, "Bones" Boyce . . . measures each new landing in terms of relative annoyance, rather than excitement.

All of which pretty much sums up the personality of Leonard "Bones" McCoy.

The First Lieutenant—The captain's right-hand man, the working level commander of all the ship's functions . . . His name is "Mister Spock." And the first view of him can be almost frightening. . . . Probably half Martian, he has a slightly reddish complexion and semi-pointed ears. But strangely, Mister Spock's quiet temperament is in dramatic contrast to his satanic look. . . .

Spock would indeed become the captain's right-hand man, replacing Number One as the first officer. His ears would remain semi-pointed, but he would be born on a different world, resulting in skin of an altered hue.

The Captain's Yeoman—"Colt" . . . blonde and with a shape even a uniform could not hide . . . Serves as Robert April's secretary, reporter, bookkeeper . . . she is not dumb; she is very female, disturbingly so.

In "The Cage," Yeoman Colt was a strawberry blonde; when *Star Trek* eventually went to series, Yeoman *Rand* was a flashier, more traditional blonde. As for "a shape even a uniform could not hide," both actresses followed that direction to perfection.

Within his pitch to Herb Solow, Gene Roddenberry provided the germs for twenty-five different adventures. Some of the following may sound strangely familiar; it's clear that many future *Star Trek* episodes sprang from these wafer-thin descriptions.

THE NEXT CAGE. The desperation of our series lead, caged and on exhibition like an animal, then offered a mate.

THE DAY CHARLIE BECAME GOD. The accidental occurrence of infinite power to do all things in the hands of a very finite man.

PRESIDENT CAPONE. A parallel world, Chicago ten years after Al Capone won and imposed gangland statutes upon the nation.

THE WOMEN. Duplicating a page from the "Old West"; hanky-panky aboard with a cargo of women destined for a far-off colony.

TORX. An alien intelligence . . . pure thought and no body, which "devours" intelligence . . . Near starvation for eons, it has been frantically seeking precisely the type of "food" the Earth could supply in quantity.

THE CAGE

"When dreams become more important than reality, you give up travel, building, creating. You even forget how to repair the machines left behind by your ancestors. You just sit, living and reliving other lives left behind. . . ."
—Vina

The *Enterprise* picks up radio transmissions that indicate there are survivors from a crashed spacecraft on the surface of Talos IV. A landing party, including Captain Pike, Lieutenant Spock, and Dr. Boyce, beams down to find an encampment of elderly male scientists—and a beautiful young woman named Vina. The group claims to have been marooned on the planet for nearly twenty years; Vina was an infant at the time of the crash, which killed her parents, and the scientists have cared for her ever since. When Boyce expresses some skepticism about how the group has survived in such perfect health, Vina offers to show Pike their secret. Instead, she lures him to a secluded ledge . . . and then vanishes into thin air! Before Pike can comprehend what has transpired, a door opens in the rock face and some aliens with oversize craniums emerge, rendering

Pike unconscious and taking him to an underground chamber. As his crew attempts to rescue him, Pike awakens to find himself trapped in a cage, observed by more of the aliens he briefly glimpsed on the surface. They are Talosians—natives of this world—and they possess extremely powerful telepathic abilities. They created the illusion of the encampment and its inhabitants—all but one, that is. Vina is real, the only survivor of that crash from two decades ago. Apparently, she, too, is an involuntary "guest" of the Talosians—another inhabitant of their intergalactic zoo. The Talosians force Pike to experience a series of fantasies, all of which feature some incarnation of Vina. For some reason, the aliens seem determined to make Pike grow fond of his fellow prisoner. But why?

When NBC programming executives first signed the production deal with Desilu to create a *Star Trek* pilot, they had little faith that the relatively small company actually possessed the know-how to complete such a complicated project. Desilu, after all, was known for much simpler fare, light comedies such as *The Lucy Show*, *Make Room for Daddy*, and *The Andy Griffith Show*. But after Roddenberry and company screened a print of "The Cage," NBC execs were surprised by their own reactions: It was, they realized, far better than they'd ever expected. In fact, it was *too* good. "It's too cerebral," they explained, showing little faith in the intelligence of their own viewers. They were nervous about the Orion slave girl's gyrations—and even more nervous about the character of Mister Spock, whose satanic countenance might lose the network important viewers in the Bible Belt states. And so the pilot was rejected.

But surprisingly, those same executives were willing to admit that they'd been wrong about Desilu's production capabilities, and in a move that was unprecedented at the time, they offered to finance a *second* pilot for *Star Trek*. The offer included caveats. The network wanted changes in the cast, including the actors playing the yeoman and the doctor, and insisted that two characters be eliminated altogether: the female named Number One (because who would take orders from a female officer?), and the alien Mister Spock (those ears!).

Roddenberry figured that he could eventually talk the network into keeping one of the two characters, but not both. He liked his devilish-looking alien. But he also liked actress Majel Barrett. And so, quipped Barrett, years after the fact, Roddenberry decided to keep the Vulcan and marry the woman, "because Gene didn't think Leonard [Nimoy] would have it the other way around."

Concerns about time and money inadvertently caused the *Star Trek* producers to stumble into a spectacular case of "less is more." They realized that landing a ship the size of the *Enterprise* on a planet at the beginning of every episode would take up far too much "story" time, and that same activity would burn up far too much of the visual effects budget. Gene Roddenberry, proving once again that he was a visionary, suggested that the crew simply "dematerialize" and then reappear in another location. He called the technology to accomplish this the "transporter," and the act of doing it "beaming." At first, they considered including an animated beam extending from the ship to the planet surface, but those same budgetary concerns eliminated that possibility. In the end, dematerializing and rematerializing was deemed the best idea.

In order to sell the trick, the Howard A. Anderson Company, a Hollywood optical company, photographed backlit grains of shiny aluminum powder dropped in front of a black backdrop. With the help of a matching musical cue written by Alexander Courage, the transporter effect would go on to win the hearts not only of viewers, but of scientists and other technology advocates worldwide.

By the way, James T. Kirk never said, "Beam me up, Scotty," on the show, regardless of what you may have heard. He *did* say, "Two to beam up," and other variations of that, but the best "remembered" bit of *Star Trek* dialogue seems to have evolved on its own.

The role of Captain Christopher Pike required an actor with personal warmth and physical attractiveness. Plus he had to be athletic, believable as a leader—and acceptable to the network, the studio, and the sponsors. Seasoned actor Jeffrey Hunter fit the bill: His many film credits included a costarring role alongside John Wayne in director John Ford's masterpiece *The Searchers* and the lead role of Jesus Christ in the biblical epic *King of Kings*.

Pike's dialogue in "The Cage" includes lines that convey the character's desire to resign his commission and retire from Starfleet. By the conclusion of the episode, he's changed his mind—unlike Jeffrey Hunter, who chose to return to feature film work rather than stay aboard Roddenberry's wagon train to the stars. A few years later, Hunter was injured while shooting a movie in Spain; within a few weeks, he had suffered multiple strokes and a cerebral hemorrhage, and a skull fracture was discovered after he had a fall. He died during surgery on May 27, 1969, a week before the final episode of *Star Trek* aired.

Gene Roddenberry originally wanted Spock's skin to have a red tint, but early tests showed that red makeup didn't translate well on black-and-white television (it appeared to be jet black!). Since the majority of the public watched TV in black and white in the mid-1960s, Fred Phillips suggested a change from red to Max Factor's "Chinese Yellow" makeup. The color—a kind of yellowish green—appeared a nice neutral gray in black and white, while on color TV sets it made Spock look distinctly alien.

For the episode's other aliens, the Talosians, Roddenberry initially had even more extravagant plans: He wanted them to resemble crabs. But as they were being developed, the production staff realized that crabs might come across as too "1950s horror movie," which was the antithesis of what Roddenberry wanted the series to project. Making the Talosians humanoid served two purposes: Humanoid Talosians were likely to have more empathy for an injured human female, and, perhaps more important, they would be far less expensive to create. To enhance their "alien-ness," diminutive actresses were cast and their dialogue dubbed by male actors. Legendary sculptor and prop designer Wah Chang took on the task of fabricating oversize foam latex heads for the Talosians. To give the highly advanced aliens a truly cerebral look, Wah Chang placed rubber bladder "veins" just beneath the latex "skin." By connecting the bladders via tiny hidden tubes to squeeze bulbs held just off camera, crew members could pump the bulbs on cue, creating a convincing portrait of pulsing neural activity as the Talosians telepathically communicated with one another.

The role of Vina had not yet been cast when the filmmakers began conducting preproduction makeup tests. Actress Majel Barrett, already set to play Number One, offered to wear the green "Orion slave girl" makeup for one test, so the producers could see how the color looked on film. The day after the sample footage had been shot, the producers gathered to view the results. To their surprise, Barrett's skin didn't look at all green; it appeared to be her normal skin tone. Concerned that the Eastman film stock they were using couldn't distinguish that particular shade of green, the filmmakers conducted the test again, this time smearing much darker green greasepaint onto the actress's face. But the next day, once again the test came back with Barrett "in the pink"—with perhaps just a hint of a green tinge. A frantic call to the film-processing lab revealed the problem: Lab technicians had assumed that the cinematographer got the camera settings wrong . . . and they had "stayed up all night trying to color-correct the film."

Vina could rely on the Talosians' powers of illusion to transform her instantly from one manifestation of beauty to another. Her alter ego, actress Susan Oliver, had no such luck; for her, the transformations took much longer—particularly the changes in skin color. Roddenberry's script to "The Cage" described the Orion slave girl as "Wild! Green skin, glistening as if oiled." Little did anyone know how prophetic the word "oiled" would be. Prior to filming, makeup designer Fred Phillips would carefully slather a pigmented mixture of Max Factor greasepaint across the areas of Oliver's body that weren't covered by her skimpy costume (and there was *far* more skin than costume). However, there are always some sections of skin that are oilier than others, and the green makeup had a tendency to blotch, cake, and crack. At times, repairing the damage seemed to take as much time as applying the makeup had taken in the first place. Finally, Phillips was assigned a makeup assistant whose sole purpose was to be at the ready whenever the cameras stopped rolling—and then rush in to help Phillips touch up Oliver before filming started again.

The large metal spearhead that Christopher Pike uses to kill the Kaylar on Rigel VII was a recycled prop from defunct studio RKO. Once a major player in Hollywood film production and distribution, RKO eventually fell on hard times, closing down for good in 1957. Later that year, Desi Arnaz and Lucille Ball (who once had been an RKO contract player) purchased the studio's Hollywood and Culver City facilities for their company. In 1967, Ball sold Desilu to Gulf & Western, where it was merged into another recent acquisition, Paramount Pictures. RKO's props apparently were included in the transaction, because they were available when *Star Trek*'s prop master came looking.

The spearhead measures approximately thirty inches in length and is seven and a half inches wide.

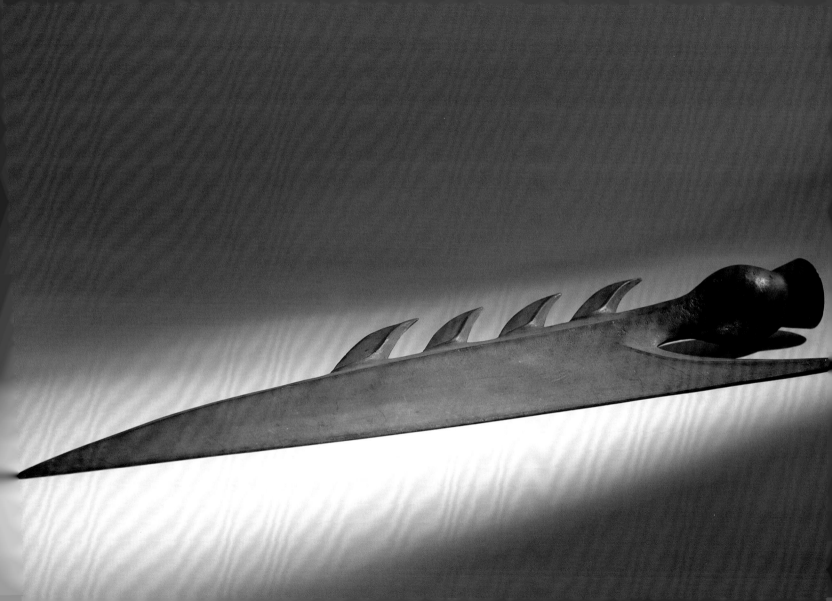

WHERE NO MAN HAS GONE BEFORE

The *Enterprise* finds the flight recorder of the *Valiant*, a starship reported lost two centuries earlier. The content of these records worries Captain Kirk: The *Valiant* suffered damage and casualties when it crossed an energy field located at the edge of the galaxy—and not long after, the *Valiant*'s captain ordered the self-destruction of his own vessel. Kirk wants to provide a full report to Starfleet of the danger at hand, so he orders the *Enterprise* into the same energy field. Like the *Valiant*, the *Enterprise* sustains physical damage and loses several crewmen. Lieutenant Commander Gary Mitchell, the *Enterprise's* helmsman and a friend of Kirk's since Starfleet Academy, emerges from the experience a changed man, with phenomenally increased intelligence and dangerous powers. First Officer Spock quickly grasps what Kirk does not wish to: that Mitchell is mutating into a being with godlike abilities. The captain must deal with Mitchell before he becomes even more powerful—or the *Enterprise* will suffer the same deadly fate that befell the *Valiant*.

"Where No Man Has Gone Before" was actually the second pilot NBC ordered for *Star Trek*. Many elements of the sets and wardrobe that had been used in the first pilot, "The Cage," were recycled here, but there were a few "cosmetic" adjustments. Jeffrey Hunter, who'd sat in the command chair as Captain Pike for "The Cage," chose not to reprise his role. William Shatner replaced him, bringing to the newly created character of Captain Kirk an energetic intensity that emphasized the physical nature of the man in the captain's chair. And right from the start, James T. Kirk's willingness to resolve a bad situation with his fists—more often than not ripping his shirt in the process—made him a perfect action icon for the era.

Despite the network's desire to get rid of "the satanic guy with the
pointy eyebrows," the character of Mister Spock returned for the series' second pilot—but he was still a work in progress. His personality
is more developed in this episode, though, than it was in "The Cage":
He's less emotional, he doesn't shout as much, and he manages
to limit the intensity of his smile to a small smirk as he politely exchanges gibes with Kirk in the ship's rec area. Spock even mentions
for the first time that yes, one of his ancestors *did* marry a human,
but apparently he is too embarrassed to explain that the "ancestor"
is his father and the "bad blood" comes from his mother.

"There's never been a visual effects artist to match Albert Whitlock," says *Star Trek* graphic artist Michael Okuda. "*Star Trek* was astonishingly lucky to have had his talent."

Matte painter Albert Whitlock is universally acknowledged as one of the greatest visual effects artists of all time. His motion picture career began in England, where he worked with Alfred Hitchcock on *The 39 Steps* and *The Lady Vanishes*. After moving to the United States, Whitlock created amazing imagery for such films as *Darby O'Gill and the Little People* before rejoining Hitchcock for *The Birds*, *Torn Curtain*, and many other projects. Throughout the 1960s and 1970s, Whitlock's matte paintings enhanced dozens of films, from *The Sting* to *The Man Who Would Be King*; he won two Academy Awards, the first for his work on *Earthquake* and the second for *The Hindenberg*.

Whitlock also created numerous mattes for *Star Trek*. Shown here is his portrayal of the automated lithium-cracking facility of Delta Vega, where Kirk hoped to exile Gary Mitchell. Whitlock's painting conveyed what the filmmakers could not: an eerie alien landscape that would have been impossible—or impossibly expensive—to duplicate on the studio lot.

The *Enterprise* crew looked slightly different when they first embarked on their trek across the stars: Spock, who had worn the blue of the sciences division in "The Cage," found himself garbed in gold—the color of command personnel—for "Where No Man Has Gone Before," and Sulu, who would later wear gold as the ship's helmsman, was uniformed in blue. At least Sulu had a plausible excuse: For this one episode only, Sulu is shown working as a physicist in the sciences department. Scotty, making his first appearance as the ship's engineer, also wears a gold uniform, as opposed to the red that later would be designated "ship's services."

In the beginning, all of the crew's tunics were made of velour—a favorite fashion fabric during the 1960s. But velour has the unfortunate habit of shrinking with every cleaning. So the shirts got smaller and smaller . . . and soon vanished entirely from the series.

Doctor McCoy, who would join the crew in "The Corbomite Maneuver" (the first episode filmed after the two pilots, but the tenth broadcast), dodged these troubles for a time by being one of the few characters to sport a second set of threads: While working down in the ship's sickbay, he wore a short-sleeved shirt of a more durable synthetic fabric. Note that, while his hair hasn't quite hit the JFK-esque length that it would remain for the rest of the series, DeForest Kelley already has the good doctor's sardonic attitude down pat in this early publicity still.

"THE VESSEL: The *U.S.S. Enterprise* is a spaceship, official designation 'starship class.' Somewhat larger than a present-day naval cruiser, it is the largest and most modern-type vessel in the Starfleet Service. It has a crew of 430 persons, approximately one-third of them female. . . .

"The Saucer Section of the vessel (at the top of which is our command bridge) is eleven decks thick at the middle. The Engineering Section (to which the two engine nacelles are attached) is equally large and complex. . . . At the rear [is] a hangar deck large enough to [hold] a whole fleet of today's jetliners. Turbo elevators, which can run both vertically and horizontally, interconnect every deck and compartment of this huge vessel. . . .

"The *Enterprise*'s engines use matter and antimatter for propulsion, their annihilation of dual matter creating the fantastic power to warp space and exceed the speed of light. . . . Hyper-light speeds or space warp speeds are measured in 'Warp Factors.' Warp factor one is the speed of light—186,000 miles per second (or somewhat over six hundred million miles per hour). . . . Maximum safe speed is warp six. At warp eight, the vessel begins to show considerable strain. . . . Warp seven or eight are used only in emergencies. . . .

"The main weaponry of the *U.S.S. Enterprise* is its banks of 'ship's phasers,' which are artillery-sized versions of the hand phaser."
    —from the *Star Trek* writers' guide, third revision, dated April 17, 1967

This sketch, one of hundreds that Matt Jefferies drew while designing the *Starship Enterprise*, has a spherical main section and a hull that rides high above the two engine nacelles. For the final version, Jefferies modified the shape of the main section and moved the nacelles so that they rode high above the hull. Gene Roddenberry and the execs at Desilu quickly approved the new design, but the ship still had to receive a thumbs-up from NBC's executives. Jefferies asked the studio's woodworking department to build a rough model from balsa wood that could be displayed at an upcoming meeting scheduled with the network. Unfortunately, when he went to pick up the model, he discovered that while most of the starship's parts already had been lathed, the nacelles had not yet been cut. Rather than wait for the workers to form the missing pieces from balsa, Jefferies took two birch dowels and quickly glued them in place. At the NBC meeting, Roddenberry proudly displayed the new iteration of his ship, holding it by a string that Jefferies had tacked to the top. But just as Scotty would later state, you can't change the laws of physics; birch is heavier than balsa, and the weight of the nacelles made the comparatively lightweight model flip over. Roddenberry, who was focusing most of his attention on the executives in the room, hadn't noticed—leaving Jefferies in the awkward position of explaining to all that the ship was upside down.

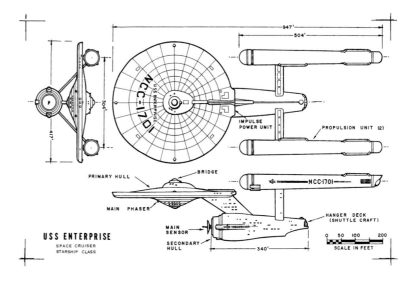

USS ENTERPRISE
SPACE CRUISER
STARSHIP CLASS

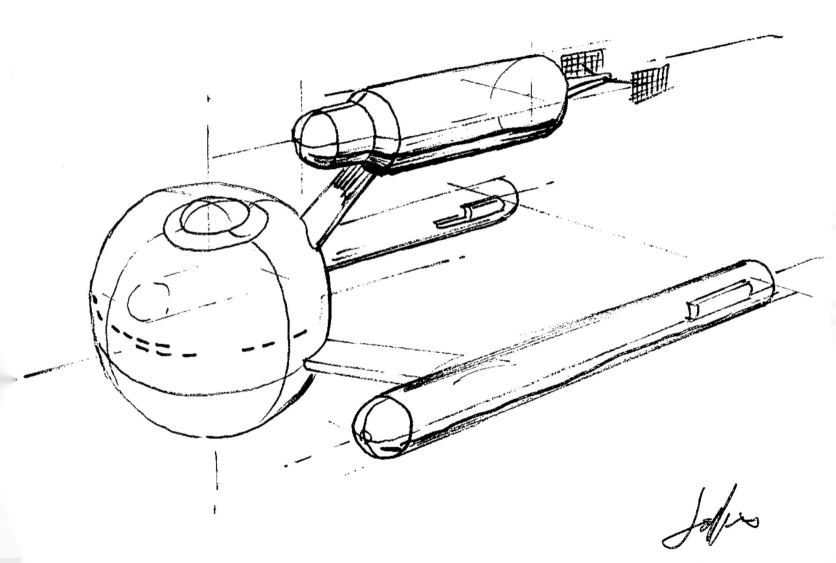

"THE CREW: International in origin, completely multiracial. But even in future century we will see some traditional trappings, ornaments, and styles that suggest the Asiatic, the Arabic, the Latin, etc. So far, Mister Spock has been our only crewman with bloodlines from another planet. . . .

"We like ways of using the crewmen (extras as well as actors) to help suggest the enormous diversity of our vessel. For example, playing a scene in leisure attire as our people pass in sports gear, obviously going to or coming from a gymnasium or such. Life aboard the *Enterprise* (believably, as in a present-day naval cruiser) is not all hard work and stern devotion to duty."

—from the *Star Trek* writers' guide, third revision, dated April 17, 1967

"CAPTAIN JAMES T. KIRK: Played by William Shatner, Kirk is about thirty-four, an academy graduate, rank of starship captain. A shorthand sketch of him might be 'a space-age Captain Horatio Hornblower' constantly on trial with himself, a strong, complex personality.

"With the starship out of communication with Earth and Starfleet bases for long periods of time, a starship captain has unusually broad powers over both the lives and welfare of his crew, as well as over Earth people and activities encountered during these voyages. . . . Kirk feels these responsibilities strongly and is fully capable of letting the worry and frustration lead him into error.

"He is also capable of fatigue and inclined to push himself beyond human limits, then condemn himself because he is not superhuman. The crew respects him, some almost to the point of adoration. At the same time, no senior officer aboard is fearful of using his own intelligence in questioning Kirk's orders and can themselves be strongly articulate up to the point where Kirk signifies his decision has been made. . . .

"Our captain is a veteran of hundreds of planet landings and space emergencies. He has a broad and highly mature perspective on command, fellow crewmen, and even on alien life customs, however strange or repugnant they seem when measured against Earth standards. . . .

"Aboard ship, Captain Kirk has only a few opportunities for anything approaching friendship. One exception is Mister Spock, a strange friendship based on logic, high mutual respect, and Spock's strong Vulcan loyalty to a commander. Another is with the ship's surgeon, Doctor McCoy, who has a legitimate professional need to constantly be aware of the state of the captain's mind and emotions. But on a 'shore leave,' away from the confines of self-imposed discipline, Jim Kirk is likely to play pretty hard, almost compulsively so. . . . He is, in short, a strong man forced by the requirements of his ship and career into the often lonely role of command, even lonelier because starship command is the most difficult and demanding task of the century."

—from the *Star Trek* writers' guide, third revision, dated April 17, 1967

"MISTER SPOCK: Played by Leonard Nimoy, this is the ship's science officer, in charge of all scientific departments aboard. As such, he is the ship's number two ranking officer and holds the rank of commander.

"His bridge position is at the library-computer station, which links the bridge to the vessel's intricate 'brain,' a highly sophisticated and advanced computer that interconnects all stations of the ship. From his central panel, Spock can tap resources of the entire computer system—including a vast micro-record library of man's history . . . plus all known information on other solar systems, Earth colonies, alien civilizations, a registry of all space vessels in existence, personnel information on any member of the *U.S.S. Enterprise*, or almost anything else needed in any of our stories. . . .

"Mister Spock's mother was human, his father a native of the planet Vulcan. This alien-human combination results in Mister Spock's slightly alien features, with the yellowish complexion and satanic pointed ears. . . . He has a strange Vulcan 'ESP' ability to merge his mind with another intelligence and read the thoughts there. He dislikes doing so since it deprives him of his proud stoic mannerisms and reveals too much of his inner self. . . .

"We now realize that Spock is capable of feeling emotion, but he denies this at every opportunity. On his own planet, to show emotion is considered the grossest of sins. He makes every effort to hide what he considers the 'weakness' of his half-human heredity."

—from the *Star Trek* writers' guide, third revision, dated April 17, 1967

U.S.S. ENTERPRISE
NCC-1701

"DOCTOR LEONARD 'BONES' McCOY: Played by DeForest Kelley, Doctor McCoy is senior ship's surgeon of the *U.S.S. Enterprise*, head of the Medical Department. As such, he has medical responsibilities for the health and welfare of the crew of the *Enterprise* and broad medical science responsibilities in areas of space exploration.

"Bones McCoy is the one man who can approach Captain Kirk on the most intimate personal levels relating to the captain's physical, mental, and emotional well-being. Indeed, he has the absolute duty to constantly keep abreast of the captain's condition and speak out openly to Kirk on this matter. McCoy is a very, very outspoken character, with more than a little cynical bite in his attitudes and observations on life. He has an acid wit, which results in sometimes shocking statements—which, under close scrutiny, carry more than a grain of truth about medicine, man, and society.

"Of all the men aboard our starship, McCoy is the least military. He is filled with idiosyncrasies, which fit the character and are his trademark. . . . McCoy is highly practical in the old 'general practitioner' sense, hates pills except when they are vitally needed, is not above believing that a little suffering is good for the soul. . . .

"McCoy is forty-five years of age, was married once—something of a mystery that ended unhappily in a divorce. He has a daughter, Joanna, who is twenty and in training as a nurse somewhere. . . . We suspect that it was the bitterness of this marriage and divorce which turned McCoy to the Space Services. He was born in Georgia in the United States and can be something of the gallant Southern Gentleman in social life, particularly with females. When the moment is right, a trace of his Southern accent will be heard."

—from the *Star Trek* writers' guide, third revision, dated April 17, 1967

"ENGINEERING OFFICER MONTGOMERY SCOTT: Played by James Doohan, Scott holds the rank of lieutenant commander, senior engineering officer on the *U.S.S. Enterprise*. With an accent that drips of heather and the Highlands, he is known to most as 'Scotty.'

"Scotty came up through the ranks, and his practical education is as broad as his formal training in engineering. He has rare mechanical capacity—many claim he can put an engine together with baling wire and glue . . . and make it run. He regards the *U.S.S. Enterprise* as his personal vessel and the engineering section as his private world, where even Captain James Kirk is merely a privileged trespasser.

"Engineering and spaceships are his life. His idea of a pleasant afternoon is tinkering in any engineering section of the vessel; he is totally unable to understand why any sane man would spend reading time on anything but technical manuals. He is strong minded, strong willed, and not incapable of telling off even a Starfleet captain who intrudes into what Scotty regards as his own private province and area of responsibilities.

"LIEUTENANT UHURA: Played by Nichelle Nichols, Communications Officer Uhura was born in the United States of Africa. Quick and intelligent, she is a highly efficient officer and expert in all ships' systems related to communications. Uhura is also a warm, highly female female off duty. She is something of a favorite in the Recreation Room during off-duty hours too, because she sings—old ballads as well as the newer space ballads—and she can do an impersonation at the drop of a communicator."

—from the *Star Trek* writers' guide, third revision, dated April 17, 1967

"LIEUTENANT SULU: Played by George Takei, Ship's Helmsman Sulu is mixed oriental in ancestry, Japanese predominating, [but] contemporary American in speech and manner. In fact, his attitude toward Asians is that they seem to him rather 'inscrutable.' Sulu fancies himself more of an Old World 'D'Artagnan' than anything else. He is a compulsive hobbyist; one week he may be fascinated by botany with the intention of that becoming his lifelong avocation, then another week we'll find he has switched to a determination of acquiring a galaxy-famous collection of alien firearms. And like all 'collectors,' he is forever giving his friends a thousand reasons why they, too, should take on the same hobby. . . .

"Although these bursts of enthusiasm make him something of a chatterbox, Sulu is a top officer and one of the most proficient helmsmen in the Starfleet Service. When the chips are down, he immediately becomes another character, a terse professional, whose every word and deed relate solely to the vessel and its safety. He has never had to receive the same order from Kirk twice."
—from the *Star Trek* writers' guide, third revision, dated April 17, 1967

"ENSIGN CHEKOV: Played by Walter Koenig, Ship's Navigator Pavel Andreievich Chekov is extremely proud of his Russian heritage. So proud, in fact, that he attributes—correctly or incorrectly—most scientific discoveries to that country and praises the virtues of native Russian products over all others. One of the *Enterprise*'s youngest officers, Chekov has a plucky sense of bravado. He is an excellent navigator—despite the fact that his internal magnetic needle seems to be permanently stuck on his homeland."

"TRICORDER: A portable sensor-computer-recorder, about the size of a large rectangular handbag, carried by an over-the-shoulder strap. A remarkable miniaturized device, it can be used to analyze and keep records of almost any type of data on planet surfaces, plus sensing or identifying various objects. It can also give the age of an artifact, the composition of alien life, and so on. The tricorder can be carried by Uhura (as communications officer, she often maintains records of what is going on), by the female yeoman in a story, or by Mister Spock, of course, as a portable scientific tool. It can also be identified as a 'medical tricorder' and carried by Doctor McCoy."
    —from the *Star Trek* writers' guide, third revision, dated April 17, 1967

"THE PHASERS: Hand weapons. We have two phasers, the 'hand phaser,' which is hardly much larger than a king-sized package of cigarettes, and the 'phaser pistol,' which consists of the hand phaser snapped into a pistol mount, the handle of which is a power pack, which greatly increases the range and power of the weapon.

"The reason for two phasers: In some instances, such as friendly calls and diplomatic missions, our landing party would not want to beam down to a planet with the larger phaser pistols hanging from their belts. The hand phaser (along with the communicator) is worn on a belt hidden under the shirt. At other times, the story does require that the landing party be conspicuously armed. . . .

"Both the hand phaser and the phaser pistol have a variety of settings. The ones most often used are 'stun effect,' which can knock a man down and render him unconscious without harming him, and 'full effect,' which can actually cause an object to dematerialize and disappear. The phaser is also capable of being set to cause an object to explode, or to burn a clean hole through an object. . . . Phasers can also be set to 'overload,' resulting in a power buildup and explosion, which destroys the phaser and anything in close proximity."

—from the *Star Trek* writers' guide, third revision, dated April 17, 1967

Matt Jefferies's early training as a mechanical artist served him well in his later career as a production designer, as this schematic drawing of the hand phaser and pistol mount shows. The intricately detailed design proved too complicated for Desilu's in-house property department, so the production turned the task of building them over to Wah Chang, who already had been contracted to design and manufacture both the communicator and the tricorder. In less time and at less expense than the Desilu prop staff could have managed, Wah Chang delivered several "working" models of the phaser (used in close-ups), along with a quantity of dummy mock-ups (useful for distance shots and stunt work).

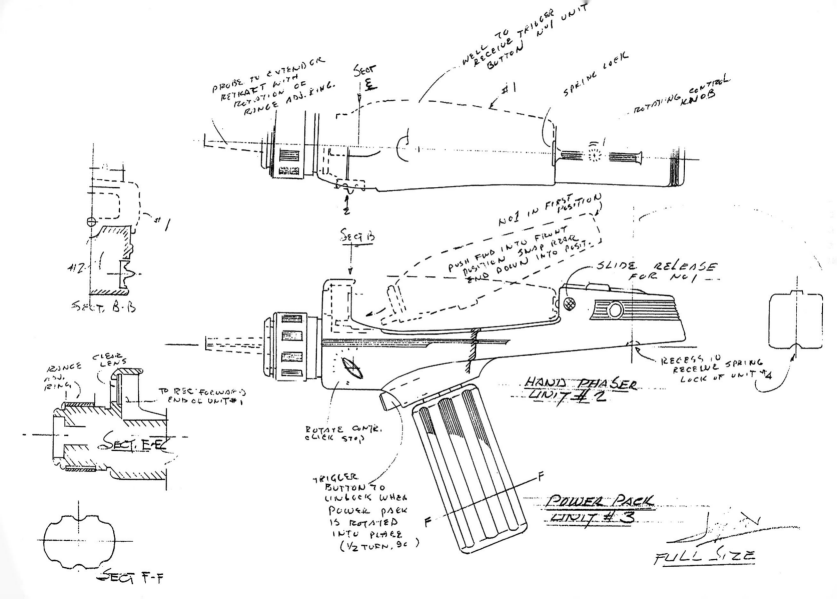

PROBE TO EXTENDER RETRACT WITH ROTATION OF RANGE ADJ. RING.

SECT E

WELL TO RECEIVE TRIGGER BUTTON NO1 UNIT

#1

SPRING LOCK

ROTATING CONTROL KNOB

SECT B

#1

#2

SECT. B·B

NO1 IN FIRST POSITION

PUSH FWD INTO FRONT POSITION SNAP REAR END DOWN INTO POSIT.

SLIDE RELEASE FOR NO1

RANGE ADJ. RING.

CLEAR LENS

TO REC FORWARD END OF UNIT #1

SECT. E·E

HAND PHASER UNIT #2

RECESS TO RECEIVE SPRING LOCK OF UNIT #4

ROTATE CONTR. CLICK STOP

POWER PACK UNIT #3

TRIGGER BUTTON TO UNLOCK WHEN POWER PACK IS ROTATED INTO PLACE (1/2 TURN, 9c)

F

F

FULL SIZE

SECT F·F

"COMMUNICATOR: A portable 'intercom,' about the size of a hand phaser. Not generally used aboard the vessel, since there are communications panels strategically located everywhere on the ship. The principal use of the communicator is between elements of a landing party on a planet surface, or from them to the *U.S.S. Enterprise* in orbit. The communicator, activated by lifting the antenna grid, also pinpoints that person's position on the planet surface, so that the transporter crew aboard the vessel can beam that person or the entire landing party up aboard the vessel."

　—from the *Star Trek* writers' guide, third revision, dated April 17, 1967

While contemporary science fiction series often have lavish production budgets to create a believably exotic universe and jaw-dropping effects, *Star Trek*'s producers had to keep their belts cinched tight right from the start. But the people behind the scenes at *Star Trek* were a particularly clever group who relied on wit to fend off deeper concerns over things like a skimpy budget. With the series premiere slightly more than a month away and a season's worth of episodes bearing down on them, the team already had been schooled to watch their pennies—and therein lay the possibilities for the lamest of practical jokes. Case in point: a series of memos, shown here, sent back and forth regarding the authorization of cast haircuts. Whether the culprit was ever found is lost to history (as is the two-and-a-half-buck haircut).

Desilu Productions I .

Inter-Department Communication

TO __GENE RODDENBERRY__

FROM __BOB JUSTMAN__

DATE __JULY 21, 1966__

SUBJECT __UNAUTHROIZED EXPENDITURES__

Dear Gene:

Is it true that you told the Desilu barber to tell all our actors that STAR TREK would pay for their haircuts? Is it true that you also told our barber that STAR TREK would pick up the cost of haircuts for Mr. Shatner's standin? I have received a bill for various haircuts at $2.50 a copy from the Desilu Smoke Shop and Barber Shop, 780 North Gower, Hollywood, California.

I have questioned Mr. Solow about whether the Desilu barber has the authority to tell thespians that we will pay for haircuts. Mr. Solow became quite incensed and intimated that you were definitely the culprit.

Being a fair-minded person, I would not go so far as to say that you were definitely the culprit. But I would go so far as to say that you are probably the culprit.

Are you the culprit?

ANXIOUS

RHJ:sts
cc: Herb Solow

HERB SOLOW

BOB JUSTMAN

JULY 24, 1966

UNAUTHORIZED EXPENDITURES

Dear Herb:

I have been informed by Mr. Roddenberry that he did not authorize the Desilu Smoke Shop and Barber Shop, 780 North Gower, Hollywood, California, to notify various thespians and standins that the STAR TREK Company would pick up the cost of haircuts for the show. I therefore enclosed a bill from the Desilu Studio Smoke Shop and Barber Shop, 780 North Gower, Hollywood, California in the amount of Five ($5.00) Dollars.

I would appreciate your handling same.

Your friend,

ROBERT H. JUSTMAN

RHJ:sts
cc: Gene Roddenberry
John D.F. Black

Nearly as many "tests" are conducted on a soundstage as on a college campus. In filmmaking, however, the tests come at the beginning of production, rather than at the end of a semester. Each department performs its own series of tests, be it screen tests (for casting), wardrobe (costuming), makeup, effects (both physical and visual), film stock, camera, or an endless array of equipment tests.

Arguably the most important component that figures into any and all of these tests is lighting. The choice of lamp, brightness, and angle can shade and shadow the wardrobe, makeup, and set design, allowing the director and cinematographer to finesse subtle intangible elements that will enhance the story they are filming.

Pictured is a test to establish the best ways to illuminate the eleven-foot-long *Enterprise* model. It inadvertently reveals an implicit fact about set lighting: The lamps throw heat as well as light, as the clapper board handler's open shirt attests.

Following NBC's approval of *Star Trek*'s second pilot, "Where No Man Has Gone Before," the production team began gearing up for the actual series. As the man responsible for the look of the *Enterprise*'s standing sets, Matt Jefferies found that his work was frequently interrupted by directors assigned to upcoming episodes. The interruptions were understandable: The directors needed a walk-through so they could familiarize themselves with the lay of the land and prep their shooting schedule accordingly. Unfortunately, the sets in question were not permanently installed, because the soundstage was not large enough to hold them all at once. But Jefferies managed to accommodate every request by showing the directors a three-dimensional scale model that he'd built, depicting each of the *Enterprise*'s permanent sets with design specifications down to the last detail.

Pictured here, the inexpensive four-foot-long model depicts sickbay, along with its futuristic beds, labs, and diagnostic area, in the upper left corner. On the opposite side of the circular corridor that divides the design, Engineering occupies the upper right. The circular bridge set rests in the lower right corner; next to the bridge stands the little-used auxiliary control room; the conference room (note the three-sided computer monitor on the oddly shaped table) is located just above auxiliary control. In the lower left, the transporter room, with console and circular "pad" area, awaits the arrival of the landing party. Although Jefferies built the model on a single level for simplicity, he reminded everyone that the various rooms actually would be located on different levels of the starship.

Thirty-two years after the series wrapped, Jefferies sold the model at auction, donating the proceeds to the entertainment industry's Motion Picture & Television Fund.

THE CORBOMITE MANEUVER

"Interesting game, this poker."
—Spock

At the uncharted edge of the galaxy, the *Enterprise* is blocked by a large spinning cube, a warning buoy that won't let the ship pass. After Kirk is forced to destroy the buoy, a gigantic spherical spaceship appears, manned by a sinister-looking alien named Balok. Balok accuses the captain of trespassing and threatens that, as punishment, he will destroy the *Enterprise* in ten minutes. Tension mounts on the *Enterprise*, and bridge officer Lieutenant Bailey loses control of his emotions, prompting Kirk to dismiss him from the bridge. Kirk, however, remains cool, employing a poker strategy to save his crew. The *Enterprise*, Kirk tells Balok, is equipped with a self-destruct system called "corbomite" that will destroy any attacker's ship. The question is, will his bluff work?

"I know, I know—many questions. But first, the tranya."
—Balok

In the pantheon of *Star Trek* villains, Balok doesn't stand as tall as Apollo, the Gorn, or even the diminutive Talosians. And in the end, he isn't even much of a villain—although he sure is entertaining. The sinister face that threatens the crew throughout the episode turns out to be a harmless puppet, its visage projected to the *Enterprise*'s viewscreen by a friendly, child-sized life-form. Eight-year-old actor Clint Howard played the humanoid version of Balok; coincidentally, Clint's brother Ron was working at a different soundstage on the same lot, playing Opie on *The Andy Griffith Show*.

Although childlike in appearance, Balok was intended to be an adult alien. Thus, young Clint's vocal track was excised after the episode had been filmed and replaced by that of well-known voice actor Vic Perrin, most familiar to viewers as the "Control Voice" from *The Outer Limits*.

The vocalizations of Balok's frightening alter ego also required a postproduction fix. Conveniently, actor Ted Cassidy, whose basso intonations had been heard as Lurch on *The Addams Family*, was about to begin filming the *Star Trek* episode "What Are Little Girls Made Of?" His deep voice fit the bill, so the producers asked Cassidy to record the puppet's threatening lines.

035

The effigy of Balok was created by noted sculptor Wah Chang. Chang began his career as the youngest artist to work on Walt Disney's *Pinocchio*. He later formed his own firm, Projects Unlimited, where he created and built the puppets for George Pal's groundbreaking stop-motion photography in *tom thumb*, as well as the titular vehicle for Pal's *The Time Machine*. Over the course of his career, Chang would create key props for a host of motion pictures, including *The King and I* and *Cleopatra*. He also designed advertising icons and mascots, such as the Pillsbury Doughboy.

Chang created many of the iconic props used in *Star Trek*: the communicator, the tricorder, and the Vulcan lute, not to mention the tribbles, the costumes and masks for the M-113 creature (the salt vampire), and the Gorn. After retiring from Hollywood, Chang segued into fine art, eventually becoming one of America's preeminent bronze sculptors.

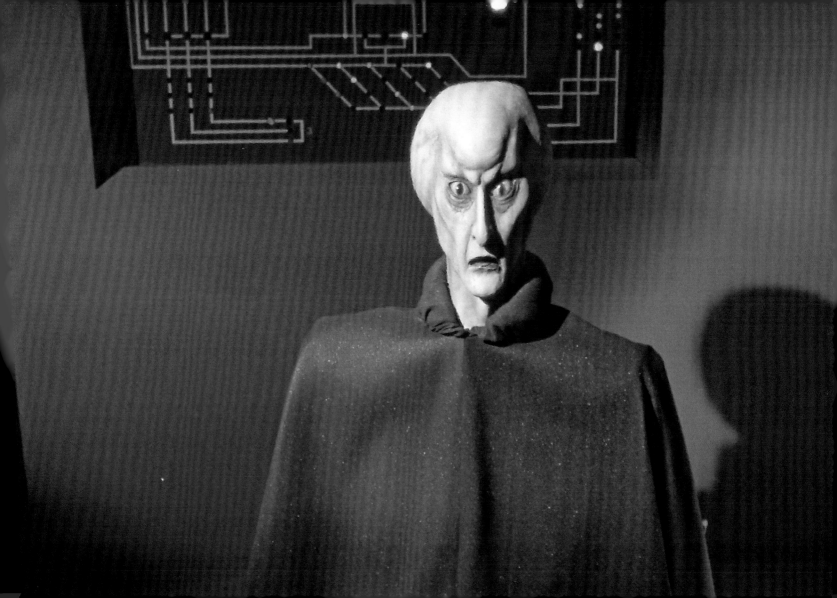

"Hailing frequencies open."
—Uhura

"The Corbomite Maneuver" is an episode of firsts. As the first episode shot after the second pilot (but held back in the original broadcast schedule to be aired as the tenth installment of the series), it marks the first time that Uhura appears, providing actress Nichelle Nichols with her signature line, "Hailing frequencies open"—which she says, with slight variations, *seven* times in this episode. It's also the first episode in which Doctor McCoy appears. Interestingly, the relationship between Kirk and McCoy seems already established here, with McCoy stepping into what would be his traditional role: giving voice to Kirk's conscience. Finally, it is the first episode in which Mister Spock drops one of his signature observations: "Fascinating." Although the Vulcan's stoic personality wasn't yet entirely established—at one point he lowers his eyes in defeat and begins to say "I'm sorry" to the captain—his fascination with all things new seems to be well fleshed out.

The fact that many first-season episodes initially were broadcast out of shooting order is easily discernible by the characters' uniforms: In "Corbomite," Uhura wears a gold command uniform, but in "Charlie X," which aired prior to this, she wears her traditional red ship's services uniform.

MUDD'S WOMEN

"Is this the kind of wife you want?"
—Eve McHuron

The *Enterprise* beams aboard the captain and "cargo" of a fleeing space vessel just before the ship is destroyed in an asteroid field. The vessel's captain, Harry Mudd, is a con man who's guilty of a variety of criminal offenses. His precious cargo is a trio of the most beautiful women Kirk and his crew have ever seen—pulse-quickeningly, heart-poundingly gorgeous. Mudd claims that his current profession is "wiving settlers," that is, matching up lonely women with financially appealing single men on colony worlds. Kirk is uninterested in the disreputable captain's career-of-the-moment; Mudd's past infractions have earned him a lengthy stay in the brig. Unfortunately, retrieving Mudd and company has destroyed all of the *Enterprise*'s lithium crystals, which are required to power its warp drive. Learning that Kirk's ship is heading for a mining colony on Rigel XII to replenish its lithium supply, Mudd quickly sends a covert message to the planet's wealthy miners. When the *Enterprise* limps into orbit, the miners inform an astonished Kirk that he won't get his crystals

until he sends those three alluring women down to the surface of Rigel XII—and frees Harry Mudd from the brig.

Out in the intergalactic boonies live three unattached women without any prospects for a husband. Along comes con man Harry Mudd, with his quick tongue and something called the "Venus drug," and *wham!* Suddenly they are three of the most alluring females in the quadrant. Ask any red-blooded male who gets within a parsec of them.

When it comes to *amour*, the Venus drug is the beauty pageant equivalent of a performance-enhancing drug. Not even Captain Kirk is immune to the profound effect the drug has on a woman's charms; fortunately, he does have the ability to pull himself together when the *Enterprise*, the real ladylove of his life, is in danger.

"There's only one kind of woman. . . . You either believe in yourself or you don't."
—Kirk

For a TV show that prides itself on its idealistic vision of the future, the original *Star Trek* series was not above treating women as "sex objects"—that is, when the plot requirement arose. And there was a logical reason for that: It was produced during the 1960s. Skirts were running short. Libidos were running high. And the upcoming battle over the most recent iteration of the Equal Rights Amendment was still just a gleam in the average mad housewife's eye.

Still, judging by the plot of "Mudd's Women," none of Mudd's conscripted ladies would have voted for the amendment—assuming, of course, that they ever would have heard of it on their backwater worlds. Take Eve, the most rational of the three women. After spending most of her life cleaning up after a bunch of unappreciative male siblings, all she wants is the opportunity to connect with a good man. Even after learning that she doesn't need the Venus drug to appear desirable, Eve can't foresee a future that doesn't involve snaring a man. The thought of serving aboard a starship never occurs to her—except perhaps as the captain's wife. So she consigns herself to life on barren Rigel XII, cleaning up for another unappreciative male (miner Ben Childress) and listening to the winds blow day and night.

"Mudd's Women" was the third episode of *Star Trek* to be produced, and it displays some of the same minor growing pains as "The Corbomite Maneuver." Uhura still wears a gold uniform, and the men's shirts have slightly oversize collars. This is particularly noticeable on Spock's shirt, which reportedly had a looser collar so that actor Leonard Nimoy could slip in and out of it without removing his Vulcan ears.

Greater care appears to have been taken with the wardrobe fashioned for Mudd's women. Their garments provide an early glimpse at what was to become a signature element of William Ware Theiss's design philosophy for the show's costumes. It's not that Theiss's creations were scandalously revealing—it's that they often revealed areas of the body typically unseen in public. Case in point: The large diagonal slit running from shoulder to waist in the garment worn by the dark-haired character Ruth reveals the gentle curve of the underside of her breast, a highly unanticipated area of display, and one that magnetically drew everyone's eye.

Well, everyone but Spock's, at any rate.

THE ENEMY WITHIN

"I'm Captain Kirk!"
–Kirk

A standard geological survey mission becomes a nightmare for the crew when a transporter malfunction splits Captain Kirk into two beings: a violent character who's all animalistic id, with a dangerous desire for Yeoman Rand, and a compassionate, indecisive man, psychologically incapable of making a command decision. Compounding matters, the malfunction has trapped the ship's landing party on the surface, where temperatures will drop to a deadly –120 degrees Fahrenheit overnight. With the lives of the crewmen in the landing party at stake and his own life on the line, the "good" Kirk must decide whether he wants to allow Scotty and Spock to use the transporter to reintegrate him with his "evil" counterpart.

042

*"The imposter had some interesting qualities, wouldn't
you say, Yeoman?"*
—Spock

"The Enemy Within" is best remembered for William Shatner's
bravura dual performance, particularly for his take on the dark side
of Captain Kirk. As the captain's gentle twin notes in disgust, the
"evil" side of Kirk is "a thoughtless brutal animal," barely capable of
communicating beyond guttural threats and demands. The shot that
first reveals him to the audience, dynamically staged by director Leo
Penn (father of actor Sean Penn) and dramatically lit by director of
photography Jerry Finnerman, emphasizes that bestial quality, as
"evil" Kirk looks around warily and flares his nostrils to scent the air, a
predator in unfamiliar territory. This science fiction twist on the story
of Jekyll and Hyde was written by Richard Matheson, the well-known
author/screenwriter behind such films as *Duel*, *I Am Legend*, *The
Incredible Shrinking Man*, and *Somewhere in Time*, as well as one of
The Twilight Zone's most popular episodes, "Nightmare at 20,000
Feet" (which, coincidentally, features William Shatner in another
scenery-chewing performance).

043

As *Star Trek*'s art director, Matt Jefferies devised many of the now-familiar elements envisioned by the show's producers. Sometimes instructions to Jefferies were vague, sometimes quite specific. Gene Roddenberry, Jefferies claimed, was a wonderful dreamer. He'd imagine a starship or a hand-held weapon and count on Jefferies, the self-described "nuts-and-bolts man," to bring that vision into reality. A conversation between the two men about thermodynamics, for example, led to the development of the phaser, a device that Roddenberry felt should be far more multipurpose than a traditional Buck Rogers-style ray gun. Jefferies was instructed to come up with a small device that would emit a beam of energy. This energy could then be adjusted to interact with the wave pattern of any molecular form; the particular energy phase required was contingent upon the nature of the target—it could convert matter into energy, stun or disintegrate a living being, or slam someone into a wall, depending on the setting. It could also speed up the molecular activity of an inanimate object, heating a rock to molten temperatures. Which is why it's a good thing that Sulu—as depicted in this sketch by Jefferies—had a phaser with him while trapped on the frigid surface of Alfa 177.

SULU HEATS ROCK
"THE ENEMY WITHIN"
'05

"I've seen a part of myself no man should ever see."
—Kirk

The "good" Kirk has a tough time making command decisions, or even having tough talks. He's soft-spoken, wishy-washy, and indecisive. During a conversation with Sulu, who is trapped on the surface below, Kirk is unable to tell the helmsman that Scotty has made no progress on repairing the transporter. Spock steps in and delivers the bad news in his usual dispassionate manner. Later, when Kirk is presented with a possible, albeit dangerous way to rejoin with his alter ego, he seems more concerned about integrating with the ugly side of himself than he is about the possibility of dying in the process. "I can't survive without him [but] I don't want to take him back," Kirk says. "He's like an animal." Spock reminds Kirk that it is the negative side of him that wields the ability to command, while McCoy points out that the good side has the courage, the compassion, and the intelligence that a captain needs to lead.

Star Trek traditionally steers clear of product placement, but borrowing an exotic-looking item from the real world and cleverly transforming it into an on-set prop is another story. A few examples: Scandinavian-modern salt-and-pepper shakers purchased from a local department store were incorporated into Doctor McCoy's arsenal of surgical implements; McCoy used a twentieth-century handheld microphone as a "white sound device" in the episode "Court Martial"; and Captain Kirk's Saurian brandy, in its very unique bottle, was actually a commemorative "powder horn" whiskey decanter produced by the George Dickel Distillery of Tennessee in 1964. Although featured most prominently in "The Enemy Within," the bottle would show up in several other episodes, including "Journey to Babel," "Space Seed," "By Any Other Name," and "Elaan of Troyius." Similar powder horn decanters fetched a pretty penny in the dealers' rooms of early *Star Trek* conventions—even without the whiskey.

THE MAN TRAP

The *Enterprise* travels to the planet M-113 to deliver supplies to that desolate world's only two inhabitants: archaeologists Robert and Nancy Crater. Nancy is an old flame of McCoy's, and the good doctor is admittedly nervous about seeing her again. But Nancy looks wonderful. In fact, she looks better than wonderful—"not a day over twenty-five," according to McCoy. Curiously, Kirk sees her as a woman in her forties, and Crewman Darnell swears she's the spitting image of a girl he knew on Wrigley's Pleasure Planet. Professor Crater makes no secret of the fact that he'd like the landing party to leave as soon as they drop off a much-needed shipment of salt. But before that can be arranged, Darnell is found dead, his body depleted of salt, and Nancy has disappeared. While Kirk searches for the answer to Darnell's death, two more crewmen are killed on M-113. And as word spreads that an intruder may have boarded the *Enterprise*, the unresolved question of Nancy's whereabouts becomes the most pressing issue on everyone's minds.

The M-113 creature—referred to by fans as "the salt vampire" for obvious reasons—is both horrific and strangely pitiable. With its snout-like mouth, studded with spiky teeth, and long suckered fingers, the beast is truly frightening. Yet its downturned eyes and deeply lined face seem to suggest an inner sadness.

While masquerading as Doctor McCoy, the salt vampire mockingly refers to itself as a "creature," but this highly intelligent life-form, "the last of its kind" according to Crater, was undoubtedly capable of comprehending the results of its actions. Unfortunately, it *wasn't* capable of controlling its hunger long enough to bargain for long-term survival. Perhaps, after years of near-starvation and lack of contact with others of its kind, it was too far gone to want to try.

"What's in a name? That which we call a rose by any other name would smell as sweet."
  —*William Shakespeare*, Romeo and Juliet

Sulu calls the bright pink exotic plant specimen in the *Enterprise*'s life sciences lab "Gertrude." Janice Rand prefers to call it "Beauregard," claiming that a woman "knows about these things." *Star Trek*'s prop department called it a hand puppet, although exactly whose hand gave the plant his—or her—personality seems to have been lost to posterity.

049

It's a quintessential moment from the series. Mister Spock is temporarily in command of the *Enterprise* and in total control—or so he thinks—until Lieutenant Uhura, feeling a bit neglected at the communications console, steps over to initiate a conversation with him. And what does she choose to discuss with the ever-logical Vulcan?

"Why don't you tell me I'm an attractive young lady?" she suggests. "Or ask me if I've ever been in love? Tell me how your planet Vulcan looks on a lazy evening when the moon is full."

As she speaks, her tone warm and inviting, Spock tugs uncomfortably at his collar—the only time in the series that he descends to a fidgety, almost human gesture. Is he, perhaps, feeling a bit warm? By the time Uhura finishes her onslaught of coquetry, Spock has postulated what seems like the appropriate answer. "Vulcan has no moon, Miss Uhura," he states. His expression betrays a bit of concern, as if he's worried that she may have missed one of the astronomical prerequisites at Starfleet Academy.

"I'm not *surprised*, Mister Spock," she responds, holding his gaze just long enough to let him know he's not fooling anyone.

From this scene, it takes only a small leap to arrive at the same intriguing conclusion about Spock and Uhura's relationship that the writers of 2009's *Star Trek* movie did.

050

"Lord forgive me."
—McCoy

Hard-core Trekkers have a weakness for episodes that provide intimate glimpses into familiar characters' otherwise well-fortified souls.
A well-loved example is "The Naked Time," which provides an en
masse look at the chinks in the crew's psychological armor, but other
episodes effectively prod the psyche of individual characters. In "The
Man Trap," poor McCoy finds himself caught in a waking nightmare.
Tossed emotionally off balance by the opportunity to experience a
brief reunion with Nancy, "that one woman" in his life, McCoy barely
has a chance to say hello before the lady vanishes. A few hours later, Nancy shows up at the door to McCoy's cabin on the *Enterprise*.
Perhaps her sudden reappearance should have warned McCoy that
something wasn't right—as should Nancy's insistence that he take a
powerful sedative to get some rest—but love can blind a man to the
obvious. A short time later, his mind muzzy from the sedative, Mc-
Coy's waking nightmare becomes all consuming as he finds himself
confronted by: a terrified Nancy, begging for his protection; a grim
Kirk, weapon drawn, ordering McCoy to step away from his former
love; and an urgent Mister Spock, demanding that McCoy ask himself
if the being before him is truly Nancy. When, at long last, McCoy manages to see Nancy for what she is, he utters a heartfelt prayer for for-
giveness and fires Kirk's phaser at something he *knows* is a monster,
but that *feels*, at least in his aching heart, like the last vestige of his
beloved Nancy.

It's the right thing to do, of course. And yet it's unlikely that McCoy
enjoyed an untroubled night's sleep *without* those sedatives for quite
some time.

The Gorn and the M-113 creature (aka the salt vampire), two of designer/sculptor Wah Chang's most famous—and most popular—*Star Trek* creations.

THE NAKED TIME

The *Enterprise* travels to Psi 2000 to pick up a group of Federation researchers before the planet disintegrates. But when Spock and Crewman Joe Tormolen beam down, they find that the scientists are dead, the apparent victims of their own extremely peculiar behavior. Not long after, members of the *Enterprise* crew begin acting strangely—the result of a highly contagious virus that the landing party brought back to the ship. Tormolen, a latent depressive, commits suicide, while Lieutenant Sulu, under the delusion that he's a French musketeer, attacks imagined enemies with a fencing sword. Navigator Kevin Riley, who fancies himself the descendant of Irish kings, seizes control of the ship by commandeering engineering; from there he informs the crew of their new responsibilities under his rule—and then he shuts down the ship's engines. Since the *Enterprise* is trapped within a decaying orbit around Psi 2000, it's only a matter of time before the ship will be destroyed along with the planet—unless Spock can help Scotty change the laws of physics by developing a method to restart the cold engines in record time. Unfortunately, Spock, too, has been hit by the virus, and he's more concerned about his mother's hurt feelings than he is about the ship's imminent destruction.

Ask an eager young actor whether he's good at something—from riding a horse to speaking French—and the actor typically will swear on a stack of Bibles that he's an expert. And then, of course, he'll immediately have to go out and actually *become* one. So it was for George Takei when screenwriter John D. F. Black asked the man who was normally shackled to the ship's helm console if he could fence. Takei swore that he could—then rushed over to Falcon Studios on Hollywood Boulevard to sign up for lessons. Takei's excitement over the scenes in "The Naked Time" that Black had written for Sulu was nearly overshadowed by his discovery that fencing instructor Ralph Faulkner had choreographed the famous fencing scene between Errol Flynn and Basil Rathbone in one of Takei's favorite childhood movies: 1938's *The Adventures of Robin Hood*. In fact, Takei learned that Faulkner had doubled for Rathbone during the sequence!

Following a few frenetic weeks of lessons, "The Naked Time" went before the cameras. On the first day of shooting, Takei was in his trailer eating a bowl of cereal when director Marc Daniels stepped in and asked the actor to take off his shirt. After a glance at Takei's bare torso, the director informed him that they'd film his fencing scenes "shirtless." The actor didn't return to his cereal; instead, he immediately hit the floor and spent any free time over the next three days doing push-ups to pump up for his pectoral debut.

Bruce Hyde was twenty-four years old when he appeared in "The Naked Time" as Kevin Riley. Today Hyde is a professor of acting at a Minnesota university, with fond memories of those days in 1966.

   "I had a contract with Desilu Studios," Hyde says. "I'd done a pilot for them, and they were paying me enough to keep me available in case the pilot got picked up. Part of the deal was that they could use me up to two or three times on whatever series Desilu already had airing. They had three shows at the time: *The Lucy Show* was ongoing, and *Star Trek* and *Mission: Impossible* had just started. That's how I wound up in *Star Trek*. My family has never traced our genealogy back, and I don't even know that I'm actually Irish, so that had nothing to do with my getting the part of Kevin Riley! But I *was* lucky: 'The Naked Time' was a really good episode, one that everyone remembers. I got to sing and joke around, which was unusual for the series."

"In 1966, I was a theater actor and hadn't done much television, so I was somewhat ill at ease in the studio," recalls Bruce Hyde. "When you're onstage and what you're doing is funny, people *laugh*. But on a TV soundstage, they're not supposed to. I remember doing all of that stuff [as Riley] in engineering, staggering back and forth, and singing 'Kathleen.' What I was doing was *supposed* to be funny, but everybody was just quiet. That was difficult for me, so the director, Marc Daniels, started choking me kind of playfully, trying to get me to loosen up and make me comfortable on the set. He was kind of a father figure to me at the time, because he'd directed a play that I had a lot of success with (*The Girl in the Freudian Slip*), first touring and then for a short time on Broadway. Marc was a really wonderful guy. I've had this photo for years. It's a really nice memento."

CHARLIE X

Captain Kirk gives passage to seventeen-year-old Charlie Evans, sole survivor of a vessel that crash-landed on the unexplored planet of Thasus fourteen years ago. Kirk finds Charlie ill-informed about some basic rules of etiquette, but friendly and eager to learn. He's even more eager to become acquainted with the fairer sex. Unfortunately, he becomes fixated on the captain's yeoman, Janice Rand, who is unsuccessful in her efforts to redirect his interest. Janice learns the hard way that Charlie has serious problems accepting rejection, and soon other members of the crew experience Charlie's wrath for perceived slights. By the time Kirk realizes the danger Charlie represents to the *Enterprise*, it's too late to do anything about it. The boy possesses extremely powerful mental abilities, which Spock hypothesizes he may have learned from the rumored inhabitants of Thasus. And those abilities, unchecked, could spell disaster for Kirk's crew.

"No laughing!"
—Charlie Evans

Hotheaded Charlie encounters a few members of the crew laughing over some private joke in an *Enterprise* corridor. Because he is a
teenager, Charlie has a tendency to assume that everything is about
him. But unlike other teenagers, Charlie has the power to stop bullies,
even perceived ones, dead in their tracks. We see only the shadows
of Charlie's tormentors in this sequence, cleverly staged by director Lawrence Dobkin. Charlie commands that the laughing cease and
then stalks away, but after he leaves, one victim, her whimpered cries
of terror strangely muffled, feels her way into the corridor, and it's revealed that her face . . . is *gone*. No eyes. No nose. And perhaps most
horrifying, no mouth—so not only is she unable to scream, or, from
Charlie's perspective, laugh, she is unable to *breathe*. Today's audiences, accustomed to the unlimited magic of CGI, may not find the
effect all that realistic, but to 1960s audiences, the image was pro-
foundly unsettling

"I want to stay!"
—Charlie Evans

Although Charlie represents as much of a threat to the crew as the
mutated Gary Mitchell, the sense of sadness and regret that the crew
experiences as the Thasians take Charlie off their hands is far more
profound. Charlie is not a man with delusions of godhood, nor is he
a villain—he is a teenage boy, full of all the sweetness and naïveté,
excitement and uncontrollable rage that every hormonal adolescent
experiences. At some point or another, what parent hasn't wished
that he or she could send a temperamental child away to live with
someone who could teach that teenager to behave? There are Horse
Whisperers and Dog Whisperers. Where are the Teenager Whisperers?

"Oh, on the Starship Enterprise, *there's someone who's in Satan's guise, whose devil ears and devil eyes will rip your heart from you!"*
—Uhura

First there was Uhura's rather blatant invitation for Spock to chat her up in "The Man Trap," and now she's singing a love song about the ship's first officer. What could Uhura have in mind?

You'd think that Spock would be annoyed by the communication officer's attempt to refocus every eye in the rec room on him. After all, who needs all that pressure when you're minding your own business, trying to put in some serious practice time with that beautiful Vulcan lute?

But strangely enough, Spock almost seems to enjoy being the object of Uhura's musical gibes, despite the song's references to his "victimizing alien love" and his spooky hypnotic gaze. There's actually a hint of a smile on his face as she sings, and isn't that just a touch . . . illogical?

BALANCE OF TERROR

"Leave any bigotry in your quarters. There's no room for it on the bridge."
—Kirk

When several Federation outposts along the Neutral Zone—the border between Federation and Romulan territories—suddenly go silent, Kirk suspects that the Romulans are responsible. Two centuries earlier, Earth fought a fierce battle against that aggressive alien society; the Neutral Zone was a result of the peace treaty that resolved the conflict. A distress call from yet another outpost serves to confirm Kirk's suspicions, and the *Enterprise* arrives just in time to witness the destruction of Federation Outpost 4, incinerated by a blast fired from a Romulan ship. The small vessel quickly disappears under cover of an invisibility cloak. Although the power of the enemy's new weapon is alarming, Kirk learns that the Romulan ship has a number of weaknesses. While it is invisible, its crew can no more see the *Enterprise* than Kirk's crew can see them. And the small craft *must* become visible in order to fire its weapon. As Kirk engages in a deadly game of cat and mouse with the Romulan captain, the *Enterprise*'s

sensors provide a startling glimpse of the mysterious species. The Romulans—never before seen by human or Vulcan—look *exactly* like Vulcans, which leads one crewman to doubt Spock's loyalty to the Federation.

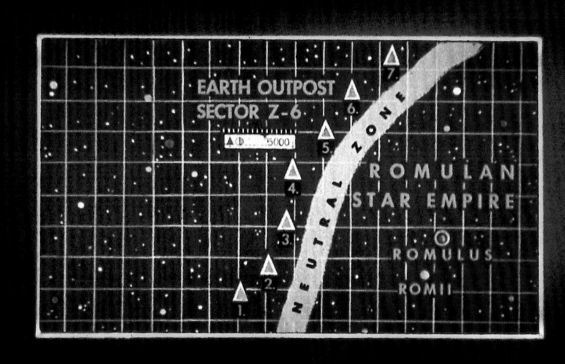

061

Even though the wedding ceremony in "Balance of Terror" never reached its anticipated conclusion, it still set an important precedent in the *Star Trek* universe. Years later, Captain Jean-Luc Picard would repeat the wedding vows first spoken here by Captain Kirk when Picard performs a wedding ceremony aboard his *Enterprise* in an episode of *Star Trek: The Next Generation*, "Data's Day." A few years after that, the vows appeared again, modified only slightly for the wedding of Captain Benjamin Sisko and his beloved Kasidy Yates in the *Star Trek: Deep Space Nine* episode "'Til Death Do Us Part."

The matrimonial verbiage, much loved within *Star Trek* fandom, has been spoken at many real-life wedding ceremonies around the world. In the interest of those who wish to hang on to it for future reference, here are the first few lines. You're on your own for the rest, lost to posterity when the red alert was sounded in "Balance of Terror":

"Since the days of the first wooden vessels, all shipmasters have had one happy privilege—and that is uniting two people in the bonds of matrimony. And so, we are gathered here today, with you, (fill in the blank), and you, (fill in the blank), in the sight of your fellows, in accordance with our laws."

062

Kirk: "Are you suggesting we fight to prevent a fight?"
Spock: "If the Romulans are an offshoot of my Vulcan blood—and I
think this likely—then attack becomes even more imperative."
McCoy: "War is never an imperative."

Once again, McCoy and Spock take diametrically opposed positions on a critical decision. McCoy, always the humanitarian, argues
against the *Enterprise* crossing into the Neutral Zone to hunt down
the Romulan ship, since that act could trigger a devastating war.
Spock, ever practical, says Kirk should run the risk of starting a possible war in order to prevent a probable one, and Kirk ultimately yields
to that cold bit of logic. Later, Kirk privately admits to McCoy that
he's having second thoughts. "When we're on that bridge," the captain says, "I see the men waiting for me to make the next move. And
Bones, what if I'm *wrong*?"

   Although this could be an opportunity for McCoy to swing Kirk
to his side, the good doctor instead counsels Kirk to avoid second-
guessing himself. "In this galaxy," he says, "there's a mathematical
probability of three million Earth-type planets. And in all of the
universe, three million million galaxies like this. And in all of that,
and perhaps more, only one of each of us. Don't destroy the one
named Kirk."

063

"I regret that we meet in this way, Captain. You and I are of a kind. In a different reality, I could have called you 'friend.'"
—the Romulan commander

There are striking parallels between "Balance of Terror" and a pair of World War II films made in the late 1950s: *Run Silent Run Deep* and *The Enemy Below*. Each film deals with a U.S. vessel facing off against the formidable vessel of an Axis power (Japan in the former and Germany in the latter). The *Star Trek* episode, written by Paul Schneider, cleverly weaves together key elements from each movie, and Matt Jefferies's set for the Romulan bridge effectively conveys the cramped feel of a World War II submarine, complete with a periscope-like monitor.

 Run Silent Run Deep may have inspired the plot thread about an officer who longs for vengeance (in "Balance of Terror," a role held by Stiles, the episode's navigator-of-the-week), and also the idea of releasing wreckage and bodies from a damaged vessel to mislead the opposition. In *Run Silent Run Deep*, it's the Allies who command the sub. In *The Enemy Below*, however, it's the Germans who operate underwater in a U-boat. *The Enemy Below* influenced many of the "human" elements that make "Balance of Terror" such a memorable episode, particularly the respect that the two captains gain for each other over the course of their encounter.

064

Another memorable creation that originated in the fertile imagination of artist Wah Chang, the Romulan bird-of-prey drifts in and out of view in "Balance of Terror," a phantom ship that made a strong impression upon *Star Trek* fans, even though it never received the screen time it deserved. Wah Chang's model was presumably put out to pasture after this episode; the brief glimpse of a similar Romulan vessel the following year, in "The Deadly Years," simply reused footage shot for this episode. The next time Kirk's crew had a close encounter with the Romulans, in "The *Enterprise* Incident," the secretive species was traveling aboard a consignment of Klingon battle cruisers. The name "bird-of-prey" would live on, however, assigned to a similarly stealthy enemy ship introduced in *Star Trek III: The Search for Spock*. That bird, however, was a Klingon vessel.

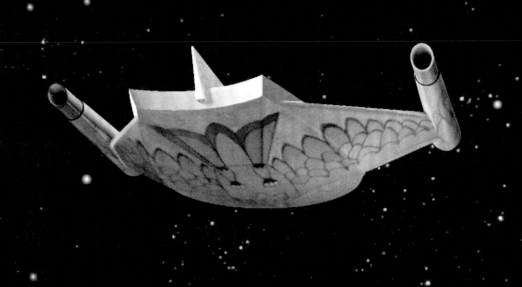

WHAT ARE LITTLE GIRLS MADE OF?

The *Enterprise* travels to the icebound planet of Exo III to learn the fate of Dr. Roger Korby, a renowned researcher in archaeological medicine who disappeared five years ago. Previous search missions found no trace of Korby or his research party, yet Nurse Christine Chapel, Korby's fiancée, remains hopeful that he is alive. Against all odds, the *Enterprise* establishes communication with Korby, who is alive and well, living beneath the frozen surface of the planet within the remains of a research facility built by "the Old Ones," the long-extinct natives of Exo. After Kirk and Chapel beam down, they discover that Korby is not alone—with him are two aides, middle-aged Dr. Brown, whom Chapel knows, and Andrea, an extremely beautiful young woman who is a stranger to Chapel. But even more disconcerting is Ruk, a frightening giant who, Korby explains, has lived in the underground caverns for millennia. The Old Ones left Ruk behind to watch over their equipment, equipment that Korby has plans for—once he takes over the *Enterprise*.

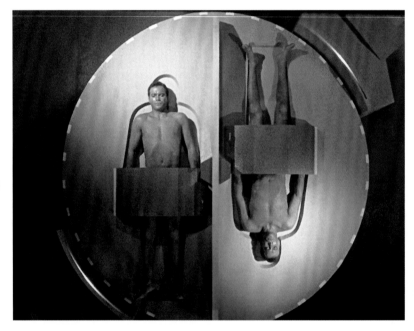

Perhaps the title "What Are Little Girls Made Of?" is a bit misleading. Andrea (Sherry Jackson) is indeed a girl—a girl android, at any rate—and to look at her, one has to assume that all of the "everything nice" ingredients went into creating her. On the other hand, Ruk is definitely more of a "snips and snails" creation, a monster right out of the classic novel *Frankenstein*. While one might be tempted, then, to cast Dr. Korby in the role of Dr. Frankenstein, keep in mind that Ruk is the creation of "the Old Ones"; he merely *worked* for Dr. Korby, and then only until he remembered his true heritage. There's still a lot of *Frankenstein* in this Robert Bloch script, as Kirk and Chapel feel their way through underground tunnels reminiscent of haunted castle catacombs, and in Korby's own resurrection from the grave. Also in the mix is more than a snippet of H. P. Lovecraft—a mentor to horror writer Bloch. Many of Lovecraft's tales made reference to "the Old Ones"—unearthly alien beings from long ago who left behind vestiges of their civilization. As in "What Are Little Girls Made Of?" Lovecraft's Old Ones ultimately were destroyed by their own monstrous creations.

"Mind your own business, Mister Spock. I'm sick of your half-breed interference—do you hear?"
—Kirk/Kirk android

The dictionary defines "half-breed" as "the offspring of parents of different races, especially the offspring of a Native American and a Caucasian." An earlier generation of moviegoers heard the term often, almost always in a derogatory way. Half-breed characters were pivotal to the plotlines of pulp novels and socially relevant big-screen westerns, the latter often cast with actors who elicited feelings of empathy from the audience, such as Elvis Presley in *Flaming Star*, Audrey Hepburn in *The Unforgiven*, and even *Star Trek*'s Captain Pike, Jeffrey Hunter, in *The Searchers*.

Although the term is virtually absent from common usage today, replaced, for the most part, by the more euphemistic "mixed race," it was still fairly common during the 1960s. The writers' guide for the series even used it to describe Mister Spock's half-human heredity: "He is biologically, emotionally, and even intellectually a 'half-breed.'" And indeed, Spock's status as a "half-breed" on his homeworld is the reason he chose to attend Starfleet Academy rather than the Vulcan Science Academy. His background was never an issue to anyone on the *U.S.S. Enterprise*, which is why Kirk's effort to imprint his android double's consciousness with the expression "half-breed"—a ver- bal cue to his first officer—was a very clever way to make the Vulcan prick up his ears.

Kirk would use the expression one additional time in *Star Trek*, when he deliberately sought to infuriate the spore-addled Vulcan in the episode "This Side of Paradise."

Actress Majel Barrett appeared in the first *Star Trek* pilot, "The Cage," as Number One, a by-the-book female officer and Christopher Pike's second-in-command on the *Starship Enterprise*. When NBC rejected that pilot, the network also rejected the notion of such a high-placed female officer. It allowed Gene Roddenberry the opportunity to produce a second pilot, stipulating that Number One not be included as a member of the crew. That might have been the end of Barrett's *Star Trek* career, except for the fact that Roddenberry liked the actress. She had appeared in his previous series, *The Lieutenant*, and he wanted to keep her onboard the ship and on the show. Thus, Nurse Christine Chapel was created.

Barrett's new character first appeared in the episode "The Naked Time," but viewers would not learn her back-story until three weeks later, in "What Are Little Girls Made Of?" Here, they discovered, she had abandoned a promising career on Earth in order to join the *Enterprise* crew in their trek through space—all in the name of love. It was a case of art imitating life: Several years later, Roddenberry and Barrett married, and they remained together until his passing in 1991.

Despite *Star Trek*'s notoriously slim budget, William Theiss never failed to deliver costumes with the unique look befitting a show set three hundred years in the future. Each of the distinctive blue and green uniforms worn by Kirk, Dr. Korby, and Dr. Brown in "What Are Little Girls Made Of?" was stitched together from separate jumpsuits of blue and green. The beautiful female android Andrea was dressed in a revealing pantsuit that seems to owe a nod to designer Rudi Gernreich, whose 1964 design for a topless bathing suit also featured a daring use of "V" straps stretched across the female torso—albeit with much less fabric.

DAGGER OF THE MIND

The penal colony at Tantalus V is known far and wide as a progressive facility, but when Kirk speaks of both it and its director, Tristan Adams, in glowing terms, Doctor McCoy can't help voicing his opinion that "a cage is a cage." Kirk, who greatly admires Adams's efforts to humanize prisons and the treatment of prisoners, insists that McCoy is wrong, even after a deranged inmate from Tantalus manages to sneak aboard the *Enterprise*. Upon learning that the inmate is *Dr. Simon Van Gelder*, a member of Adams's staff, McCoy insists that Kirk conduct a complete investigation. As McCoy and Spock attempt to get to the bottom of Van Gelder's apparent psychosis, Kirk tours Tantalus with *Enterprise* psychiatrist Dr. Helen Noel. However, Kirk's introduction to the facility's "neural neutralizer"—a device that supposedly eliminates malfeasant thoughts from criminal minds—quickly changes the captain's opinion about Adams's benevolent practices.

"Dagger of the Mind" is notable for introducing the Vulcan mind-meld. Spock describes it as "an ancient Vulcan technique," one that he has not previously used on a human. The mind-meld, he explains, is "a highly personal thing to the Vulcan people, to our private lives"—but, as we would come to learn in later episodes, there's little about *any* Vulcan ritual that isn't highly personal.

The mind-meld allows two persons to become linked telepathically, literally sharing each other's consciousness. Far more reliable than any truth serum, it can also get to the source of a deeply repressed psychological problem faster and more efficiently than psychother- apy, hence its logical use here to plumb the depths of Simon Van Gelder's damaged mind.

Spock's finesse—or perhaps actor Leonard Nimoy's finesse—in performing the technique would become far more precise in subse- quent episodes. Here he positions and repositions his hands, touch- ing numerous spots on the patient's skull as he makes "pressure changes in nerves and blood vessels." Later in the series, Spock presumably learns that it is possible to restrict his penetrating touch to the region between his human subject's temples and sinus cavi- ties, although a few times Spock actually manages to perform a mind-meld—or at least implant a suggestion—without touching the subject at all, through a wall ("By Any Other Name") and in one instance, via eye contact ("The Omega Glory").

She's a beautiful girl, and she and Kirk obviously like each other. What's wrong with this picture?

One big thing: It never happened. Kirk met Dr. Helen Noel at the *Enterprise* science lab's Christmas party. They "danced and talked about the stars," Dr. Noel recalls—but afterward, to her great disappointment, she went back to her quarters alone.

Dr. Noel clearly was uninformed about Kirk's personal rules of engagement. Despite his legendary appetite for the fairer sex, he makes it a point never to hunt within his own fold. U.S. naval regulations, which provide a loose basis for Starfleet's fictional regulations, contribute compelling motivation for Kirk's standard: "Personal relationships . . . that are unduly familiar and that do not respect differences in rank and grade violate the long-standing custom and tradition of the U.S. Naval Service and are prohibited."

The kiss shown here is a fantasy that was inspired by the Tantalus colony's neural neutralizer. Kirk had instructed Dr. Noel to test the device by implanting an "unusual suggestion" within his mind. Dr. Noel, in a flagrantly unprofessional moment, suggested that the aftermath of the Christmas party had gone differently, that Kirk had swept Helen up in his big strong arms and carried her to the boudoir, where, presumably, Kirk had his way with her. Or actually, considering this was *her* fantasy, it might be more accurate to say Dr. Noel had her way with *him*.

The writers for *Star Trek* were, by and large, a scholarly lot, not shy about dropping classic literary references into their scripts. Character and place names used in "Dagger of the Mind" suggest that writer S. Bar-David (the pen name of Shimon Wincelberg) was an aficionado of Greek mythology. Tantalus, the penal colony Kirk visits, was the name of a misbegotten son of Zeus—misbegotten in both senses of that word: illegitimate *and* bad. As punishment for a string of deeds including cannibalism, human sacrifice, and parricide, Tantalus was consigned to live in an eternal state of temptation without satisfaction. The English word "tantalize" is derived from his name.

 Lethe, an assistant at the Tantalus colony, is a former patient of Dr. Adams who opted to stay on after being cured. Her blank expression and eerily emotionless demeanor suggest that Adams has wiped out more than her criminal tendencies with his machine. In Greek mythology, Lethe was a river in Hades; anyone who drank from it experienced complete forgetfulness. The name is the source for the English word "lethargy," meaning sluggish or indifferent. Lest we forget.

No, it's not déjà vu. We *have* been here before—or at least Kirk has. The establishing shot for the Tantalus Penal Colony facility in "Dagger of the Mind" is a modified version of the matte painting depicting Delta Vega's lithium-cracking station in "Where No Man Has Gone Before." The towering refinery tanks in the background of the Delta Vega operation were eliminated, and the entrance door to the "administration building" was changed.

Matte paintings were often reused in *Star Trek* episodes, sometimes with modifications and sometimes without. In an era when television episodes were traditionally repeated in rerun form only once, and when the dawn of home video lay nearly a decade in the future, no one worried about reusing a set or a prop or a matte painting once, twice . . . or more.

MIRI

The *Enterprise* comes across a planet that resembles Earth as it was in the mid-twentieth century. Kirk, Spock, McCoy, and Yeoman Rand beam down and find that the planet's only inhabitants are a tribe of prepubescent children who, somewhat fittingly, refer to themselves as the Onlies. But where, Kirk wonders, are their parents? Before long, he finds the chilling answer. The children are the only survivors of a scientific experiment gone terribly wrong, a misguided attempt to develop a virus that would extend the human life span. The virus worked as theorized on the children—who are all more than three hundred years old—but the adults died from the virus's terrible side effects. And the children, who are aging slowly, will face the same fate once they reach puberty, at which point they will deteriorate rapidly and die in extreme agony. The adult members of the *Enterprise* landing party, already showing symptoms of the virus, are likely to die sooner than that, unless McCoy can develop a cure. But when the children band against the adults and steal the equipment that would allow McCoy to test a potential vaccine, only the adolescent Miri—torn between her loyalty to her young friends and her developing feelings toward Kirk—can save their lives.

Pundits of the day called it "the generation gap." During the three-year period that *Star Trek* was in production, a unique generational conflict found sociological footing. Burgeoning "baby boomers" began asserting themselves politically just as events of the day—an unpopular war in Vietnam, the rise of psychedelic drugs, the popularity of rock 'n' roll, the immediacy of television news—united them in an unprecedented manner. The establishment saw these young people as challenging and confrontational, dubbing them and their activities "counterculture." The boomers responded defiantly, tossing back slogans such as "Question authority" and "Don't trust anyone over thirty."

Schisms between parents and children, teachers and students, administrators and young voters, were not new, but this period of social unrest was far more widespread than ever before, which inspired screenwriters in search of subject matter. "Miri" writer Adrian Spies drew inspiration from current events—the generational gap between Kirk (the landing party's ostensible "father figure") and the self-sufficient children—and from William Golding's novel *Lord of the Flies*. It's easy to correlate the Onlies' fear of violent "grups" (grownups) with *Flies*' "littluns," frightened of the unknown, which is realized in the book as "the beast." While the novel paints a vivid image of how separation from societal restraints, and parents, can turn even the most innocent children into killers, "Miri" provides a softer but equally cautionary tale for contemporary audiences.

"Bonk, bonk on the head!"
–the Onlies

Actor Phil Morris was seven years old when he appeared in "Miri" as one of the Onlies, an anonymous boy wearing an army helmet. Morris has since appeared in numerous *Star Trek* productions, including *Star Trek III: The Search for Spock*, *Star Trek: Deep Space Nine*, and *Star Trek: Voyager*. His long résumé also includes a prominent recurring role on *Seinfeld* as lawyer Jackie Chiles and, as an ongoing cast member, in revivals of *Mission: Impossible* and *The Love Boat*. During the 1960s, Phil's father, Greg Morris, costarred as Barney Collier in *Mission: Impossible*, another Desilu production. "The producers tapped the pool of talent then working on the Paramount lot and got them to bring in their kids," Phil Morris explains. "They got me, my older sister Iona, two of William Shatner's daughters, ["Miri"] director Vincent McEveety's kids, and more. It was cool, man, working with Michael J. Pollard! And it was a lot of fun—until my foot got run over by a camera dolly," he laughs, "which made it both the highlight and the lowlight of my career!"

Lisabeth Shatner and her older sister, Leslie, were in the group. Ms. Shatner notes that she was too young to understand why they were doing the things asked of them, but that she eventually realized everything was "pretend." And there's one particular detail that never left her memory: Janice Rand's unique hairdo. "I was utterly fascinated by it," she recalls. "It was woven into a checkered pattern on top, and I stared at it for a long time, wondering if it was possible to actually play checkers on it."

*"Captain's Log, Stardate 2713.5. In the distant reaches of our gal-
axy, we have made an astonishing discovery. Earth-type radio signals
coming from a planet which apparently is an exact duplicate of the
Earth. It seems impossible, but there it is."*
—Kirk

Why does Miri's world look so much like Earth? And why do the
streets that she and her friends play in look so much like the streets
of Anytown, USA (circa the mid-twentieth century)?

The word "budget" is extremely important in Hollywood. No genre-
based television series—be it a western, cop drama, or space exploration show—has ever had a budget large enough to create all the par-
aphernalia so vital to the ideal "look" of a series. Or so the producers
say. In the 1960s, it was relatively easy to find a ranch with horses for
actors to ride, or a city street in Los Angeles that could fill in for any
U.S. urban center. Alien worlds, however, were not quite so common.
So producers of science fiction series were forced to be creative, to
tailor their shows to what was easy to fabricate.

As the producers of *Star Trek* instructed potential writers in the
show's 1967 series guide: "Be creative, but practical. Remember,
'Class M' planets [a *Star Trek* term that designates planets with
oxygen-nitrogen atmospheres capable of supporting 'life as we
know it'] will often be similar to many parts of Earth, with societies

duplicating or intermixing almost any era in man's development.
Jungle backgrounds exist on back lots, so what about primeval
worlds? Or a pioneer-Indian type culture? Lovely parkland exists
locally, so do unusual highly modern buildings, so do farms."

And so did a ready-made city set (regularly used by *The Andy
Griffith Show*) at the Desilu Culver back lot in the Culver City neigh-
borhood of Los Angeles. Available set, meet television production
seeking available set. We now pronounce you "planet which apparently is an exact duplicate of the Earth."

THE CONSCIENCE OF THE KING

Research Scientist Thomas Leighton is certain that Anton Karidian, part of a traveling Shakespearean troupe, is actually "Kodos the Executioner," the infamous former governor of Tarsus IV who sent four thousand people to their deaths twenty years ago. Leighton and his friend James Kirk were both on Tarsus at the time of the massacre; Kirk has put the past behind him, while Leighton's scars run deep, both physically and psychologically. Although Kirk is skeptical of the accusation, his curiosity is piqued, and he attends a party for the Karidian acting company at Leighton's home. There, he encounters Karidian's beautiful daughter Lenore—and, not long after, the dead body of Dr. Leighton. Now concerned that his deceased friend may have been on to something, Kirk offers the troupe passage aboard the *Enterprise* to their next performance while he attempts to investigate further. In the meantime, Spock learns that with the death of Dr. Leighton, of the nine people who actually saw the face of Kodos two decades ago, only two remain alive—Kirk and Lieutenant Kevin Riley, both on the *Enterprise*. And when Riley is poisoned—almost fatally—while stationed alone at his post, it seems logical to Spock that his captain is about to become the next, and final, target of a killer.

"The character who gets poisoned in 'The Conscience of the King' wasn't originally written to be Kevin Riley," notes actor Bruce Hyde. "But when they decided to use me a second time on the show [following his appearance in 'The Naked Time'], they turned him into the same guy I played before."

And thus, Kevin Riley was upgraded from a "guest star" in one episode to a "regular" character aboard the *U.S.S. Enterprise*, at least in the minds of his many fans.

"I guess it was a memorable glass of milk," chuckles Hyde. "I only acted professionally from 1964 to 1970, traveling back and forth between New York and L.A. Then I was cast into the San Francisco company of *Hair*, and at the end of that year, I decided to drop out of acting and stay in San Francisco. I really left the whole arena. So it was a surprise to me a few years later when I read this article in the *New Yorker* about a big *Star Trek* convention in New York. Apparently there was a trivia contest, and they ran a sample question: 'What was the poison put in Lieutenant Riley's milk?' And I thought, 'Oh my God, I can't believe they're really thinking about *that*!' It was the first inkling I had that *Star Trek* would be such an issue for years to come.

"And I can still remember the name of the poison—tetralubisol!"

081

"The play's the thing wherein I'll catch the conscience of the King."
—William Shakespeare, Hamlet

References to the works of Shakespeare are common in *Star Trek*. The episode title "Dagger of the Mind" refers to a phrase spoken by Macbeth, "By Any Other Name" calls to mind Juliet's famous turn of phrase, and *Star Trek*'s characters quote Shakespeare regularly throughout the entire series. But no episode draws so heavily on the Bard's work as does "The Conscience of the King." The episode opens with Kirk watching a performance of *Macbeth*, and savvy viewers soon recognize that the plotline borrows liberally from *Hamlet*, as even the episode's title suggests. In the play, Shakespeare's melancholy Danish prince used a visiting theater troupe to expose a criminal; here, actors in the troupe are the ones who are actually guilty of criminal behavior. For this episode's finale, the untethered Lenore delivers the longest Shakespearean speech of the entire series as she leans over her dead father's body. Although she is dressed as *Hamlet*'s Ophelia, Barbara Anderson's performance is pure Lady Macbeth—after she's lost her mind, of course.

082

Nichelle Nichols began her career as a singer and dancer, touring while still a teenager with Duke Ellington, and later with Lionel Hampton. After segueing into acting, she displayed her vocal talents in the *Star Trek* episodes "The Changeling," "Charlie X," and "The Conscience of the King." Nichols's singing remains an integral part of her many personal appearances at *Star Trek* conventions. She does not, however, play the Vulcan lute at these events, admitting that she doesn't really know how to play it. No matter—her a cappella voice sounds just fine.

THE *GALILEO* SEVEN

"That thing out there has ionized this complete sector. None of our instruments work. There's four complete solar systems in the immediate vicinity, and out there, somewhere, a twenty-four-foot shuttlecraft, off course and out of control. Finding a needle in a haystack would be child's play!"
—Kirk

En route to Makus III, the *Enterprise* passes the beautiful—and dangerous—quasar-like formation known as Murasaki 312. Since the *Enterprise* has standing orders to investigate all cosmic phenomena of Murasaki's type, Kirk decides to launch a manned shuttle into the formation. Galactic High Commissioner Ferris is infuriated by Kirk's action: The *Enterprise* is carrying emergency medical supplies to Makus, and from there they are to be transferred to the plague-ridden New Paris colonies. But Kirk reminds Ferris that the rendezvous won't take place for five days, and Makus III is only three days away—in short, there's time. However, the simple research mission goes horribly wrong. The radiation in Murasaki 312 affects the *Shuttlecraft Galileo*'s controls, and the small ship carrying Spock,

McCoy, and five others crashes on Taurus II, an unexplored planet within the quasar. With the *Enterprise*'s sensors blinded by the same radiation, Kirk can't even begin to guess where to start looking for his crew. Suddenly, that cushion of time available before the *Enterprise* is due at Makus III is looking very thin—and Ferris is pushing Kirk very hard.

The *Galileo* shuttlecraft owes its existence to a plastic model-making company called AMT, one of the very first *Star Trek* licensees. In 1966, AMT, excited by early footage of the soon-to-debut television series, acquired the merchandising rights to manufacture and market a scale model plastic kit of the *U.S.S. Enterprise*. The company later would produce models of the Klingon battle cruiser, the Romulan bird-of-prey, and the *Galileo*. In fact, AMT not only manufactured the *Galileo* shuttlecraft model, but the company also constructed the life-size *Galileo* exterior and the interior set seen in "The *Galileo* Seven" (and other episodes), reportedly one of the terms of its deal with the studio.

It was a particularly sweet arrangement for the series' producers. "It was a full-scale model that the actors could walk and talk in," explains coproducer Robert Justman. "All it cost us was the expense to truck it from Arizona to the set in Los Angeles."

star
trek

amt U.S.S. ENTERPRISE SPACE SHIP MODEL KIT

Modèle réduit pour assembler ● Un-assembled hobby kit

amt

STAR TREK

U.S.S. ENTERPRISE

Galileo 7

SHUTTLECRAFT

NCC-1701/7
U.S.S. ENTERPRISE

Galileo

U.S.S. ENTERPRISE

Galileo

NCC-1701/7

U.S.S. ENTERPRISE NOT INCLUDED

"Strange. Step by step I've made the correct and logical decisions, and yet two men have died."
—Spock

Spock receives a harsh but useful lesson in leadership in "The *Galileo* Seven." Typically, he's an exemplary first officer, prepared to give the captain insightful, rational advice on all matters—scientific or not. Onboard the *Enterprise*, that advice is sometimes tempered by Doctor McCoy's emotional counterpoint. But in this situation, as the highest-ranking officer on the shuttlecraft, Spock must make his own decisions, without obligation to consider the opinions of McCoy or the majority. His charges on the ill-fated *Galileo* shuttlecraft seem to resent his ultra-logical approach from the start, but they grudgingly accept their superior's decisions, some good, some not so good. McCoy even has the grace to compliment Spock on making the right call in the nick of time. But this doesn't mean that the two men will never butt heads again. It's safe to predict that viewers will find Spock and McCoy at odds in any random episode in which Kirk is missing in action or presumed dead (such as "The Tholian Web," "Arena," "Bread and Circuses," and several others).

COURT MARTIAL

When Captain Kirk is put on trial, his career hangs on the courtroom skills of attorney Sam Cogley. The case against Kirk is strong: He is accused of jettisoning an observatory pod during an ion storm without giving Lieutenant Commander Ben Finney, the crewman manning it, time to escape. The captain remembers the incident differently, but computer records support the accusations—and they don't lie. Or do they? Prosecuting attorney Areel Shaw—who is an old girlfriend of Kirk's—seems to have an ironclad case against the captain, but the eccentric Cogley is unconcerned, as he places more faith in his old books than in any computer. Aboard the ship, McCoy worries when First Officer Spock seems more interested in taking on the ship's computer at chess than in helping to prove the captain's innocence.

"Books, young man, books—thousands of them. This is where the law is. Not in that homogenized, pasteurized synthesizer. Do you want to know the law? The ancient concepts in their own language? Learn the intent of the men who wrote them, from Moses to the tribunal of Alpha 3? Books!"
—Samuel T. Cogley

That actor Elisha Cook Jr.'s portrayal of attorney Samuel T. Cogley would be nothing less than scene-stealing is hardly surprising: During his sixty-year career, Cook managed to hold his own opposite such heavyweight actors as Humphrey Bogart (in *The Maltese Falcon*) and Alan Ladd (in *Shane*), and he was lauded for dozens of equally challenging roles.

It's easy to believe that Cook is speaking for both himself and Cogley when he delivers the speech championing the value of books over computers, and not surprisingly, the episode built around his character features the most prominent appearances that "ancient" paper artifacts make in all of *Star Trek*. Kirk reads the accusations against him on printed paper, and soon finds his quarters crowded with stacks of law books. Ultimately, Spock's riposte to the accusations is tangible proof that the computer was wrong, while Cogley's books were right. The message may be even more relevant in today's Internet-driven world than it was in the 1960s, but Kirk, at least, seems to have

taken it to heart. In the *Star Trek* motion pictures that feature the original crew, we learn that Kirk subsequently gains a great appreciation of real, leather-bound books. In fact, Spock gifts him a precious copy of *A Tale of Two Cities* in *Star Trek II: The Wrath of Khan*.

Another classic aspect of "Court Martial" is its plotline, which is reminiscent of the lavish Cecil B. DeMille film *Reap the Wild Wind*. In that film, John Wayne is accused of wrecking his ship, and a missing woman is assumed to have been killed in the wreck (just as Kirk is accused of destroying the pod containing Finney). Although Paulette Goddard, the ship's owner, is Wayne's accuser, she falls in love with him (just as Kirk's prosecutor, Areel Shaw, seems to retain a soft spot for her old flame). And as in "Court Martial," the story ends in hand-to-hand combat—although Wayne's final showdown is with a giant squid.

Even though no official rules were ever established for the game, fans worldwide have taken up the gauntlet and developed rules for their own "noncanonical" enjoyment of three-dimensional chess. Judging by its appearance in six original-series *Star Trek* episodes— "Where No Man Has Gone Before," "Charlie X," "By Any Other Name," "The Corbomite Maneuver," "Whom Gods Destroy," and, of course, "Court Martial"—tri-level chess appears to be Spock's favorite pas- time, although Kirk beats him at it in at least two of those episodes, thanks to his unpredictable, illogically human decisions.

The first matte painting on record was created by director Norman Dawn for his 1907 film *Missions of California*. Dawn placed a pane of painted glass between the camera and his subjects and then photographed them together. Numerous techniques for combining matte shots with live-action photography have been developed in the century since, from stacked multi-planes of glass to double exposure to blue screen processing. Beginning in the 1990s, digital imaging increasingly has replaced matte painting, and today, literally hundreds of computer programs offer ever-expanding tools and techniques. And yet, as this matte of "Court Martial's" Starbase 11 shows, the creativity of early matte artists has rarely been surpassed. Albert Whitlock painted the work with oils on Masonite, revealing the timeless precision and skill of his brushwork, as well as his affinity for imaging futuristic landscapes.

THE MENAGERIE (PARTS 1 & 2)

"Captain Pike has an illusion, and you have reality. May you find your way as pleasant."
—Talosian Keeper

The *Enterprise* diverts to Starbase 11 after Spock reports that Christopher Pike, the *Enterprise*'s former commander, has requested their presence at the station. When they arrive, the station's commander, Commodore José Mendez, tells Kirk that Pike couldn't possibly have issued the summons, as he was severely disabled in a recent accident and can't move or speak. While Kirk meets with Mendez, Spock returns to the ship and beams up Pike—whom he served under for more than eleven years—and then locks the *Enterprise* on course for the planet Talos IV, a planet that the Federation has forbidden starships to visit. Years earlier, Captain Pike was captured by the planet's inhabitants, a race of powerful telepaths who have the dangerous ability to make illusion seem real. Pike had managed to convince the Talosians to release him, but now it seems as if Spock is determined to deliver the helpless captain into their hands. And he's willing to risk both his career *and* Kirk's in order to do it.

Producing episodes of a television series, week after week, is a huge responsibility, particularly when it comes to staying under budget and on schedule. Filmmakers are always on the lookout for novel ways to stay ahead of the curve, and *Star Trek*'s producers were no exception. They couldn't help thinking about the show's original pilot, which was sitting in a film vault, apparently destined for obscurity. After all, "The Cage" represented an episode that had already been shot and paid for. If only there was a way to *use* it—think of the time and money they'd save!

And so a script was devised, a "frame," in literary parlance, that could be wrapped around the existing footage in an interesting way. By producing *one* hour of television, the producers could fill *two* hours of airtime. That would give them more time to develop additional episodes and recoup some of the money they'd spent on the pilot. As a bonus, since the existing footage contained plenty of action, the frame didn't need to, so it could be frugally shot almost entirely on existing sets, with no location shooting and a minimum of additional actors to hire.

The frame worked brilliantly. For once *Star Trek* found itself both a few days and a few dollars ahead. And to top it off, "The Menagerie" (which had been Gene Roddenberry's original title for "The Cage") won the 1966 Hugo Award—science fiction's most prestigious honor—for Best Dramatic Presentation.

092

Desilu and NBC executives had discussed the possibility of airing "The Cage" as a movie-of-the-week if *Star Trek* did not go forward as a series. When the pilot was nixed, Desilu approached actor Jeffrey Hunter with a request to rejoin the cast in order to shoot enough additional footage to make the movie option viable. But Hunter, who wanted to return to feature films, declined. This meant that Roddenberry had to devise a way to make Christopher Pike look very different in the frame story that would ultimately envelop the first pilot. Thus, it was decreed that Pike, following an act of heroism befitting his character, had been burned beyond recognition. This gave newcomer Sean Kenney (the man behind the disfiguring makeup) some very subdued screen time in "The Menagerie." Happily, it was not Kenney's only role in the series. He also appeared as Lieutenant DePaul, alternately a navigator and a helm officer in the episodes "Arena" and "A Taste of Armageddon."

Appearing with Sean Kenney in this still is Malachi Throne. In addition to costarring in dozens of movies and television shows, Throne has an ongoing career as a "voice-over artist," lending his vocal tones to commercials ranging from Revlon to Goodyear. Which is why he was originally heard, but not seen, in "The Cage"; Throne's voice replaced the female voice of the actress playing the Talosian Keeper, thus enhancing the character's alien quality. When he was later cast as Commodore Mendez in "The Menagerie," the sound department electronically modified the original voice-over recording to make sure that the Keeper's voice was different from that of Mendez.

093

The magic of visual effects allows a set designer to build a minimal amount of background, which later will give the impression of a maximal degree of scope. After actress Julie Parrish and two extras were photographed in front of a simple "block" facade, the effects department superimposed the image onto a matte painting depicting Starbase 11. Without the beautiful matte, the "outer space" beyond the facade would have been the empty space of the soundstage.

One minute—or rather, one stardate—she was there, standing at the captain's side, handing him an electronic clipboard to initial, pouring him a cup of coffee, serving him a plate of those multicolored veggie cubes. The next, she was gone.

Clearly, NBC had been hoping that Yeoman Janice Rand (Grace Lee Whitney) would be a big hit with *Star Trek* viewers. The network featured her in the early promotional photography for the series and played up her role in their press releases. To judge from these items, the Big Three of *Star Trek* were Kirk, Spock, and Rand. The back cover for the first official tie-in book—a collection of short stories adapted from *Star Trek* episodes by science fiction author James Blish—even described Rand as "the most popular member of the crew, the truly 'out-of-this-world' blonde [who] has drawn the important assignment of secretary to the captain on her first mission in deep space."

Despite the network's early enthusiasm for the character, Janice Rand no longer served on the *Enterprise* after "The Conscience of the King." There are several conflicting rumors about why Whitney left the show. The one most often repeated is that the network found Kirk to be too constrained by her presence. After all, the captain was a virile man who needed space to roam—and to engage in a new romantic tryst every week. It was good for the ratings. But how could he do that with this "secretary" keeping track of his every move? And so, the story goes, Rand was "transferred to another ship."

Rand (still played by the vivacious Whitney) would later return to the fold for several *Star Trek* films, serving as the *Enterprise*'s transporter chief in *Star Trek: The Motion Picture*, an emergency operations officer at Starfleet Command in *Star Trek IV: The Voyage Home*, and a communications officer on the *U.S.S. Excelsior* under Captain Sulu in *Star Trek VI: The Undiscovered Country*.

SHORE LEAVE

"The more complex the mind, the greater the need for the simplicity of play."
—Kirk

An idyllic yet curiously uninhabited world in the Omicron Delta region of space appears to be the perfect place for Kirk's crew to get some much-deserved rest and recreation. Then McCoy encounters a large talking rabbit, Sulu runs into an ancient samurai warrior, and Kirk's attention is split between a former nemesis from Starfleet Academy and a beautiful ex-girlfriend. Still, it all seems like harmless fun and games, until McCoy is mortally wounded—skewered by the lance of a knight on horseback while defending a maiden in distress. As other crew members become embroiled in deadly scenarios of their own making, Kirk realizes that the planet is no wonderland. But who—or what—is behind the bizarre manifestations?

The original story outline for "Shore Leave," by famed science fiction author Theodore Sturgeon, was completed in May 1966, months before *Star Trek*'s debut. As filming approached in the fall, a rewrite was deemed necessary to make the script fit within what had become the show's established parameters for the characters, technology, and story style. Sturgeon was unavailable, so another writer was given the assignment. Unfortunately, that writer was unaware of additional changes the network had requested.

And so it would fall to Gene Roddenberry to rework the script—after shooting had begun. Legend has it that he did it on location while sitting beneath the shade of a tree at Africa U.S.A., a six-hundred-acre ranch in Acton, California. With beautiful scenery, a lake, and a whole contingent of wild animals on call, Roddenberry saw the facility, frequently used by Hollywood filmmakers in the 1960s, as the perfect setting for this quasi-fantasy story. Today the location is the home of Shambala Preserve, a wild animal sanctuary founded by actress Tippi Hedren, of *The Birds* fame.

Additional location sequences for the episode—easily distinguishable by the jarring switch to a desert-like terrain—were shot at craggy Vasquez Rocks in nearby Agua Dulce, California.

There's no denying that Captain Kirk can be hard on his wardrobe. Time after time, his garments have been exposed to the kind of sartorial mayhem that would make even a seasoned seamstress weep. But in "Shore Leave," Kirk's shirt actually seems to rend *itself*. Case in point: Kirk's tussle with old rival Finnegan is definitely rough-and-tumble, but his gold tunic is clearly intact throughout the sequence in which Finnegan slams the captain to the ground. Nevertheless, when the camera moves in for a tight close-up, Kirk's garment is mysteriously torn to shreds.

Script supervision is usually one of the most steadfast aspects of television and film production. It's the supervisor's difficult job to oversee continuity from scene to scene, noting everything from the way an actor is standing to the way the scene is lit. But given that "Shore Leave's" script was being rewritten as it was shot, every department had its hands much too full. Here and there, wardrobe continuity became a bit, well, noncontiguous (Yeoman Barrows's uniform, which suffers damage following an attack by Don Juan, shows some similar inconsistencies from scene to scene). And a last-minute name change for actress Barbara Baldavin—from "Mary Teller" to "Angela Martine," the character she'd played in "Balance of Terror"—somehow didn't get dubbed in during postproduction for scenes shot prior to the name change; hence, she is referred to by different names at different points in the story.

Compounding matters, everyone in the production seemed to have a pet element to work into this story about a planet where thoughts became reality. Some made it into the script, some didn't. A live tiger was rented, but although William Shatner reportedly hoped to wrestle it to the ground, the idea was nixed. The tiger's appearance was brief and relegated to the sidelines. An elephant was also rented but never got its moment on camera.

Despite the topsy-turvy nature of the production, however, "Shore Leave" is inarguably one of *Star Trek*'s most popular episodes.

098

"I've got a personal grudge against that rabbit, Jim."
—McCoy

McCoy is the first *Enterprise* crew member to experience the wonders of this strange "amusement park" planet. In a world where idle thoughts instantly manifest into reality, McCoy finds himself face-to-face with the White Rabbit from Lewis Carroll's fanciful tale *Alice's Adventures in Wonderland*. Unaware that he himself is the "author" of this fantastical scenario, McCoy can't help feeling resentful when his report to the captain is met with good-natured skepticism on Kirk's part. Later that day, after he's gotten the hang of how the place works, McCoy conjures up two scantily clad young ladies from a Rigel II cabaret—"bunnies" of a very different kind—much to the jealous Yeoman Barrows's displeasure.

   Ironically, this episode would not be DeForest Kelley's sole encounter with giant rabbits. Six years later, the actor would run into them again, in the horrific 1972 B movie *Night of the Lepus*. This time, however, the shoe's on the other foot—or rather, paw—as the overly large beasts (the result of—what else—man's infernal tampering with nature) develop a taste for flesh and start munching on the locals in his town.

099

THE SQUIRE OF GOTHOS

As the *Enterprise* passes through a supposedly empty sector of space, sensors pick up a previously uncharted and presumably uninhabitable planet. Seconds later, Kirk and Sulu vanish from the bridge. A landing party equipped with survival gear beams down to find an inexplicably lush and habitable environment, as well as a huge medieval manor. Inside, Kirk and Sulu are being held as the prisoners—or, more accurately, the playthings—of a being named Trelane, who calls his world "Gothos." Although Trelane appears to be human, he clearly isn't: He possesses the remarkable ability to transform energy into matter. Despite his power, Trelane displays the temperament of a spoiled child, demanding that members of Kirk's crew play games he associates with the customs of eighteenth-century Earth. In an attempt to placate their captor, Kirk challenges Trelane to a hunting game—and finds himself in a battle for his life.

"Ah. A Nubian prize. Taken on one of your raids of conquest, no doubt, Captain."
—Trelane

Star Trek regularly conveyed messages decrying racial prejudice and included sharp dialogue pointing out the inappropriate thinking of unenlightened species. As often as not, Uhura was the character utilized to put others in their place. For example, when Trelane approaches the two women he's transported from the *Enterprise*, he refers to Uhura as "a Nubian prize," assuming she is a possession belonging to Kirk. In contrast, Trelane likens the blonde Yeoman Teresa Ross to "fair Helen [of Troy]," calling her visage "the face that launched a thousand ships." Kirk quickly points out that Trelane's prejudice reveals "an immature, unbalanced mind."

A subtler—and more amusing—reference to race quickly slips past the ear in the episode "The Naked Time." During his swashbuckling delusional state, Sulu puts his arm around Uhura and tells her, "I'll protect you, fair maiden." Pushing him away, she responds, "Sorry, neither."

Perhaps the most interesting exchange takes place in "The Savage Curtain," when Uhura lets "Abraham Lincoln" (or rather, an alien presence standing in for Abe) off the hook for referring to her as a "charming negress." Lincoln, apparently realizing his mistake, at-tempts to correct himself: "Forgive me, my dear. I know in my time some use that term as a description of property." But Uhura graciously responds, "In our century, we've learned not to fear words."

The name of Trelane's species is never mentioned in "The Squire of Gothos." And while Kirk and company would encounter quite a few quasi-omnipotent entities down the road (the Organians, the Metrons, and the Melkotians, just to name a few), there were none with Trelane's childlike enthusiasm for making mischief on a cosmic scale. That is, until *Star Trek: The Next Generation*. Fans of both shows have wondered for decades, "Was Trelane a Q? Is the Q that made Picard's life miserable a grown-up version of Trelane?" Gene Roddenberry never answered either question, but he was reportedly amused by the notion. As writers and producers are known to draw water occasionally from the same creative well, it's a possibility worth considering, if only for the fun of it.

Some production design drawings consist of a series of abstract lines and are meant to provide a general idea of what the writers have in mind. Others are detailed and shaded to the point that they become minor works of art, suitable for framing. This beautiful Matt Jefferies design for the entrance to Trelane's manor was re-created onstage with exquisite attention to detail.

EXT. TRELAINE MANOR
STAR TREK 18

ARENA

Upon discovering the destruction of a Starfleet base on Cestus III, the *Enterprise* gives chase to the Gorn spaceship that's responsible for the damage. As the two ships cross into uncharted territory, they are halted by a powerful species known as the Metrons, who accuse Kirk and the Gorn commander of trespassing. The Metrons opt to settle the conflict by forcing Kirk to fight the Gorn commander in hand-to-hand combat on a nearby planet. The winner will go free, while the loser will be destroyed, along with his ship and crew. Kirk realizes that the Gorn are immensely strong, man-sized reptiles, and that their commander would readily defeat him if strength alone were to determine the winner. Is the captain resourceful enough to prevail through other means?

"No, I won't kill him. Do you hear? You'll have to get your entertainment someplace else."
—Kirk

Despite Kirk's justifiable anger over the destruction at Cestus III, he finds that he can't bring himself to kill the Gorn commander, even in the face of the Metrons' assurance that the Gorn "surely would have destroyed you." Kirk has come to understand the Gorn's actions; he's even willing to admit that the Federation colonists may have been in the wrong.

The theme of compassion appears repeatedly throughout *Star Trek*: It's what makes "us" (representatives of the Federation) better than "them" ("bad guys" like the Klingons, the Gorn, etc.). Kirk is willing to admit that he is a barbarian (and he does so, in several episodes), but he also is quick to point out that he's an *enlightened* barbarian, meaning he can choose *not* to kill—and therein lies the advancement of his (and thus our) civilization.

Given that the show first aired during an era when U.S. conflicts in Southeast Asia were escalating, the audience could have easily related to Kirk's philosophy. He wasn't a pacifist, by any means, but he trusted his instincts and avoided killing when he could. His reward was that the all-powerful Metrons paid him a compliment: "We feel that there may be hope for your kind. Therefore you will not be destroyed."

105

On December 29, 1913, a young filmmaker named Cecil B. DeMille started shooting Hollywood's first full-length motion picture, *The Squaw Man*, in a barn on Vine Street. Since that day, Los Angeles and the surrounding area have served as the location for countless films and television episodes. These days, oft-filmed streets, buildings, hillsides, parks, and cemeteries are readily recognized by astute viewers. During the 1960s, however, the general public was not thought to be quite as savvy or traveled. A shot of the jet age architecture of the Theme Building at Los Angeles International Airport could pass for the exotic headquarters of a mysterious spy agency. And the very unique strata of Vasquez Rocks passed for many an alien world on *Star Trek*.

Standing proudly just north of Los Angeles, the rock formation—named after the famed bandit Tiburcio Vasquez—was the backdrop for hundreds of early westerns, featuring vigilantes such as Zorro (a character originally based on Vasquez) and cowboys like Tom Mix, Buck Jones, and Tim Holt. Gene Autry shot numerous episodes of his television show here, as did the producers of *The Lone Ranger*, *Gunsmoke*, *Bonanza*, *The Wild Wild West*, *The Six Million Dollar Man*, and, more recently, *Monk*, *Bones*, and *NCIS*. But *Star Trek* is very likely the show that is most closely associated with the location. Four episodes featured prominent exterior scenes shot at Vasquez Rocks: "Arena," "The Alternative Factor," "Shore Leave," and "Friday's Child."

106

On an episode popularity scale, "Arena" stands somewhere in the middle of the pack. What makes it memorable is not Gene L. Coon's script, which was an adaptation of a well-known short story by science fiction writer Fredric Brown—it's the big green guy.

The Gorn is one of the prolific Wah Chang's best-known designs—and it's his design that people remember, not the plotline. Yes, the Gorn is yet another man in a rubber, zippered suit. But original viewers, particularly young ones, took to the bipedal lizard with an affection they never extended to the Mugato, the creature in the zippered suit from "A Private Little War." The Gorn became an instant classic, and to this day it remains one of the most popular action figures based on a *Star Trek* character.

The lines separating departmental responsibilities in a film or television production sometimes appear arbitrary. For example, the costume department is responsible for creating rubber creature suits like that of the Gorn, but if that costume requires any special accommodations, such as waterproofing or rigging to keep the actor comfortable while wearing it, those needs are the responsibility of the special effects department. The distinction between departments grows even fuzzier when differentiating between such items as pieces of jewelry. Earrings belong exclusively to the costume department, while wedding rings and watches are supplied by the property department. The property department also is responsible for any type of helmet, even though the helmet wearer may be dressed in a matching uniform created by the costume department. And, demonstrating that the distinction can be extremely arbitrary, a purse is a part of a costume, while a briefcase (even if carried by a woman *as* a purse) is a piece of property. These odd distinctions developed and were codified throughout the history of film production; in general, the very first time an item was needed for a production, the department that supplied it became responsible for similar items evermore.

THE ALTERNATIVE FACTOR

"How would it be, trapped forever with a raging madman at your throat? Until time itself came to a stop, for eternity. How would it be?"
—Kirk

While orbiting a lifeless planet, the *Enterprise* is rocked by a powerful energy pulse. The ship's sensors can't interpret the phenomenon, and Spock can describe it only in vague terms: For a brief moment, space itself "winked" out of existence. Starfleet Command confirms that the phenomenon was felt across the entire quadrant and believes that the massive disruption could represent the prelude to an invasion from outside the galaxy. With orders to find the source of the pulse, Kirk investigates the planet below, where sensors now show the presence of a human. There, Kirk finds Lazarus, an odd zealot who claims to be hunting a creature bent on the destruction of all life. Lazarus possesses a small ship that provides passage between our universe and its antimatter counterpart, where his enemy—actually an antimatter version of himself—awaits. Lazarus's initial attempt to travel between the two universes apparently caused the bizarre cosmic disruption that the *Enterprise* experienced. Now

Lazarus wants the *Enterprise*'s dilithium crystals so that he can "recharge" his ship and continue his hunt—and Kirk's refusal to provide them isn't about to stop him. Lazarus's insane obsession may endanger more than the *Enterprise*, for if he succeeds in crossing universes and confronting the antimatter Lazarus, Spock hypothesizes that *both* universes will be annihilated.

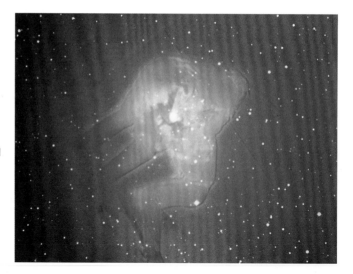

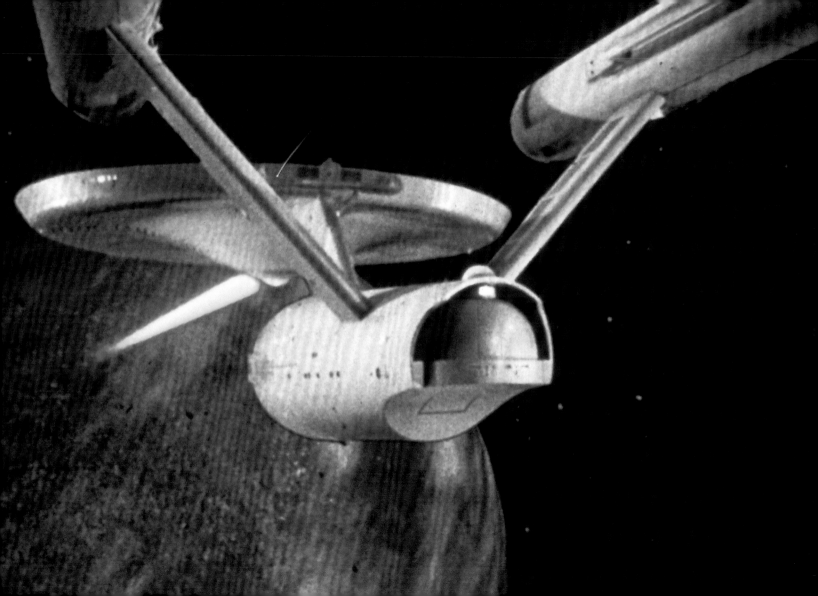

"Another universe, perhaps another dimension, occupying the same space at the same time."
—Kirk

This episode introduces an intriguing concept to *Star Trek* fans: Could a parallel universe, similar and yet different from our own, possibly exist? Unfortunately, this theme isn't even hinted at until the episode is half over. By that time, the viewer is thoroughly entangled in what appears to be a retelling of *Moby-Dick*, with Lazarus as Ahab, pursuing a cosmic white whale as he shouts, "Find my enemy! Find the beast! I'll have my vengeance!"

But while the production of every episode had its own unique set of problems—and "The Alternative Factor" was cursed with more than its fair share—the severest damage seems to have arisen from an unfortunate early choice in casting.

The role of Lazarus was awarded to up-and-coming actor John Drew Barrymore, scion of the famous Barrymore clan and father to actress Drew Barrymore. Although Barrymore showed up for initial meetings and costume fittings, he was nowhere to be found on the first day of production. The role was hastily recast with future *Here Come the Brides* star Robert Brown, but such disruptions always create a ripple effect, triggering costume alterations, script revisions, rescheduled location days, and so on. The episode went a day over schedule, requiring the cast to be carried, in terms of pay, over the Thanksgiving holiday, extremely pricey for a show struggling to remain within a tight budget.

Spock: "Captain, the universe is safe for you and me."
Kirk: "But what of Lazarus? What of Lazarus?"

An early draft of the script for "The Alternative Factor" features a plotline in which Lazarus becomes romantically involved with a female engineer on the *Enterprise*; he later manipulates her into stealing the dilithium crystals he needs. Although the character, Lieutenant Charlene Masters, remains in the filmed version of the episode, she never encounters Lazarus, aside from when he knocks her out so that he can steal the crystals. There are several probable reasons for the change.

For one thing, the subplot, as originally conceived, is very similar to a subplot in "Space Seed," which was scheduled to go into production a few weeks later. The romance between Marla McGivers and Khan is a much more compelling and plausible one than that between Masters and Lazarus, so if a decision had to be made between two similar subplots, the producers seem to have made the right one.

A second possibility returns once again to casting. The actress chosen to play Masters was Janet MacLachlan, who was intelligent and attractive, and who also possessed the right amount of gravitas to play the female officer in charge of a division of engineering. Coincidentally, MacLachlan was also an African American. The romantic entanglement between her and Lazarus (who was *not* African American) could conceivably have caused some television stations in the South to reject airing the episode.

Whatever the reason, the excision of the romance left some large holes in the script and airtime to fill, which may explain why there are an inordinate number of scenes featuring Lazarus falling off cliffs, getting injured, and wrestling with his counterpart in the "corridor" between the two universes.

TOMORROW IS YESTERDAY

"Whatever this thing is, it's big. Two cylindrical projections on top, one below. Purpose: undetermined."
—Captain Christopher

After the gravitational forces of a black star toss the *Enterprise* back in time, the crew awakens to find the ship orbiting Earth in the twentieth century. When the U.S. Air Force's radar spots the ship over Nebraska, a small fighter jet goes up to investigate—and then the *Enterprise* is forced to beam the pilot aboard after the starship inadvertently destroys his plane. Now Kirk has a problem. If he returns Captain John Christopher to Earth, the pilot will report everything he's seen, which could change history. Making matters worse: Spock isn't sure that the *Enterprise* can make it back to the twenty-third century.

Captain Christopher: "I never have believed in little green men."
Spock: "Neither have I."

"Writing should be about characters," says screenwriter D. C. Fontana. "I like the action, too, but the foundation I work from is always the characters." Whether drawn from the germ of an idea that she originated or from a story concept she's been asked to expand and transform, Fontana's scripts always emphasize the human element of an adventure.

The concept for "Tomorrow Is Yesterday" originated with *Star Trek* producer Robert Justman. The basics are all there in a short memo Justman sent to Gene Roddenberry: An accident flings the *Enterprise* into the past, where it is spotted on twentieth-century Earth radar and identified as a UFO. Kirk realizes that knowledge of the *Enterprise*'s existence could alter the course of history, and, as Spock puts it in the aired episode, "If it is changed, Captain, you and I, and all that we know, might not even exist."

Roddenberry assigned the story idea to Dorothy Fontana. She, in turn, created a memorable teleplay that gave meaty roles both to the regulars and to guest star Roger Perry as Air Force Captain John Christopher—a man who is, at various times, amusing (reacting to the Vulcan first officer), irksome (stubbornly refusing to accept Kirk's decree that he cannot return home), and sentimental (absorbing the news that his not-yet-conceived son will someday head a mission to Saturn). In short, he's as human as they come. Fontana added plenty of action and humor to the mix—and showed a touch of precognition when she had Kirk cite from memory that Earth's "first manned moon shot was in the late 1960s": Earth's first manned moon landing occurred in 1969, just three years *after* this episode hit the airwaves, and just a few short months after *Star Trek* aired its final first-run episode.

"Tomorrow Is Yesterday" marks the second time that the *Enterprise* travels back in time. But whereas the first trip, in "The Naked Time," was very short—a mere seventy-one hours—this one sends the crew three hundred *years* into the past, necessitating some precise calculations from Spock and Scotty in order to get the *Enterprise* home. Afterward, Kirk realizes they have come up with a tool that will allow the *Enterprise* to make controlled trips through time, whenever such travel is deemed required. You'd think this would have resulted in starships from every world initiating their own journeys in time and space, but apparently Starfleet kept the methodology of the so-called slingshot effect very hush-hush. Kirk and company would again use the technique to revisit Earth of the 1960s in "Assignment: Earth" and later, Earth of the 1980s in the film *Star Trek IV: The Voyage Home*.

"Computer, you will not address me in that manner."
—Kirk

Although NBC executives had given Gene Roddenberry an unprecedented second chance to sell them on his *"Wagon Train* to the stars" concept, they instructed him to eliminate the character of the *Enterprise*'s female first officer, known as "Number One," from all future *Star Trek* offerings. Still, veteran television writer Samuel A. Peeples, who'd been tagged by Roddenberry to write the second *Star Trek* pilot, felt there might be a way to retain the intriguing character, not as a human female but as the personality of the ship's computer. Peeples postulated that in the future, astronauts (presumably all male) might experience psychological problems on extended space missions sans female companionship. Giving a ship's computer a female voice, he reasoned, as well as programming it for simple conversation, might assuage this problem. Peeples even pushed the envelope a little further, suggesting that an upgrade gone awry might give the *Enterprise*'s computer a "personality circuit," allowing her to fall in love with her captain. This female computer, named "Number One," would be fully capable of thinking for herself: She would "watch out for the entire ship's complement . . . even to the point of going contrary to their wishes, if it is in their best interests." In such cases, "she becomes all machine—with potentials no human can ever approach."

Number One would sometimes be "vain," "jealous," and "capable of pouting like any female when things don't work out her way."

Peeples's particular take on Number One never made it onto the *Enterprise*. However, something very like his pouty computer did make a brief appearance in "Tomorrow Is Yesterday," wherein viewers learn that the ship's computer has received a less than satisfactory upgrade that irritates Captain Kirk to no end. The late Majel Barrett, who played Number One in "The Cage," provided the respectably dispassionate female voice of the *Enterprise* computer throughout the entire run of the series, and also in the spin-off *Star Trek* shows and films. Her last performance as the voice of the *Enterprise* computer was in the 2009 *Star Trek* movie.

THE RETURN OF THE ARCHONS

One hundred years ago, a starship known as the *Archon* traveled to Beta III—and was never heard from again. Kirk takes the *Enterprise* to Beta III to investigate the fate of the *Archon*'s crew and discovers a society, collectively known as "the Body," that is stagnant and non-productive. The Body is under the strict mental control of Landru, a seemingly omniscient computer that's been in charge for thousands of years. It was Landru that destroyed the *Archon* and "absorbed" its crew into the pathologically tranquil populace of Beta III. The same fate awaits Kirk's crew if the captain can't find a way to stop Landru.

The people of Beta III believe Kirk and company to be "Archons," the name collectively given to the survivors of the *Archon*, a Starfleet ship that Landru destroyed a hundred years ago.

The name "Archon" doesn't really fit within Starfleet's traditional pattern of ship nomenclature. Most often, the starships mentioned in *Star Trek* are named after historic Earth naval vessels; the *Enterprise*, for example, is one of the top-of-the-line starships designed for long-range exploration, among them *Constitution*, *Constellation*, *Defiant*, *Endeavor*, *Excalibur*, *Exeter*, *Hood*, *Intrepid*, *Lexington*, *Potemkin*, *Republic*, and *Yorktown*. "Archon," however, is a Greek word that means "ruler," containing the same root as "monarch" and "hierarchy"—not really a snug fit within a fleet dedicated to peace and exploration.

Why the anomaly? It was apparently a bit of whimsy on the author's part. The story for "The Return of the Archons" was written by Gene Roddenberry, the same Gene Roddenberry who, while in college, belonged to a debate team called "the Archons."

"The evil must be destroyed. That is the Prime Directive. And you are the evil. Fulfill the Prime Directive!"
—Kirk

Speaking of debate teams (see previous spread), clearly there was one at Starfleet Academy. James T. Kirk positively excels at using common debate tactics against his opponents, revealing errors or omissions in his opponent's facts and/or logic in order to win an argument. This skill is particularly powerful when dealing with opponents of the inanimate kind, as on Beta III. When Kirk believes Landru to be a powerful humanoid of some sort, he is briefly stymied. But once Spock points out that Beta III's society has "the tranquillity of the machine, all parts working in unison," Kirk knows what he's up against. If he can find the computer that's running things, it's a goner, because his glib tongue can easily tie knots in a computer's logic, ultimately confusing it into self-destruction.

"The Return of the Archons" is the first of four episodes in which Kirk literally talks a computer to death; he pulls it off again in "The Changeling," "I, Mudd," and "The Ultimate Computer."

"It's almost the Red Hour," a man on the street informs Kirk's landing party. Then the clock strikes six and all hell breaks loose. The people of Beta III, suddenly cast free of their imposed apathy, erupt into a "festival" of violent, lustful chaos. Twelve hours later, the party's over, and people go back to whatever boring things they were doing before the animalistic shindig. No explanation is given for why the Red Hour takes place, and although it gives the episode an exciting first act, in truth it has little to do with the rest of the episode.

Many viewers, however, took the concept of "Red Hour" to heart, perhaps none more so than comic actor and self-proclaimed *Star Trek* fan Ben Stiller. In 2001, Stiller named his motion picture production company "Red Hour Productions," and under that logo almost a dozen movies have been released to date, including *Zoolander*, *Starsky & Hutch*, and *Tropic Thunder*. As cowriter of *Zoolander*, Stiller named the film's white-haired evil fashion czar "J. Mugatu" (after the white-haired ape in the *Star Trek* episode "A Private Little War") and the female lead character Matilda Jeffries (after *Star Trek* production designer Matt Jefferies).

119

A TASTE OF ARMAGEDDON

"I'm a barbarian."
—Kirk

Against the stated wishes of Eminiar VII's governing faction, Federation Ambassador Robert Fox orders Kirk to establish diplomatic contact with the planet. Upon arrival, Kirk learns that Eminiar VII has been at war with the neighboring world of Vendikar for more than five hundred years, even though there's no sign of any damage that could be attributed to such prolonged conflict. The surprising reason: Eminiar VII and Vendikar are engaged in a virtual war. Computers on each world project the weapons strikes and resulting casualties. Those unlucky citizens who are declared "dead" must report to vaporization booths for *actual* destruction—and the war's latest victims are the crew of the *Enterprise*.

"We're human beings, with the blood of a million savage years on our hands. But we can stop it. We can admit that we're killers, but we're not going to kill today. That's all it takes. Knowing that we're not going to kill . . . today."
—Kirk

Star Trek was always a "message" show, and more often than not in an era when the Vietnam War was on the mind of every American, the message was that "war is *bad*." It would be said often over the course of seventy-nine episodes, but perhaps never as eloquently as Kirk puts it in "A Taste of Armageddon":

"Death, destruction, disease, horror—that's what war is all about. That's what makes it a thing to be avoided. But you've made it neat and painless—so neat and painless, you've had no reason to stop it, and you've had it for *five hundred years*."

This episode is a perfect counterpoint to the one that preceded it, "The Return of the Archons." There, a computer keeps peace in the society it oversees by restricting the emotions of the planet's inhabitants. Here, the governing council of Eminiar VII has nearly eliminated the populace's emotional response to death by allowing a computer to run its five-hundred-year war with a neighboring world.

The FSNP (for "Famous Spock Nerve Pinch," as it was referred to in scripts for *Star Trek*) originated very early in the show's first season. In "The Enemy Within," Spock was to KO "evil" Kirk with a karate chop, but actor Leonard Nimoy felt that it was out of character for Spock. He suggested to the director that the Vulcan, who knew something of human anatomy, would realize that if he applied pressure to the nerve complex at the base of the neck, he could render someone unconscious instantly and nonviolently.

As with his mind-meld technique, Nimoy's FSNP would get better the more his character practiced it. Although Spock often applied the pinch from behind his victim (as in "The Enemy Within" and "Tomorrow Is Yesterday"), the writers began giving him lines that allowed him to walk right up to the intended and apply the FSNP—as he does here, telling the gullible guard that "there is a multi-legged creature crawling on your shoulder" and then reaching forward, as if to helpfully brush the creature away.

While many *Star Trek* tableaux were "reenvisioned" a few years ago for the remastered release of *Star Trek* in high definition, some were so iconic that the producers merely color-corrected them and cleaned them up. Albert Whitlock's original matte painting of Eminiar VII's futuristic cityscape—seen here—received little alteration. The new CGI version followed the lines of the old painting very closely but added a few moving elements, such as a hover-train and several tiny humans walking in the deep background, to make it less static. Members of the crew that worked on the remastered series played the humans.

"When CBS announced that they had remastered the original *Star Trek* series in high definition, they also announced plans to redo the visual effects," recalls Michael Okuda, one of the remastering project's three visual effects producers, along with Dave Rossi and Denise Okuda. "Of course, we knew fans would be skeptical. We shared their concern, and we were determined to respect the artistry and the storytelling of those who made that classic show back in the 1960s."

This photo of the CBS Digital crew was taken in November 2006. The occasion was "green screen day," when the crew would shoot images of the humanoid life-forms (in other words, themselves) that would appear, typically in unrecognizably tiny form, within a number of the completed mattes. Standing in the back row, far right, is the project's visual effects supervisor, Niel Wray. Also in the back row, matte artist Max Gabl is seen in a brown T-shirt and producer Dave Rossi in a gold Starfleet tunic. Producers Michael and Denise Okuda, also in Starfleet garb, kneel side by side in the center of the front row. Sitting cross-legged in the very front, the cheerful figure in black is the project's executive producer, David LaFountaine.

SPACE SEED

The *Enterprise* comes upon an old "sleeper ship" from Earth's late twentieth century. The vessel, labeled *Botany Bay*, carries a crew of men and women, all in suspended animation. The group's presumed leader, a charismatic man who gives his name only as "Khan," is revived, but Kirk puts off awakening the others until he can learn more about Khan and his ship. But Khan Noonien Singh—a genetically perfect specimen who managed to conquer a quarter of the planet during Earth's so-called Eugenics Wars—still has all the ambition, strength, and cunning that made him a formidable tyrant centuries earlier. With the help of the ship's historian, who has fallen in love with him, Khan awakens his followers and takes control of the *Enterprise*, giving its crew an ultimatum: yield to his leadership . . . or die.

"It would be interesting, Captain, to return to that world in a hundred years and learn what crop had sprouted from the seed you planted today."
—Spock

Be careful what you wish for, Spock. Long after the end of their five-year mission, the *Enterprise* and its crew would again encounter Khan Noonien Singh and learn that circumstances on Ceti Alpha V had sprouted a very bitter crop. Once a rational, albeit power-hungry ty-rant, the Khan that Kirk encounters in 1982's *Star Trek II: The Wrath of Khan* is a madman, driven insane by the hardships he has endured on the hellish planet to which he was consigned.

The person behind the return of Khan is Harve Bennett, producer and cowriter of *Star Trek II*. It was Bennett whom Paramount Pictures turned to when the studio decided to make a sequel to *Star Trek: The Motion Picture*. He was known more for his success on network tele-vision (*The Mod Squad*, *The Six Million Dollar Man*, and *The Bionic Woman*) than his motion picture acumen, but Paramount was count-ing on Bennett's reputation for producing well-made, action-packed adventures on time and within a set budget.

When he got the assignment, Bennett admits, "I was an ignoramus about *Star Trek*. So I spent three months watching episodes, with an eye to potential source material."

Bennett wanted to create a classic story, pitting the hero, Kirk, against a strong villain. The stronger the antagonist, he reasoned, the greater the achievement of the protagonist. And when he saw "Space Seed," Bennett recalls, "I had one of those 'Eureka!' moments. I can't think of a stronger antagonist in the history of *Star Trek* than Khan." All the elements that he needed were right there, he continues. "A superman in exile, a guest actor who was still available—it all made such sense."

"Open your heart. Will you open your heart?"
—Khan

There are times when *Star Trek*'s wonderful vision of the future isn't quite so forward-thinking. Race relations, an unpopular war, the social divide between hippies and the establishment—all were fair game when it came to poking holes in the status quo. But when it came to women, well, consider the "How to Marry a Millionaire" mind-set of "Mudd's Women," the flirty computer (created by female engineers!) with "an unfortunate tendency to giggle" in "Tomorrow Is Yesterday," or even poor Uhura, stuck opening and closing hailing frequencies for much of the series.

But if certain parts of "Space Seed" come across as Harlequin romance (ship's historian Marla McGivers's fascination with the living embodiment of her warrior-prince fantasies leads her to throw away her career and commit mutiny), it's not just a sign of the era's inequality between the sexes. Just about *everyone* on the *Enterprise*, with the exception of Spock, is struck by Khan's tremendous charisma. As McCoy tells Kirk, "He has a magnetism, almost electric—you've felt it." Even Kirk, who should have known better, yields to Khan's seemingly innocent request to peruse the technical manuals for the *Enterprise*. And the entire senior staff (all male) thoroughly confounds Spock when they express open admiration for Khan.

And if the words on the script page established Khan as a man of influence, the charisma of the actor who portrayed him certainly closed the deal. "Ricardo Montalban *is* power," declares Harve Bennett, producer of *Star Trek II: The Wrath of Khan*. "He's one of the most underrated actors in the past fifty years." The Latino actor's turn as the magnificent tyrant, reprised fifteen years later in the motion picture, secured Montalban his position as *Star Trek*'s most memorable villain, bar none.

"Well, either choke me or cut my throat—make up your mind."
—McCoy

By the latter part of the first season, Doctor McCoy had become a strong presence on *Star Trek*. The once occasional verbal jabs between McCoy and Spock were now a regular feature, clearly fun to write and equally fun to watch. Viewers were also learning about McCoy's eccentricities—like the fact that he disliked having his atoms "scattered back and forth across space" by the transporter. But beyond comic relief, and beyond sheer utility as the guy who was there to patch up the crew, it was clear that McCoy could hold his own in a dramatic setting, even up against a villain as incandescent as Khan Noonien Singh. McCoy's cool-under-fire persona comes to the forefront in a memorable scene from "Space Seed," as Khan grabs him by the throat and threatens him with a knife. This move provokes only a wry surgical tip from McCoy, delivered with whispered intensity: "It would be *most* effective if you would cut the carotid artery, just under the left ear."

The comment has the desired effect: Khan respects McCoy's willingness to meet his challenge, mano a mano, so to speak, and he tells the doctor that he is "a brave man."

While Shatner and Nimoy were, by this time, drawing in an impressive amount of fan mail each week, DeForest Kelley also had a devoted following, thanks to his consistently strong performances in scenes like these. Associate producer Bob Justman recognized that the actor deserved better than the contractual "featuring DeForest Kelley" end credit that he was receiving. Justman therefore took it upon himself to discuss the matter with NBC, and the following season, DeForest Kelley's name was moved up front to a "starring" credit in the main titles.

Blue screen technology in the 1960s was an analog process that required an extraordinary amount of care and skill. Replacing the blue area in a shot with an additional image required use of an optical printer—essentially a camera that looks directly into a projector—and photochemical processing. Effects technicians took numerous steps to sandwich together pieces of film and rephotograph them using filters and other forms of manipulation. Given the digital tools used today, it seems astonishing that these efforts, at the time, were considered "bleeding-edge" technology.

The eleven-foot-long *Enterprise* model, shown here along with the *Botany Bay* spacecraft from "Space Seed," now sits in the Smithsonian Institution (see spread 361).

THIS SIDE OF PARADISE

The *Enterprise* is sent to Omicron Ceti III to report on the fate of a group of colonists who have been exposed to the region's deadly Berthold radiation. To the surprise of Kirk and the rest of the landing party, the colonists are all alive and in perfect health. Among them is Leila Kalomi, a former acquaintance of Spock's who harbors feelings for the Vulcan. Leila demonstrates the secret of the group's survival by exposing Spock to the spores of an alien plant species. The plants have established a passive symbiotic relationship with the colonists: Their spores immunize the humans against the Berthold radiation and, at the same time, provide the host with perfect health and a feeling of serene tranquillity. As the spores work on Spock, he yields to his long-suppressed emotional side and falls in love with Leila. Before long, the entire crew has been exposed to the spores and opted to abandon the ship in exchange for a pastoral life on the planet—leaving a frustrated Kirk wondering how he can get the mutineers to return to the *Enterprise*.

Many of the female characters who graced the *Star Trek* screen were given hairstyles plied into bizarre architectural configurations and garments that left little to the viewer's imagination. "This Side of Paradise"'s Leila Kalomi, as portrayed by Jill Ireland, was a noteworthy exception to the rule. Her beauty spoke of a different feminine ideal—the "nature girl," refreshingly free of artifice, garbed in practical yet chic overalls. Leila was smart, gentle, and self-sufficient—but apparently not opposed to communal living, given the right group of people. Even the camera adored her: Director of photography Jerry Finnerman's painterly hand cast her in a radiant glow that seemed to highlight each individual strand of her golden hair. The stoic Spock somehow managed to resist Leila prior to his exposure to the spores, but he made up for lost time after he inhaled.

According to D. C. Fontana, who reconceived the story that had been credited to Nathan Butler (a pseudonym used by science fiction author Jerry Sohl), Leila was initially conceived as "a woman of color." "She was supposed to be Hawaiian, and she was going to have a relationship with Sulu," says Fontana. Scripts, however, typically go through many iterations, and ultimately it was Spock, not Sulu, who wound up being paired with Leila. "Then they cast Jill Ireland, an amazingly beautiful woman, to play Leila," says Fontana, recalling the delicate-featured, blue-eyed, blonde actress. "I thought, well, *some* Hawaiians may look like her," Fontana jokes.

"We weren't meant for [Paradise]. None of us. Man stagnates if he has no ambition, no desire to be more than he is."
—Kirk

If there's one thing James Kirk can't stomach, it's Paradise. His passion for the *Enterprise* is all-consuming. No woman can hope to stand between Kirk and his ship, so what chance does an odd-looking botanical specimen have? The spore-shooter does its best, showering the captain with a full charge of happy dust, but it only pacifies the captain for a short while. All it takes is a glimpse at one of his medals for bravery to create cracks in his superficially peaceful facade. By the time he gets to the transporter room with his suitcase, the captain doesn't look like a man eager to spend the rest of his life tilling the soil, let alone abandon the love of his life. Pounding his fist against the transporter controls, Kirk forces out three emphatic words: "*I . . . can't . . . leave!*" After that, the score is Kirk one, spores *nada*.

The first draft of the script, reports writer D. C. Fontana, indicated that all the spore plants were located in a cave on the planet. *One* cave. Laughing, she says, "Well, *obviously* the characters would quickly figure out: '*Do not go in the cave!*' And that's one of the first things I changed when Gene [Roddenberry] gave the script to me to rewrite. I put those spores all over the place."

"For the first time in my life, I was happy."
—Spock

Finding extraterrestrial spores on one's planet usually is a bad thing. They may have traveled to your world to expand their grazing territory— and you're the blue plate special (as in *The Day of the Triffids*). Or they may have come with some peculiar master plan that involves replacing you and all of your neighbors with a populace of look-alike, emotionless drones (*Invasion of the Body Snatchers*). But the nonnative spores of Omicron Ceti III don't seem to have a malicious agenda. They actually make living on that irradiated planet possible, and they provide a nice bonus package: feelings of peace, tranquillity, and yes, love. The "emotionless" Mister Spock initially experiences some painful side effects as the spores infiltrate him—presumably because he is engaged in a ferocious internal battle against all that force-fed sweetness and light. Once he yields, however, he's as blissful as the rest of the colonists, and he seems to genuinely regret being freed from their influence. The spores, once banished, leave all the colonists with perfect health, though they also seem to leave Spock with a broader sense of compassion. He is remarkably kind to Leila when he reveals that he can no longer love her; we sense that the emotion he experienced was genuine. But turning his back on that emotion is his duty, he explains, describing it as his "self-made purgatory."

Viewers who have studied all seventy-nine episodes of *Star Trek* know there are only two scenes that depict the empty *Enterprise* bridge, bereft of personnel. The one that most fans think of is in "This Side of Paradise": just a few seconds of footage that convey the sense of isolation Captain Kirk feels as he steps out of the turbolift and comprehends at last that his entire crew has deserted him. The other scene, briefer and less iconic, is in "The Mark of Gideon."

It was the "Paradise" shot that the producers of *Star Trek: The Next Generation* turned to when they decided to honor *The Original Series* by re-creating Kirk's bridge for a *TNG* episode called "Relics." The filmmakers quickly learned what a difficult task they'd taken on: The original bridge was long gone, and there wasn't even an accurately scaled drawing of the set to use as a reference. Compounding the problem was the fact that building an entirely new bridge set for a single sequence would not be cost-effective. Enter serendipity: The producers found the "Paradise" footage and used it as part of their blue screen process. That allowed the designers to build a smaller piece of set that came within budget, a pie-shaped wedge containing a captain's chair and helm/navigation console borrowed from model maker and long-time *Star Trek* fan Steve Horch.

THE DEVIL IN THE DARK

The *Enterprise* travels to the planet Janus VI to determine what is killing workers in an underground mining facility. Doctor McCoy scoffs when Spock surmises that a silicon-based life-form may be behind the deaths, but Spock is proven correct: The killer is found to be a rocklike beast that excretes acid at will, allowing it to tunnel swiftly through solid rock—or to disintegrate a man. The miners want the creature destroyed, yet Spock believes that it may be an intelligent being with a rational motive behind its actions. But with Kirk's life in the balance, there may not be time to prove his theory.

Kirk: "Mister Spock, give us a report on life beneath the surface."
Spock: "There is no life. At least, no life as we know it."

In the late 1960s, segregation and the civil rights movement in the
United States were featured on the evening news as often as not. The
producers of *Star Trek* never openly stated which side of that argument they supported, but they consistently staged stories that suggested how prejudice originates from misunderstanding, from a refusal to recognize the value of others who may be "different." For
"The Devil in the Dark," they created the most "different" alien ever
encountered by the crew of the *Enterprise*. Of course, it took Spock,
the outsider, to recognize that the "silicon nodules" were eggs—the
offspring of a very intelligent and vengeful being. The conclusion for
all is that the "devil" down in the mines was not the Horta, but the
mob mentality of the frightened miners.

Television production is as much about budget as it is about story-telling, a fact never more apparent than in the production of early science fiction shows. In an inventive, frugal attempt to create an alien landscape on a tiny budget, *Star Trek*'s writers set the story for "The Devil in the Dark" underground, allowing production designers to create rocks and tunnels by simply covering handy items with fabric, fiberglass, and papier-mâché. To assist in selling the concept, a matte painting depicting the facility was hung in the background for several shots. The result: effective sci-fi on a shoestring.

"The Devil in the Dark" is one of *Star Trek*'s most beloved episodes, due in part to a unique creature known as the Horta. Hoping to bring an alien to the screen that didn't look like just another man in a fuzzy costume with a zipper down the back, the producers offered a challenge to independent effects makeup and costume designer Janos Prohaska: If he could create "a really great creature," they'd rent it from him and let him play the role. Prohaska was known at the time for creating more earthly animal costumes such as bears, so when he returned carrying a large, lumpy, "goopy thing," recalls D. C. Fontana (the show's script supervisor), everyone from Roddenberry to the episode's writer, Gene L. Coon, had understandable reservations. "He got us all outside to take a look at it in action," says Fontana. "I remember he laid this rubber chicken on the ground and then he put on the costume." Prohaska then proceeded to "get into character" as the Horta. He scooted around, quivering and rotating, and then, Fontana continues, "he jumped right on the rubber chicken—crawled right over it—and out the back end of the costume came a bunch of chicken bones!" Coon reportedly was so impressed that he quickly ran to his typewriter to refine the script.

Over the years, fans of the show most often have likened the Horta to "an extra-large pepperoni pizza." Always with the proper respect, of course.

ERRAND OF MERCY

"As I stand here, I also stand upon the home planet of the Klingon Empire, and the home planet of your Federation, Captain. I'm putting a stop to this insane war."
—Ayelborne

The Federation stands on the verge of war with the Klingon Empire, and Kirk travels to the planet Organia, hoping to convince its inhabitants to allow Starfleet to establish a presence on their strategically located world. The strangely placid Organians, however, refuse to cooperate, even when Commander Kor's Klingon occupation force invades. As the *Enterprise* and a Klingon vessel square off in preparation for battle, the Organians demonstrate why they don't need help from the Federation—or anyone else—to keep their territory conflict-free.

Kor: "You of the Federation, you are much like us."
Kirk: "We're nothing like you. We're a democratic body."
Kor: "I'm not referring to minor ideological differences. I mean that we
are similar as a species. Here we are on a planet of sheep, two tigers.
Predators. Hunters. Killers. And it is precisely that which makes us
great. And there is a universe to be taken."

Considering the Klingon species' eventual importance within the *Star
Trek* pantheon of characters, "Errand of Mercy" is a curiously gentle
episode to have introduced "the warrior species." Although Klingons
live for battle, the closest Kor gets to it is his verbal sparring with Kirk.
When a violent confrontation doesn't ensue, Kor laments, "It would
have been glorious." One suspects that Kirk feels the same.

However glorious it may have been, the episode really isn't about
war—it's about the tensions that lead up to war. By the end of its first
season, *Star Trek* was coming into its own, taking twentieth-century
subjects and stealthily transforming them via the future tense. It was
"message television," if you knew how to decode it. In writer Gene L.
Coon's hands, the Cold War between the United States and the
Soviet Union became the standoff between the Federation and the
Klingons—or, on more intimate terms, the one between Kirk and Kor.
But as the Organians predicted, the Federation and its Klingon counterpart would eventually become "fast friends" and work together.

Again, a bit of accurate foresight from the *Star Trek* writers: The Cold
War would end, and the Soviets would allow the Berlin Wall to fall.

Rather than fade into the background, the warrior race of the Klingons would grow in popularity, gaining even *more* fans as the aggressive allies of the Federation than they had as its enemies. Vulcans
notwithstanding, today they are the *Star Trek* franchise's most popular alien species.

The real stars of "Errand of Mercy" are the Organians, calmly smiling through what appears to be an escalating crisis in their own backyard. But isn't this the flash point for a heated interstellar war? Well, no . . . because the Organians have the ability to douse that flame at any point they wish. A staunch believer in free will, Kirk is amused to learn that what he had thought was a battle of wits was nothing of the sort. "We didn't beat the odds," he tells Spock. "The Organians raided the game."

Although their name would be woven into the fabric of *Star Trek* continuity, the Organians would not become *Star Trek* regulars. Having an omnipotent species around to take care of complex problems would not be good for ongoing story lines; jeopardy, after all, is the engine that drives drama, and with the Organians standing in the wings, there would be no jeopardy. Still, the *threat* of their intervention would play an important role in keeping the peace between the Federation and the Klingons. The "Organian Peace Treaty"—note the similarity to the so-called nuclear peace treaty that was much in the news during the late 1960s—would be referred to in later episodes "The Trouble with Tribbles" and "Day of the Dove," and again in the motion pictures *Star Trek II: The Wrath of Khan* and *Star Trek VI: The Undiscovered Country*.

Etymology often consists of fun little stories about people. Famous examples: Nineteenth-century temperance advocate Amelia Bloomer promoted women's right to wear pants; the eighteenth-century Earl of Sandwich asked his servant to bring him a slab of meat tucked between two pieces of bread; and nineteenth-century plumber Thomas Crapper developed ways to improve washroom facilities. These names spontaneously became commonly used nouns, but when a name falls under the pen of a writer, it can take on a new meaning by design. For instance, when screenwriter Gene L. Coon created a villainous new species for the episode "Errand of Mercy," a name for the blackguards didn't immediately come to mind—until that of an old acquaintance of Gene Roddenberry's came into earshot. Roddenberry, who had been a proud member of the Los Angeles Police Department, served with an officer named Wilbur Clingan. The production staff liked the sound of the name, so Coon altered the spelling and used it in this episode.

142

THE CITY ON THE EDGE OF FOREVER

"A question. Since before your sun burned hot in space and before your race was born, I have awaited a question."
—the Guardian

Two drops of cordrazine can save a man's life. But when Doctor Mc-Coy accidentally injects himself with a hundred times that amount, he becomes a delusional madman, fleeing the *Enterprise* via the ship's transporter. On the planet below, Kirk and a landing party find the Guardian of Forever, a living machine that seems to be the source of the mysterious time distortion waves the *Enterprise* had been investigating prior to the accident. As the Guardian demonstrates its abilities by showing Kirk the history of Earth via a large portal, Mc-Coy leaps through and disappears into the past. At that instant, the *Enterprise* disappears from orbit, stranding the landing party on the Guardian's world. McCoy has done something to change Earth's history, explains the Guardian, and that, in turn, has altered the present of Kirk and company. It's up to Kirk and Spock to follow McCoy into the past and prevent him from effecting that change.

143

"One day soon, man is going to be able to harness incredible energies, maybe even the atom. Energies that could ultimately hurl us to
other worlds in some sort of spaceship."
—Edith Keeler

The character of Edith Keeler was loosely based on real-life twentieth-
century evangelist Aimee Semple McPherson, who preached conser-
vative gospel in progressive ways, via radio, movies, and stage acts.
During the era in which most of "The City on the Edge of Forever"
takes place, McPherson was instrumental in opening soup kitchens
and free clinics for the poor.

Keeler is a far more secular character than McPherson, preaching
the benefits of hard work, sobriety, and love of one's fellow man, rather
than strict Christianity. She's a forward thinker (unlike McPherson,
who spent much of her life rallying the masses to oppose Charles
Darwin's theory of evolution), speculating about man's exploitation
of the atom and his future in the stars. Although Kirk clearly believes
that Edith is intuitive, Spock scoffs at any suggestion of clairvoyance
and categorizes her observations as mere "gifted insight."

Whatever she's got, however, she seems to have it in spades. Had
McCoy succeeded in saving her life, she would have gone on to influence no less than Franklin D. Roosevelt with her idealistic and paci-
fistic beliefs.

Or she might have made a good detective. Her powers of perception are quite astute, particularly when it comes to sizing up Spock.
Keeler deems the Vulcan's position in the universe to be "at [Kirk's]
side, as if you've always been there and always will." And indeed,
Spock would fulfill that prediction, in one way or another, for much of
the next several decades.

Kirk: "Spock, I believe I'm in love with Edith Keeler."
Spock: "Jim, Edith Keeler must *die."*

The score for "The City on the Edge of Forever" was written by Fred Steiner. Although Steiner contributed more scores to *Star Trek* than any of the show's other composers, his best-known television-related work is a cool jazz piece called "Park Avenue Beat," which was used as the theme to *Perry Mason* for that show's entire nine-year run. Like many television shows of the era, *Star Trek* was economical in its use and reuse of its scores: Steiner's score for "City" was a partial one, with many of the musical cues pulled from earlier episodes. Steiner's original work in the episode underscores the bittersweet romantic relationship between Kirk and Edith Keeler. The old classic "Good Night, Sweetheart," by composer Ray Noble and lyricists Jimmy Campbell and Reg Connelly, plays a prominent role in the episode, initially heard playing on a radio as Kirk and Keeler stand talking about the stars, and later, as a lamentful string adaptation that underscores Kirk's emotions in the aftermath of Keeler's death.

   A grace note: Can there be time travel without anachronism? Apparently not. The scenes on Earth supposedly take place in 1930, but the song "Good Night, Sweetheart" was not released until 1931.

"Let's get the hell out of here."
—Kirk

"The City on the Edge of Forever" ranks at the top of almost everyone's list of favorite *Star Trek* episodes—*Star Trek* fans, *Star Trek* actors, *Star Trek* producers, you name it. Just about everyone loves it, *except* for the man who wrote it—or didn't write it, as the legend goes.

The man credited with writing the episode is Harlan Ellison, a brilliant author of speculative fiction whose work has been much in demand by television producers since the early 1960s. By all accounts—and there are many—the script Ellison delivered for "City" did not work within the established *Star Trek* format and, as written, would have been prohibitively expensive to produce. Those who read the script were effusive in their praise; it was, they said, outstanding, worthy of its own segment in an anthology-type television series such as *The Outer Limits* or *The Twilight Zone*. But, to paraphrase Spock, it was "not Star Trek as they knew or understood it." Hence, not usable as is.

So who is responsible for what viewers wound up seeing on the screen? The basic framework of Ellison's story remains, as do some of the characters and some of the best lines. But the script went through the hands of no less than four additional writers, and each added his or her own touches. Too many cooks, as is generally said, spoil the broth. But somehow, in the case of "The City on the Edge of Forever," the work of five "cooks" came together serendipitously, creating a final product that would go on to become one of the most acclaimed hours in television history.

OPERATION: ANNIHILATE!

An inexplicable interplanetary epidemic of mass insanity is sweeping across a section of the galaxy. If the outbreak follows its most recent trajectory, the planet Deneva—home to Kirk's brother Sam and his family—is next in its path. By the time the *Enterprise* arrives, Deneva's inhabitants are already infected, enthralled to some unknown agent that uses pain to bend them to its collective will. Kirk's brother has already perished, and his sister-in-law Aurelan dies in agony after revealing that "horrible things" are forcing the populace to build spaceships—but to what purpose? While investigating the infestation, Spock is attacked by a strange parasite that infiltrates his entire nervous system within a matter of minutes. Only Spock's rigid Vulcan mental discipline allows him to withstand the pain it inflicts. Spock reveals to Kirk that he is being pressured to take control of the *Enterprise* in order to spread a large colony of these parasites across the galaxy. For now, he says, he can resist, but if McCoy can't expedite a cure, Kirk must send the Vulcan down to Deneva—and exterminate everyone on the planet.

Always on the lookout for futuristic architecture, *Star Trek* production took advantage of aerospace and automotive corporation TRW's ultramodern "Space Park" headquarters in Redondo Beach, California, for key scenes in "Operation: Annihilate!" Filming commenced on February 15, 1967, just outside the facility's cafeteria, where the *Enterprise* landing party was attacked by a band of Deneva's parasite-crazed residents. Founded in 1953 by Simon Ramo and Dean Wooldridge, two former Hughes Aircraft employees who felt there was a future in developing advanced electronic systems for aircraft, TRW became part of Northrop Grumman Space Technology in 2002.

"It is my brother. Was my brother."
—Kirk

The original draft of the script for "Operation: Annihilate!"—the only episode of *Star Trek* to feature an exclamation point in the title—did not mention Kirk's family. The character of Aurelan was present, but instead of being Kirk's sister-in-law, she was the girlfriend of the man who flew his ship into the Denevan sun. Matching Aurelan up with Sam Kirk and adding their son Peter to the mix gave the episode a poignancy that had been lacking previously, and it gave the show a sense of continuity that somehow made the familiar characters seem more "real."

Viewers had heard of Sam just once before: In the episode "What Are Little Girls Made Of?" the real Kirk tested the android Kirk's memory by quizzing him about Sam:

KIRK: Tell me about Sam.
KIRK 2: George Samuel Kirk, your brother. Only you call him Sam.
KIRK: He saw me off on this mission.
KIRK 2: Yes, with his wife and three sons.
KIRK: He said he was being transferred to Earth Colony 2 research station.
KIRK 2: No, Captain. He said he was continuing his research and that he wanted to be transferred to Earth Colony 2.

What happened to Sam's other two sons is unclear, but it's just as well they weren't on Deneva when the neural parasites arrived.

Once again, William Shatner found himself performing a dual role in an episode, as producers decided that the best person to play Sam . . . was Bill. This time, at least, there were no lines to memorize. All Shatner had to do was play dead—and wear a dapper little mustache.

"It's not life as we know or understand it."
—Spock

During the 1950s and 1960s, magic shops, dime stores, and cheesy comic book ads used to provide children and adolescents with outlets through which they could exchange their hard-earned allowance money for all sorts of gag items—the grosser the better. X-ray glasses, joy buzzers, and whoopee cushions were all very popular, but only one novelty item hit the big time by becoming a prop in a *Star Trek* episode: a rubbery pile of fake vomit, typically sold under the name "Whoops!" or some other euphemism.

According to venerable gag manufacturer Fun Inc., more than sixty thousand fake vomits were produced annually in America during the 1960s. Some looked at them and thought, "Great way to gross out Susie!" Others—OK, maybe just Wah Chang—looked at them and thought, "Great neural parasite!" Chang modified the novelty vomits slightly, covering them with a clear, inflatable bladder to make them "pulse" and stringing them with wires so the crew could manipulate the little critters like marionettes.

A scene that had already been filmed, in which Kirk shares a tender moment with his nephew Peter, was ultimately cut from "Operation: Annihilate!" In the scene, Peter informs Kirk that he'd like to remain on the colony world rather than return to Earth to live with his grandmother. "Dad thought Deneva here is the best place in the whole galaxy," explains Peter. Kirk observes, "Well, your father's partner said he and his wife always wanted a boy," and lets the boy know that they're waiting for him in the transporter room. They shake hands and Peter exits in his mini Starfleet uniform. After he's gone, Scotty wonders if the lad will want to attend Starfleet Academy, like his uncle. "I hope he decides not to," Kirk replies somberly. "If there was no other choice, Scotty, I would have had to give the order to destroy this planet. I don't want him to ever have to make that choice."

Television production is a serious business. Behind the fortified walls of each studio, a huge amount of money is invested in productions that studio executives expect to be both entertaining and profitable. The careers of hundreds of employees, from behind-the-scenes specialists (sound engineers, makeup artists, grips, carpenters, and so forth) to on-camera actors, are at stake in such ventures.

In short, there's no time for frivolity. And yet . . . such moments happen.

Once upon a time, the public was oblivious to the fact that actors periodically blew their lines, dropped props, or walked into doors that should have whisked open, resulting in much cursing and much laughter from everyone on the set. However, *Star Trek*'s producers often held on to such takes, editing them into a "blooper reel" of on-set goofiness later unveiled for cast and crew at the series' seasonal parties. Fandom became aware of the silliness when, following the series' cancellation, Gene Roddenberry began carrying the blooper reel to *Star Trek* conventions.

There also were deliberate pranks, primarily played on the actors. Fandom became aware of such incidents via published behind-the-scenes accounts. The most infamous gag was reported in the seminal book *The Making of Star Trek* (written by Stephen E. Whitfield with Gene Roddenberry) and repeated at countless *Star Trek* conventions by the subject of the prank—the "prankee," if you will—Leonard Nimoy.

This was the tale of the missing bicycle.

Studio lots are large, and employees expend a great deal of time getting from one location to another. These days, the trip may occur via battery-powered golf cart. During the production of *The Original Series*, however, it often was made by bicycle, typically one provided by the studio. Nimoy had a bicycle, and according to Whitfield, cast and crew regularly took a fiendish delight in hiding it from the actor in an ever-escalating series of heists. Finally, Nimoy, in an attempt to quash the shenanigans, took to bringing his bicycle onto the soundstage during filming. But the actor's actions instead served to push the culprits to a new level of ingenuity. One minute the bicycle was there, and the next—it wasn't. A perplexed Nimoy ultimately found his bicycle high overhead, suspended from the rafters of the soundstage.

BB 95¢

A BALLANTINE ★ ORIGINAL 73004

NCC-1701

THE MAKING OF
STAR TREK

What it is — how it happened — how it works!

Stephen E. Whitfield • Gene Roddenberry

Although pioneers in television development had begun experimenting with color transmissions as early as 1904, the U.S. Federal Communications Commission did not approve a standardized system for broadcasting in color until 1953. The approved system had been developed by electronics company RCA. American viewers, however, remained content to watch programming in monochrome, or "black and white," for another decade. By then, RCA, also the home company of broadcast network NBC, had invested an estimated $130 million in perfecting color television sets. Hoping to see its investment pay off, RCA began a campaign to promote color viewing. By 1966, it was promoting NBC as "the Full Color Network" and had commissioned the A. C. Nielsen Company to survey television viewers about their preferences. While the survey results indicated that top-rated shows maintained loyal viewers who watched in either black and white or in color, it also showed that the series most watched specifically in color was *Star Trek*. Recognizing this as an opportunity to sell color TV sets, RCA executives placed an ad in the hugely popular *Life* magazine. Sporting a copy line that could be seen as referring to either the brand name or the series, "When you're first in Color TV, there's got to be a reason," the ad shows RCA's family-sized "Hathaway" console set. On the Hathaway's screen is a color picture of Kirk and Spock, while the background of the ad features a spectrum of colors that incorporate two additional pictures of the space-traveling duo. And

in a nudge pointed directly at the viewers Nielsen had discovered, a smaller copy line reads, "See '*Star Trek*' on RCA Victor Color TV." Throughout the following decade, known as the "replacement period" in TV merchandising parlance, national sales doubled as families upgraded from their older black-and-white sets to color, with RCA proving a major player during the transition.

When you're first in Color TV, there's got to be a reason.

See "Star Trek" on RCA Victor Color TV. Shown above, The Hathaway

- Like Automatic Fine Tuning that gives you a perfectly fine-tuned picture every time.
- A new RCA tube with 38% brighter highlights.
- Advanced circuitry that won't go haywire.
- And over 25 years of color experience.
- You get all this and more from RCA VICTOR.

The Most Trusted Name in Electro

In September 1967, just days before the debut of *Star Trek*'s second season, the first *Star Trek* fanzine—or fan-produced magazine—appeared at that year's World Science Fiction Convention in New York. Other than by its very existence, *Spockanalia* wasn't an attention grabber: It consisted of forty-five pieces of mimeographed paper, hand-folded into a ninety-page pamphlet and bound with heavy-duty staples. On the plain white cover was a drawing of Mister Spock. Within its pages were a polite letter from Leonard Nimoy ("I sincerely hope that your magazine will be a success, and want to thank you very much for your interest in STAR TREK and MISTER SPOCK."); some thoughtful essays related to Vulcan physiology, psychology, and culture; several poems; and a short story entitled "Star Drek." The editorial page included a choice bit of news provided by *Star Trek* producer Robert Justman about the upcoming episode "Amok Time" and a clarion call from Bjo Trimble, soon to become *Star Trek*'s best-known fan advocate, warning fans that if they wanted to ensure the show's long-term survival, they must send letters to the powers that be at NBC.

Ostensibly a one-shot, *Spockanalia* was priced by coeditors Devra Langsam and Sherna Comerford at fifty cents each. And although the newcomer faced stiff competition from the established science fiction zines sold on nearby tables, sales were brisk. Of course, none of those zines had Mister Spock on the cover. "Most general science fiction zines at the time were book reviews and descriptions of trips to recent science fiction conventions," recalls Langsam. "They didn't do fiction; the feeling was that if your fiction were good enough to print, then you should try to sell it [professionally]. But of course, you *couldn't* sell *Star Trek* fiction that way; there was no market for it."

The one-shot would go on to spawn four more editions, by which time there was a burgeoning market for *Star Trek* fan fiction. Within a few short years, despite the fact that the *Star Trek* series was no longer running on network television, the *Star Trek* fanzine universe exploded, with literate fans across the United States doing what they could to keep *Star Trek* alive.

!INTERPHASE

WARPED SPACE 9

BOSH

THE COMPLEAT FAULWELL / LANDING PARTY 6

VOL. I

Menazerie

NO. 6

154
CATSPAW

McCoy: "Three witches, what appears to be a castle, and a black cat."
Kirk: "If we weren't missing two officers and a third one dead, I'd say someone was playing an elaborate trick or treat on us."
Spock: "Trick or treat, Captain?"
Kirk: "Yes, Mister Spock. You'd be a natural. I'll explain it to you one day."

Kirk is concerned when the *Enterprise* loses track of a landing party sent to explore the planet Pyris VII, especially after one of the men beams up dead. With Scotty and Sulu still missing on Pyris, Kirk, Spock, and McCoy form a search party and retrace the missing men's steps. The trio soon finds a foreboding castle occupied by Korob and Sylvia—apparent practitioners of witchcraft—and also the two missing officers, who have been transformed into zombies. Upon learning that Korob and Sylvia are part of an advance team for an alien culture's mission of conquest, Kirk attempts to charm Sylvia in order to uncover the real source of her power.

The second season of *Star Trek* introduced fans to Ensign Pavel Chekov, who would permanently fill what previously had been the rotating position of ship's navigator. With an eye toward attracting more teenage girls to *Star Trek*'s audience, Gene Roddenberry had decided to add another character to the bridge crew: someone young and slightly irreverent, someone Beatle-ish . . . or at least Monkee-ish. But a timely snipe against the series from the official newspaper of the Communist Party would transform Roddenberry's vision of a cheeky Brit into a humorously ethnocentric Russian.

Star Trek, it seems, had leaked through the Iron Curtain. An article appeared in *Pravda* slamming the "typically capitalistic" mind-set behind the show. Why, the paper wondered, were there no Russian crewmen aboard the *Enterprise*? Were Americans so ill-informed about the achievements of the Soviet space program?

It was a valid point and an unintentionally clever suggestion. In the same way that the presence of Uhura and Sulu served to demonstrate that integration would be commonplace in the not-so-distant future, the presence of a Russian officer would demonstrate that petty disagreements between Earth's nations would become a thing of the past. *The Man from U.N.C.L.E.* (which debuted in 1964, two years before *Star Trek*) already had blazed a trail in that direction with the character of Russian agent Illya Kuryakin; clearly, the viewing public had no problem accepting characters with differing ideologies, working side by side for a common cause—particularly if they were "cute."

Thus, Walter Koenig was cast in the role of Ensign Pavel Chekov. Roddenberry still liked the idea of the character sporting a Beatles-style haircut, even if the character had a Muscovite accent, so the actor wore a "mop-top" wig until his own hair grew to an appealingly shaggy length.

"Catspaw," written by Robert Bloch, shares a number of common elements with "Broomstick Ride," a short story that Bloch penned in 1957. In "Broomstick Ride," a starship commander on a survey mission comes across a strange world inhabited by superstitious peasants, their somewhat more advanced ruler, a bevy of witches, and the dark "Master of the Sabbath." After witnessing demonstrations of what appears to be old, Earth-style black magic, the commander departs, unconvinced of the authenticity of what he's seen. The Master of the Sabbath and the planet's ruler, worried that the commander's report will bring more Earth ships, burn an effigy of the spaceship, which, although thousands of miles away from their planet, explodes.

Bloch obviously drew upon "Broomstick Ride" for his second *Star Trek* script, but he worked within the required *Star Trek* formula, providing scientific explanation for the teleplay's odder happenings and Gothic accoutrements. Rather than minions of a mythical dark lord, Korob and Sylvia were visitors from another galaxy who took up residence on Pyris as the advance team for an invading force. They sought to drive away the crew of the *Enterprise* by exploiting the visitors' ancient fears—although they were as misinformed about the beliefs and predilections of twenty-third-century humans as Trelane in "The Squire of Gothos." Their "magic" is actually transmuter-based thought-conversion technology— *much* more plausible than black magic!

"He doesn't know about trick or treat."
—McCoy

Typically, the start of a new season is the only conceivable time when spare production cash is available to embellish the look of a somewhat "needy" episode. But *Star Trek*'s producers never had a great deal money in their coffers, and a lot of what they did have was allocated to the upcoming production of "Amok Time." The effects in "Catspaw" reflect the tight budget. The "real" forms of Korob and Sylvia—an odd cross between tiny birdlike creatures and crustaceans—were depicted through the use of marionettes constructed from pipe cleaners, crab claws, and other bits of flotsam and jetsam. The strings, alas, were a bit too evident, even though the pair was never seen in tight close-up.

Sylvia's rampage as the fearsome "giant" cat was primarily conveyed by sending a trained kitty down a miniature version of the castle corridor and by casting its shadow on the wall in front of Kirk. It was neither convincing nor scary, despite the script's attempt to make it so. "Why a [giant] cat?" Kirk asks Spock. "Racial memories," Spock replies. "The cat is the most ruthless, most terrifying of animals, as far back as the saber-toothed tiger."

Still, "Catspaw" was unique in one sense. Although it was the first episode produced for *Star Trek*'s second season (1967-68), it didn't air until the final week of October—just in time for Halloween. And that, apparently, was a deliberate choice. For the first and only time in its history, *Star Trek* produced a seasonally themed episode, complete with black cats, skeletons, iron maidens, haunted castles, and three creepy witches who recite, as Spock observes, "very bad poetry."

This tiny silver model of the *Enterprise* was used as a prop in the episode "Catspaw." To subdue Captain Kirk, the witchlike character Sylvia dangles this charm over a flame and then suggests he contact the *Enterprise*. Upon hearing that his ship and crew are likewise being roasted, Kirk surrenders and hands over his phaser. Sylvia's companion, Korob, then seals the miniature within an impenetrable force field, thus trapping the real *Enterprise* as well.

The actual prop, which is only about four inches long, was donated to the Smithsonian Institution's National Air and Space Museum in 1973 by *Star Trek* designer Matt Jefferies.

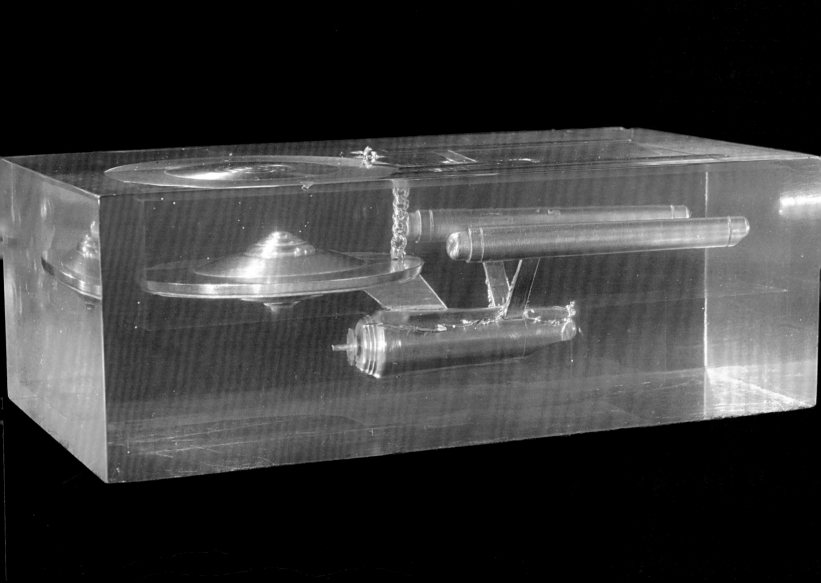

METAMORPHOSIS

After Federation Commissioner Nancy Hedford contracts a deadly virus during a critical peace negotiation, Kirk, Spock, and McCoy attempt to rush her to medical facilities on the *Enterprise* via the *Shuttlecraft Galileo*. En route, the shuttlecraft is hijacked by a mysterious cloudlike entity and forced to land on a small planet inhabited by a single human being: Zefram Cochrane, inventor of the warp drive. Cochrane, presumed dead for one hundred and fifty years, explains that the cloud creature brought them to his world because it knew that he was lonely for others of his own kind. Unfortunately, the Companion, as Cochrane refers to the entity, has no intention of allowing any of them to depart, even if the extended stay costs Hedford her life.

"The name of Zefram Cochrane is revered throughout the known galaxy. Planets were named after him. Great universities. Cities."
—Spock

As the inventor of the single most important device in the history of manned spaceflight, Zefram Cochrane is an important role model for Starfleet cadets, but the accompanying fame and celebrity make him uncomfortable. When Kirk, Spock, and McCoy encounter him in "Metamorphosis," Cochrane barely resembles the historical portrait of a brilliant scientist who made faster-than-light space travel possible; rather, he comes across as a mild-mannered shipwreck victim who'd be content to sit out the rest of his life on a tiny planetoid in the Gamma Canaris region of space. A later incarnation of Cochrane, in *Star Trek: First Contact*, confirms the initial impression garnered in "Metamorphosis"; he's the most reluctant astronaut to grace the big screen since Don Knotts. Which should, perhaps, serve as warning to students of history: Legendary figures are prone to feet of clay.

161

"Now we are human. We know the change of the days. We will know death. But to touch the hand of man, nothing is as important."
—Nancy Hedford/the Companion

Although typically categorized as "science fiction," *Star Trek* is actually a vehicle for traditional stories staged within genre settings. If you ignore the magenta sky in "Metamorphosis," along with the futuristic shuttlecraft and the Companion's unearthly powers and appearance, it's easy to see that the episode is a simple romance: Boy meets girl, lives with girl, and once he gets over a few personal prejudices, falls in love with girl. Veteran composer George Duning was commissioned for the episode on the basis of his quintessentially romantic score for the 1955 film *Picnic*. His yearning, heartfelt melody provided a perfect underscore as the Companion-made-flesh expressed her feelings to Cochrane—and it would be heard under romantic scenes in several subsequent episodes of *Star Trek*.

162

Compared to the jaw-dropping visual effects generated with today's technology, the tech available in the 1960s was, as Spock might say, all "stone knives and bearskins." The downside of low-tech effects was that aliens often looked like men in rubber suits. The upside was that resourceful collaborations between director, costume designer, and art director resulted in visuals that transcend their limitations. In "Metamorphosis," a seemingly inconsequential piece of wardrobe becomes a visual metaphor for Nancy Hedford's transformation. Hedford wears a multicolored head scarf (tightly wrapped, to match Hedford's tightly wrapped personality) when she first arrives on Zefram Cochrane's planetoid. She loosens it and casts it aside during her illness, and then, after she is reborn as the Nancy/Companion chimera, she drapes it across her shoulders like an elegant stole. But it isn't until the last act of the episode, when she holds the scarf before her eyes to observe Cochrane through the translucent fabric, that the viewer experiences a small epiphany. The pattern on the scarf resembles that of the alien Companion's glowing "skin." The hybrid entity, which now sees through Nancy's human eyes, is attempting to catch a glimpse of Cochrane as the Companion once saw him. It is a beautifully poetic visual metaphor that worked perfectly for an audience of the pre-CGI era.

FRIDAY'S CHILD

Kirk arrives at Capella IV to negotiate a mining agreement, only to discover the Klingons are already there, having forged an alliance with a faction that seeks to usurp Akaar, the Capellan leader. After the faction succeeds in slaying Akaar, Kirk is told that under Capellan law, the life of Eleen, Akaar's pregnant wife, is also forfeit, something the captain refuses to allow. With Eleen in tow, Kirk, Spock, and McCoy head for the hills, hunted by both Klingons and Capellans. While Kirk and Spock hold off their pursuers, McCoy sets his sights on delivering the baby that Eleen no longer has any interest in bearing.

Kirk: *"How did you arrange to touch her, Bones? Give her a happy pill?"*
McCoy: *"No, a right cross."*
Kirk: *"I've never seen that in a medical book."*
McCoy: *"It's in mine from now on."*

Doctor McCoy is clearly a highly trained physician with an inventive mind. Over the course of his five-year-mission, he figured out the antidote to the Psi 2000 virus, the counteragent to Elasian tears, and a potion that not only neutralized the neurologically devastating effects of spatial interphase, but also made a good mixer for Scotch.

However, McCoy liked to downplay his skills, even going so far as to describe himself as "just an old country doctor"; it's possible that he may have yearned for a more low-tech practice. As he emerged from his drug-induced delirium in "The City on the Edge of Forever," McCoy took in his surroundings (New York City, c. 1930) and expressed a heartfelt desire to see a hospital of the era, even though he despaired of the fact that it was a place where they used needles and sutures "to cut and sew people like garments."

The events in "Friday's Child" finally gave McCoy the opportunity to prove his worth without the electronic assistance of sickbay's shiny gizmos and gadgets. With a minimum of tech and a maximum of bedside manner, McCoy delivered Eleen's baby in a cave and convinced her to accept the child.

Spock: "Fortunately, this bark has suitable tensile cohesion."
Kirk: "You mean it makes good bowstring."
Spock: "I believe I said that."

The inspiration for the arsenal of weaponry in "Friday's Child" is derived from Earth's eastern to western hemispheres, and from the distant past to the distant future. As the episode begins, McCoy tells his compatriots about the Capellans' *kligat*, a three-sided bladed weapon that is similar to the Japanese *hira-shuriken*, or "ninja throwing star." The Capellans also possess several types of swords that are reminiscent of medieval European blades. As Kirk and Spock prepare to defend themselves, they make bows and arrows similar to Native American hunting weapons. Along with these "primitive" weapons, the Starfleet and Klingon officers carry twenty-third-century hand phasers, and back on the *Enterprise*, Scotty has ship-sized phaser banks at the ready.

But leave it to a woman to find a more efficient means of dispatch. Surrounded by all these man-made weapons of high and low tech, when Eleen needs to escape from McCoy, she simply hits him with a rock.

Poor security officer Grant; he didn't even manage to stay alive until the opening credits. Why? Ostensibly, it's because he had an itchy trigger finger. But as any respectable Trekker knows, the *real* reason is that he was wearing a red shirt, which, on *Star Trek*, is tantamount to waving a red flag in front of a bull.

The Curse of the Red Shirt is more than a myth. The *Enterprise* began its five-year mission with a crew complement of 430 men and women. Of that total, 59 (13.7%) of them died during the series. Among the dead, 6 (10%) wore gold shirts, 5 (8%) wore blue, 4 (7%) wore engineering smocks—and 43 (73%) wore red. Think about it: Of all the crew members who drew their last breath, 73% wore red.

Grant's chances of survival would have been better if he'd applied to officers' school. They get to wear gold.

By the second season of *Star Trek*, costume designer William Ware Theiss's iconic designs were receiving their due from an appreciative public. Carolyn Palamas's pink Grecian gown—beautifully worn by actress Leslie Parrish in "Who Mourns for Adonais?"—looked resilient enough from the front, while a side view suggested that the faintest whisper of a breeze could send it cascading to the ground. Which leads one to wonder what happened when they switched on that wind machine. . . .

Theiss's clever designs influenced costumers of the 1960s and beyond. Robert Blackman, costume designer for all of the *Star Trek* series that followed, readily acknowledges Theiss's influence on his own exotic pieces. "I sort of got away with murder," he says with a smile, "revealing parts of the body that people don't usually look at. And that actually follows the concepts of Bill Theiss. He was always thrilled to find a place he could open up that would suggest 'naughty' to viewers—but really it was just that he had closed up one area and opened up a different one, using cutouts and weird sheer fabrics wrapped in gold cord and marabou. It's amazing that he was able to do that stuff during the era he was working in."

But one thing Theiss *couldn't* do during that era was display much of statuesque actress Julie Newmar's body when she appeared in "Friday's Child." Newmar, who'd thrilled male viewers with her scantily clad appearance as Stupefyin' Jones in both the stage and screen

versions of *Li'l Abner*, played an extremely pregnant woman in "Friday's Child." Thanks to Lucille Ball's groundbreaking prepartum appearances in *I Love Lucy*, *Star Trek* producers had no problem featuring a pregnant character on the show. But putting Eleen in a revealing pregnancy smock would have been a bit too scandalous for NBC's Standards and Practices.

WHO MOURNS FOR ADONAIS?

"If you want to play god and call yourself Apollo, that's your business—but you're no god to us, Mister!"
—Kirk

Near the planet Pollux IV, the *Enterprise* encounters an unlikely phenomenon: a giant green hand that materializes in front of the starship and holds it motionless. The hand is actually a manifestation of energy generated by the powerful entity that resides on the planet below. He calls himself "Apollo" and claims to be one of the beings that inspired the ancient Greek legends of Earth. Upon beaming down to Pollux IV, Kirk and rest of the landing party learn that Apollo misses the blind adoration he once experienced as one of the Olympian gods. He wants Kirk's crew to stay with him—forever—and worship him in the manner of their ancestors. But Kirk has no intention of letting Apollo force his will on the men and women under his command, even though this "god" has the ability to inflict severe punishment for disobedience.

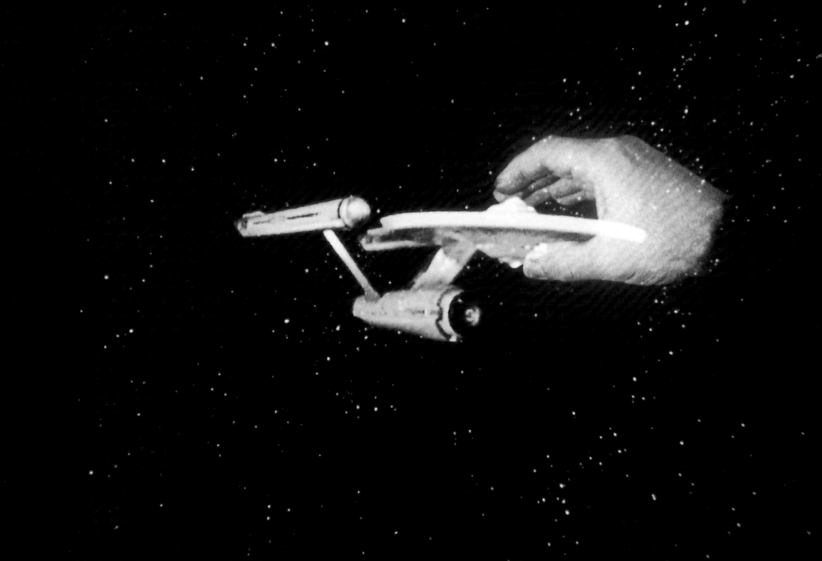

169

"To coin a phrase—Fascinating."
—McCoy

Screenwriter Gilbert Ralston had a way with characters. In 1965, he combined a James Bond-type character with the western genre to create the hybrid hero James West, star of the Ralston-scripted pilot for *The Wild Wild West*. Ralston was equally adept at creating villainous—or perhaps just "tragically flawed," depending on your point of view—characters. When he wrote the story for "Who Mourns for Adonais?" in 1967, he chose the Greek god Apollo as Kirk's nemesis of the week. It was a novel idea at the time; Erich von Däniken's *Chariots of the Gods*—which popularized the idea that the myths about Earth's early gods had been inspired by visits from powerful space aliens—would not be published for another year.

Apollo was a curious choice for the god of the hour. It's true that Apollo, like his father, Zeus, had a definite eye for the ladies (Carolyn Palamas is lucky that she wasn't turned into a laurel tree when she ran away from him), but few male gods *didn't* have such interests. In terms of his abilities, the mythical Apollo was best known for his day job: driving the golden chariot of the sun across the sky each day. Tossing lightning bolts was his father's predilection, not Apollo's.

The title, by the way, has more to do with classic English poetry than it does with the residents of Mount Olympus. Drawn from a line in Percy Bysshe Shelley's poem "Adonais: An Elegy on the Death of John Keats," the piece likens the deceased poet Keats to Adonis, a mortal male associated with rebirth and fertility within Greek mythology.

170

Although many actors prefer to perform their own stunts, studio insurance policies demand that doubles replace them for the most dangerous physical bits. Actor and stunt double Jay D. Jones stood in for Jimmy Doohan as Scotty in a number of *Star Trek* episodes. The stunt profession is a difficult one: Doubles regularly get punched, tossed, set aflame, rolled in vehicles, and dropped from high places. They must know how to ride, surf, ski, skydive, box, and most important of all, *land*. During the shooting of "Who Mourns for Adonais?" Jones was the one wearing the body harness attached to a wire that jerked him aloft as Apollo struck Scotty with one of his lightning bolts. It looked amazing on-screen, but Jones paid a price. The stunt landed him in the hospital, with a slight concussion.

AMOK TIME

"It is said thy Vulcan blood is thin. Are thee Vulcan or are thee human?"
–T'Pau

When the typically staid Spock begins behaving erratically, Kirk orders him to undergo a thorough medical examination. McCoy's diagnosis is a stunner: Spock will die if he isn't taken home to Vulcan within a matter of days. But why? Spock reluctantly reveals that he has entered the Vulcan *Pon farr*—an overwhelming biochemical process that compels members of his race to return home and take a mate . . . or die from the tremendous pent-up physical and mental stresses within. Defying his standing Starfleet orders, Kirk changes course for Spock's homeworld, unaware that aspects of the primitive mating ritual soon will put his own life in peril.

"How do Vulcans choose their mates? Haven't you wondered?"
—Spock

Theodore Sturgeon's script for "Amok Time," which kicked off the series' second season on NBC, provided a plethora of information about the insular Vulcan civilization, answering questions that not even the most avid *Star Trek* fan would have considered asking.

Why not? Well, for one thing, it would have been extremely rude.

Rather than deliver a thoughtfully staid piece about Vulcan civilization, Sturgeon created a drama about a subject typically not discussed in polite company: biology. That is, biology of the Vulcan reproductive kind.

Like Kirk, audiences probably had assumed that when adult Vulcans felt it was time to increase the population, they went about it . . . logically. But Sturgeon came up with a far more interesting theory. Two thousand years earlier, he explained, the Vulcan race purged emotion from their daily lives and pressed logic to their collective bosoms. As a result, the species entered a prolonged period of peace and intellectual enlightenment, but for which they would pay an extremely high price. The Vulcans became absolute masters of their passions, but every seven years they would become slaves to the basest of passions, required to mate—or die.

"It strips our minds from us. It brings a madness which rips away our veneer of civilization. It is the Pon farr. *The time of mating."*

For such an earthy subject, the story drew surprisingly few complaints, quite remarkable considering that NBC's Standards and Practices watchdogs regularly instructed *Star Trek*'s producers to avoid any scenes involving "open-mouthed kissing." Perhaps Spock's simile likening Vulcan *Pon farr* to the plight of Earth's salmon swimming upstream to spawn made it seem as if the subject matter really *did* concern plain old biology rather than S-E-X. Reportedly, only one station refused to air the episode "as is." ZDF, a German television channel, is said to have cut several scenes and to have rewritten dialogue for the voice actors who dubbed the American lines into German. Thus, in Germany it appeared that Spock was suffering from a malady referred to as "Weltraumfieber" (space fever).

Frederick Beauregard Phillips was *Star Trek*'s makeup man for seventy-eight of the series' seventy-nine episodes, the exception being the second pilot. After Phillips did "The Cage," Robert Dawn, son of MGM's makeup maestro Jack Dawn, sat in for him on "Where No Man Has Gone Before." Phillips returned for the first regular episode to be filmed, "The Corbomite Maneuver."

Gene Roddenberry had requested Spock's pointed ears, but Phillips is credited with devising and refining the Vulcan's look—not to mention the look of the Klingons, the Romulans, the Talosians, and every other alien species (sans rubber suits) that the *Enterprise* came across. (Phillips later was responsible for the Klingons' updated appearance in *Star Trek: The Motion Picture*, where he added the dental appliances and knobby skull ridges that only a movie's longer shooting schedule and larger budget could make possible.)

Leonard Nimoy typically spent ninety minutes in the makeup chair. This gave Phillips the requisite time to apply the actor's specially molded latex ear tips, yellowish face, body makeup, and yak-hair eyebrows, as well as to style his hair. On occasion, Phillips could nearly cut that time in half—but such occasions were a rarity. As is the case with most production-department heads, Phillips typically worked with assistants who could take on the "low-maintenance" members of that week's cast, but some days there couldn't possibly be enough hands.

"Amok Time" is a perfect case in point. Applying the full complement of ears to the contingent of actors hired as Vulcans at Spock's "wedding" might have blown the entire season's budget for materials and labor. Thankfully, costume designer William Ware Theiss came to the rescue. Recycling the helmets worn by the Romulans in season one's "Balance of Terror," Theiss covered the heads of many extras, saving Phillips hours of work. Of course, what the production saved on ears was spent on the episode's wardrobe budget: Aside from the helmets, all the exotic duds were made from scratch and never used again.

T'Pau: "Live long and prosper, Spock."
Spock: "I shall do neither. I have killed my captain . . . and my friend."

The Vulcan salute, along with the accompanying phrase "Live long and prosper," first appeared in "Amok Time." The salute had not been mentioned in the script; Theodore Sturgeon had written only that Spock would approach Vulcan matriarch T'Pau and greet her. While preparing to shoot the scene, actor Leonard Nimoy felt that he should lead with some type of respectful gesture, the equivalent of a salute, a handshake, or a bow. Director Joseph Pevney agreed and suggested that Nimoy create the gesture. In doing so, the actor fell back on a curious hand-and-finger configuration he recalled from childhood. Some viewers assumed that the "salute" was a variation of the two-fingered peace sign so popular in the 1960s, but years later Nimoy revealed that he actually based it on something he'd witnessed long ago during a high holy days service at synagogue. His family had instructed young Leonard to cover his eyes respectfully during the delivery of the sacred blessing, but being a small curious boy, he peeked. Nimoy observed the rabbi raise and spread the fingers of both hands to form the Hebrew letter "shin," which stands for the word "Shaddai," or "Almighty."

Nimoy relates that he found the experience both moving and magical. It remained with him for life, and he drew upon it when he filmed "Amok Time," adapting the two-handed blessing into a one-handed salute, with his fingers split into the familiar "V."

Other than the main theme, the fight music for "Amok Time" is perhaps the most recognizable theme from *Star Trek*. Composed by Gerald Fried, the Stravinsky-esque piece, titled "The Ritual/Ancient Battle," represents the full spectrum of activity encompassed within the ancient Vulcan *koon-ut-kal-if-fee* (literally, "marriage or challenge") ceremony. We first hear this theme played softly under the dialogue as Spock describes the source of his "malady" to Kirk; a short time later, the measured but slightly dissonant strains accompany the processional leading to the joining ceremony. Then, after Spock learns that he must fight for his betrothed's hand, the melody explodes into a frenzy of savagery, beloved by all fans of violently choreographed free-for-alls. The theme has been borrowed to accompany on-screen fights in *The Simpsons, The Cable Guy*, and *Futurama*. As described by author Jeff Bond in his book *The Music of Star Trek*, the theme is "a model of action scene bombast, wildly percussive and bursting with exclamatory trumpet, flute and woodwind trills to accentuate the hammering of the brass-performed fanfare."

Those who work closely with *Star Trek* have a tendency to discuss aspects of the series from what may seem, to outsiders, a peculiar perspective. Although we *know* it's "just a television show," the characters, ships, creatures, and civilizations all exist within our minds as extensions of an actual living history. At times, there doesn't seem to be much difference between the world outside the metaphor and the world within it.

For Michael Okuda, who contributed to every *Star Trek* movie and television series from *Star Trek IV: The Voyage Home* through *Star Trek: Enterprise*, and his wife, Denise, who cowrote the *Star Trek Encyclopedia* with him while working on many of the same shows, the distinctions are particularly fine. Invited to say a few words about some of the stunning images they helped to create for the remastered release of *Star Trek*, they choose to do it "within the metaphor," as with this description of a rendering from "Amok Time":

> *The nuclear holocaust two millennia ago not only shattered Vulcan civilization, but it laid waste to the planet itself. Few traces remained of life before the "time of the awakening," save for a few ancient temples and statues, mostly ensconced in the once-verdant mountains. Yet those decaying stone edifices embodied the inherent contradictions of Vulcan society: the determined efforts of a violent people to live a life of serene logic in defiance of their animal passions. Some believed it impossible to change a*
> *people's very nature, choosing instead to abandon their homeworld. But those that remained proved equal to the challenge. The teachings of Surak brought about a new rebirth to Vulcan society, one free of the scourge of warfare whose scars still marred the planet.*

THE DOOMSDAY MACHINE

"Gentlemen, I suggest you beam me aboard."
—Kirk

While investigating the destruction of several planetary systems, the *Enterprise* detects the crippled hulk of the *U.S.S. Constellation*, drifting lifeless in space. But one of the ship's crew remains aboard, and alive: the *Constellation*'s commander, Commodore Matt Decker. In a state of shock, Decker claims his vessel encountered a gigantic mobile weapon that was pulverizing the planets around it and swallowing them up. The *Constellation* attempted to destroy this monstrosity, only to suffer severe damage from its energy rays. In an effort to save his crew, Decker admits that he beamed the entire complement down to one of the worlds in the system, which was later destroyed by the berserker. The *Enterprise* soon tracks down this planet killer, and Spock reveals that the machine is on course for one of the most densely inhabited regions in the galaxy. Clearly, it must be stopped. But with Kirk and Scotty off the ship repairing the *Constellation*, Decker takes it upon himself to go after the planet killer with the *Enterprise*.

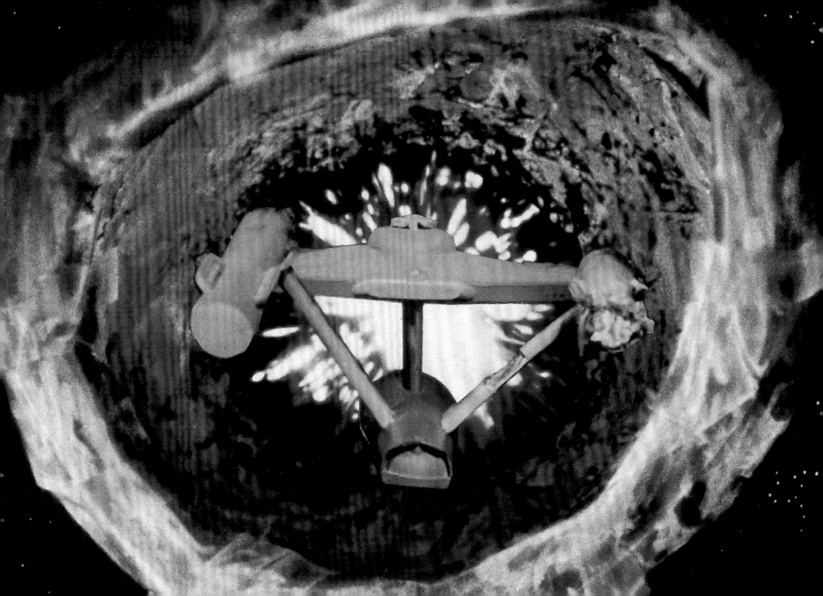

Star Trek was always running out of money, which explains a lot about the series' production values. With few exceptions, landing party missions almost always were shot on a soundstage, with colored-gel filters providing the unearthly hues of alien worlds. Costumes, sets, props, and episodic musical cues often were recycled for later episodes to stretch the show's budget just a little further.

Thus when Gene Roddenberry contacted writer Norman Spinrad and asked him to pitch an episode for *Star Trek*, it's not surprising that the executive producer also gave him a proviso: Think of a story that would use only the show's standing sets. As it turned out, Spinrad had long toyed with the idea of doing a science fiction take on Herman Melville's *Moby-Dick*, and that was the idea he pitched. Roddenberry liked it, and Spinrad set to work on what became "The Doomsday Machine." With a redress of the *Enterprise* sets standing in for those of its sister ship, the *Constellation*, the only new element the producers needed to source was the planet killer itself. Spinrad provided a few inspirational sketches and then went on to work on something else.

The writer was surprised when he saw the aired episode. Why, he wondered, did the planet killer look less like a high-tech, insanely powerful berserker than a wind sock dipped in cement?

"Ran out of money," Roddenberry apologized. Spinrad had a good eye: The planet killer *was* a wind sock that had been dipped in cement.

"They say there's no devil, Jim, but there is. Right out of hell—I saw it!"
—Decker

At the time Norman Spinrad received the assignment to write his *Star Trek* homage to *Moby-Dick*, he was told that actor Robert Ryan had expressed an interest in appearing on the series and would likely be cast as the story's Ahab, Commodore Decker. It seemed like a good fit. Ryan, once a Marine drill instructor at Camp Pendleton, California, made a career out of playing "tough-as-nails" characters, from an anti-Semitic killer in *Crossfire* to a fierce, aging gunfighter in *The Wild Bunch*.

So Spinrad shaped Decker's persona with Ryan in mind, only to learn later on that actor William Windom had been given the role. Apparently Ryan's schedule had precluded his appearance in the series. Windom's take on Decker was softer than the writer had anticipated; rather than a vengeful force of nature, his Ahab was a tortured soul whose guilt over the death of his crew drives him to deadly obsession. Nevertheless, Windom's performance is strikingly powerful and made a lasting impression on viewers. At eighty-six years old, he remains a popular guest at *Star Trek* conventions.

Sol Kaplan's score to "The Doomsday Machine" is one of the few that actually qualifies as a full *Star Trek* soundtrack. Many of the musical cues written for this episode eventually would be scattered throughout later ones, but here they work together as a unified piece, like a symphonic score. The episode opens to the sound of a muted trumpet, conjuring connotations of a military funeral, then joins with mournful cellos as the *Enterprise* gets its first view of the mortally wounded *Constellation*. Later, the trumpet pairs with a snare drum's fast roll, giving a martial feel to the escalating conflict between Spock and Decker onboard the *Enterprise*. In fact, each component of the story gets a theme, from the variations on Alexander Courage's familiar fanfare for the *Enterprise* (which also, by extension, represents Kirk in his scenes on the *Constellation*) to the cacophonous mix of low woodwinds, trumpeting horn blasts, and nervous piano that represents the planet killer itself, pounding relentlessly as the thing comes closer and closer, maw stretched wide to swallow up all in its path, like a shark approaching its victim. . . .

The blockbuster movie *Jaws,* with its iconic theme painting a vivid portrait of a sleek voracious killer on the prowl, was still eight years in the future; Kaplan's theme for the planet killer seems eerily prescient. Could John Williams be a secret Trekker?

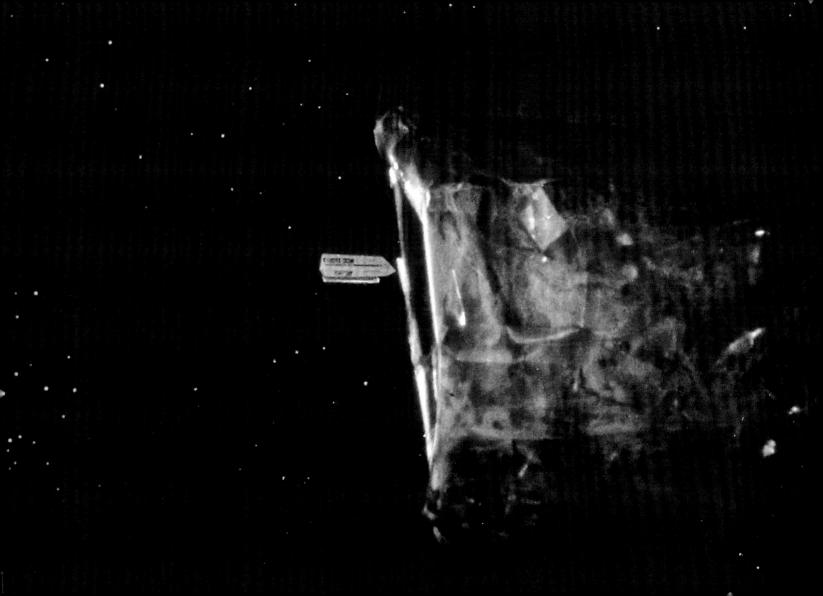

WOLF IN THE FOLD

After Chief Engineering Officer Scott suffers an on-the-job head injury, Captain Kirk and Doctor McCoy take him down to Argelius II, a renowned hedonistic pleasure planet, for some therapeutic time off. Just as Scotty begins to enjoy himself, however, a local woman in his company is brutally slain, and he becomes the primary suspect. As Kirk and McCoy investigate, a yeoman from the *Enterprise* is murdered—and again Mr. Scott seems to be the only person nearby. Scotty claims to have no memory of his actions during the time frame of either crime, and Argelius's Chief Administrator Hengist wants to arrest him. The planet's Prefect Jaris delays Hengist, noting that Jaris's wife, Sybo, who is gifted with the power of empathic insight, may be able to assist in the investigation. But when Sybo is murdered while attempting to draw out the truth, Scotty, again, is found at the scene.

"Wolf in the Fold" was the last of Robert Bloch's trilogy of *Star Trek* stories to be produced, although it originally aired before his Halloween-inspired tale, "Catspaw." Bloch's penchant for revisiting favorite themes once again influenced his choice of subject matter. This time around, it is "the lone psychopath who leaves a trail of murdered women in his wake." Bloch's short story of the occult, "Yours Truly, Jack the Ripper," published in *Weird Tales* magazine in 1943, had already been adapted as an episode of the TV series *Thriller* in 1961, but with significant changes it served as the springboard for an effective *Star Trek* murder mystery. Throughout his career, Bloch wrote about numerous historical villains, including the Marquis de Sade and Lizzie Borden, but Jack the Ripper was clearly a favorite.

At first glance, actor John Fiedler may not seem the most likely personage to portray one of history's most infamous serial killers. The actor with the "helium-high" voice is better known for playing such gentle, shy characters as Juror #2 in the classic *12 Angry Men* and the diminutive Mr. Peterson on *The Bob Newhart Show*. He also served a forty-year tenure as the voice of Winnie the Pooh's best friend, Piglet, for Walt Disney. And yet, his appearance here is not "casting against type": There's method to the madness. Mr. Hengist is a simple administrator holding a less than glamorous job—pure John Fiedler. When Hengist is possessed by a bloodthirsty entity, Redjac, one suspects that it was as much a treat for the actor to perform double duty as it is for audiences to watch him.

"I know a café where the women are so . . ."
–Kirk

When Tania Lemani, who portrays Kara, the belly dancer, was twelve years old, her family moved from Iran to the United States. At the time, she was fluent in Russian and Persian and had been studying ballet since the age of three. She never suspected that a simple comprehension mistake in her newly acquired third language would have a profound impact on her life and career. "I was sixteen, dancing in a ballet show, when someone offered me a job in Las Vegas. I took a bus there, and when I got to the Flamingo Hotel, I asked for the ballet troupe. They told me, 'Oh no, we don't have *ballet* dancers, we have *belly* dancers,'" she jokes. "I didn't know what belly dancing was, and when I found out I said, 'I can't do that—my father would *kill* me.' But I danced there for six weeks, and as time went on, the more I belly danced, the more offers I got to do that kind of work in Hollywood.

"My childhood dream had been to become the next Bette Davis," Lemani recalls, "and when I was cast on *Star Trek*, they said they wanted someone who could both dance *and* act, so I was very excited. They sent me to the makeup department because they wanted to do something extravagant with my look. The first day, they put feathers of different colors all over my face—on my eyelashes, my eyelids, my nose. Then they took me to the director, Joe Pevney, and he said, 'No.

No. Less!' The makeup people kept trying to match his vision for four days, with less and less feathers and fewer colors each time, but Joe kept saying, 'No.' *Finally*, on the fifth day, I came in with no makeup and he said, 'That's it. *That's* what I want to see—her *face*.' After that, the actual filming only took a couple of days."

As was the practice of the era, a certain, surprisingly innocent part of the body was banned from the television screen. Cher experienced the same censorship on her variety show, as did Barbara Eden on *I Dream of Jeannie*. And, of course, so did Lemani. "They let me do all of the choreography myself," Lemani says. "But they wouldn't let me show my belly button. They made me cover it with a jeweled flower."

During the 1960s, several exotic ingenues began appearing regularly on American screens both large and small. Some, such as France Nuyen, who costarred in *South Pacific*, and Nancy Kwan, who appeared in *The World of Suzie Wong* and *Flower Drum Song*, would become widely recognized by the public. But others, such as Pilar Seurat, did not become household names but were equally busy. A Filipina American born in Manila, Seurat had a unique beauty that allowed her to play a variety of "Asian" roles. She already had costarred with Burt Lancaster and Shelley Winters in the feature *The Young Savages*, as well as in numerous TV shows, from *Maverick* to *The Alfred Hitchcock Hour*, when Gene Roddenberry cast her in his first series, *The Lieutenant*. Pleased with her performance, he asked her to appear in *Star Trek* as Sybo, the lovely Argelian empath who reveals Redjac's presence and pays the price for doing so.

Seurat retired from the entertainment business in the early 1970s, but her son, Dean Devlin, would grow up to become one of Hollywood's most successful writer/producers, with hits such as *Stargate*, *Independence Day*, and *Godzilla* (with then-collaborator Roland Emmerich) to his credit. A science fiction aficionado, Devlin has always professed a personal delight in his mother's appearance in the original *Star Trek*. His production of *Eight Legged Freaks*, which premiered the year after Seurat died, is dedicated to her memory.

THE CHANGELING

Four billion inhabitants of the Malurian system have been ruthlessly eliminated. As the crew of the *Enterprise* investigates the cause behind this holocaust, they encounter a small, self-contained computerized device that identifies itself as Nomad. Once a Terran exploratory probe sent into space to seek out new forms of life, Nomad has been transformed into a hybrid device, the result of its union with an alien probe programmed to collect sterilized soil samples. Nomad now believes that its mission is to sterilize, or rather eradicate, imperfect life-forms, like the imperfect inhabitants of the Malurian system—and the crew of the *Enterprise*.

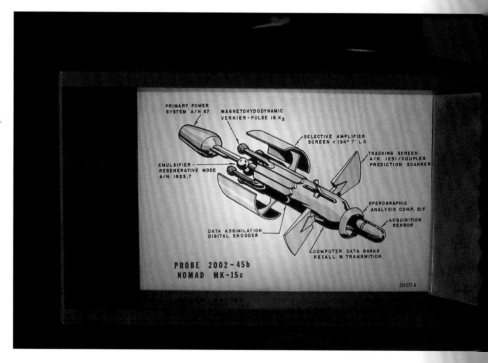

PRIMARY POWER
SYSTEM A/N 57

MAGNETOHYDODYNAMIC
VERNIER-PULSE 16 K₃

SELECTIVE AMPLIFIER
SCREEN + 134° 7' L D

TRACKING SCREEN
A/N 1231/COUPLER
PREDICTION SCANNER

EMULSIFIER-
REGENERATIVE MODE
A/N 1623.7

SPEROGRAPHIC
ANALYSIS COMP. 21F

ACQUISITION
SENSOR

DATA ASSIMILATION
DIGITAL ENCODER

COMPUTER DATA BANKS
RECALL & TRANSMITION

PROBE 2002-45b
NOMAD MK-15c

196372 A

Poor Uhura. She loves to sing, but every time she does, something *terrible* happens. In the episode "Charlie X," Charlie doesn't like the teasing little ditty she makes up about him, so he closes up her throat, choking off the song (fortunately, there was no permanent damage that time). In "The Conscience of the King," Riley is so entranced by Uhura's singing that he allows himself to get poisoned (no permanent damage that time either, although it was a close call). Then, in "The Changeling," Uhura's singing so intrigues Nomad that he scans her brain in a rather clumsy attempt to discover whence the melodic urge arises. Unfortunately, this time there *is* permanent damage: The probe inadvertently purges the communication officer's brain of all knowledge! Fortunately, she's quickly reeducated. And none of these misfortunes had an impact upon the considerable musical talent of Uhura's alter ego, Nichelle Nichols.

"Bridge to captain. That mechanical beastie is up here."
—Scotty

When Nomad comes aboard, it tells Kirk that it has "the capability of movement within [the] ship." But the probe may have been a bit overconfident. Observant viewers have noted that as Nomad moves through Engineering late in the fourth act of "The Changeling," it seems to swing back and forth a bit unsteadily. Was Nomad hitting the Saurian brandy that day?

   Nope. It was simply experiencing a little glitch that the editors neglected to nip from the final print. Nomad's mobility came courtesy of a special effects man, or perhaps more properly, a "puppeteer," who controlled the probe's forward motion as it dangled on a wire and he walked on the overhead soundstage rafters. Of course, the puppeteer had to stop from time to time, allowing the probe to "hit its mark" and pause as it followed Scotty's course around the room. The man in the rafters simply didn't have enough leverage to halt the dangling object's forward momentum in that scene.

In the same sense that Nomad became a "changeling," this episode was destined to become a changeling as well. Eleven years after NBC canceled *Star Trek*, Paramount Pictures released the film *Star Trek: The Motion Picture*. As noted by many Trekkers, significant similarities exist between this episode and the movie. In "The Changeling," a damaged Terran exploratory probe programmed to find new life-forms unites with an alien space probe designed to sterilize soil samples; the hybrid probe thinks that it is supposed to eliminate all "biological infestations" and, following its earlier programming, seeks to return to the home of its "creator." Kirk knows that he has to stop it because once Nomad gets to Earth, it will find a planet full of biological infestations—and destroy them. In the film, a Terran space probe named *Voyager* has been damaged and subsequently repaired on a "planet of living machines." The probe, which now calls itself "V'Ger," seeks to sterilize all "carbon units" that it encounters, including those on the *Enterprise* and Earth, where it hopes to meet its "creator." In each iteration, Spock learns the full background of the hybrid machine by performing a Vulcan-to-machine mind-meld.

Little wonder that some fans referred to the motion picture as "Where Nomad Had Gone Before."

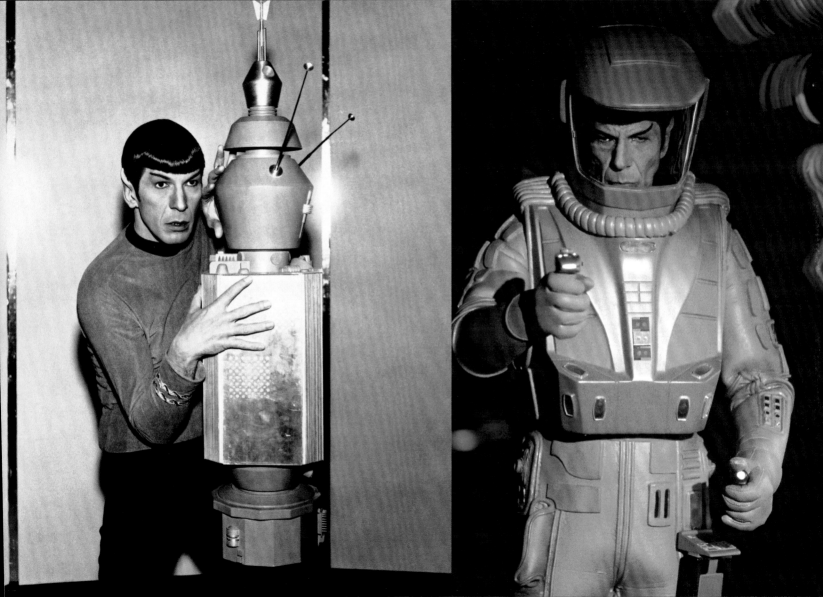

THE APPLE

"A Garden of Eden, with land mines."
—Kirk

Kirk's landing party discovers firsthand that a seeming paradise can be a very dangerous place to visit. Within the first few hours on Gamma Trianguli VI, Kirk loses three crewmen to poisonous plants, exploding rocks, and non-weather-related lightning bolts. To make matters worse, he can't beam the landing party back to the ship; something is draining the ship's power, rendering the transporter useless. The inhabitants of the planet are a simple, gentle people who make daily offerings of "food"—actually fuel—to the sophisticated computer they know only as the serpent god Vaal. In return, Vaal carefully controls living conditions on the planet, providing an Eden for its inhabitants. But Kirk and his crew, including those up on the *Enterprise*, are quite another matter. Vaal is determined to eradicate their presence from its sphere of influence—unless of course, Kirk destroys Vaal first.

Doctor McCoy often teases Spock about his green blood, but never about his recuperative powers. In "The Apple," security officer Hendorff quickly dies from a flower's poisonous darts, yet Spock, similarly poisoned, recovers (of course, receiving an injection of Masiform D from McCoy may have had something to do with that). Lieutenant Kaplan is struck and disintegrated by a lightning bolt, but when Spock is struck, he suffers only second-degree burns. Spock also is thrown through the air by a powerful force field, but he suffers injury only to his pride. Perhaps it's because he grew up in Vulcan's high gravity and thin atmosphere, or perhaps it's because of his importance to the cast, but it seems—at least in Spock's case—you can't keep a good man down.

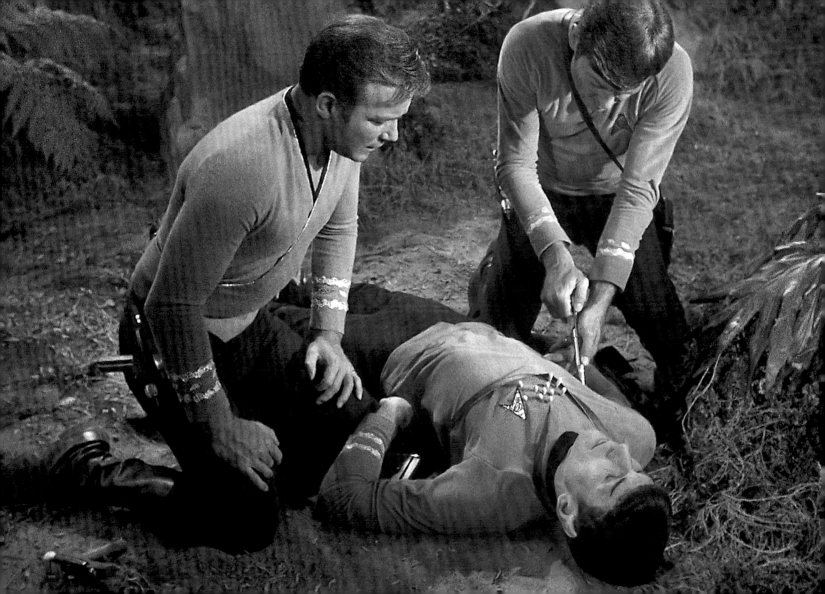

The note on Matt Jefferies's conceptual drawing of Vaal reads, "Reynolds Wrap on 1x3 frame (all angular facets)." Luckily for Jefferies, aluminum foil was cheap and available, because when NBC reluctantly renewed *Star Trek* for a second season, executives included a provision that would allow the network to dump the series after sixteen episodes if the show wasn't meeting their ratings expectations. Regardless, the producers had to plan their budgets around the twenty-six episodes they *hoped* to shoot. Every department felt the pinch, and Jefferies was forced to work with less than $10,000 per episode, regardless of what sets a script might call for. Creating Vaal's "dragon's head" from tinfoil worked surprisingly well, and the inadvertent "crinkles" created while working with the foil added texture to the "reptile skin."

120°

EXIST.
CLIFF

Reynold's Wrap
ON 1x3 FRAME
(ALL ANGULAR
FACETS)

JADE GREEN
LACQUER —

GREENS

+20'

+14'

+11½'

+3'

STAGE. FLR. 516.10

YAAL
"THE APPLE" 038

192

Makora: *"The way they touched. I do not understand."*
Sayana: *"They were not angry. I think it was pleasant for them."*
Makora: *"But what is to be gained? It is not a dance. It gathers no food. It does not serve Vaal. But it did* seem *as though it was pleasant to them."*

Young love is difficult, but no more difficult than young film careers, which is why it's possible to play a game called "What ever happened to . . . ?" In "The Apple," the lovely Sayana was played by Shari Nims, whose career was confined to only three roles, all in the year 1967. She first appeared in the feature film *Easy Come, Easy Go*, a rather forgettable Elvis Presley project. Shortly afterward, she played Sayana in "The Apple" and later appeared, uncredited, in an episode of *The Wild Wild West* before apparently changing careers. For the actor who played Makora, however, Hollywood had other plans. He'd already appeared in *Flipper* and *I Dream of Jeannie* before stripping down for his one role in *Star Trek*. He spent the next two years costarring in *Here Come the Brides* and subsequently took on dozens of roles in series ranging from *Ironside* to *Murder, She Wrote*. But perhaps viewers best remember him for the character he played on television from 1975 to 1979, and reprised in a feature-film cameo in 2004. Both the series and the feature were titled *Starsky & Hutch*. The character was Detective Ken "Hutch" Hutchinson. And the actor? David Soul.

193

MIRROR, MIRROR

An ion storm creates a transporter malfunction, swapping Kirk, Mc-Coy, Scotty, and Uhura with their counterparts from another universe. The mirror universe has the same technology as their own, but the civilization there has evolved along a quite different path. *Enterprise* crew members there rise in rank by practicing intimidation and assassination, and Kirk is expected to execute anyone who challenges his authority, including the Halkans, the peaceful inhabitants of the planet below. As Scotty searches for a way to get the landing party home, Kirk attempts to save the Halkan populace. But can he do so without forfeiting his own life?

"What will it be? Past or future? Tyranny or freedom? It's up to you."
—Kirk

Viewers seldom get to find out what happens to the characters in a television episode after the final credits roll. Fortunately, *Star Trek* is the longest-lived franchise in television history. With five series following in the flagship's wake over the decades, it was inevitable that at least one of those shows would pick up the gauntlet from where Kirk tossed it at the end of "Mirror, Mirror."

And in 1994, *Star Trek: Deep Space Nine* did, in an episode called "Crossover." The taut episode placed two of the *DS9* regulars into that gritty alternate universe—as in the original, the result of a bizarre accident.

The script was cowritten by Peter Allan Fields (a veteran of 1960s-era television, having written numerous scripts for *The Man from U.N.C.L.E.*) and *DS9*'s executive producer, Michael Piller. However, it was writing staff colleague Robert Hewitt Wolfe who would provide the historical details linking "Mirror, Mirror" to "Crossover."

"I came up with the idea that the Mirror Spock took over after our Kirk left their universe, and that turned out to be a mistake," says Wolfe. "Empires aren't usually brutal unless there's a reason—internal or external pressures that cause them to be that way. And the reason, in this case, was that the barbarians (the fierce alien species who opposed the Terran Empire) were at the gate."

Under the Mirror Spock's more peaceful reign, the Terran Empire no longer kept things in tight check. As a result, its enemies joined forces and took the empire's place in dominating the galaxy—enslaving most of the Earth and Vulcan peoples at the same time.

It seems that no good deed goes unpunished, Captain Kirk.

Have you ever wondered why the *Starship Enterprise* almost always flies from left to right across your TV screen? After completing the show's two pilots and receiving the green light that allowed them to go to series, *Star Trek*'s producers decided to retrofit the eleven-foot model of the ship by adding more running lights. This was long before the use of space-saving fiber optics for such purposes, so the only way the technicians could accomplish the change was by drilling numerous holes in the model and running electrical wires through those holes. The model makers drilled from the left-hand side, which meant, of course, that the port side of the ship, riddled and perforated by wires, was rendered forever unusable for filming.

For the rest of the series, whenever the *Enterprise* was depicted flying from right to left, viewers were almost certainly looking at footage from the second pilot, "Where No Man Has Gone Before"—and it's easy to tell. Just as Mister Spock looked different in that episode, so does the *Enterprise*. That version of the eleven-foot model has a taller bridge dome, a bigger sensor dish, unlit nacelle caps, louvers on the back ends of the nacelles, and of course, fewer running lights.

The producers opted to use this footage in "Mirror, Mirror" to visually suggest the landing party's trip to the alternate universe. Viewers first see the ship traveling left to right, as usual, then, following a jarring series of quick cuts, they see the ship orbiting from right to left. And although viewers' eyes interpret it as the same ship (or at least the mirror universe version of the same ship) that was flying from left to right, it's actually the one from "Where No Man Has Gone Before."

Years later, when the eleven-foot *Enterprise* model was presented to the Smithsonian Institution, the damage done by *Star Trek*'s well-meaning, hardworking techs finally was repaired as part of a major restoration (see spreads 359–361).

The Spock of our universe once described the Vulcan mind-meld as "a highly personal thing to the Vulcan people." Although he would perform melds with many different species—and even a few machines—Spock virtually always asked permission before he pressed his fingers against a "meldee's" head.

The reasons are twofold. For one thing, melding always carries a risk. It can be physically draining to both parties, even painful, and when linking with a dynamic mind, there is the chance that one or the other individual might find it difficult to "let go."

The other reason has to do with ethics. When a link is *forced* upon an unwilling individual, there is little moral distinction between the *mental* duress the "melder" causes his or her victim and an act of *physical* violation. Because of the savage world in which he exists, the mirror universe Spock has no compunction about forcing his way into McCoy's mind—he needs the information and he needs it *now*. It's hard to imagine our universe's Spock behaving in this manner— except that he does so in not one but *two* of the *Star Trek* movies: forcing his *katra*, or living spirit, into McCoy's mind in *Star Trek II: The Wrath of Khan*, and dragging the names of collaborators from the mind of his traitorous protégée Valeris in *Star Trek VI: The Undiscovered Country*.

THE DEADLY YEARS

"I'm thirty-four years old."
—Kirk

Members of a scientific expedition based on Gamma Hydra IV have been afflicted with a radiation-induced illness that triggers highly accelerated aging—and now members of the *Enterprise* landing party that beamed down to the planet are showing signs of the same malady. All, that is, except for Chekov, who seems unaffected, while Kirk, Spock, Scott, and McCoy grow older by the hour. As McCoy tries to unravel the riddle behind Chekov's immunity, the increasingly forgetful Kirk is judged unfit to maintain command of the *Enterprise*. But Commodore Stocker, who takes Kirk's place, has never commanded a starship, a fact made painfully obvious by his decision to cut across Romulan territory on the way to Starbase 10.

"Bones, I believe you're getting gray."
—Kirk

If you think old age is a pain, you should try old-age makeup! "The Deadly Years" forced key actors to spend from three to six hours in the makeup trailer each day. Some, like easygoing DeForest Kelley, simply accepted that this particular episode would require him to spend more time sitting than acting. William Shatner, like others, would bear the challenge like a trouper but find himself understandably frustrated when, after suffering through three boring hours of carefully applied latex sags, penciled age lines, and a special hairpiece, he arrived on the set to be told that production was closing down for the day. That moment was captured for posterity on one of *Star Trek*'s infamous "blooper reels," humorous outtakes that the producers would string together to run at each season's wrap party. (Gene Roddenberry later brought the reels to numerous *Star Trek* conventions.) In the clip, Shatner, in old-age makeup, addresses the powers that be—in this case, the coproducer—declaring: "Bob Justman, I'm going home now, after spending three hours putting this [expletive deleted] makeup back on . . . and it's *your* fault!"

The makeup looked fairly realistic for its time, but it's interesting to note that the actors aged far more gracefully over the years than their *Trek* alter egos did in "The Deadly Years."

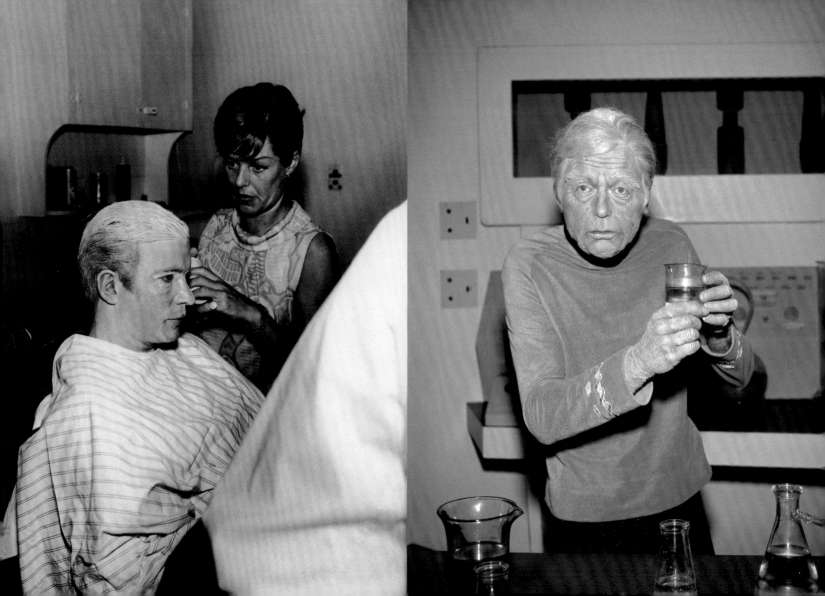

The original script for "The Deadly Years" would have allowed the viewers to see Kirk, after he is given the curative serum, grow younger as he rushes from sickbay to the bridge. The restoration would have happened en route. But the actors' performances as old men were apparently *too* realistic; their slower delivery of lines and halting physical movements bogged down the show's normally crisp pacing. In order to make the episode come in at the correct length, the rejuvenation sequence was scrapped, replaced by footage that implied Kirk did all of his de-aging while strapped to the bed in sickbay.

"Some more blood, Chekov. The needle won't hurt, Chekov. Take off your shirt, Chekov. Roll over, Chekov. Breathe deeply, Chekov. Blood sample, Chekov. Marrow sample, Chekov. Skin sample, Chekov. If I live long enough, I'm going to run out of samples."
—Chekov

One of the unsolved mysteries of *Star Trek* is how Khan recognized Chekov when he first laid eyes upon him in *Star Trek II: The Wrath of Khan*. After all, "Space Seed," the episode that introduced Khan, aired during *Star Trek*'s first season, and actor Walter Koenig, who plays Chekov, didn't join the show until season two. So, isn't it logical to think that Chekov wasn't posted to the *Enterprise* until then? Well, you can believe that, or if you prefer to think otherwise, you can pick up a hint dropped in "The Deadly Years."

Arriving on the bridge during the episode's final act, the once-again youthful Kirk quickly assesses the situation at hand (the *Enterprise* is surrounded by Romulan ships, with no way to get back across the Neutral Zone unless some of them give way) and sends a message to Starfleet that he knows the Romulans will decode: Since escape is impossible, he's going to implement the *Enterprise*'s "recently installed corbomite device," which will destroy all matter within a 200,000-kilometer diameter.

As Kirk initiates this clever ploy, Sulu and Chekov exchange conspiratorial grins that *seem* to show they know exactly what Kirk is doing because they recall the last time he did it—way back in season one's "The Corbomite Maneuver."

Now, just as fans know that Sulu was not initially a member of the *Enterprise*'s bridge crew (he was a physicist in "Where No Man Has Gone Before"), this little sight gag gives them reason to suspect that Chekov *might* have been assigned to the *Enterprise*'s lower decks when Khan came aboard. Which means, of course, that Khan certainly *could* have encountered him. Why not?

I, MUDD

Norman, an *Enterprise* crewman revealed to be an android, catches Kirk unawares when he takes control of the ship and locks it on course for a planet entirely occupied by androids—and one human being, Kirk's former nemesis Harry Mudd. It was Mudd who sent Norman on the mission to shanghai Kirk and his crew; he's been trapped on the android world since his own ship crash-landed there, and he plans to escape in the *Enterprise*. But the androids, who'd previously been very accommodating to Mudd, have their own plans for the starship. They've decided to use it to travel across the galaxy, "protecting" humankind from its lowest impulses, and they intend to leave Mudd, Kirk, and the crew of the *Enterprise* behind.

While *Star Trek*'s dramatic episodes won all the critical accolades, the show did occasionally venture into the realm of slapstick comedy. Although there were subtle threads of humor shot through many of the episodes, only three of the seventy-nine were outright comedies: "I, Mudd," "The Trouble with Tribbles," and "A Piece of the Action." All three rank quite high in terms of audience affection, possibly because of the cast's apparent willingness to poke fun at their traditionally staid characters.

"I, Mudd" features one of the show's most popular villains, Harcourt Fenton Mudd (played memorably by Roger C. Carmel). While there was a touch of menace to his persona in "Mudd's Women," here Harry serves primarily as a comic springboard for the regular cast's atypical antics, with Kirk serving as ringmaster while Chekov and Uhura waltz to the unheard music of Scotty and McCoy's "air orchestration," and deadpan Spock effectively demonstrates that he can out-droll the best of them. It's the broadest of humor, proving that even a series revered for its serious social messages can have a joke at its own expense, from time to time.

The end credits for "I, Mudd" list costar Alyce Andrece "as Alice #1 through 250" and her twin sister, Rhae Andrece, "as Alice #251 through 500." Those designations may have been a convenient way to credit the actresses, but they weren't adhered to on the set. In one scene, the sisters appear together as #3 and #11, and in another as #66 and #99. Perhaps the end credits were intended as one final joke meant for the private enjoyment of the viewers at home.

Star Trek casting director Joe D'Agosta found that hiring multiple sets of twins to play identical androids wasn't as easy as he'd figured. Only days before "I, Mudd" was ready to go before the cameras, D'Agosta, still searching for talent, was ecstatic to observe a pair of twin girls walking down the street in Hollywood. Leaping from his car, he accosted them with the question, "Can you act?" The shocked—and understandably suspicious—eighteen-year-olds had just arrived in town, but they eventually accepted his invitation to a casting session. When D'Agosta brought them to producer Gene L. Coon's office, the girls were dressed in miniskirts and wedgies—and they had their pet bobcat with them. Coon volunteered to hold the cat on his lap while the girls read aloud several pages of dialogue. As it turned out, the girls didn't have much talent, and their kitty had few social graces; Coon's shirt, pants, and *skin* were much the worse for wear. Nevertheless, the sisters were hired as extras—with the proviso that they leave the cat at home when they reported for filming.

During the Cold War, the Russians often boasted that everything of importance had been invented in Russia first. Some of their claims had basis in fact; for instance, it's true that Alexander Popov experimented with radio waves before Guglielmo Marconi sent wireless messages—but that doesn't necessarily make him the father of radio or Russia the mother of invention. But as the Communist Party continued such claims, it inspired a new genre of jokes among humorists, and *Star Trek's* writers joined the fray as they shaped the persona of Ensign Pavel Andreievich Chekov.

After taking in his beautiful surroundings in "The Apple," Chekov states, "It makes me homesick. Just like Russia." To McCoy's retort that the scenery bears more of a resemblance to the Garden of Eden, Chekov replies, "Of course, Doctor. The Garden of Eden was just outside Moscow." In "The Trouble with Tribbles," Chekov explains his familiarity with quadrotriticale by noting that the hybrid grain is "a Russian invention." Later, when Scotty declares that Scotch, as opposed to vodka, "is a drink for a *man*," Chekov chidingly responds, "Scotch? It was invented by a little old lady from Leningrad."

Of course, there were times when even Chekov had to admit that his homeland couldn't beat his current circumstances; when the lovely Alice androids indicate that they are programmed to cater to his every whim in "I, Mudd," Chekov can't help murmuring an appreciative "This place is even *better* than Leningrad."

THE TROUBLE WITH TRIBBLES

"One million, seven hundred seventy-one thousand, five hundred sixty-one. That's assuming one tribble, multiplying with an average litter of ten, producing a new generation every twelve hours over a period of three days."
—Spock

Responding to a distress call, the *Enterprise* diverts to Deep Space Station K-7, where Kirk discovers that the station's "emergency" was triggered by the demands of an obnoxious Federation bureaucrat named Nilz Baris. Baris insists that Starfleet—more specifically, the *Enterprise*—protect an important shipment of grain that is being stored at the station. Kirk isn't inclined to comply, but when a Klingon ship arrives at the station, demanding recreational privileges for its crew, Kirk decides to stick around, granting his own crew the same privileges. On the station, Uhura encounters a trader who offers her a sample of his wares: an innocuous little creature called a tribble. And that's when Kirk's problems begin to escalate, rapidly. One tribble becomes thousands of tribbles before anyone knows it, infesting the

Enterprise, the space station, and the all-important grain bin that Kirk has promised to protect.

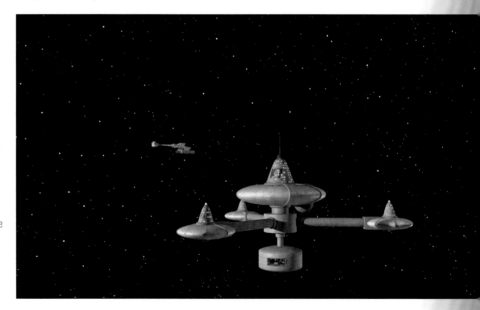

"I want to know who put the tribbles in the quadrotriticale and what was in the grain that killed them."
—Kirk

What a piece of work are tribbles, those small purring marvels wrapped in a fur coat. "The only love money can buy," according to space merchant Cyrano Jones, although he admittedly has a stake in selling the sweet little creatures. A more precise definition than that would depend entirely on whom you ask. They remind Spock of the lilies of the field: "They toil not, neither do they spin." He sees no practical use for them, although he allows that their pleasant trilling seems to have a tranquilizing effect on the human nervous system. Doctor McCoy completes a medical analysis of one and declares that the little balls of fluff are bisexual, able to reproduce at will—and, in fact, they appear to be born pregnant. After one tribble quickly becomes 1,771,561 tribbles, McCoy figures out that if you stop feeding them, they stop breeding. *Now* he tells 'em!

Consistently voted *Star Trek*'s most popular offering, "The Trouble with Tribbles" wasn't all that popular with the late Robert Justman, coproducer of *Star Trek*. Like the tribbles themselves, Justman felt the premise was just "too cute" and that the cast's performances skated dangerously close to parody.

Justman admitted that he was, however, a minority of one.

In 1788, eleven ships known as the First Fleet sailed from England to Australia to establish a convict settlement. Among the goods carried by that fleet: live rabbits, presumably destined as food stock. But a number of the rabbits escaped, and before long, their offspring had overrun the continent, eating to extinction an unknown number of native plants. That, in turn, left the land vulnerable to devastating erosion—an ecological disaster in the making that greatly affects Australia today.

Writer David Gerrold hoped to sell an outer space version of that story to the producers of *Star Trek*, and when he observed a friend's key chain topped with a pink ball of fluff, he knew what inexpensive-to-produce prop would serve as his space rabbits. The script sold, and special effects genius Wah Chang accepted the challenge of designing the "tribbles" from pieces of artificial fur. Chang then paid seamstress Jacqueline Cumeré $350 to stitch up five hundred of the fluff balls.

The script called for a number of the tribbles to move about, and that's where special effects man Jim Rugg, who handled the "mechanical effects" for the series, sprang into action. Rugg stuffed some of the tribbles with surgical balloons attached to air hoses that ran offstage. As hidden crew members squeezed rubber bulbs, the pulsating results made the tribbles seem to breathe. Rugg also placed tiny windup spring motors into some of the tribble props so

that they could "crawl" across the floor, and into others he inserted battery-operated motors cannibalized from toys. And that's how tribbles are conceived—regardless of what Doctor McCoy has to say on the subject.

In 1996, the producers of *Star Trek: Deep Space Nine* decided to craft a special episode of their show that would honor the original *Star Trek*, which was about to celebrate its thirtieth anniversary. Showrunner Ira Steven Behr charged his writing staff with the creation of something truly unique, and after a series of brainstorming sessions, the team hit upon an idea that seemed to fit the bill: The characters from *Deep Space Nine* would time-travel back to the twenty-third century—specifically to Deep Space Station K-7, the locale of "The Trouble with Tribbles"—to prevent the assassination of Captain James T. Kirk by disguised Klingon agent Arne Darvin.

Everything about the concept was daunting (particularly the thought of expense), but they tackled the most basic potential hurdle first: They'd need new footage of Arne Darvin. So many guest stars from the original series had passed away over the decades; was Charlie Brill, the actor/comedian who'd played Darvin, still alive? The group was pondering this subject over pizza one day when fate stepped in—literally—in the form of Mr. Brill, who walked into the pizza parlor. He certainly *seemed* alive.

Following this bit of serendipity, the writers were nearly convinced that their concept was blessed. However, the story would also require cutting-edge technology. Could they seamlessly "marry" the *DS9* characters into footage from the earlier show? They assigned Gary Hutzel, *Deep Space Nine*'s visual effects supervisor, to conduct a test. Days later, Hutzel arrived at the office to show the producers some footage from an old *Trek* episode. The producers were unimpressed, until Hutzel revealed that one of *his* assistants was standing near the turbolift, mingling with Kirk's crew on the bridge of the *Enterprise*. That sealed the deal, and after being given budget approval from Paramount, they began fleshing out their story. The resulting episode, "Trials and Tribble-ations," features remarkable scenes where 1990s-era *Star Trek* characters join the 1960s-era *Star Trek* crew in the classic bar fight with the Klingons, the lineup wherein Kirk chews out his men for participating in that fight, and the famous storage bin scene, where tribble after tribble tumbles out to land on Kirk's head (because *DS9*'s Captain Sisko is *in* the bin, tossing tribbles out of the open hatch). The episode was a labor of love for the actors and the staff, and a pure delight for fans.

According to John Dwyer, set decorator for the second and third seasons of *Star Trek*, only a few original tribbles remain from the production of the classic episode "The Trouble with Tribbles." Dwyer provides a word to the wise for fans who hope to add one of these rarest of rare commodities to their personal collection.

"If you see one at a convention and the dealer claims it's authentic, here's the way to tell," Dwyer states. "If it looks good, it's most likely a fake! Because these things look terrible! They're practically bald. The phony fur technology of the 1960s was not all that great. Actually, if you've ever seen a gray-haired lady who dyed her hair red, and it was half-grown out on top, you've got the picture. And they kind of look like a rat might have chewed on them."

So there you have it. If it looks *really* pretty, keep your cash in your pocket and walk the other way!

What will businessmen of the twenty-third century wear? Judging by the threads that William Theiss created for Nilz Baris and Arne Darvin in "The Trouble with Tribbles," professionals of Kirk's era will don attire that the men of our own era wouldn't find all that intimidating. Which is to say, a nice gabardine in a color that doesn't call too much attention to itself.

BREAD AND CIRCUSES

On the hunt for survivors from the *S.S. Beagle*, a lost Federation vessel, the crew of the *Enterprise* arrives at planet 892 IV, where the civilization closely resembles that of Earth's ancient Rome—albeit a Rome whose culture has advanced to technological levels matching those of Earth's twentieth century, with fast cars and brutal, televised gladiator matches. Upon arrival, Kirk, Spock, and McCoy question members of the "Children of the Sun," peaceful dissidents who have forsworn violence, and discover that the *Beagle*'s Captain R. M. Merik has become the right-hand man to the empire's Proconsul Claudius Marcus. Confronting Merik, Kirk learns that the former captain allowed the proconsul to enslave the *Beagle*'s crew and throw them into the arena, where most of them were slaughtered in battle. And now the proconsul expects Merik to convince Kirk to do the same with the crew of the *Enterprise*.

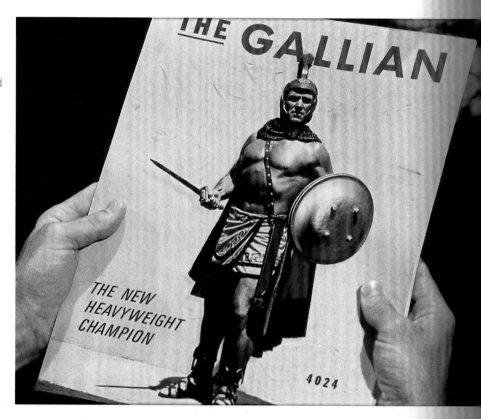

From the earliest days of Hollywood cinema, the fates of Paramount Pictures and Cecil B. DeMille, the studio's first preeminent filmmaker, were tightly intertwined. DeMille had a lifelong passion for lavish historical epics, and he directed a slew of them for Paramount, from *Joan the Woman*, a 1916 silent "super-spectacle" about Joan of Arc, to 1956's *The Ten Commandments*, DeMille's final film as a director. Just prior to his death in 1959, DeMille was making plans to direct a story about space travel. He never had the opportunity to film his science fiction epic; nevertheless, he managed to make an impression on the twenty-third century—via *Star Trek*. As "Bread and Circuses" was about to go into production, the producers were given permission to borrow props from Paramount's storage vaults. They chose a number of costumes and props made for the DeMille extravaganzas *The Sign of the Cross, Cleopatra*, and *The Crusades*: for example, the costumes worn by the *Star Trek* episode's centurion guards.

Like Vasquez Rocks, scenic Bronson Canyon, located just minutes from the front gates of Paramount Pictures, has been featured in hundreds of films and television shows. It initially was developed as a quarry that supplied crushed rock to Los Angeles's road builders at the beginning of the twentieth century, but that ceased operation in the 1920s. The burgeoning Hollywood entertainment industry soon discovered the craggy canyon, perfect for westerns as well as science fiction and adventure films. Early movies featuring stars as disparate as Tom Mix, John Wayne, and Rin Tin Tin were shot there, as well as later genre classics like the original *Invasion of the Body Snatchers*. By the 1960s, Bronson had become the darling of the television industry, so often in need of a desolate-appearing—but conveniently located—outdoor filming arena. Every incarnation of televised *Star Trek* (with the exception of the animated series) filmed at least one episode there, as did the film *Star Trek VI: The Undiscovered Country*.

Besides its rocky slopes, the canyon is also known for Bronson Caves, which is actually a short, forked tunnel through a hill. The origins of the man-made cave are a bit murky: Some say the developers of the quarry, the Union Rock Company, blasted it out of the hill, while others claim that filmmakers did, with the producers of the first *Robin Hood* feature film (1922) most often mentioned.

Most of the verbal darts that McCoy launched at Spock over *Star Trek*'s three-year run bounced off the Vulcan's seemingly impenetrable hide. But during an exchange in "Bread and Circuses," one of those lancet sharp insults apparently hits its mark, and McCoy, as if detecting the scent of blood (green variety) in the air, quickly moves in for the kill:

> *"Do you know why you're not afraid to die, Spock? You're more afraid of living. Each day you stay alive is just one more day you might slip and let your human half peek out. That's it, isn't it? Insecurity."*

The blocking in this sequence is unique to the series. Typically, when the doctor launches into one of his tirades against the Vulcan, the two are face-to-face, with Spock regarding McCoy impassively. And that *is* the way things start out here, but as McCoy nears the truth, Spock deliberately turns his face *away*—leaving only the viewers at home to witness his countenance . . . and his true feelings. He seems troubled by McCoy's accusations—perhaps this is something he hasn't realized about himself. But ultimately, it doesn't matter. Spock quickly recovers his composure and turns back to regard McCoy with the usual well-practiced disdain.

And that's that for Spock's brief moment on the psychiatrist's couch—at least in "Bread and Circuses." But the events of the following episode, "Journey to Babel," would reveal to one and all the primary source of those apparent chinks in his emotional armor.

JOURNEY TO BABEL

The *Enterprise* has been assigned to convey a group of Federation representatives to an important conference on Babel, and Kirk suspects he will have his hands full keeping peace among the eclectic group of guests. Last to arrive onboard is the Vulcan contingent, led by Ambassador Sarek, who is accompanied by his human wife Amanda. The ambassador and his wife are Spock's parents, but the reunion between father and son is surprisingly chilly. Amanda explains to Kirk that a disagreement over Spock's choice of career has kept the two men from speaking for eighteen years. As the ship gets under way, however, the family feud becomes the least of Kirk's worries. The assorted planetary reps have wildly differing opinions about the Babel Conference's central issue: the admission of the planet Coridan to the Federation. Even Sarek, with his restrained Vulcan temperament, is drawn into a heated argument with a Tellarite ambassador—and a short time later, the Tellarite is found dead, his neck snapped via a Vulcan technique called *tal-shaya*. Sarek claims to have been incapacitated at the time of the murder, and indeed, McCoy reveals that the ambassador *is* suffering from a life-threatening cardiovascular malfunction. If Sarek is to survive the voyage, he must have immediate surgery. The operation will require a large quantity of Vulcan blood, which McCoy can obtain only from Spock—*if* the younger Vulcan submits to a hazardous experimental procedure. But after Captain Kirk is critically injured in an attack by one of the conference attendees, Spock turns McCoy down—effectively sentencing his father to death.

"Logic! Logic! I'm sick to death of logic!"
—Amanda

To a generation of baby boomer children who'd grown up watching *Father Knows Best*, actress Jane Wyatt was the quintessential "mom"; to the parents of those children, she was the "perfect" wife or girlfriend, invariably paired in films with a major-league actor such as Cary Grant, Randolph Scott, or Gary Cooper. And, of course, to fans of classic film, she was the charming young woman Ronald Colman had the misfortune to leave behind—but the good sense to return to—in Frank Capra's *Lost Horizon*. Wyatt's delicate features and good-natured grace served her well over a lengthy career. And *Star Trek*'s producers showed similar grace in crediting the actress as "Miss Jane Wyatt" in the episode's end credits. It was a rare, old-fashioned gesture, even in the 1960s: the showbiz equivalent of a tip of the hat to a woman with a long and distinguished career.

Wyatt's warm and affectionate performance as Amanda, Spock's human mother, made it easy to comprehend how she could melt the Vulcan reserve of both father and son. D. C. Fontana, who wrote this episode, says that she named Spock's mother "Amanda" because the name means "worthy of being loved." Could there be a better reason to marry someone?

Of course, when warmth alone didn't do the trick, Amanda had in reserve a human mother's gift for emotional manipulation to make an impression on a stubborn child:

"When you were five years old and came home stiff-lipped, anguished, because the other boys tormented you, saying that you weren't really Vulcan, I watched you, knowing that inside the human part of you was crying. And I cried too. There must be some part of me in you. Some part that I still can reach. If being Vulcan is more important to you, then you'll stand there, speaking rules and regulations from Starfleet and Vulcan philosophy, and let your father die.

And I'll hate you for the rest of my life."

Well, no one ever said that mother-son relationships were easy . . . on any planet.

Casting Mark Lenard as Spock's father, Sarek, was likely a no-brainer for *Star Trek*'s producers. As the Romulan commander in "Balance of Terror," he'd made a strong impression both on the show's audience and on its cast and crew. A talented character actor, Lenard bore a fortuitous resemblance to Leonard Nimoy, quite possibly due to the fact that both men's parents were Jewish immigrants who came from the same part of the world: neighboring states in the Soviet Union. The fact that they were playing father and son was a bit more of a stretch, however; at the time Lenard was cast as Sarek, he was only forty-three, just seven years older than the man who played his son.

As gracious to the fans he encountered at *Trek* conventions as he was on set, Lenard became extremely popular with *Star Trek* fans—and they had plenty of opportunities to see him over the years. He was one of the few actors to play the same character in more than one incarnation of *Star Trek*. A few years after the series ended, he would voice Sarek in an animated episode called "Yesteryear." Two decades later, he would reprise the role in a pair of episodes on *Star Trek: The Next Generation*. In between those appearances, he played Spock's father in the films *Star Trek III: The Search for Spock*, *Star Trek IV: The Voyage Home*, and *Star Trek VI: The Undiscovered Country*, as well as a Klingon commander in *Star Trek: The Motion Picture* (he also dubbed the voice of a younger actor who played Sarek in *Star Trek V: The Final Frontier*).

Chief Engineer Scott once lamented, "I can't change the laws of physics!" Even miracle workers like Scotty, who could no doubt repair a malfunctioning deflector shield with a paper clip, apparently yield to what they see as the inviolable hurdles of reality.

Not so with Doctor McCoy, who has no compunction about shattering an equally impenetrable metaphysical barrier at the end of "Journey to Babel."

What was McCoy's shocking lapse in judgment? He broke *Star Trek*'s fourth wall!

There's an unwritten rule in entertainment: Performers are not supposed to address the audience directly from within the confines of their theatrical stage or soundstage. To do so is to "break the fourth wall," that is, pierce the "invisible screen" that separates the audience from the goings-on within the context of the show they are watching. It's an intangible understanding between two parties, part of the willing suspension of disbelief that allows an audience to fall under the spell of a fictional work.

While comedies occasionally break this fourth wall (possibly because it inspires additional laughs), dramas seldom do. It tends to jerk audiences out of the aforementioned spell that the producers have worked so hard to cast. But here, at the end of "Journey to Babel," is the unthinkable:

SPOCK: *Doctor, I'll return to my station now.*

MCCOY: You *are at your station, Mister Spock.*
KIRK: *Doctor McCoy, I believe you're enjoying all this.*
SPOCK: *Indeed, Captain. I've never seen him look so happy.*
MCCOY: *(to Spock) Shut up. (to Kirk) Shh. Shh! (to camera) Well, what do you know? I finally got the last word.*

It's an unprecedented moment in *Star Trek*, somehow forgivable because it's the very last moment in the episode, and the series already had established a precedent of periodically ending the show by having one or more characters deliver a jokey one-liner. Then, too, McCoy's obvious delight at this fleeting opportunity to control both his captain *and* his arch-nemesis, combined with DeForest Kelley's endearingly goofy grin, make this a moment that *Star Trek* fans savored rather than scolded.

"Tellarites do not argue for reasons. They simply argue."
—Sarek

Whether makeup artist Fred Phillips took his cue for the Tellarite makeup from Sarek's assertion that the species is argumentative or from his own creative mind, there's little doubt that the species introduced in "Journey to Babel" was pigheaded, visually as well as culturally.

Phillips began his career during the golden era of movies, applying cosmetic makeup to a rainbow of stars, including Loretta Young, Barbara Stanwyck, and Shirley Temple. Glamour aside, he excelled at another level of makeup: creating exotic alien features.

Phillips sculpted and molded the Tellarites' facial features into foam latex prosthetic appliances. While wearing the pictured nose and cheek appliance for his portrayal of Ambassador Gav, actor John Wheeler found that he couldn't see properly though the eye holes, so he tilted his head back in an attempt to adjust his line of vision. By holding his snout high, Wheeler inadvertently added a pertinent level of arrogance to the character's demeanor.

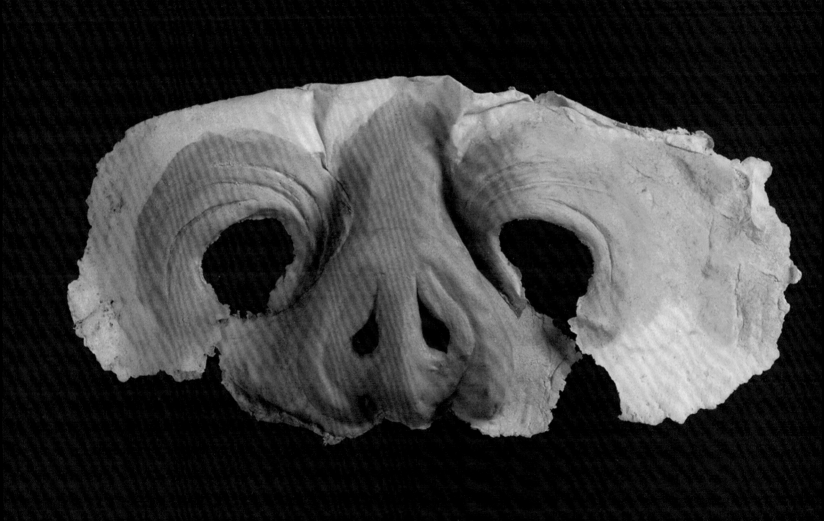

221

A PRIVATE LITTLE WAR

Kirk: "Bones, do you remember the twentieth-century brush wars on the Asian continent? Two giant powers involved, much like the Klingons and ourselves. Neither side felt it could pull out."
McCoy: "Yes, I remember. It went on bloody year after bloody year."

Returning to a primitive world that he first visited thirteen years earlier, Kirk finds the peaceful land of his friend Tyree, leader of the "hill people," much changed. Tyree's antagonistic neighbors, the "villagers," are now armed with flintlock rifles, weapons that, at their current stage of development, they shouldn't have. The rifles have been provided by conniving Klingons, who aim to take control of Tyree's planet by helping one ignorant group of natives defeat the other. Kirk feels the only rational way to help Tyree is to provide him with similar weapons and level the playing field—much to pacifist McCoy's dismay.

222

The clapperboard reads:

DESILU STAR TREK 60345
DIR MARC DANIELS
CAM LEROY PINKERMAN
DATE 10-3-67

48A

The United States became involved in military operations in Vietnam during the 1950s, but it wasn't until the mid-1960s that the American public took notice. North Vietnam, backed by its Communist allies, was battling South Vietnam, which had the support of the United States and other nations. As President Lyndon Johnson began sharply escalating troop buildup in 1965, antiwar activists got busy, and protests became the main fodder of the news cycle. Writer Don Ingalls (using the pseudonym Jud Crucis), a former Los Angeles police officer and writer on *Have Gun Will Travel* like Gene Roddenberry, wrote a *Star Trek* script permeated with Vietnam references. A subsequent rewrite eliminated many of the most blatant comparisons, but the analogy to the war remained, with Kirk and the Klingons standing in for the United States and its Communist foes, both arming two closely situated indigenous peoples against each other. The result, an escalation in violence cloaked within the guise of a supposed balance of power, leaves Kirk with a much fuller understanding of the bitter lessons of history, and *Star Trek* with one of its most "political" episodes—although the "Sonny and Cher" look of Tyree and his witchy woman Nona may have partially obscured the point.

"... *To explore strange new worlds* ..." One of NBC's dictums was that the *Star Trek* producers live up to the captain's weekly prologue by producing a "planet show," with the crew visiting a new alien world every week, or at least as often as the limited budget made location shoots possible. While that sounds like a fine premise for a series, it ignores the fact that without a healthy budget for hair, wardrobe, and makeup, the crew might beam down to a planet where the natives wear really bad wigs and the wildlife sports an evolutionarily ridiculous horn, giving it the look of an episode of *Monty Python's Flying Circus.*

Strange new world, indeed!

THE GAMESTERS OF TRISKELION

"Who said anything about a mutiny, you stubborn, pointy-eared . . . ?!"
—McCoy

Kirk, Uhura, and Chekov disappear off the *Enterprise*'s transporter pad and wind up on the planet Triskelion, far from their intended destination. Realizing that the trio has been abducted, Spock, McCoy, and Scotty attempt to track them down—but it's an awfully big galaxy, and they have few clues. On Triskelion, Kirk learns that they've been snatched by the Providers, three disembodied brains that intend to turn the *Enterprise* crew members into warriors fit for the gladiatorial ring. Having evolved beyond the need for physical activity, the Providers have little to do with their time other than wager on the outcome of such contests of strength and skill. The kidnapped Starfleet officers are trained for their new lives by other captives who serve as "drill thralls." As Kirk learns more about life on Triskelion, he formulates a plan that would free him and his comrades—and the thralls as well—if he can just survive a match that will determine everyone's fate.

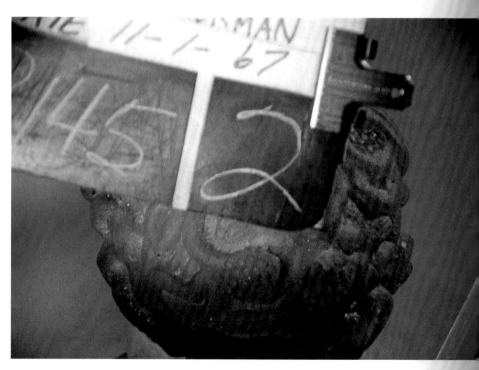

Kirk should have been used to it by now; after all, the Triskelions were not the first nigh-omnipotent aliens to pit him in a battle to the death. In "Arena," the good captain was forced into hand-to-hand combat with an oversize lizard known as the Gorn. In "The Squire of Gothos," Kirk found no recourse but to challenge the irksome but dangerous Trelane to a duel. The Triskelions, however, were the first to get their kicks by placing wagers on the outcome of Kirk's experience in the ring. Still, one can't help but wonder: What the heck is a "quat-loo?" And what can a disembodied brain do with one—not to mention thousands—of them?

In retrospect, it's not surprising that "The Gamesters of Triskelion" provided part of the inspirational fodder for "Where No Fan Has Gone Before," an especially *Star Trek*-reference-heavy episode of *Futurama*. Suffice it to say that amid the dozens of *Trek* references that fill the half hour, there are wagers in quatloos and series regulars being "pit[ted] against each other in armed combat—to the death," as seen in *Star Trek* "episodes 19, 46, 56, 66, and 77," per the *Futurama* writers.

Nice homage, but they left episode 34 off their list!

Does Galt, the master of the drill thralls, look familiar? He should. From a simple visual standpoint, of course, he represents a link in a villainous chain that includes such memorable bad guys as Fu Manchu and Ming the Merciless. But beyond that sinister goatee and shiny pate, there may be a different reason that viewers sense a familiarity. The role of Galt was filled by character actor Joseph Ruskin, who had appeared in more than one hundred roles on television *prior* to appearing on *Star Trek*, and who would appear in another one-hundred-plus afterward. The *Star Trek* franchise has a notoriously long memory, and besides Ruskin's recent performances in shows and films such as *Bones*, *ER*, *Smokin' Aces*, and *Alias*, he's portrayed a fascinating variety of aliens in later versions of *Star Trek*, including a Son'a (*Star Trek: Insurrection*), a Klingon (*Star Trek: Deep Space Nine*), a Vulcan (*Star Trek: Voyager*), and a Suliban (*Star Trek: Enterprise*).

"Goodbye, Jim Kirk. I will learn, and watch the lights in the sky, and re-member."
—Shahna

Captain Kirk famously talked computers and computer-like enti-ties into going against their "primary function" many times over the course of his Starfleet career. But that's nothing compared to the number of times his glib tongue achieved similar results with the op-posite sex. As Scotty once observed, it pays to have "the right tool for the right job," and James Kirk clearly finds seduction a very use-ful tool, particularly when it comes to getting out of a jam. In "The Gamesters of Triskelion," Kirk teaches drill thrall Shahna the mean-ing of love—then, while she's entranced, he slugs her and steals the key to his cell.

Over the seasons, Kirk similarly managed to sidetrack an astound-ing number of appreciative females, including adolescent Miri, an-droid Andrea, catty Sylvia, Andromedan Kelinda, the mirror universe captain's woman Marlena Moreau, and Deela, the quick and easy Scalosian queen. Generally, these moments of bliss were contrived to assist the stalwart captain in saving his ship or his crew. But fate sometimes would demand payback for all of this kissing without con-sequence. Kirk's career stood between him and some of the women he truly cared about, and the grim reaper made short work of that un-

lucky pair for whom he just might have sacrificed that career: Mira-manee and Edith Keeler.

Shahna was lucky—he left her, but at least she was still breathing!

Star Trek was never a ratings behemoth during its three years on network television. Nevertheless, it did generate a certain amount of heat. People talked about the show. Television audiences recognized the characters, even if they didn't tune in to the show each week. And when Leonard Nimoy appeared on the popular new series *The Carol Burnett Show* in 1967, no one—except possibly the character Carol was playing—mistook Mister Spock for Dr. Spock.

Although NBC didn't seem to have much faith in the series, Kaiser Broadcasting did. Owner and operator of a string of UHF broadcast television stations from the late 1950s through the 1970s, Kaiser appreciated the small but passionate viewing audience that *Star Trek* attracted. In fact, Kaiser began negotiating with Paramount for syndication rights to the series in 1967, a full year and a half before the series was canceled. When *Star Trek* went off the air, Kaiser got moving, setting in motion plans to run uncut episodes on its stations in time slots opposite its competitors' dinner hour newscasts. In doing so, Kaiser nabbed the majority of younger viewers in such major cities as Chicago, Philadelphia, Boston, Detroit, and Cleveland. When independent stations across the country caught wind of Kaiser's tremendously successful syndication efforts, they too lined up to carry the series. The end result was a true phenomenon: a series that became more popular in syndication than it had ever been in first run.

Although Paramount television execs were delighted with *Star Trek*'s success in syndication, so few of them watched the show that the press kit issued by the syndication division featured an illustration of Mister Spock wearing the wrong-colored tunic. The mistake went uncaught until after distribution of the kit, instantly transforming the item into a future collector's item.

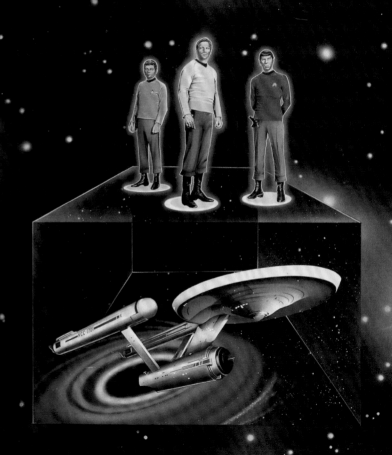

STAR TREK

THE PHENOMENON

OBSESSION

Spock: "I need your advice."
McCoy: "Then I need a drink."

The reappearance of a deadly cloudlike creature that Kirk encountered while he was a lieutenant on the *U.S.S. Farragut* triggers within him an obsession that alarms Spock and McCoy. Eleven years ago, the creature killed half the *Farragut*'s crew, including Garrovick, the ship's captain. Kirk has always believed that if he hadn't hesitated in firing at the creature, he could have saved the lives of all who perished. Now one of Kirk's crewmen on the *Enterprise*—ironically, the son of Captain Garrovick—has inadvertently committed the same "sin" as Kirk: He froze at the precise moment when he should have fired on the cloud. Kirk blames Garrovick for the deaths that ensued; he relieves the young officer from duty and sets out to destroy the creature. This time, he promises himself, it won't get away.

As *Star Trek* historians have noted, James T. Kirk was "the quintes-sential Starfleet officer, a man among men and a hero for the ages." Nevertheless, he was *human*, and susceptible to many human frailties—including, as Doctor McCoy put it, "the greatest monster of them all . . . guilt." The death of Garrovick, "one of the finest men [Kirk] ever knew," haunted the captain for years. The reappearance of the entity that killed his former commander triggered within Kirk an "obsession" that would lead him to endanger not only his own crew, but the populace of an entire planet desperately in need of medical deliveries. Kirk initially couldn't help believing that he'd been given a chance to redeem himself for that long-ago mistake in judgment. Instead, he realized that he'd been wrong about his role in Garrovick's death, which made finding a way to eliminate the deadly cloud crea-ture not an act of exculpation, but one of everyday heroism.

Everyday, that is, if you're James T. Kirk.

Most of the memorable creatures from early movies and television—
from *Creature from the Black Lagoon* to *Godzilla*—sported two arms,
two legs, and a zipper down the back. And that's the way it remained,
until the digital age made it easier to construct alien creatures via
computer graphics. But even "back in the day," *Star Trek* contracted
with several effects studios—among them Van der Veer Photo Effects,
the Howard A. Anderson Company, the Westheimer Company, and
Cinema Research—and the show also had on staff Jim Rugg, a very
inventive physical effects man. Thus, on occasion, the producers were
able to "think outside the zipper" for the alien of the week. In "Obsession," a smoke-making machine hidden behind the rocks teased the
viewers into thinking there was more going on than there was, as
did simple process shots created by layering footage of smoke and
sparkles over the action. In the end, however, it wasn't the visual image
that sold the "dikironium cloud creature," but something that triggered
a different sense. "Do you smell that?" Kirk asks, ostensibly of his crew,
but of the viewer as well. "A sweet odor, like honey . . . a thing with an
odor like that." And when the dying security officer Rizzo whispers,
"A smell. A strange smell. It was like being smothered in honey," the
viewer has little choice but to imagine he smells it too. This particular
creature was fleshed out with dialogue. There wouldn't be a more effective "depiction" of odor on the small screen until the Food Network
came into existence some thirty years later.

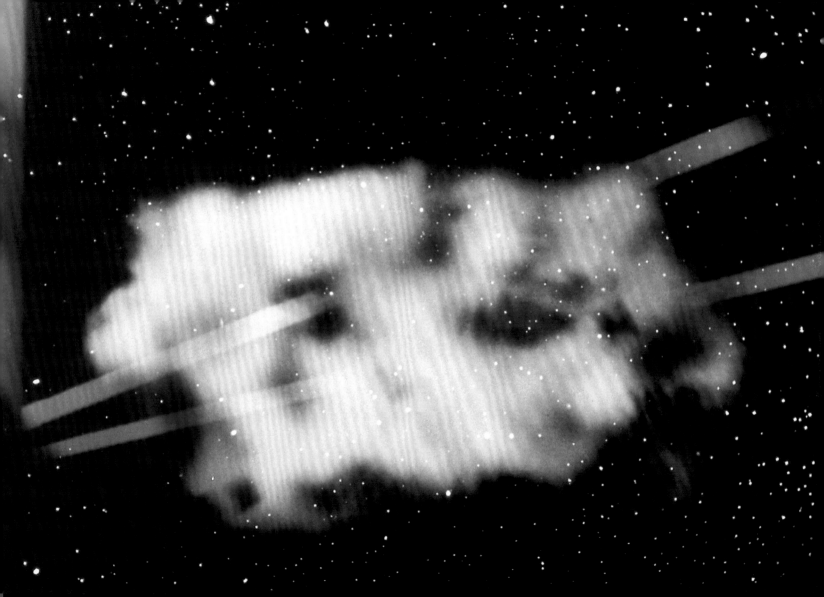

The seemingly simple clapper board is one of the most important pieces of equipment used on a film set. Without the information on it, a film editor would have a difficult time figuring out which snippet of footage he was viewing at any given time. Essentially, the board is a slate; the upper portion lists the name of the production company (in this case, Desilu), the production (*Star Trek*), the series production number (603), immediately followed by the episode number (47), the director's name (Ralph Senensky), the cinematographer's name (Jerry Finnerman), and the date. Below that, on the chalkboard, are the scene (53C) and "take" (2) numbers. The name "clapper" relates to the sound the device makes when the hinged bar across the top is loudly "clapped" shut. The sound is as important as the visual; it's the editor's prime clue for synchronizing the audio track with the visual track.

Scene 53 of "Obsession" consisted of a serious discussion between Spock and McCoy. In the master shot (53A), the camera captured both actors as they went through the action and dialogue from beginning to end. The camera was then re-situated to shoot Spock in close-up (53B), wherein Leonard Nimoy repeated the entire scene while DeForest Kelley responded from off camera. In the image at right, the slate indicates that the lens has been focused on Kelley, who is about to repeat McCoy's lines in close-up for the second time; apparently the director wanted Kelley to perform a second take. Thus Scene 53C, Take 2.

The camera department crew member who handles the clapper board is called the film loader. The tasks that person performs include everything physical about the film stock, from loading raw film into the camera to marking it correctly (via the slate information), to placing the exposed film into the marked film can and then placing that can into secure, dark storage until the loader delivers it to the editor. It's a highly responsible position, not for the faint of heart, although it does have one interesting perk: By the end of a production, the film loader's hands have become very recognizable, if only to the person in the editing room.

DESILU "STAR-TREK 60347
DIR RALPH SENENSKY
CAM JERRY FINNERMAN
DATE 10-16-67
53C
2

THE IMMUNITY SYNDROME

"It's a disease, like a virus in the body of our galaxy."
—McCoy

After losing contact with solar system Gamma 7A and the *Starship Intrepid*, Starfleet dispatches the *Enterprise* to the region. At the same time, Spock is blindsided by a psychic bolt from light years away; the *Intrepid*—a ship manned entirely by Vulcans—has just been destroyed, and all four hundred members of its crew along with it. When the *Enterprise* reaches Gamma 7A, sensors reveal that every one of the system's billions of inhabitants is also dead, destroyed by what appears to be a gigantic single-celled organism that most resembles an impossibly oversize amoeba. The amoeba-like entity feeds on the energy of living beings, and it's gathered enough to reproduce; it's up to Kirk to destroy it before that can happen. But how? Spock and McCoy each volunteer to take a shuttlecraft into the "heart" of the life-form to determine and convey the information Kirk will need—but that solution leaves Kirk with an extremely unpleasant decision to make.

"Which of my friends do I condemn to death?"
—Kirk

The ongoing verbal feud between Spock and McCoy escalates to a new level in "The Immunity Syndrome," as each attempts to convince Kirk that he is the best man to conduct what is likely to be a suicidal exploratory mission. They are both men of science, equally qualified to take a shuttlecraft into the "heart of the beast" (or, more accurately, the nucleus of the protoplasmic mass), but the captain ultimately assigns Spock, presumably because of his superior physical stamina, to the task.

   Although Spock and McCoy's one-on-one exchanges contain the traditional amount of species bashing (for example, "You speak about the objective hardness of the Vulcan heart, yet how little room there seems to be in yours"), the most heated dialogue seems to arise when the two are vying for Kirk's recognition, like children battling for a father's attention. Nevertheless, McCoy worries about Spock the whole time he's out in the shuttle (despite his wicked delight in telling the Vulcan, "Shut up, we're rescuing you!"). And in later episodes, Spock would subtly express similar concern about the doctor's threatened well-being.

   So is it love or is it hate? As Kirk once observed when asked if the two men were enemies: "I'm not sure *they're* sure."

The label on the panel reads: HANGER DECK PRESSURE — CLOSED

"Captain—the Intrepid . . . *it just* died. *And the four hundred Vulcans aboard . . . all dead!"*
—Spock

Vulcans are considered "touch telepaths," meaning they generally cannot perceive the thoughts of another individual unless they are in physical contact. There are exceptions, however; Spock occasionally has been able to plant suggestions into another's mind through a wall, and even as far as across a room. But in "The Immunity Syndrome," he actually experiences the deaths (or, as he describes it, the "death screams") of a ship full of Vulcans from light years away. When Doctor McCoy expresses appropriate skepticism over this newfound ability, Spock attempts to explain it in simple terms: "Call it a deep understanding of the way things happen to Vulcans." Later, he clarifies the sensation he experienced, defining it as "the touch of death." But the *Intrepid*'s ill-fated Vulcans apparently were even bigger skeptics than McCoy; what they experienced as they died, according to Spock, was sheer astonishment.

"No speculation, no information—nothing. I've asked you three times for information on that, and you've been unable to supply it. Insufficient data is not sufficient, Mister Spock. You're the science officer. You're supposed to have sufficient data all the time."
—Kirk

As you may suspect, the one-celled organism that attacks the *Enterprise* isn't actually an amoeba—it's a visual effect, created by Van der Veer Photo Effects. While the exact process that Frank Van der Veer and his team used is undocumented, it appears to be a colored liquid, most likely mineral oil, pressed between two closely spaced, nearly parallel sheets of glass. By moving one of the sheets very slightly, the effects artist could make the liquid undulate a bit—just enough to make the thing look alive.

This rather low-tech technique was used extensively during the 1960s, primarily during the "light shows" that were a part of the era's enhanced rock 'n' roll concerts. While the bands were onstage performing, techs from lighting companies would sit in the rear of the hall, beaming wavelike swirls of bright colors onto the musicians and the screen behind them. The effect was similar to, but much more basic than, that practiced by Van der Veer: A mixture of mineral oil and food coloring was dripped onto a large piece of glass, and the glass was then placed under an overhead projector. As the glass was tilted, wildly psychedelic patterns would form and appear to spread across the stage in a wave of "living color." Occasionally the techs would add brine shrimp to the mixture, and the elastic flow would shimmy with tiny living dots darting to and fro. (This excursion through time and space brought to you by a survivor of the 1960s.)

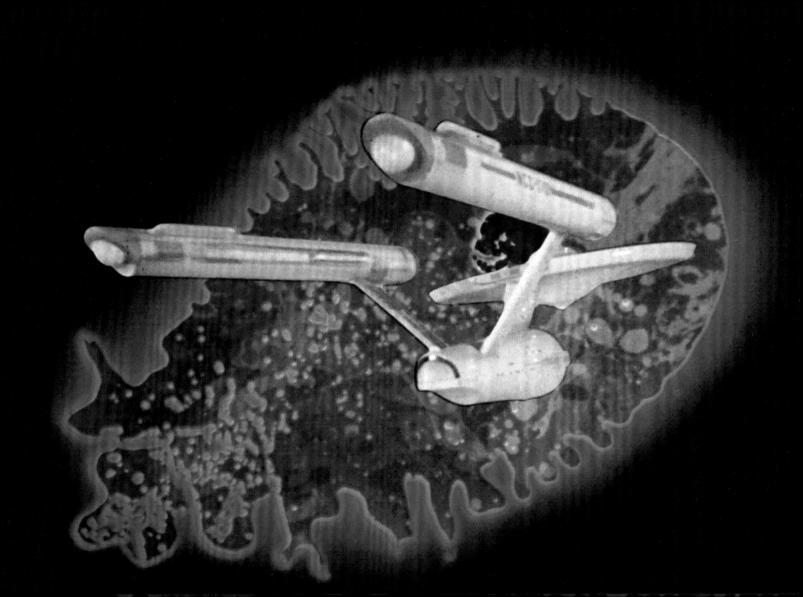

A PIECE OF THE ACTION

"The most cooperative man in this world is a dead man. And if you don't keep your mouth shut, you're going to be cooperatin'."
—Bela Oxmyx

It's been one hundred years since the planet Sigma Iotia II received a visit from a Federation vessel. Back in those days, there was no Prime Directive, and the crew of the *Horizon* inadvertently contaminated the planet's cultural development by leaving behind a book entitled *Chicago Mobs of the Twenties*, which the populace apparently took to heart. When the *Enterprise* arrives for a follow-up visit, Kirk discovers a society patterned exclusively on that book: a world of gangsters and their molls, all looking to obtain the best "piece of the action," whatever it happens to be at any given moment. The captain quickly realizes that the only way to clean up the contamination is to do as the natives do and launch his own unique brand of counter-contamination.

238

After spending nine years as a writer and producer on *Star Trek: The Next Generation* and *Star Trek: Deep Space Nine*, Ronald D. Moore would go on to garner even greater public attention by developing and executive producing (with colleague David Eick) the highly acclaimed revival of *Battlestar Galactica*. But one of Moore's best *Star Trek* ideas was never produced—by choice. In 1996, the writing staff of *Deep Space Nine* was searching for inspiration. The thirtieth anniversary of *Star Trek* was coming up, and *DS9* wanted to produce an episode that would serve as a tribute to the franchise. After sifting through his memory of the original series, Moore hit upon the idea of having the *DS9* characters visit the planet Sigma Iotia II from "A Piece of the Action." His thought was that the crew would discover that the imitative Iotians, whose society initially had been contaminated by the visit of one starship, had been further contaminated by Kirk's visit with the *Enterprise* crew. As a result, they'd traded in their mob culture and gangster garb for pseudo-Starfleet uniforms and gear. In short, the entire civilization now revolved around the Iotian perception of *Star Trek*. Moore saw the episode as a tongue-in-cheek tribute to the lifestyle that many of *Star Trek*'s most devoted fans had adopted: dressing up like crew members from the *Enterprise*, creating their own version of Starfleet technology, and perhaps even gathering at conventions.

After thinking it through, however, the writing staff began to worry that some of the fans might take the homage the wrong way and assume they were being ridiculed. And so the writers dropped the idea, opting instead to build the tribute around a different episode, "The Trouble with Tribbles."

Three years later, in 1999, the movie *Galaxy Quest* premiered. The film's core premise is that the cast of a cult science fiction television show is kidnapped by a geeky alien species that has based its culture on the episodes they've been following via long-range broadcast. Clearly, the movie was intended as a comic tribute to *Star Trek* and its fans, in much the same way that Moore had envisioned the *DS9* episode. Ironically, *Galaxy Quest* was a great hit with all segments of the moviegoing public, perhaps nowhere more so than with the *Star Trek* fan base, who, as it turns out, were anything but insulted.

239

"Captain, I do have reservations about your solution to the problem of the Iotians."
—Spock

The Prime Directive, or Starfleet General Order no. 1, decrees: "No identification of self or mission. No interference with the social development of said planet. No references to space or the fact that there are other worlds or more advanced civilizations." In other words, Federation crew members are not to disturb the natural cultural growth of unaware civilizations that haven't yet developed warp capability. Unfortunately, the Prime Directive wasn't being enforced when the *Horizon* visited Sigma Iotia II a hundred years prior to the *Enterprise*'s arrival. The *Horizon*'s unthinking crew not only told the Iotians about spaceships and transporters, but they left behind physical evidence of their presence. What arose from this carelessness is, as Spock describes it, a very clear example of the "contamination of the normal evolution of the planet."

   Of course, Kirk and his crew weren't responsible for the cultural contamination of Sigma Iotia II; they observed the consequences of the damage caused by the *Horizon* and attempted to contain what that crew had wrought. However, over the course of *his* five-year mission, Kirk wasn't exactly a paragon of compliance with the Prime Directive, as evidenced in the episodes "The Return of the Archons,"

"A Taste of Armageddon," "The Apple," "Friday's Child," "Patterns of Force," and "A Private Little War." Which might be bad news for the Federation, but in *our* world, allowing Kirk to bend, break, or otherwise mutilate Starfleet General Order no. 1 served to provide *Star Trek*'s writing staff with a whole litany of interesting story ideas.

The gamblers on Beta Antares IV have no time for kid's card games. They play a *real* game, a *man's* game—or at least, that's the way Captain Kirk tells it. The game's called "fizzbin," and although it requires actual intelligence, it's not too difficult.

Each player gets six cards, *except* for the player on the dealer's right, who gets seven. The second card is turned up, except on Tuesdays. If a player gets two jacks, he has a half-fizzbin. But if he gets another jack, what he's got is a sralk, and he gets disqualified. What he really needs are a king and a deuce—except at night, of course, when he'd need a queen and a four. If he gets only a king, then he gets another card—unless it's dark, in which case he'd have to give it back. The last card in a hand is called a kronk—but what everyone really wants is a royal fizzbin. And the odds of that happening—well, they're so astronomical that Spock hasn't ever bothered to compute them.

BY ANY OTHER NAME

After responding to a fake distress call, the *Enterprise* is hijacked by a group of Kelvans from the Andromeda galaxy. Inherently non-humanoid, the Kelvans have taken human form to assess our galaxy's suitability for their purposes: Increasing radiation levels throughout the Kelvan Empire eventually will make life there impossible for their species, and they've decided that ours is ripe for conquest. But before that, they must travel home to make their report. That's where the *Enterprise* comes in; the Kelvan ship was irreparably damaged during the voyage through the galactic barrier, and with a few adjustments, Kirk's ship will make a more than satisfactory trade-in. Because direct resistance will result in the Kelvans destroying members of the crew, Kirk explores a more subversive way of defeating the invaders. The human forms the Kelvans have adopted have plenty of human weaknesses, which Kirk, Spock, McCoy, and Scotty eagerly exploit.

During Scotty's heroic effort to get Tomar toasted, he provides the Kelvan with the name of each alcoholic beverage that he serves. However, as time passes and many bottles of hard liquor are shared, Scotty has a wee bit of trouble remembering the name of one particular bottle. Thus, when Tomar asks him, "What is it?" Scotty eyeballs it, sniffs it, and finally tells him, "It's green."

The joke would be transported to *Star Trek: The Next Generation*, with James Doohan reprising the role of Scotty nearly a quarter of a century after filming "By Any Other Name." In the *TNG* episode "Relics," Data, the *Enterprise*-D's android science officer, offers Scotty a drink from an unlabeled bottle of alcohol, and when similarly unable to identify the substance within, he tells Scotty, "It is green."

"This is the essence of what they were. The flesh and brain and what you call the personality, distilled down into these compact shapes."
—Rojan

To the general public, the curious geometric objects that litter the corridors of the *Enterprise* after the Kelvans have their way with Kirk's crew may look like oversize dice from a board game or, to the somewhat better educated members of the audience, dodecahe-drons—solid figures with twelve faces. To the *much* better educated members of the audience, they are referred to as cuboctahedrons: poly-hedrons whose faces consist of six equal squares and eight equal equilateral triangles.

To the *Star Trek* writers, however, they were a clever way to tempo-rarily get rid of the *Enterprise* crew.

After Rojan and his band of Kelvans take over the *Enterprise*, they require the services of just four crewmen: Kirk, Spock, Scotty, and McCoy. So, what were the writers supposed to do with the other 425 (Yeoman Thompson having been dispatched by Rojan during Act One)? They didn't want to have the Kelvans kill anyone else, and beaming everyone down to a planet was neither efficient nor time ef-fective. According to D. C. Fontana, it was Gene Roddenberry who hit upon the solution when she went to his office to ask for some input. As he listened to her explain the problem, Roddenberry toyed with an onyx paperweight that sat on his desk. After a moment of thought, he suggested that the Kelvans transform the crew into small objects that would still contain their basic essence, perhaps objects that looked something like his paperweight—which was, of course, a do-decahedron.

While these geometric objects may not have been the most interesting props ever created for *Star Trek*, they *did* resonate with certain members of the public. Predictably, math majors liked them; references to the "multifaceted" transformed crew members in "By Any Other Name" seem to abound on math-oriented Internet sites. TV writers liked them too; characters in a segment of *Good Eats*—a humorous, semi-scientific cooking show—referred to the *Star Trek* cuboctahedrals in a memorable episode about lentils, in order to launch a discussion about the basic components of the human body and the need for certain proteins.

RETURN TO TOMORROW

Deep beneath the surface of a long-dead world, Kirk finds a vault containing the vestiges of an ancient civilization and that civilization's last three survivors—Sargon, his wife, Thalassa, and Sargon's former enemy, Henoch—their conscious minds stored within orblike receptacles. Sargon needs Kirk's help; he and his two compatriots require the temporary use of three human bodies in order to construct android shells that ultimately will house their minds. Kirk agrees, and his mind is transferred to the orb as Sargon moves into his body. Henoch's mind takes Spock's body, and Thalassa receives that of a female astrobiologist. All goes well until Henoch privately decides that he wants to keep Spock's body. Of course, to do so, he'll need to destroy both Sargon *and* Captain Kirk.

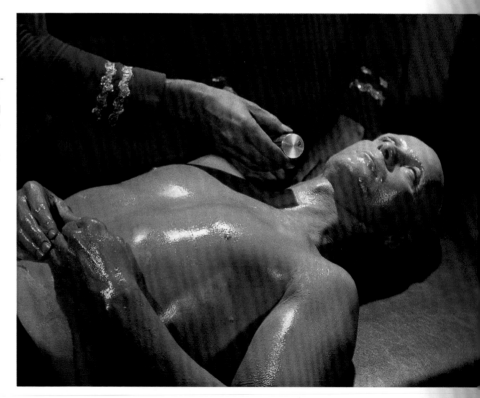

When asked why he climbed Mount Everest, George Mallory, the 1920s British mountaineer who died on his third attempt at conquering the peak, supposedly answered, "Because it's there." While that's a clever retort, it's not a satisfactory answer to the broader question implicit in the reporter's query: "Why does man bother to do difficult things?" The answer to that would require more seriousness, more philosophy, more insight. It's a question that was posed regularly on *Star Trek*, but never so poignantly as in the episode "Return to Tomorrow." Given the opportunity to participate in a questionable scientific endeavor, the *Enterprise* crew gathered to go over the pros and cons. Their discussion resulted in what may well be James T. Kirk's greatest speech, one that encompasses the philosophy of Starfleet, the five-year mission, and the series itself:

> *"They used to say if man could fly, he'd have wings. But he did fly. He discovered he had to. Do you wish that the first Apollo mission hadn't reached the moon, or that we hadn't gone on to Mars, and then to the nearest star? That's like saying you wished you still operated with scalpels and sewed your patients up with catgut like your great-great-great-great-grandfather used to. I'm in command. I could order this. But I'm not, because Doctor McCoy is right in pointing out the enormous danger potential in any contact with life and intelligence as fantastically advanced as this. But I must point out that the possibilities, the potential for knowledge and advance-* *ment, is equally great. Risk . . . risk is our business. That's what this starship is all about. That's why we're aboard her."*

"Your captain has an excellent body, Doctor McCoy. I compliment you both on the condition in which you maintain it."
—Sargon

Much has been written about William Shatner's acting style—the tortured physical mannerisms, the hurried, almost urgent phrasing, the unexpected pauses. The style, unique among actors, as evidenced by countless, instantly recognizable imitations, had an auspicious beginning. As a young, hopeful thespian in the Stratford Shakespeare Festival at Ontario, Canada, Shatner held the position of understudy in the Bard's *Henry V*. One evening, with only a few hours' notice and no rehearsal time, he found himself on the stage playing the lead role. His pauses that night were inadvertent—he was struggling to recall the difficult dialogue—but following the performance, critics and audience members alike praised the newcomer for his passionate portrayal of the king. The young actor apparently recognized a good thing when he saw it, and he systematically modified the technique into the style that has kept him in the spotlight for half a century.

PATTERNS OF FORCE

"Note the sinister eyes and the malformed ears. Definitely an inferior or race. Note the low forehead, denoting stupidity. The dull look of a trapped animal."
—Melakon

Communication has ceased between the Federation and John Gill, the cultural observer they sent to study the planet Ekos. In attempting to find out what happened to Gill, who was once a professor at Starfleet Academy, the crew of the *Enterprise* learns that he conducted an unauthorized social experiment that went very badly—or much too well, depending on your point of view. Gill applied the efficient model of Earth's Nazi Germany to Ekos's chaotic political structure. The result: a picture-perfect re-creation of Hitler's regime, right down to plans for launching a "Final Solution" against the troublesome Zeons.

Strange as it seems, even the buildings that appear in movies and TV programs have "stand-ins." Much of the action in "Patterns of Force" centers on two buildings that are part of the Ekosian Nazi headquarters complex. In reality, they're located on Earth, right in the middle of the Paramount lot in Hollywood. At the time the episode was produced, they were known by the rather mundane names "the Directors' Building" and "the Producers' Building." In front of the two buildings was a paved parking lot; over the course of the episode, you can see the assorted tanks and government vehicles pulling in and parking. Located nearby was the famed Bronson Gate, which may be familiar to fans of the film *Sunset Boulevard* (at one time the gate served as the main automotive entrance to the lot). But studios change with shifts in management. Following *Star Trek*'s cancellation, many of the buildings on the lot were rechristened with names that evoked the men and women who'd first made the studio famous. The Producers' Building became the Lubitsch (for the director, Ernst) Building and the Directors' Building was renamed Schulberg (producer B. P. Schulberg was head of Paramount in the 1930s). The Bronson Gate was transformed into a pedestrian portal for Paramount employees, and the parking lot around the corner was torn up to create Producers' Park, a tranquil grassy oasis in the midst of administrative and production offices where employees can relax in the shade of graceful jacaranda trees. To misquote Joni Mitchell,

it was, perhaps, one of the few times in history when someone *un-paved* a parking lot to put up a bit of paradise!

Prior to *Star Trek*, it's fair to say that fans of science fiction literature were predominantly male. Aficionados of science fiction movies and the rare sci-fi television show were similarly gendered.

Then came *Star Trek*. And while the males in the viewing audience likely tuned in to see episodes written by well-known authors such as Theodore Sturgeon, Harlan Ellison, and Richard Matheson (and—fess up, guys—also to admire the sleek ships, futuristic hardware, and alien babes in revealing attire), women were surprisingly quick to pick up on the series. They liked the premise, the characters, and the depiction of strong friendships between the shipboard comrades-in-arms. They also liked the actors who played the male leads, as fan mail to the studio would attest.

"Patterns of Force" features the one and only time in *Star Trek* that Leonard Nimoy appears on camera sans shirt. William Shatner already had doffed his tunic—or parts of his tunic—numerous times on the show, and he definitely had his admirers in the audience. But the sight of *Spock* semi-clothed triggered a different wave of female adulation, primarily expressed in *Star Trek* fanzines, fan-produced publications devoted to a particular genre, TV series, or film. The vast majority of *Star Trek* fanzines are written, published, and read by women, which may explain the popularity of titles featuring artwork that utilized Spock's shirtless appearance in "Patterns of Force" as an anatomical point of reference.

"You mean the Fuhrer is an alien?"
—Daras

Due to post-World War II sanctions against the depiction of Nazi symbols and uniforms, "Patterns of Force" is the one episode of *Star Trek* that was withheld from broadcast in Germany for many years. It aired for the first time in 1999, albeit late at night on a pay-TV station. In other parts of the world, the show drew mixed reactions. Some lauded Roddenberry and the actors for approaching the subject matter at all in an era when the Holocaust typically was not touched upon in public school curricula. Others criticized fictional character John Gill's premise that Hitler's Germany was "the most efficient state Earth ever knew," a belief that leads him to transform the fractured civilization he finds on Ekos into an alien version of the Third Reich . . . with predictable results. Efficient or not, what bonehead would think it was a *good* idea to teach fascism to a populace already known to be antagonistic and warlike?

THE ULTIMATE COMPUTER

"Computers make excellent and efficient servants, but I have no wish to serve under them. Captain, a starship also runs on loyalty to one man, and nothing can replace it, or him."
—Spock

Informed that the *Enterprise* is to serve as the test vehicle for the experimental M-5 supercomputer, Kirk worries that Starfleet's need for human captains and crews may be at an end. But while the M-5 handles its first test flawlessly, it soon begins to act erratically, destroying an unmanned drone vessel and, not long after, dozens of the innocent crew members involved in the war games being conducted by Starfleet. With the computer's own inventor unable to pull the plug on what he sees as his greatest creation, Kirk realizes that Starfleet may have no choice but to destroy M-5 and with it, the *Enterprise*.

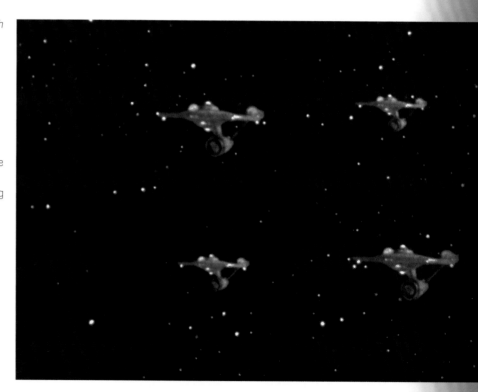

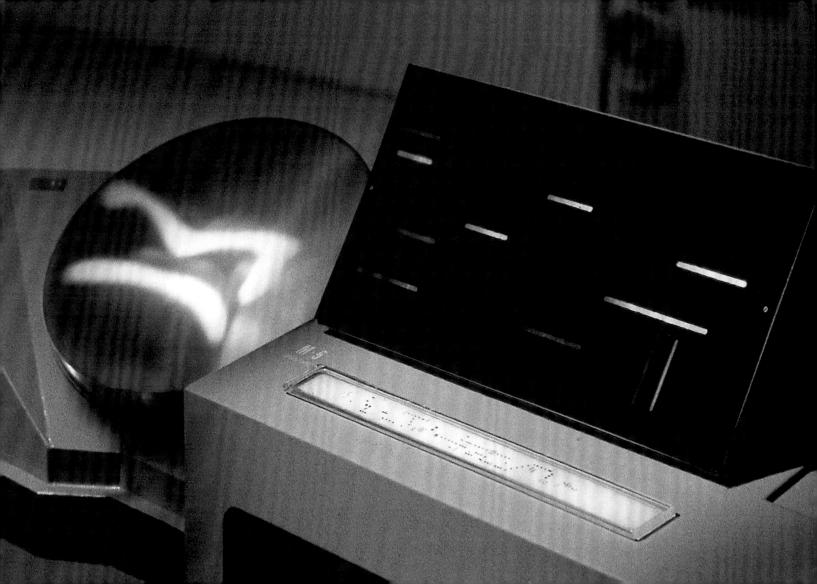

As season two headed toward the finish line, production money became tighter and tighter. But with "The Ultimate Computer"'s intellectually taut, emotionally engrossing script (teleplay by D. C. Fontana, story by Laurence N. Wolfe) to keep the audience's minds engaged, the producers were able to avoid "going back to the well" for additional money to create engaging visual elements. They had some existing footage from earlier episodes that would work just fine. The brief visual of the Federation starbase where Kirk meets Commodore Wesley was a reuse of Deep Space Station K-7 from "The Trouble with Tribbles." The ill-fated *Woden* ore freighter was actually the *Botany Bay*, Khan's sleeper ship from "Space Seed." And the *Enterprise* itself should probably have been drawing overtime pay for its multiple appearances in the episode as the *Hood*, the *Excalibur*, the *Potemkin*, and the *Lexington*, particularly in the scenes where they all appear together, neatly arranged in battle formation—courtesy of an optical printer.

"Do you know the one, 'All I ask is a tall ship'? Twentieth-century Earth. 'All I ask is a tall ship and a star to steer her by.' You could feel the wind at your back in those days. The sounds of the sea beneath you. And even if you take away the wind and the water, it's still the same. The ship is yours. You can feel her. And the stars are still there, Bones."
—Kirk

Although Kirk has, by this point in the series, established his literary cred with the audience, he demonstrates in this episode that he has read *more* than Shakespeare's best-known works. He quotes John Masefield's "Sea Fever" here, a poem that is certainly a good fit for this future incarnation of Horatio Hornblower. Kirk may be a man of the twenty-third century, but he will always be a man whose feet are firmly anchored in the romantic haze of a simpler era, which is why Wesley's "Captain Dunsel" snipe—a reference implying that men like Kirk may no longer be needed aboard starships—hurts like hell.

Kirk would quote the same line from "Sea Fever" again in *Star Trek V: The Final Frontier*. McCoy would incorrectly attribute it to Melville, but then, the good doctor has always been a better psychologist (not to mention mixologist) than a lit major.

After completing the first season of *Star Trek*, George Takei took advantage of the series' hiatus by accepting an offer to appear in *The Green Berets* with legendary actor John Wayne. The film's shooting schedule indicated that Takei would be back in Hollywood in time to resume his role as Sulu in *Star Trek*'s season two. Things didn't work out as planned—the movie went over schedule, and the actor was absent during the filming of fourteen *Star Trek* episodes. During his absence, many of the scenes originally written for Sulu were adapted for a new character, Chekov, played by Walter Koenig. Three thousand miles away, Takei couldn't help but develop a grudging resentment for the person he knew only as the usurper of his position. When he finally returned to the *Star Trek* set, just in time to shoot "Return to Tomorrow," he learned that Koenig, as Chekov, wasn't in the episode. The dreaded confrontation had been delayed.

But while Koenig was set to appear in the following episode, "Patterns of Force," Takei, as Sulu, was not. It wasn't until the third script following Takei's return, "The Ultimate Computer," that he finally would have the opportunity to meet the interloper who had taken his place. Prepared to dislike Koenig, Takei stepped into the trailer that the two men were being asked to share for the day and heard Koenig complaining loudly about . . . something. Takei initially assumed that it was about sharing the trailer, a situation that he was equally prepared to complain about. But he quickly learned that Koenig

was complaining about the moplike "Beatles wig" that he'd been ordered to wear until his hair grew longer. In a flash of insight, Takei understood that his rival was simply a fellow actor feeling much the same angst and insecurity about his job that he himself was feeling. After that, the two became fast friends, and Sulu and Chekov became an iconic team throughout the rest of the series and the subsequent movies.

THE OMEGA GLORY

Upon finding the *U.S.S. Exeter* hanging in orbit over the planet Omega IV, Kirk, Spock, and McCoy beam over to the vessel and discover there's no one aboard. No one *alive*, that is; the *Exeter*'s crew has been reduced to dust, the results of a virulent disease they contracted on the planet's surface—and now Kirk's landing party has also been exposed. Unable to return to the *Enterprise*, they beam down to Omega IV and encounter Ron Tracey, the *Exeter*'s captain. Tracey informs them that the disease will remain dormant if they remain on the planet, but Kirk's not satisfied with that prognosis. Nor is he pleased to learn that Tracey has opted to provide advanced weaponry to one side in a fierce civil war between the planet's inhabitants, a serious breach of the Prime Directive.

Kirk: "These words, and the words that follow, were not just written for the Yangs, but for the Kohms as well!"
Cloud William: "But the Kohms—"
Kirk: "They must apply to everyone, or they mean nothing! Do you understand?"
Cloud William: "I . . . do not fully understand, one named Kirk. But the Holy Words will be obeyed. I swear it."

"The Omega Glory" arguably holds the inglorious title of the "least-liked" episode of *The Original Series*. Gene Roddenberry hadn't expected this; in fact, his script was one of three, along with "Mudd's Women" and "Where No Man Has Gone Before," that the producers had submitted to NBC as a potential second pilot after the network rejected "The Cage." One complaint cited by fans is that a society located so far from Earth couldn't have spontaneously developed along lines so historically similar to Earth, with names like "the Yangs" for Yankees and "the Kohms" for Communists, not to mention the Yangs possessing an American flag (the tattered old "Glory" of the title) and the Preamble to the U.S. Constitution. Curiously, the similarities of the Romanesque planet that the *Enterprise* visited in "Bread and Circuses" didn't bother them nearly as much.

It's likely the producers assumed that the audience would draw the logical conclusion that the inhabitants of Omega IV were descendants of Asian and American space explorers. But apparently the viewers needed that information laid out a bit more explicitly, as it was in an earlier version of the script:

> *MCCOY: Jim, the parallel's too close. They seem so completely human. Is it possible that . . . ?*
> *KIRK: The result of Earth's early space race?*
> *SPOCK: Quite possible, Captain. They are aggressive enough to be human.*

Total body water content in the human male is approximately 60 percent, in the female, 55 percent. So when Doctor McCoy tells Kirk that "water . . . makes up 96 percent of our bodies . . . ," he's a bit off—by 36 percent! (He'd be a lot closer if he were referring only to water content of lean muscle tissue.) As for the "white crystals" left behind by the dehydrated crew of the *U.S.S. Exeter*, he says, "Jim, the analysis of this so far is potassium 35 percent, carbon 18 percent, phosphorous 1.0, calcium 1.5 . . ." The good doctor might have included 65 percent oxygen, 9.5 percent hydrogen, and 3.3 percent nitrogen—plus a plethora of trace chemicals. But he was close enough for TV; after all, he does say "so far," implying that he'll do a more thorough breakdown once he's back in his research lab on the ship. Presumably while there, he'll modify his original estimate of carbon content to the actual 18.5 percent.

One can't help but think that Gene Roddenberry was chiding NBC executives when he wrote the scene in which the Yangs think Mister Spock resembles a painting of Satan. After all, the Vulcan's "satanic appearance" was the very argument those execs used when (strongly) suggesting that the character be excised from the cast while the series was in development. But as the series progressed, Mister Spock quickly emerged as the show's (arguably) most popular character—and what good producer *wouldn't* jump at the chance to slip in an inside joke when given the opportunity?

Haggai reproveth the people's negl...

...and poor people, and they shall trust in the...
of the Lord.

13 The remnant of Israel shall not do in...
nor speak lies; neither shall a deceitful ton...
found in their mouth: for they shall feed...
down, and none shall make them afraid.

14 ¶ Sing, O daughter of Zion; shout, O...
be glad and rejoice with all the heart, O dau...
of Jerusalem.

15 The Lord hath taken away thy judg...
he hath cast out thine enemy: the King of...
even the Lord, is in the midst of thee: thou...
not see evil any more.

16 In that day it shall be said to Jerusalem...
thou not; and to Zion, Let not thine hands be...

17 The Lord thy God in the midst of thee is...
he will save, he will rejoice over thee with jo...
will rest in his love, he will joy over thee with...

18 I will gather them that are sorrowful f...
solemn assembly, who are of thee, to whom...
reproach of it was a burden.

19 Behold, at that time I will undo all that a...
and I will save her that halteth, and I gather her that...
driven out; and I will get them praise and fa...
every land where they have been put to sha...

20 At that time will I bring you again, even...
time that I gather you: for I will make you a nam...
a praise among all people of the earth, when I...
back your captivity before your eyes, saith the L...

HAGGAI.

10 Therefore, the heaven over you is st...
from dew, and the earth is stayed from her fr...

11 And I called for a drought upon the land...
upon the mountains, and upon the corn, and...
the new wine, and upon the oil, and upon that w...
the ground bringeth forth, and upon men, and...
cattle, and upon all the labour of the hands.

12 ¶ Then Zerubbabel the son of Shealtiel...
Joshua the son of Josedech, the high priest...
all the remnant of the people, obeyed the voic...
the Lord their God, and the words of Haggai...
prophet, as the Lord their God had sent him...
the people did fear before the Lord.

13 Then spake Haggai the Lord's messeng...
the Lord's message unto the people, saying...
with you, saith the Lord.

14 And the Lord stirred up the spirit of Ze...
babel the son of Shealtiel, governor of Judah...
the spirit of Joshua the son of Josedech, the...
priest, and the spirit of all the remnant of...
people; and they came and did work in the ho...
of the Lord of hosts, their God,

15 In the four and twentieth day of the s...
month, in the second year of Darius the king.

CHAP. II.

1 Haggai encourageth the people to the work; 10 He sheweth that their sins hindered the work, &c.

IN the seventh month, in the one and twent...
day of the month, came the word of the L...
by the prophet Haggai, saying,

ASSIGNMENT: EARTH

The *Enterprise* travels back in time to the year 1968 to determine how Earth managed to avoid a pending nuclear crisis that year. While in orbit around the planet, the ship intercepts a powerful transporter beam that apparently had been carrying a humanoid named Gary Seven to Earth. The mysterious Seven explains that he's a twentieth-century man trained by aliens to deal with the situation. Kirk doesn't trust Seven or his extremely advanced equipment . . . or the strangely intelligent black cat that accompanies him. However, if he doesn't let Seven do his job, he runs the risk of changing Earth's history—and not for the better.

Star Trek was not the only idea for a TV series to germinate within Gene Roddenberry's fertile imagination. Throughout his career, he conceived many interesting tales, most of which fell under the category of "speculative fiction." One such idea had to do with an Earthman named Gary Seven, who traveled from the future to the twentieth century in order to fight evil shape-changing Omegans out to change history to their advantage. Roddenberry penned a pilot script toward the end of 1966, during *Star Trek*'s first season, but apparently it didn't sell. However, a year later, with *Star Trek*'s cancellation a very real threat, Roddenberry must have thought there might be a way to raise a phoenix from the existing series' embers. He dusted off the Gary Seven tale and reworked it with writer Art Wallace, transforming it into a *Star Trek* episode that he hoped would serve as a springboard for a brand-new series.

The bad news was that NBC wasn't interested.

The good news was that *Star Trek* was renewed for a third season.

In "Assignment: Earth," much of the action takes place at a fictional stand-in for the Kennedy Space Center in Florida, dubbed "McKinley Rocket Base." However, the base exteriors seen in the episode were themselves a stand-in; the location Kirk and Spock beam down to was actually the back of an office building on the Paramount lot. Named for Marlene Dietrich, the beautiful German actress who appeared in *The Blue Angel* and many other Paramount films over the decades, the Dietrich Building is located just opposite the Commissary, the studio's upscale dining facility.

*"Well, how do you expect me to type, with my nose? Did you see that?
The machine typed everything I—it's typing everything I'm saying!
Stop it. Stop it! STOP IT!"*
—Roberta Lincoln

Some people view the fanciful predictions foretold in old science fiction movies and television shows and say, "Where is the *flying car* I was supposed to have by the dawn of the twenty-first century?"

Other people—primarily writers—say, "Where is that amazing voice-activated electric *typewriter* that types everything we say?"

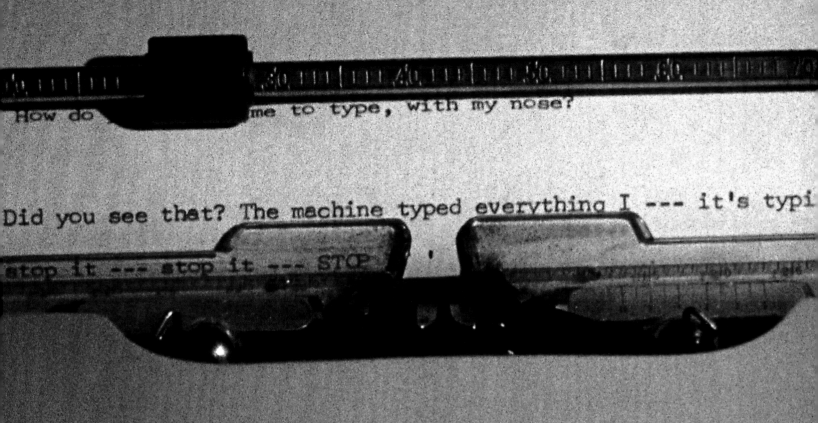

How do ___ me to type, with my nose?

Did you see that? The machine typed everything I --- it's typi

stop it --- stop it --- STOP

In 1951, Betty JoAnne Conway attended a gathering of science fiction fans and met her destiny. Bjo, as her friends called her, quickly became a fixture of the fan community, a "BNF" ("Big Name Fan") well known for her skills at organizing art shows and costume displays for conventions. But it wasn't until 1967 that Bjo and her husband, fellow fan John Trimble, became BNFs to a much larger community.

Star Trek captivated the Trimbles from the very beginning. After Bjo realized that the Desilu production office was just a few miles from her home, she wrote a letter asking to meet the producer. Gene Roddenberry, complimented that his show had at least one loyal viewer, agreed to meet with her. Impressed with her intelligence and enthusiasm, Roddenberry wisely said, "Yes," when Bjo volunteered to help out by opening the stacks of fan mail that were beginning to pile up at the Star Trek offices.

By the middle of Star Trek's second season, the producers were convinced that NBC intended to cancel the series. That was unacceptable to the Trimbles, who hoped to see the show live on in reruns (this was before the days of home video). They knew that if Star Trek didn't produce at least seventy episodes, it wouldn't be sold into rerun syndication and would disappear forever.

Bjo had an idea: She would start a letter-writing campaign to NBC—a "Save Star Trek" campaign. As she had done at dozens of science fiction conventions, she orchestrated the activity in an efficient and professional manner. Bjo had found many fan letters to be poorly written, demanding, and even rude. So she created a "how-to" memo, which included the names and office addresses of NBC executives, and distributed it to her friends throughout the fan community. Among the instructions were several strategic hints, such as: Use a legal-size envelope, don't mention Star Trek on the front of the envelope, and don't include a return address on the outside of the envelope (thus ensuring that the studio would be required to open it). Fans also were asked not to send form letters, so the recipients at NBC would understand that each letter came from an individual viewer. And, the memo stressed, be polite.

In the following weeks, the Trimbles received requests for copies of the how-to memo from fans across the country, from the membership of the high-IQ organization Mensa, and even from employees of Polaroid—a Star Trek sponsor—who then sent letters not only to NBC, but to everyone at their own company. As momentum grew, the Kansas City Star interviewed the Trimbles; the resulting story generated hundreds of additional requests for the memo.

The exact number of letters that NBC received is not recorded—estimates range from tens of thousands to a million—but whatever the count, NBC was so impressed by the response that on March 31, the network included a special announcement after one of the episodes.

The upshot: Star Trek would return for a third season.

In historical accounts—some accurate, some apocryphal—related to the demise of *Star Trek*, NBC executives typically are cast as the unthinking villains, cutting down this classic series in its prime. But no company is entirely populated by "black hats." The truth is, there were many NBC execs who supported *Star Trek* over the years. Both David Tebet, NBC's vice president for talent, and Mort Werner, chief programming executive at the network during the 1960s, are considered "white hats" by most who knew them.

David Tebet was well liked by most of the talent he oversaw (comedian George Burns referred to him as "the vice-president in charge of caring"). It was Tebet's job to spot and recruit stars for the network, and to keep them happy so they would stay. Among the entertainers he brought to NBC were Michael Landon, James Garner, Dean Martin, and a young, little-known comedian named Johnny Carson.

During his tenure at NBC, Mort Werner oversaw the premieres of *Bonanza*, *Rowan & Martin's Laugh-In,* and three series that featured minority actors in prominent roles for the first time: *Star Trek*, *I Spy*, and *Julia*. Although he had been at the studio when *Star Trek* was canceled, Werner was a strong advocate of relaunching the *Starship Enterprise* in a ninety-minute TV movie as early as 1970.

LASS OF SERVICE
is a fast message
ss its deferred char-
is indicated by the
er symbol.

WESTERN UNION TELEGRAM

W. P. MARSHALL
CHAIRMAN OF THE BOARD

R. W. McFALL
PRESIDENT

SYMBOLS
DL = Day Letter
NL = Night Letter
LT = International Letter Telegram

The filing time shown in the date line on domestic telegrams is LOCAL TIME at point of origin. Time of receipt is LOCAL TIME at point of destination

A PDT SEP 20 68 LA151
LLT226 (TELEX 049) PD NEW YORK NY 20 1024A PDT
OBERT H JUSTMAN
236 LORING AVE LOSA
OU AND YOUR SHOW HAVE DONE CREDIT TO US ALL, SO WELCOME. ALL
EST WISHES FOR THE NEW SEASON. WARMEST REGARDS
DAVID TEBET VICE PRESIDENT TALENT NBC-TV NETWORK
1046).

2-65)

CLASS OF SERVICE
This is a fast message unless its deferred character is indicated by the proper symbol.

WESTERN UNION TELEGRAM

W. P. MARSHALL
CHAIRMAN OF THE BOARD

R. W. McFALL
PRESIDENT

SYMBOLS
DL = Day Letter
NL = Night Letter
LT = International Letter Telegram

The filing time shown in the date line on domestic telegrams is LOCAL TIME at point of origin. Time of receipt is LOCAL TIME at point of destination

1040A PDT SEP 20 68 LA140
L LLS166(TELTEX 055) PD NEW YORK NY 20 1025A PDT
ROBERT H JUSTMAN
236 LORING AVE LOSA
236 WELCOME TO ANOTHER NEW SEASON AND OUR THANKS FOR YOUR HARD WORK
AND COOPERATION. ALL BEST WISHES
MORT WERNER VICE PRESIDENT PROGRAMS NBC TELEVISION NETWORK
(1038).

SF1201(R2-65)

SPECTRE OF THE GUN

"They are shadows. Illusions. Nothing but ghosts of reality. They are lies. Falsehoods. Specters without body. They are to be ignored."
—Spock

As punishment for trespassing in Melkotian space, Kirk and four members of his crew are forced to participate in a surrealistic reenactment of a historical event drawn from Kirk's memory: the gunfight at the O.K. Corral. Unfortunately, Kirk, Spock, McCoy, Scotty, and Chekov have been cast in the roles of the Clanton gang, the losing side of that epic confrontation with Wyatt Earp, two of his brothers, and Doc Holliday—which means the Melkotians expect them to die. But when certain details of the scenario don't play out as history would have it, Spock begins to suspect that a Vulcan mind-meld may be the key to their survival.

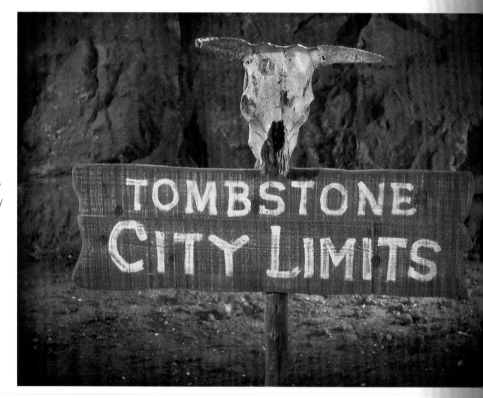

By the time DeForest Kelley appeared in "Spectre of the Gun," he
must have known the O.K. Corral saga very well; the episode represented his third theatrical visit to Tombstone. He had played Ike Clanton in a 1953 episode of the documentary series *You Are There* (nar-
rated by respected newscaster Walter Cronkite), and he had played
Morgan Earp in the 1957 motion picture *Gunfight at the O.K. Corral*, costarring with Burt Lancaster, Kirk Douglas, and Dennis Hopper.
Those performances set him on both sides of the famous rivalry,
but this time he crossed over once again to become a member of
the Clanton gang, playing Tom McLaury, one of the three gunfighters
killed during the 1881 shoot-out.

The Earp brothers are famous today, but unlike a number of their contemporaries in the "Wild West" era, they weren't legends in their own time. Men like Buffalo Bill Cody, Wild Bill Hickok, and Bat Masterson actually saw fictionalized stories about their exploits in dime novels written by authors such as Ned Buntline. Alas, other than in the local papers, the Earps didn't live to see their names in print.

Decades after his battle with the Clanton gang, Wyatt Earp settled in Los Angeles, where he found himself drawn to the burgeoning motion picture industry. He developed friendships with famous cowboy actors Tom Mix and William S. Hart, both of whom were fascinated by tales of his real-life exploits. Yet, in spite of his showbiz contacts, Wyatt's exploits remained unsung until two years after his death, when author Stuart N. Lake published a biographical novel titled *Wyatt Earp: Frontier Marshal*. After the novel was serialized in the *Saturday Evening Post*, the Earp name at last caught fire in the American imagination. In 1934, the novel was made into a movie titled *Frontier Marshal*, but inexplicably, the name of the lead character was changed to "Michael Wyatt." A few years later, a new version of the novel was made, with Randolph Scott portraying the appropriately named Wyatt Earp. Since then, the number of books, movies, and television episodes based on Earp's life have blossomed well beyond any expectations Wyatt once may have had, lending truth to the self-fulfilling message embedded in the theme song of *The Life and Legend of Wyatt Earp*, a Desilu-produced television series of the 1950s: "Long live his fame and long live his glory, and long may his story be told."

The red sky and skimpy facades constituting the "Spectre of the Gun" set decoration weren't created because the producers wanted viewers to remember that they were watching an illusion, or because they worried that the viewing audience (predominantly science fiction fans) wouldn't watch something that looked too much like a western.

No, once again the devil in the details was the same one the producers had wrestled with from the very beginning: budget. The script, originally called "The Last Gunfight," had been sitting on the corner of someone's desk since its submission early in the first season, but traveling to a rented western town location was deemed too costly. At the last minute, just before production began on the third season, Robert Justman and director Vincent McEveety agreed that pared-down (read "inexpensive") false fronts built entirely on one soundstage would serve the story. They turned, as usual, to the amazingly talented Matt Jefferies, and the result—a work of true sur-realistic beauty—serves as a fine example of "less is more."

ELAAN OF TROYIUS

"Did she cry, Jim? Did her tears touch you at any time?"
—McCoy

The planets Elas and Troyius are both considered members of the Federation, but their inhabitants have been at war with each other for many years. Now, with the Klingon Empire showing increasing interest in the region, it has become imperative for the two populations to come together in peace. To facilitate a treaty, the *Enterprise* escorts Elaan, the Dohlman—or ruler—of Elas, to Troyius, where she is to be united in matrimony to that world's leader. But the temperamental and arrogant Dohlman wants no part of the arranged union. After Elaan seriously wounds the Troyian ambassador who had been attempting to improve her social graces, Kirk is forced to take on the role of her tutor—a task made far more difficult by the Elasian woman's peculiar body chemistry, which elicits a heated response from Kirk.

"Elaan of Troyius" was indicative of many, though not all, of the episodes produced for *Star Trek*'s third season. Costumes, makeup, and script were all overblown, perhaps more suitable to sci-fi pulp than to the show's earlier attempts at straightforward storytelling in a unique setting. The most interesting element in this episode is one seen only fleetingly: the newly created Klingon D7 battle cruiser, designed by art director Matt Jefferies. He aimed at creating a vessel that would be instantly recognizable as an enemy ship, "especially," he explained, "for a flash cut. There had to be no way it could be mistaken for our guys. It had to look threatening," like the manta ray from which he drew part of his inspiration.

"Elaan" marked the D7's first appearance in *Star Trek*, and although the spacecraft represented the Klingon Empire's standard fighter spacecraft, it would briefly become the ship of choice for Romulans as well. In "The *Enterprise* Incident," Spock seems to allude to an alliance between the Romulans and the Klingons when he states: "Intelligence reports Romulans now using Klingon design." A more practical explanation might be the *Star Trek* "waste not, want not" philosophy: If you're going to spend the money on an expensive new model, you'd better be prepared to use it on camera—even when it's not exactly what the situation calls for.

Because the original model of the D7 was created for use in distance shots, it has minimal details. Nevertheless, the greenish

hull, long neck, and bulbous front bridge made it instantly identifiable. More advanced models of Klingon spacecraft derived from this design would appear in the *Star Trek* films and television series that followed *The Original Series*.

Pictured is Jefferies's original model of the Klingon D7 battle cruiser, which he donated to the Smithsonian Institution's National Air and Space Museum in 1973.

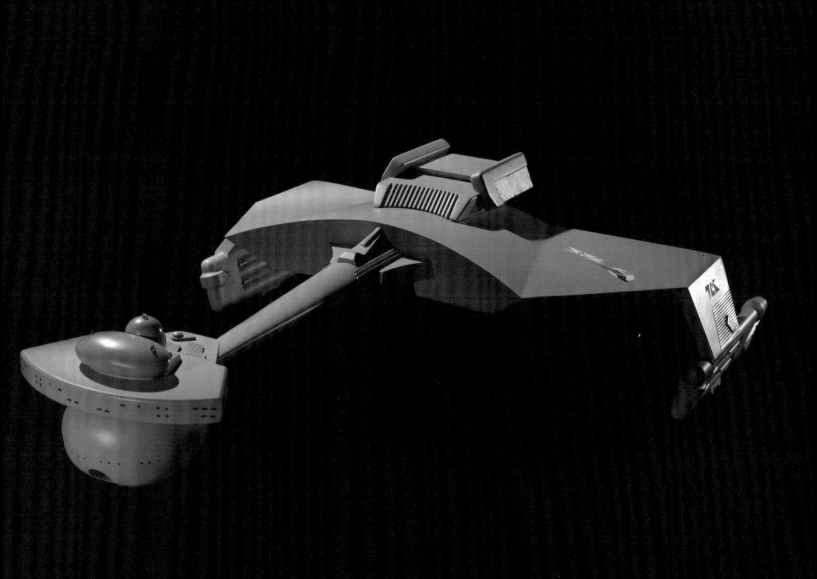

A sequence that was shot for "Elaan of Troyius" was left on the cutting-room floor. The sequence took place in the *Enterprise*'s rec room, which had apparently seen a serious upgrade since its last appearance during the show's second season. The set description notes:

"It resembles a psychedelic arboretum. The curve of the ship's bulkheads can be seen beyond the tops of trees. Flowers of all kinds flourish. A fountain sparkles in a lawn of pink grass. Members of the crew sit on benches and flat rocks, talking or playing three-dimensional chess. A group exercises. . . ."

The sequence was meant to follow Elaan's attack on Petri, the Troyian ambassador, and precede Kirk's first attempt to teach the Dohlman some manners. Kirk, McCoy, and Spock (who is playing his Vulcan lute, referred to in the scene as a lyre) discuss the need to appoint a new etiquette instructor. "Logic" dictates that Kirk, as the person aboard of highest rank, is the only appropriate choice. Kirk isn't happy about that, but perhaps if a bit of soothing music were piped into Elaan's quarters during the lesson. . . .

Kirk exits, and McCoy wanders off as well. But Uhura, who has been observing, sticks around for this rather awkward exchange with Spock:

UHURA: Mr. Spock, that music really gets to you.
SPOCK: Yes, I find it relaxing.

UHURA: Relaxing? It's . . . I don't know what to call it—but relaxing's not the word.
SPOCK: Most interesting. I suppose it works differently on non-Vulcan nervous systems.
UHURA: I'd certainly like to learn how to play that.
SPOCK: I'd be glad to give you the theory. The mathematics are somewhat complex. To my knowledge, no non-Vulcan has ever mastered the skill. You see, we Vulcans have natural rhythm.

It's unclear exactly why the sequence was cut from the episode. All that remains are some early drafts of the script and a few slides that convey the visuals. It could be that the episode was running too long and this was the most extraneous scene. Or that someone decided Uhura was paying *way* too much attention to Mister Spock. Or . . . it could be that someone on staff suddenly recalled that Uhura was no stranger to the Vulcan instrument, having accompanied Spock's playing with some vocals in the first season's "Charlie X," and played it herself when she serenaded Riley in "The Conscience of the King."

While Gene Roddenberry came up with the concept of the transporter, creating the transporter room and the unique platform within it fell to the imaginations of the individuals on the set design team. Always on the lookout for quick and less-expensive ways of doing things, the team found the perfect item for one component right on the set: a Fresnel lens from a 10,000-kilowatt set light. French physicist Augustin Jean Fresnel (pronounced "fruh-NELL") invented the lens in 1822, although it's unlikely he expected his invention would one day help in scattering molecules across the galaxy. The lens is composed of concentric glass prisms that bend and concentrate light; as a transporter "pad," it not only provided a transparent portal for the illumination that would help to sell the transporter effect, but also made a futuristic-looking spot to position a pair of feet.

THE PARADISE SYNDROME

"Behold, a god who bleeds!"
—Salish

On a serene world threatened by an approaching asteroid, Kirk, Spock, and McCoy find a settlement of what appear to be transplanted Native Americans—and a mysterious obelisk that could *not* have been constructed by the locals. While investigating the object, Kirk inadvertently triggers a trapdoor and falls into the obelisk's interior, where he is rendered unconscious by an energy jolt from a piece of alien technology. When he awakens, Kirk remembers nothing of his former life, and the friendly natives he encounters inform him that he is the god they have been awaiting. In the meantime, unable to find Kirk, Spock and McCoy return to the ship, which quickly leaves orbit in an effort to change the course of the asteroid—before it's too late.

"I have found Paradise. Surely no man has ever attained such happiness."
—Kirk/Kirok

It will not last. Sixty days—that's as much Paradise as Kirk can be allowed.

He has always known that he was not meant for Paradise. For Kirk, there is "no beach to walk on." No time to "gather a few laurel leaves" or to "stroll to the music of the lute." It actually takes an act of God—or rather, an extremely advanced civilization—to grant Kirk two months of complete bliss on a beautiful alien world. With all memories of his identity as the captain of the *Enterprise* eliminated, he accepts the proffered cloak of many-colored feathers and is born again as Kirok, medicine man to a peaceful tribe of Native American transplants and husband to the beautiful Miramanee.

But there is always a serpent in Paradise, and sometimes it is the one that lives within. Kirk cannot escape the shades of his past, barely submerged beneath haunting dreams of a "lodge that moves through the sky." He cannot escape his responsibilities, either: Once his ship returns, Spock restores the memories that the Preservers took from him. And for relinquishing those responsibilities, for daring to enjoy the sweetness of those two brief months, he will be punished . . . with bittersweet memories that will linger for a lifetime.

"The Paradise Syndrome"—originally titled "The Paleface"—may have been the most expensive episode produced during *Star Trek*'s third year, with new costumes, new sets, and an oversize alien obelisk that likely would have been difficult to work into later episodes. In addition, it was the only show of the season to take cast and crew out on location. Many of the final year's offerings were so-called bottle shows—shot primarily on the series' existing sets—but "Paradise" was lensed in the Franklin Canyon Reservoir, north of Beverly Hills in what is now the Santa Monica Mountains National Recreation Area. The reservoir has been the site of many movies and television series over the years; its most memorable usage was as the old fishing hole in the opening credits of *The Andy Griffith Show*. The trip may have been pricey, but the natural beauty of the locale meshed well with Matt Jefferies's organic designs for the tribal dwellings, set along the shore of a lake.

There was only one new (rather large) item created for the episode that the producers would be able to "recycle" before the series' end: the gigantic asteroid that Spock attempts to split with the *Enterprise*'s phasers. The big, lumpy rock would be "recast" as the asteroid-ship *Yonada* seven episodes later, in "For the World is Hollow and I Have Touched the Sky."

+15'-18'

14'-16'

LACED HIDES
ON UKIE POLES.

EXT. OBELISK

"PALEFACE"
60043·058

INT. INDIAN LODGE
STG. 10

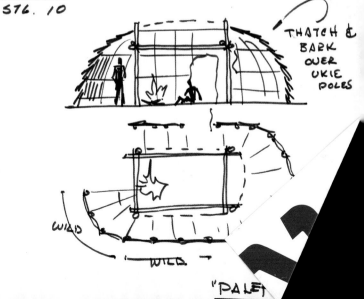

THATCH &
BARK
OVER
UKIE
POLES

WILD

WILD

"PALE

THE *ENTERPRISE* INCIDENT

Romulan commander: "It is unworthy of a Vulcan to resort to subterfuge."
Spock: "You are being clever, Commander. That *is unworthy of a Romulan*."

After an erratic Kirk takes the *Enterprise* into Romulan territory without authorization from Starfleet, the starship is immediately surrounded by Romulan vessels that demand the surrender of the captain and his crew. Kirk and Spock beam over to the Romulan flagship to meet with its female commander, but Spock refuses to confirm the captain's explanation that his trespassing was the result of an equipment malfunction. Instead, the Vulcan declares that Kirk is clearly suffering from diminished mental stability, and that he acted under his own volition. McCoy is summoned to the Romulan vessel to assess Kirk's condition, but the captain, infuriated at Spock's betrayal, attacks his first officer. Spock responds instinctively, defending himself by using the Vulcan death grip—and killing Captain Kirk.

Gene Roddenberry often stated that he disapproved of the *Enterprise* crew "sneaking around" on espionage or spying missions, but that is exactly the type of mission Kirk and Spock undertake in "The *Enterprise* Incident," an episode that seems based, at least in part, on the 1968 capture of the *U.S.S. Pueblo* in North Korean waters. Fans rate the episode among the best of the season, although they, too, seem a bit squeamish about Kirk and Spock's actions. At one point, Uhura tells Scotty that there was no order from Starfleet authorizing the *Enterprise*'s crossing into the Romulan Neutral Zone—but later McCoy tells Nurse Chapel, "Jim and Spock were operating under Federation orders."

So just who was it who sent them on this quest of theft and deception? Decades later, the series *Star Trek: Deep Space Nine* tackled similar subject matter, revealing that within Starfleet Intelligence there is a covert "black ops" unit known only as "Section 31" (think CIA but with fewer constraints from the head of state). Section 31, which has been around as long as Starfleet, is responsible for identifying and dealing with perceived threats to the Federation in whatever way its operatives deem necessary. Stealing a piece of potentially dangerous technology from a perceived enemy might just be right up this unit's alley. In fact, just to take it full circle—although it isn't canon—*Section 31: Cloak*, a licensed *Star Trek* spin-off novel, establishes that James T. Kirk *had* received orders from that very agency.

By the start of the third season, regular viewers of *Star Trek* came to expect seduction scenes between Kirk and the lovely lady of the week. But, by the same token, they did *not* expect such scenes with Spock. Yes, the Vulcan had shown romantic emotion with Leila Kalomi ("This Side of Paradise")—*after* she "drugged" him. Near the end of the final season, he would also experience passionate feelings toward Zarabeth ("All Our Yesterdays")—but only because he had been transported five thousand years into the past, where his ancestors were still uncivilized, "warlike barbarians." So it came as quite a surprise when the obviously interested female Romulan commander slipped into something more comfortable and the typically imperturbable Vulcan slipped into serious seduction mode.

Or did he?

Writer D. C. Fontana has stated that the romantic tête-à-tête in "The *Enterprise* Incident" was modified after she'd turned in her draft of the script, and that while she liked the episode, she felt that it was out of character for Spock to pretend to be romantic. While Fontana is correct—it doesn't seem ethically appropriate for the upright Mister Spock—it's interesting to consider that the commander actually may have gotten under Spock's skin. She is certainly worthy of his respect; she commands a large starship, something Spock admits to her that he hasn't yet achieved. While fans may object that male Vulcans respond romantically to females only during *Pon farr*, even Fontana admits that this is too literal an interpretation of the facts established in "Amok Time." It's true that *Pon farr* is a time for reproduction—but that doesn't discount a Vulcan male's ability to indulge in sexual interplay when such an opportunity seems . . . logical.

McCoy: "That's the Vulcan death grip for you."
Chapel: "There's no such thing as a Vulcan death grip."
Kirk: "Ah, but the Romulans don't know that."

Despite what Spock and McCoy may say about one another, the two men have absolute faith in each other's intelligence and underlying motivations—which is, perhaps, the reason Spock knew that McCoy would understand his subterfuge in "killing" Kirk in front of the Romulan commander and her guards. Up to that point, McCoy had no knowledge of Kirk and Spock's orders to steal the cloaking device, yet when Spock states, "I was unprepared for his attack. I instinctively used the Vulcan death grip," McCoy has the presence of mind to respond in kind: "Your instincts are still good, Mister Spock. The captain is dead."

The message has been delivered and received, allowing McCoy to carry on the charade and spirit Kirk off the Romulan ship. It isn't until the next scene that audiences catch up with McCoy, realizing what the good doctor grasped a few minutes earlier: that (a) Spock is never unprepared, and (b) he never blindly gives in to "instinct," particularly violent instinct.

Of course, it probably didn't hurt that McCoy, like Chapel, also knew that there is no such thing as a Vulcan death grip.

AND THE CHILDREN SHALL LEAD

"Hail, hail, fire and snow. Call the angel, we will go. Far away, for to see. Friendly Angel, come to me."
–the children

After beaming down to the planet Triacus, Kirk's landing party discovers that all the adult members of the scientific expedition based there have committed suicide. Curiously, the scientists' children are fine—in fact, a little *too* fine. They seem strangely unconcerned with their parents' deaths and are primarily interesting in playing games. The children are brought to the ship, where they promptly proceed to summon an entity they met on Triacus. Although this creature is known as "Gorgan the Friendly Angel," he is actually evil incarnate—and the being responsible for the deaths of the adults on the planet. The children's belief in Gorgan makes him powerful, and he turns that power against the crew of the *Enterprise* via the trustful children. By the time Kirk realizes that the children are under a malevolent influence, it's too late. Gorgan has taken control of the ship.

"You are my future generals. Together we can raise armies of followers. Go to your posts! The first great victories are upon us. You will see. . . . We shall exterminate all who oppose us! Our purity of purpose cannot be contaminated by those who disagree, who will not cooperate, who do not understand. They must be annihilated."
—Gorgan

The transparent fellow who called himself "Gorgan" orated his powerful closing statement with the competence of a great defense attorney—as he should have been expected to, given that the actor playing him was just that. Attorney Melvin Belli is perhaps best known for representing Jack Ruby, the Texas bar owner who killed Lee Harvey Oswald shortly after Oswald was arrested for the assassination of President John F. Kennedy. Among Belli's other high-profile clients: the Rolling Stones, following the death of a fan at their Altamont Free Concert. Belli also took a special interest in defending the underdog in personal injury cases against powerful adversaries such as Coca-Cola and Dow Corning.

While being interviewed for a profile in *Playboy* magazine, Belli noted that he might have become an actor had he not studied law. His high profile gave him the opportunity to take on his second calling, and his two career choices sometimes overlapped: He appeared as himself in the motion picture *Wild in the Streets* and again in the

cop series *Hunter*, and he played various fictitious characters in other films and TV shows. Gorgan may be his best-remembered television role, however—and it's certainly the only one in which he wore what could best be described as a fancy shower curtain.

Under the guise of "sci-fi," *Star Trek*'s writers delved into touchy subjects that otherwise might not have met with the network's approval. "And the Children Shall Lead" fits into this category of "message" episodes, with what appears to be a cautionary look at the Hitler Youth movement of the 1920s to 1940s, and an indictment of the movement's policy of teaching children to inform on their parents if they weren't following the party line. Early in his regime, Adolf Hitler stated that the future of Nazi Germany was its children. He ordered that most teenagers join the Hitler Youth, or its auxiliary for girls. These young people were taught Nazi dogma, anti-Semitic policies, and military tactics. The objective of the youth groups was to build a supportive following for Hitler; direct parallels to that objective can be heard in Gorgan's ranting, "You are my future generals. . . . Our purity of purpose cannot be contaminated. . . ." Unfortunately, in this case the message seems to have been diluted to the point that it was missed, misunderstood, or disregarded by viewers, who have consistently ranked the episode near the bottom of the seventy-nine.

Child performers often have a difficult time transitioning into successful adult careers in the entertainment industry, but three of the youngsters who appeared in "And the Children Shall Lead" moved on to such success.

Before her role as Mary, nine-year-old Pamelyn Ferdin was already well established, having appeared in many popular shows of the 1960s, such as *Bewitched*, *My Three Sons*, and *Family Affair*. Following her *Star Trek* appearance, Ferdin voiced the character of Lucy in the animated movie *A Boy Named Charlie Brown* and two specials on TV. She also voiced a character in *Charlotte's Web*, an animated version of E. B. White's classic tale, in 1973. In addition to her active career in voice-over work, she has appeared in dozens of television series, including *Mannix*, *The Odd Couple*, *Lassie*, and *The Streets of San Francisco*. Beyond her acting career, Ferdin has been recognized for her work saving neglected and abused animals.

Brian Tochi, who played Ray, was very busy after his *Star Trek* appearance, costarring in such series as *The Brady Bunch*, *Kung Fu*, and *Diagnosis Murder*. His motion picture credits include *The Omega Man*, with Charlton Heston, and the *Revenge of the Nerds* movies. Like Ferdin, he has done extensive work behind the microphone, lending his voice to Leonardo in the *Teenage Mutant Ninja Turtles* movies and voicing characters for *Mortal Kombat*, *The Iron Giant*, *Batman Beyond*, *Family Guy*, and *Avatar: The Last Airbender*.

Perhaps most impressive are the *two* career paths that Craig Hundley followed. Prior to appearing as Tommy Starnes on *Star Trek*, Hundley had been seen in series ranging from *The Beverly Hillbillies* to . . . *Star Trek*—as Kirk's nephew Peter in the first-season episode "Operation: Annihilate!" As he continued acting, he also concentrated on his musical talents; with his group, the Craig Hundley Trio, he played piano on his own jazz compositions, drawing standing ovations when performing on *The Tonight Show Starring Johnny Carson* and *The Jonathan Winters Show*. Hundley soon found himself writing and recording background music for the TV shows *Alfred Hitchcock Presents* and *Knots Landing*, as well as for the features *Dreamscape*, *Star Trek IV: The Voyage Home*, and *2010*, among many others. It's interesting to note that composer Jerry Goldsmith was nominated for an Academy Award for scoring *Star Trek: The Motion Picture*. For that score, Goldsmith turned to a singular musical instrument called the Blaster Beam to augment the V'ger probe's screen time. The Blaster Beam, a fifteen-foot-long device that uses motorized magnets and a series of artillery shell casings to produce its unique sound, was invented by Craig Hundley.

SPOCK'S BRAIN

"Brain and brain! What is brain?"
—Kara

A beautiful woman materializes on the bridge of the *Enterprise* and renders everyone aboard unconscious. When Kirk awakens, he notices that Spock is missing from his post. A few seconds later, he receives a call from McCoy, who informs Kirk that the Vulcan is down in sickbay, lying on a diagnostic bed—with his brain surgically removed! McCoy estimates that they must track down the missing organ within twenty-four hours, or Spock's body will die. Following the ion trail left by the mysterious woman's spacecraft, the *Enterprise* arrives in the Sigma Draconis system, and Kirk confronts the brain snatcher, an Eymorg named Kara. Although Kara isn't particularly bright, she refuses to be cowed by Kirk and company. Her people need "the Controller"— their terminology for Spock's brain, which is now running much of the equipment on her world—and they have no intention of returning it.

"Hers is the mind of a child."
—McCoy

Ask the average fan for his or her opinion about the best episode of *Star Trek*, and chances are you'll get a fair sampling. "The City on the Edge of Forever." "The Trouble with Tribbles." "The Cage." "Journey to Babel." "Balance of Terror."

But ask the same fan about the *worst* episode, and chances are you're going to hear one answer more than any other: "Spock's Brain."

It's hard to fault that choice. Beautiful but apparently moronic women in very short skirts steal Spock's brain so that the organ can run their planet's "central control system," circulating air, purifying water, and operating heating plants. Why? Because the old Controller is "finished," presumably on its last leg . . . er . . . hemisphere. But why choose Spock's brain? That's never made clear. Obviously, he'd be the best choice if all you had to choose from were members of the *Enterprise* crew. But of all the inhabitants *in the entire galaxy*? *Really*?

Yet, for all the reasons there are to hate this episode, there are an equal number of reasons to love it. Call it a guilty pleasure. "Spock's Brain" is so clearly wrong in every single way, from the beauty pageant smile on the face of Eymorg brain thief Kara when she first shows up on the bridge of the *Enterprise*, to the fact that Spock's brain is both removed *and* replaced over the course of the episode

without mussing a hair on his head. Perhaps he has a screw top cranium?

Which brings to mind one serious question. The opening episode of a show's new season is supposed to set the tone for the coming year and tantalize the audience into tuning in for more the following week. *Star Trek*'s first season led with "The Man Trap," an eerie episode with a scary alien creature and a lot of action. Fair enough. The second season premiered with "Amok Time." Sensational! You can't get better than that.

And then there was season three. "Spectre of the Gun" was the first episode produced, but it was held from airing until the end of October. If the episodes had been aired in production order, that's when "Spock's Brain" would have appeared. So . . . just which exec at NBC thought that "Spock's Brain" would make the *perfect* third-season opener, and *what* was the tone he was trying to set?

"He was worse than dead. . . . His brain is gone!"
—McCoy

As the decades fly by, the original *Star Trek*, with its beloved cast, familiar catchphrases, vivid primary colors, and somewhat unrealistic-appearing alien creatures, seems to become more and more retro—in a good way, of course. A fun way. Which is why it made sense when one of the country's preeminent comedy club chains, the Improv, approached Paramount Pictures in 2004 and asked to license a *Star Trek* episode for live reenactment onstage at its Irvine, California, location. It wouldn't be a spoof of the series, the club's owner promised, nor would it "put down" the show's audience. The performers would take one script and perform it *verbatim* onstage for a paying audience's enjoyment. Paramount would even be allowed to pick the episode.

For something that was going to be performed at a comedy club, it might have made sense to pick one of *Star Trek*'s three acknowledged comedies: "The Trouble with Tribbles," "A Piece of the Action," or "I, Mudd." But, the studio's licensing department reasoned, since those shows were *already* funny, they wouldn't have lent the performers much room to flex their creative muscles and give the episode a slightly different edge. Perhaps it would be better to choose something that hadn't originally been intended as a comedy . . . but that

would, nevertheless, come across as extremely amusing in the right hands.

Thus, when the comic actors at the Irvine Improv received their scripts, they discovered they had committed to perform . . . "Spock's Brain." Not surprisingly, the cast "got it" immediately—as did audiences, who drove from as far as fifty miles away to enjoy a few hours of slightly hammy nostalgia. Originally scheduled to run on Wednesday nights for four successive weeks, the show picked up several encore performances due to popular demand—and a "command performance" at that year's annual *Star Trek* convention extravaganza in Las Vegas, where the crew faced its toughest audience: hard-core Trekkers.

The outcome? The Trekkers were, by far, the most appreciative audience of all. The stunned players even received requests for autographs—which had never happened in Irvine.

IS THERE IN TRUTH NO BEAUTY?

"Who is to say whether Kollos is too ugly to bear or too beautiful to bear?"
—Miranda Jones

The navigational capabilities of the benevolent Medusan species far outpace those of any humanoid intellect, yet the appearance of these non-corporeal beings is so jarring to the human mind that it induces instant insanity. The *Enterprise* has been assigned to convey Kollos, a Medusan ambassador, back to his home world, along with psychologist Miranda Jones, a beautiful human who hopes to form a telepathic link with Kollos. Also along for the ride is Laurence Marvick, a Federation engineer assigned to aid in an exchange of technical information with the Medusan, using Miranda as "translator." Kollos travels in a shielded container to protect the humans around him, but Marvick, whose infatuation with Miranda has made him irrational, inadvertently looks at the ambassador during an attempt to eliminate his "competition." In the grip of madness, Marvick sends the *Enterprise* careening across the galactic barrier, placing the crew on course for oblivion.

Miranda Jones: "The glory of creation is in its infinite diversity."
Spock: "And the ways our differences combine to create meaning and beauty."

For much of the two thousand years that have passed since the reformation on the planet Vulcan, the concept of IDIC—an acronym for "Infinite Diversity in Infinite Combinations"—has represented the stoic race's philosophical approach to life. The visualization of the IDIC—a triangle embedded within a circle, its apex pointing to a precious stone—is, in fact, a national symbol of Vulcan.

   The concept of IDIC sprang from the creative mind of Gene Roddenberry, but he didn't introduce it until *Star Trek* production was well into its third season. By the time "Is There in Truth No Beauty?" went before the cameras, Roddenberry had stepped back from his day-to-day duties on the series; in fact, his only contributions to this episode were the lines of dialogue that introduce the IDIC to viewers, and his behind-the-scenes suggestions to designer William Ware Theiss about the design of the IDIC pendant Spock wears in the episode. Not long after the episode aired, Lincoln Enterprises, a small direct sales operation formed by Roddenberry and future spouse Majel Barrett to meet the growing demand for *Star Trek* merchandise, began supplying similar IDIC pendants to eager fans. Critics have suggested that thought of the merchandise inspired development of

the philosophy, but the IDIC concept is a sound one, profound enough to stand the test of time and become the cornerstone of Vulcan beliefs in subsequent *Star Trek* productions.

Montgomery Scott was a Scotsman—but Jimmy Doohan wasn't. The actor actually was of Irish descent and born in Vancouver, British Columbia; however, he was a superb dialectician, proficient in many accents, including British dialects, European and Asian accents, and numerous vocalizations as far afield as Rastafarian. Doohan recalled that when he went to the Desilu casting office, he had no idea that he'd wind up playing a character with a Scottish accent. "I was called one day to read for *Star Trek*, and because I do a lot of accents, they said, 'Please do a lot of accents,'" recalled Doohan in an interview with Tom Snyder on *The Tomorrow Show*. "So I read the same five or six lines in about five different accents. They picked the Scottish, and of course I was delighted with that. I think that the tradition of an engineer *is* a Scotsman, because all the great motor ships and steamships in the world were built on the Clyde [river]."

Doohan was proud of the character he'd created, and he was fond of saying, "Scotty is ninety-nine percent me and one percent accent." Viewers with a good ear for voices may have noticed that he did more than just the chief engineer's voice on *Star Trek*. He was the series' "go-to" guy when voice-over talent was needed and can be heard as Sargon in "Return to Tomorrow," the M-5 computer in "The Ultimate Computer," Trelane's father in "The Squire of Gothos," and the Oracle in "For the World is Hollow and I Have Touched the Sky." As a practical linguist, he contributed to Marc Okrand's development of both the Klingon and Vulcan languages, which were initially created for use in the *Star Trek* films.

290

THE EMPATH

With the Minaran sun about to enter a nova phase, the *Enterprise* heads for that solar system to retrieve Federation researchers Linke and Ozaba. But when Kirk, Spock, and McCoy arrive at the laboratory, they find it to be empty. A log record indicates that the scientists literally vanished into thin air, but before the trio can figure out what happened, they are apprehended in the same way—transported to a bleak underground facility occupied only by a mute woman, a pair of highly advanced aliens . . . and the lifeless bodies of Linke and Ozaba. The aliens, who identify themselves as Vians, admit that they are conducting an experiment, one that regretfully has cost the two Federation researchers their lives. But the experiment isn't over; now that the *Enterprise* crewmen have arrived, the Vians can continue their work, which may ultimately save the mute woman's entire species—but cost Kirk, Spock, and McCoy their lives.

291

The word "empathic" was not part of the average person's vocabulary in 1968—it was just the dawn of the "touchy-feely" era of the 1970s. But Gem's amazing empathic abilities clearly intrigued Gene Roddenberry, who would introduce other characters with similar abilities in both *Star Trek: The Motion Picture* (the Deltan Ilia, who is able to relieve Chekov's pain when he is burned in a shipboard accident) and *Star Trek: The Next Generation* (the human-Betazoid hybrid Deanna Troi, who can "read" others' emotions—a handy skill for a ship's counselor).

When Scotty hears about the strange experiment that the Vians orchestrated to judge the "worthiness" of Gem's people for salvation, he relates the parable of the "pearl of great price" (Matt. 13:45-46). His observation feels like a non sequitur within the script, perhaps because it is one of the very few biblical references in the original series. Roddenberry felt strongly that the *Star Trek* universe should be a secular one—not *anti*-religion, but one in which individuals were free to believe in whatever faith they cared to believe, without fear of prejudice. Hence, for the most part, no individual religion was singled out for attention, except where a biblical phrase may have slipped into common usage.

"The Empath" is an unusual episode, almost excessively violent for *Star Trek* yet extremely tender in portraying the relationships among the three lead characters, Kirk, Spock, and McCoy. This episode, more than any other, serves to establish the "trinity" element of *Star Trek* in viewers' minds via its portrait of three personalities that define a whole.

Kirk is the *soul* of the *Enterprise*—a man who cares deeply about his mission and his crew. The ship is both an extension of himself and also the only permanent "partner" he can allow himself. His courage is undeniable, his passion legendary. Without Kirk, there would be no *Star Trek*; he is the hero that every exciting saga requires. There isn't a man or woman aboard the *Enterprise* who doesn't have absolute faith in the decisions made by the brave man in the captain's chair, and they would follow him through the gates of hell.

Spock is the *brains* of the outfit, a man whose rational way of thinking balances and tempers Kirk's decisions. As good a captain as Kirk is, he needs a man like Spock to function as a carburetor, regulating the fiery impulses that drive Kirk across the Final Frontier. This captain is not a "by-the-book" officer; he typically makes decisions based on his gut instincts—brilliant, inspired, but occasionally lacking in the kind of information that only a dispassionate and eternally inquisitive mind can provide. When they work together, there is no "no-win" scenario that these two men can't beat.

And McCoy? He is the *heart* of *Star Trek*. Compassionate. Emotional. Unreasonable at times. He's a doctor—a *great* doctor—not a tactician. The heart obviously can't run a starship; in a dire situation, McCoy would be a hopeless mess. But without a heart, a starship is just a piece of metal. McCoy is the man Kirk has entrusted to be *his* ship's heart. The captain may not turn to the doctor for advice as often as he turns to Spock, but Kirk knows that McCoy will always be there for him, ready with a warm word—or a cold Finagle's Folly—to give him the insight that he needs to do his job.

THE THOLIAN WEB

"The Tholian ship has been disabled. But as a result of the battle, we must accept the fact that Captain Kirk is no longer alive."
—Spock

An *Enterprise* landing party beams aboard the *Starship Defiant*, which they find drifting powerless in space. *Defiant*'s crew is dead, the apparent victims of a widespread mutiny. Before they can determine what triggered the wave of violence, the landing party discovers that the *Defiant* is destabilizing around them due to a spatial interphase. Scotty reports that he can transport only three of the four men, so Kirk sends the others ahead with the intention of following in a few minutes. But before he can do so, the ship—along with Kirk—disappears. Now in command, Spock faces a ticking clock. The hostile Tholians have arrived, and they demand that the *Enterprise* leave their territory by the next period of interphase; at the same time, McCoy has determined that the bizarre region of space they're in has a dangerous effect on the human nervous system—if they don't leave soon, the entire crew will go mad, the way the *Defiant*'s crew did. But Spock—convinced that he can rescue Kirk—refuses to leave.

"The renowned Tholian punctuality."
—Spock

Spock's comment about the "renowned" Tholian punctuality served well as an introduction to a new alien species, giving the impression that the Federation already knew a lot about them. However, over the course of this one episode, neither the Federation nor the writers chose to share much of that information with the audience, who learned only that their governing body is the Tholian Assembly, their actions show them to be very territorial, and they are, as mentioned, quite punctual. Viewers couldn't even be certain about the true physical appearance of the Tholians. Was the faceted geometric image on the viewscreen a Tholian head, a mask, a helmet, or an artificial projection like that of Balok in "The Corbomite Maneuver"?

Decades would pass before viewers learned more about this mysterious species. Although the Tholians were mentioned several times on *Star Trek: The Next Generation* and *Star Trek: Deep Space Nine*, it wasn't until the *Star Trek: Enterprise* episode "In a Mirror, Darkly" that viewers learned that Tholians don't have much of a head at all; instead, like many arachnids and crustaceans, they have what appears to be a cephalothorax, with head and thorax united as a single part. Within their nub of a noggin, a pair of deep-set, glowing eyes are the only distinguishable feature. Two spindly arms and six spider-like legs

complete the rather disturbing package.

From the information that *Star Trek: Enterprise* presented, it appears that the image projected onto Spock's viewscreen in "The Tholian Web" was indeed that of Commander Loskene, in the flesh.

295

*Uhura: "Mister Spock? We will be able to retrieve the captain . . .
won't we?"*
*Spock: "Yes. However, the dimensional structure of each universe is
totally dissimilar. . . . If we are not extremely careful, we shall lose the
captain and become trapped ourselves."*
Chekov: "And die like him?! Aaaaaagggggghhhhhhhh!!!"

Several of *Star Trek*'s characters have signature lines of dia-
logue. Spock regularly says, "Fascinating." McCoy says, "He's dead,
Jim." Uhura says, "Hailing frequencies open." And Chekov says,
"Aaaaaagggggghhhhhhhh!!!"

   Actually, the navigator screams in only five episodes: "Mirror, Mirror" (to be precise, it is the mirror universe Chekov who screams),
"The Deadly Years," "Day of the Dove," "The Tholian Web," and "The
Way to Eden." He'd likely have screamed in the first season, too,
if he'd been created back then. And rest assured, motion picture
scripts a decade hence would offer Chekov plenty of additional opportunities to scream. Clearly, the writers thought it was a skill at
which Chekov—and "vocalist" Walter Koenig—was unrivaled.

296

"The captain's last order is top priority, and you will honor that order before you take over."
—McCoy

They listened to it—but they wouldn't admit to Kirk that they listened to it. And Spock outright *lied* about it, despite his frequent admonitions that "Vulcans don't lie."

Nevertheless, it's a fine "final" speech, and whether his best friends owned up to having heard it or not, it's worthy of remembrance:

"Bones, Spock. Since you are playing this tape, we will assume that I am dead, that the tactical situation is critical and both of you are locked in mortal combat. It means, Spock, that you have control of the ship and are probably making the most difficult decisions of your career. I can offer only one small piece of advice, for whatever it's worth. Use every scrap of knowledge and logic you have to save the ship. But temper your judgment with intuitive insight. I believe you have those qualities, but if you can't find them in yourself, seek out McCoy. Ask his advice. And if you find it sound, take it. Bones, you've heard what I've just said to Spock. Help him if you can. But remember, he is the captain. His decisions must be followed without question. You might find that he is capable of human insight and human error. They are most difficult to defend, but you will find that he is deserving of the same loyalty and confidence each of you have given me."

Most *Star Trek* episodes were set either on the ship or on "Class-M" planets where space suits aren't required. However, the taut story for "The Tholian Web" suggested suits that would allow crew members to survive in an environment with no breathable atmosphere, which gave William Theiss the opportunity to design this ingenious costume for the *Enterprise* landing party. Made primarily from silver lamé, the suit looks like something a twentieth-century astronaut—or perhaps a well-dressed beekeeper—might feel comfortable in. This particular costume, worn by DeForest Kelley in the episode, was sold at Christie's auction house in New York during *Star Trek*'s fortieth-anniversary celebrations.

FOR THE WORLD IS HOLLOW AND
I HAVE TOUCHED THE SKY

"Many years ago I climbed the mountains, even though it is forbidden. . . . Things are not as they teach us—for the world is hollow, and I have touched the sky."
—old man

Shortly after McCoy discovers that he is terminally ill, the *Enterprise* comes upon what appears to be an asteroid, headed straight toward a populated world. Sensors reveal that the asteroid is hollow and is, in fact, a spaceship. Believing the vessel to be uninhabited, Kirk, Spock, and McCoy beam inside and are promptly confronted by the people of Yonada, who are unaware that they live on a ship. The vessel is controlled by a sophisticated computer known as the Oracle, which the inhabitants consider a godlike entity. Unfortunately, the Oracle, with 10,000-year-old programming, is far more fallible than a god, and Kirk and Spock are stymied as to how to repair it without revealing the truth about the "world" to its inhabitants. As the two attempt to covertly address the problem, McCoy finds himself growing close to the beautiful high priestess who rules on behalf of the Oracle.

If the asteroid that hides a big interstellar ark looks at all familiar, it's probably because the same lumpy model was used in "The Paradise Syndrome." But the big rock is not the only similarity between the two episodes.

Some say that there are only seven basic story lines, and that all fiction is merely permutations of the seven. If so, *Star Trek* certainly managed to hit most of those story lines multiple times. The series' third season seems particularly rife with repeated motifs from earlier episodes.

The title "For the World is Hollow and I Have Touched the Sky" may be a lot longer than "The Paradise Syndrome," but many of the other details are strikingly similar. In each episode, one of the ship's key crew members is incapacitated in some way (in "Paradise," Kirk has amnesia; in "Hollow," McCoy is afflicted with a devastating blood disease). And because of this, each winds up spending time on a planet/"planet" with a woman he can't help falling for—who he, in fact, marries! But long-term happiness is not in the cards, since each respective planet/"planet" is about to be smashed to bits or is about to smash some other planet to bits, all because some high-tech piece of equipment has begun to malfunction. No one knows how to fix it, because no one remembers how it works or even that it exists. Both McCoy and Kirk leave when their medical problems subside. McCoy tells Natira that he wants to "search through the universe to find a cure for myself and others like me" (which, in fact, happens approximately *one minute later* when Spock finds it in the Fabrini library). Kirk leaves after he regains his memory—and after Miramanee dies. But the odds are that he, like McCoy, would have moved on even if she survived. During this era of television, single leading men in weekly dramas did not get to reap the benefits of nuptials. If the Cartwright men of *Bonanza* couldn't pull it off, what chance did a group of futuristic sailors whose "life, lover, and lady" was the cosmic sea?

300

Natira: "You have lived a lonely life?"
McCoy: "Yes, very lonely."
Natira: "No more, McCoy. There will be no more loneliness for you."

Although it was inevitable that his relationship with high priestess Natira would end, it was nice to see McCoy *finally* get to fall in love and kiss an extremely beautiful woman. Viewers who'd followed the show from the very beginning had witnessed McCoy's anxious reunion with a former paramour (or at least what he *thought* was a former paramour) in "The Man Trap." They'd seen his tentative flirtation with Yeoman Barrows in "Shore Leave." But that was as far as the writers seemed willing to take McCoy—until they sent Natira his way.

That McCoy has lived "a lonely life" is probably news to anyone who *hasn't* read the series' writers' guide, which offered scribes the tantalizing information that McCoy had been married at some point in the deep, dark past, and that the marriage had ended unhappily, driving him into space. But until Rik Vollaerts opted to utilize this thread in his script for "For the World is Hollow and I Have Touched the Sky," the gruff but tenderhearted doctor never seemed to behave like a man who'd led a lonely life.

Kirk promised McCoy a trip to Yonada—or rather, to the world where the Yonadans would start their new lives *outside* the space ark—in a little over a year. One hopes that he made good on the promise.

301

DeForest Kelley had the heart of a poet, a fact best known to the passel of friends he gathered throughout his life with his soft, gentle Georgian manner.

After receiving his discharge from the U.S. Army Air Force at the end of World War II, Kelley hoped to pursue an acting career, and when a talent scout from Paramount Pictures saw him in a play in Long Beach, California, his dream solidified. During the 1940s and 1950s, he co-starred in numerous motion pictures and dozens of television series, usually playing a "heavy." That villainous persona couldn't have been further from his own, and Kelley occasionally worried that he would be typecast in such roles forever. Then, in 1966, he donned the Starfleet uniform of Doctor Leonard McCoy and actually *was* typecast for the rest of his life—but not in a way that he ever regretted.

McCoy is anything but a heavy, possessing the same strong, caring demeanor of the man who portrayed him for the next thirty-three years. Kelley was fond of telling his friends that he was still living "in the same house with the same wife." The stability in that statement allowed him to pursue his poetic drive, and he wrote a long poem titled "The Big Bird's Dream." The "Big Bird" of the title wasn't Kelley, however; the poem was about the creation of *Star Trek* by Gene Roddenberry (whom the series' cast and crew had long ago dubbed "the Great Bird of the Galaxy"), and about efforts to relaunch *Star Trek* following the show's cancellation. Encouraged by the warm reception he received at *Star Trek* conventions around the world, Kelley delighted in reciting the poem to rapt listeners. Eventually, Kelley's wife, Carolyn, copied the poem in flawless, practiced calligraphy, and the actor began distributing autographed copies of his slim self-published book of verse. He was working on a sequel, to be titled, "The Dream Goes On," when he passed away in 1999.

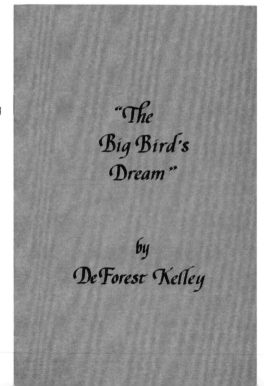

"The Big Bird's Dream"

by

DeForest Kelley

302

DAY OF THE DOVE

"Four thousand throats can be cut in one night by a running man."
—Klingon warrior

Summoned to Beta XII-A by a cry for help from the colonists on that world, Kirk and the *Enterprise* arrive to find . . . nothing. There is no sign of a colony, or aftereffects of its annihilation. As Kirk attempts to puzzle it out, a badly damaged Klingon ship arrives, its infuriated commander, Kang, blaming Kirk for the deaths of most of his crew. Kang attempts to claim the *Enterprise* as a replacement for his own crippled vessel, but although he and his crew come aboard, Kirk manages to keep them at bay until, somehow, all energy weapons aboard the ship disappear, inexplicably replaced with swords—and each side is evenly armed. Overcome by an all-encompassing sensation of bloodlust, both crews erupt into a frenzy of brutal combat aboard the *Enterprise*. But neither side is aware that a malevolent energy creature has orchestrated the entire encounter. Now this entity has come aboard to feast upon the feelings of primitive hatred and violence it has evoked.

303

Commander Kang is regarded as one of the most prominent warriors in Klingon history. Decades after the events of "Day of the Dove," he still would be making his presence known in the *Star Trek* universe, specifically in episodes on *Star Trek: Deep Space Nine* ("Blood Oath," which also featured John Colicos and William Campbell in reprisals of their earlier *Star Trek* roles) and again on *Star Trek: Voyager* ("Flashback"). Similarly, much of the strength of "Day of the Dove" in an otherwise uneven third season comes from actor Michael Ansara's powerful performance as the self-assured leader Kang.

Ansara's unique appearance (his family emigrated from Syria when he was two years old) contributed to a career in which he played a variety of ethnic roles, primarily Native Americans. Although he appeared in more than fifty productions on stage, screen, and television, his single most recognized role was as Cochise in the series *Broken Arrow*. His performance as Kang is much of a kind with the noble but fierce Apache leader. Now in his eighties, Ansara regularly voices the character of Mr. Freeze in the animated *Batman* series of TV movies.

Klingon science officer Mara wielded authority over many of the 437 warriors on Kang's battle cruiser, although some of her clout may have come from her position as Kang's wife. Aside from the respect she commands from Kang's crew, by sheer virtue of her existence Mara occupies an important role in *Star Trek* history. She is the *only*

Klingon female viewers would meet during Kirk's five-year mission (although observant viewers may spot another female, who remains anonymous, within Kang's crew). Although the concept of women in combat positions was still years in the future for Americans, female Klingon warriors apparently didn't face the same barriers. Besides Mara, the *Star Trek* audience would soon meet Valkris (in *Star Trek III: The Search for Spock*), Vixis (in *Star Trek V: The Final Frontier*), and the delightfully trashy Duras sisters (on *Star Trek: The Next Generation*). Actress Susan Howard, who played this first among Klingon females, is best remembered for her portrayal of Donna Krebbs on the series *Dallas*.

304

The entity that fed on the anger it engendered among Kirk's and Kang's crews was never identified; students of *Star Trek* history refer to the spinning, color-changing "pinwheel" as the Beta XII-A entity, after the planet where the warring parties of "Day of the Dove" first encountered it. But that designation doesn't take into account that the non-corporeal entity may not have been native to the planet. Unlike the similar creature that fed on fear vibes—most commonly referred to as "Redjac," for its role in the Jack the Ripper-related murders ("Wolf in the Fold")—the Beta XII-A entity didn't body-hop; instead, it visibly hovered above the mayhem it inspired. Which meant, of course, that someone had to tell the folks in front of the camera where it was at any given time so that they'd all be gazing at the right spot when the effects crew got to work after principal photography was completed. The problem was easily solved: Visual effects designer Mike Minor tied a multicolored beach ball to the end of a stick and held it in the appropriate spot. The actors simply had to "follow the bouncing ball." It wasn't because of the ball, however, that the entity and the characters never appeared together in the same shot—that was the fault of the budget.

305

305

PLATO'S STEPCHILDREN

Responding to a distress call from Platonius, Kirk, Spock, and McCoy beam down to find Parmen, the planet's ruler, on the verge of death from an infected leg. The Platonians, the landing party learns, have powerful telekinetic abilities, but they have no resistance to infection. When McCoy cures Parmen, the grateful leader attempts to convince him to stay on his world. McCoy politely rejects the invitation, but the Platonians won't take no for an answer. Using their powerful minds, they put Kirk and Spock through an escalating series of bizarre and humiliating performances in an attempt to pressure McCoy to change his mind.

306

It is the stuff of legend: The kiss between Kirk and Uhura in "Plato's Stepchildren" in 1968 was American television's first interracial kiss!

Except, like most legends, it's not entirely true:

1. By definition, interracial means, "relating to, involving, or representing different races." There are many races on the planet Earth, not just two. And technically speaking, prior to the episode "Plato's Stepchildren," Kirk had *already* kissed at least one woman of another race, even though television viewers were not yet aware of that fact. In "Elaan of Troyius," shot ten episodes prior to "Plato's Stepchildren," Kirk smooched Asian American actress France Nuyen; the episode, however, would not air until four weeks after "Plato" was broadcast.

2. *Star Trek* is a "dramatic program"—dramatized fiction, if you will. But there are other kinds of television programs, and other shows got to first base ahead of *Star Trek*. Actress Anne Bancroft raised eyebrows when she gave Sidney Poitier a kiss on the cheek along with his Oscar® on the Academy Awards® broadcast of 1964. And in 1967, Nancy Sinatra and Sammy Davis Jr. greeted each other with an on-screen kiss in the televised musical-variety special *Movin' With Nancy*

3. Audiences may *think* they saw Kirk and Uhura kiss in this episode, but did they really? Reportedly the network exerted quite a bit of pressure on the production to keep William Shatner and Nichelle Nichols from achieving actual lip-lock. For most of the sequence, Uhura and Kirk are in profile, but just as they are about to kiss, the camera moves in and Kirk swings Uhura ever so slightly *toward* the camera. Now the back of her head blocks part of his face, and as he leans forward, the audience can't quite see what's going on. Do their mouths touch? Probably. But do they actually kiss? Well . . . as the newspaper editor said in *The Man Who Shot Liberty Valance*, "When the legend becomes fact, print the legend!"

307

"Take care, young ladies, and value your wine.
Be watchful of young men in their velvet prime.
Deeply they'll swallow from your finest kegs.
Then swiftly be gone, leaving bitter dregs.
Ahh-ah-ah-ah, bitter dregs."
—Spock

Although the Platonians forced Kirk and Spock to engage in several bizarre activities, one can imagine that Kirk might not have objected to kissing Uhura under different circumstances. And while Spock likely wouldn't have been a big fan of flamenco dancing in any event, there's a chance that he *might* have enjoyed singing "Maiden Wine," assuming he could kick back and slip out of those pointy ears. Which is to say, if he were in his Leonard Nimoy persona, since Nimoy himself wrote the song.

Nimoy's professional singing and songwriting career began during *Star Trek*'s first season, when record executives from Dot Records— then a subsidiary of Paramount Pictures—approached the producers to inquire about releasing a *Star Trek*-themed album. Recognizing an opportunity to bring in some additional revenue, Herb Solow, then Desilu's executive in charge of production, quickly penned a memo to Desilu's business affairs office, urging the organization execs there to enter into the requested deal with Dot or, for that matter, any other record company that wanted to do anything along those lines, "be it straight dramatic music, weird music, Nichelle Nichols singing, Bill Shatner doing bird calls, or even the sound of Gene Roddenberry polishing a semi-precious stone on his grinder."

Nimoy's big break came about when the daughter of Dot arranger/producer Charles Grean encouraged her dad to put Mister Spock on that *Star Trek*-themed album. Nimoy agreed to do it, and the album— which, as a result, would be titled *Mr. Spock's Music from Outer Space*—was cut. The record was successful enough that Dot asked Nimoy to sign a long-term contract.

When Nimoy composed "Maiden Wine," he may have had one of his upcoming albums in mind. "Plato's Stepchildren" hit the airwaves in November 1968. "Maiden Wine"—a longer version with musical arrangement—would appear on the album *The Touch of Leonard Nimoy* the following year.

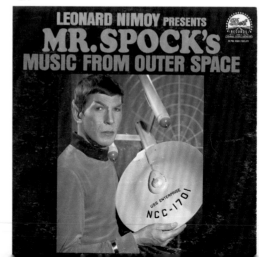

308

WINK OF AN EYE

"Your crew cannot see you or any of us because of the acceleration. We move in the wink of an eye. Oh, there is a scientific explanation for it, but all that really matters is that you can see me and talk to me, and we can go on from there."
—Deela

The *Enterprise* responds to an urgent summons from the planet Scalos, but when Kirk and company arrive, they find only a beautiful, deserted city—and a burgeoning mystery, as a member of the landing party disappears into thin air! Back on the ship, the crew finds evidence that someone has been tampering with assorted controls and equipment, but there's no sign of an intruder. Only after Kirk's coffee is spiked with Scalosian water does he find out that the ship has been infiltrated by the same beings who sent the initial distress call. However, now he, and only he, can see them. Kirk learns that long ago their metabolism had been accelerated by environmental changes on their planet, and now, thanks to the contaminant added to his coffee, so has his. Deela, queen of the Scalosians, informs Kirk that her people are in the process of taking control of the *Enterprise*; they plan to use the ship's male crew members to help Scalos deal with a severe infertility problem, one that ultimately could eradicate Deela's entire species.

Deela: "I'm glad we're both innocents. I despise devious people, don't you?"
Kirk: "I believe in honest relationships myself."

Throughout his five-year mission, James T. Kirk seduced a woman in every port—or at least it seemed as if he did. But in movies and television of the day, such activity generally remained an open question without visual proof. Up until this point in the series, the closest viewers had gotten to said visual proof was in "Bread and Circuses," when Kirk was given the beautiful slave Drusilla to use as he wished on the night before his scheduled execution. The pair kiss, the camera pans up to a burning oil lamp . . . and then that shot fades into a very similar one, except that the lamp has burned out. The camera shifts to show Kirk asleep on a cot—alone—and fully clothed. Hmmm.

That's about as much as NBC's ever-vigilant Standards and Practices department would permit in those days. It was an era desperately clinging to the mores of the 1950s, even as the sexual revolution was taking place outside the studio gates. But something seems to have changed in the year that transpired between "Bread and Circuses" and "Wink of an Eye." For apparently, while the audience was presumably distracted by cuts between scenes showing activities going on in other parts of the ship, Kirk and Deela . . . did it. The proof is in the sign of the shoe—or rather, the boot. Kirk is sitting on the side of his bed, pulling up his boot; Deela is nearby, fixing her hair in the mirror. It's clear they weren't playing three-dimensional chess. It is, undeniably, the most tantalizing moment in all of *Star Trek*. But viewers are forgiven if they missed it; given the circumstances, it was all over in the wink of an eye.

The console surfaces on the *Enterprise* bridge were studded with colored resin "buttons" laid out in a very specific pattern. After the show ended, professional model maker Greg Jein managed to acquire a box of the precious baubles—which was good news for the producers of *Star Trek: The Next Generation* when they wanted to re-create a section of Kirk's original bridge for the episode "Relics." The buttons—borrowed from Jein, who occasionally did work for the series—added a wonderful touch of authenticity to what was supposed to be a holographic reproduction . . . yet somehow, something wasn't quite right. A few years later, when *Star Trek: Deep Space Nine*'s producers once again created Kirk's bridge, this time for the episode "Trials and Tribble-ations," scenic artist Doug Drexler researched and resolved the problem. "It was a matter of placement," Drexler says. "There's a certain logic to the way they're laid out, the way they're placed, the sizes and the types. And if you don't place them in the right spot, they don't have a proper sweep to them and they don't feel right. It's a matter of degrees. But if you miss by a couple of degrees, it might as well be a mile."

311

THAT WHICH SURVIVES

Losira: "I have come for you."
Sulu: "What do you want?"
Losira: "I want to touch you."

Intrigued by the highly enigmatic readings the ship's sensors are receiving from the planet below, Kirk, McCoy, Sulu, and geologist Lieutenant D'Amato step into the transporter and prepare to beam down. But as they are dematerializing, a beautiful woman appears and kills the transporter operator. By the time the landing party materializes below, the *Enterprise* is no longer in orbit above them; the ship has been hurtled nearly a thousand light-years from its previous location. To make matters worse for Kirk's group, the mysterious woman appears on the planet and kills D'Amato with a touch of her hand. Back on the *Enterprise*, Spock attempts to plot a course back to the planet—but the same deadly female returns to the ship and kills one of Scotty's engineers in an attempt to sabotage the *Enterprise*'s return to her world.

312

312

Spock: "You have eight minutes, forty-five seconds."
Scotty: "I know what time it is, I don't need a bloomin' cuckoo clock."

Once again, *Star Trek*'s visual effects crew found a simple way to combine practical photography with the elements they could easily obtain. In order to place Scotty within an "authentic" antimatter energy stream, they photographed a number of dry, spindly tree branches laid side by side. After processing the film, they animated the image of the branches, looped it, and printed it with color film stock to create an illusion of flowing blue current.

313

At the beginning of *Star Trek*'s third season, many of the original creative staff members moved on to other projects. Perceived indifference from the broadcast network's executives and a difference in management style between the bosses at Desilu and those at Paramount prompted Herb Solow to depart; writer Gene L. Coon, whose clever ideas had contributed so much to the series, also had left. Stalwart coproducer Robert Justman, who'd been with the show since the beginning, abandoned ship halfway through the third season. Even creator Gene Roddenberry removed himself from hands-on involvement with the show he'd created, although he held on to the title of executive producer. Under new, less attentive management, the series floundered.

Although she'd given up the position of story editor at the end of season two, D. C. Fontana did her best to work under adverse circumstances, penning three stories for season three. But even that proved too close for comfort. "I didn't like the way the third season was going," Fontana says, "and I just wanted to get away. I left several stories that someone else wrote the scripts for."

Only one—"The *Enterprise* Incident"—would appear under her actual name. She removed her name from "That Which Survives" and "The Way to Eden," substituting "Michael Richards" (a combination of the first names of her two brothers) as her nom de plume.

Like Gene Roddenberry, Walter "Matt" Jefferies had flown B-17s during World War II, so they both understood the workings of flying vehicles. On the day they met, Roddenberry asked Jefferies to design a starship that was "instantly recognizable" but that had "no flames, no fires, no rockets." Jefferies, who previously had served as a designer with the *Ben Casey* series' art department, took the assignment very seriously; he drew dozens of designs before Roddenberry accepted his final version of the *Enterprise*, with its saucer, lower hull, and twin nacelles. The young production designer moved on to create many of the props and sets that visually define *Star Trek* today, including the iconic design of the *Enterprise* bridge.

One particular set is identified very closely with the art director: that narrow, cylindrical crawlway that allowed Scotty instant access to malfunctioning systems equipment throughout the ship (as seen in "That Which Survives" and numerous other episodes). The production staff jokingly referred to the cramped crawlway as a "Jefferies tube," and the name stuck—although it was never official terminology. Some two decades later, the writing staff of *Star Trek: The Next Generation* incorporated the name within a script, and when a crew member uttered it on the air, the term "Jefferies tube" at long last was rendered canon.

LET THAT BE YOUR LAST BATTLEFIELD

Bele: "It is obvious to the most simple-minded that Lokai is of an inferior breed."
Spock: "The obvious visual evidence, Commissioner, is that he is of the same breed as yourself."
Bele: "Are you blind, Commander Spock? Well, look at me. Look at me!"
Kirk: "You're black on one side and white on the other."
Bele: "I am black on the right side."
Kirk: "I fail to see the significant difference."
Bele: "Lokai is white on the right side. All of his people are white on the right side."

The *Enterprise* intercepts a stolen shuttlecraft and its sole passenger, a native of the planet Cheron named Lokai. He requests political asylum from the Federation, claiming that he is a victim of racial persecution on his homeworld. Not long after, the *Enterprise* receives a second representative from Cheron: Bele, an officer of Cheron's Commission on Political Traitors. Bele wants Kirk to turn Lokai over

to him, but Kirk refuses. A frustrated Bele attempts to convince the *Enterprise* crew that Lokai's criminal nature is inherent in his physical appearance: black on his left side and white on the right. Bele, a member of Cheron's ruling class, is black on the right side and white on the left—which apparently makes all the difference on Cheron. When Kirk and company fail to comprehend the value of that difference, Bele decides to force Kirk's hand—by taking control of the *Enterprise*.

Spock: "All that matters to them is their hate."
Uhura: "Do you suppose that's all they ever had, sir?"
Kirk: "No. But that's all they have left."

In 1965, the streets of south central Los Angeles erupted into a racial conflagration that, in the aftermath, became known as the "Watts Riots." Reacting to perceived injustices perpetrated against them by the power structure of the city, including the police, the African American residents of the area took to the streets. The result was a six-day period of violent unrest in which thirty-four people were killed, hundreds were injured, and millions of dollars' worth of property was destroyed. Memories of that event prompted *Star Trek* writer Gene L. Coon to sketch out a story outline that he titled "A Portrait in Black and White," which examined racial prejudice in the simplest terms, leaving out all politically arguable shades of gray.

Coon was not the first writer to create a portrait of a problem in such simplistic terms (here, Bele being black on the right—or "correct"—side). As early as 1726, Jonathan Swift fabricated two opposing political parties in his work *Gulliver's Travels*. The "Big-endians" and their foes were at war, fighting over which end of their hard-boiled eggs should be opened for eating. As ridiculous as that seems, it perfectly described the triviality of the real-life political problems Swift was allegorizing. Prejudice, after all, is prejudice, and injustice is

injustice, all of which Coon understood.

The executives at NBC rejected the outline, stating that the story "did not fit into the *Star Trek* concept." The rejection didn't please Coon or his egalitarian boss, Gene Roddenberry, but they set it aside, hoping that a day might come when the outline could be expanded into a script and produced.

The conglomerate that someday would be known as Gulf & Western Industries had its roots in a manufacturer of automobile bumpers in 1934; by the mid-1960s, G&W had grown into a huge diversified corporation that included clothing manufacturers, sugar plantations, cigar companies, financial services, record production, and book sales. At that point, the behemoth decided to break into showbiz, and as 1966 faded into 1967, the company purchased both Desilu Productions and Paramount Pictures. As it had with every previous acquisition, G&W management made its first order of business cutting production costs.

As *Star Trek* geared up for its third season, Paramount's new overseers, looking for ways to tighten up the show's budget, spotted what they felt was an easy target: They deemed that rather than pay for new story ideas, the rejected story ideas on file could be resurrected. Among them was an outline titled "A Portrait in Black and White." By this time, the outline's prolific writer, Gene L. Coon, had left the series, so Oliver Crawford, who previously had cowritten "The *Galileo* Seven," was hired to turn out a script. Crawford discovered that the story nugget within the outline suffered from a lack of action—and that the premise itself was a mite short for an hour-long episode. Given the reduced budget and the limited production time, the creative staff did what it could, but no one was very happy with it (and, in fact, Coon asked that they put his pen name "Lee Cronin" on the final

product). And they never did resolve the problem of "not enough story to fill the hour," which is why so much time is devoted to Bele and Lokai running though the *Enterprise* corridors, chasing . . . chasing . . . chasing. . . .

Perhaps the most suspenseful moment in all of *Star Trek* came when Captain Kirk activated the *Enterprise*'s self-destruct mechanism in "Let That Be Your Last Battlefield." The tension mounted—enhanced by cuts to extreme close-ups of the characters' eyes and mouths—as the officers recited the crucial authorization codes:

"Computer, this is Captain James Kirk of the U.S.S. Enterprise. *Destruct Sequence one. Code one, one-A."*

"This is Commander Spock, science officer. Destruct Sequence number two. Code one, one-A, two-B."

"This is Lieutenant Commander Scott, chief engineering officer of the U.S.S. Enterprise. *Destruct Sequence number three. Code one-B, two-B, three."*

"Destruct Sequence completed and engaged. Awaiting final code for thirty-second countdown."

"Code zero, zero, zero, destruct zero."

In a wonderful moment of continuity within the franchise, this sequence would be used in almost exactly the same way (except for a change in personnel, reflecting the officers on hand) in the feature film *Star Trek III: The Search for Spock*:

"Computer, this is Admiral James T. Kirk. Destruct Sequence one. Code one, one-A."

"Computer, Commander Montgomery Scott, chief engineering officer. Destruct Sequence two. Code one, one-A, two-B."

"Computer, this is Commander Pavel Chekov, acting science officer. Destruct Sequence three. Code one-B, two-B, three."

"Destruct Sequence completed and engaged. Awaiting final code for one-minute countdown."

"Code zero, zero, zero, destruct zero."

Of course, in "Battlefield," the crew (and the audience) knew that Kirk was adept at playing "poker" and likely would win the match in time to deactivate the order. In the feature film, Kirk had deadlier intentions—and fewer choices—and sadly, that beautiful ship *did* explode, in one of *Star Trek*'s most indelible visual moments.

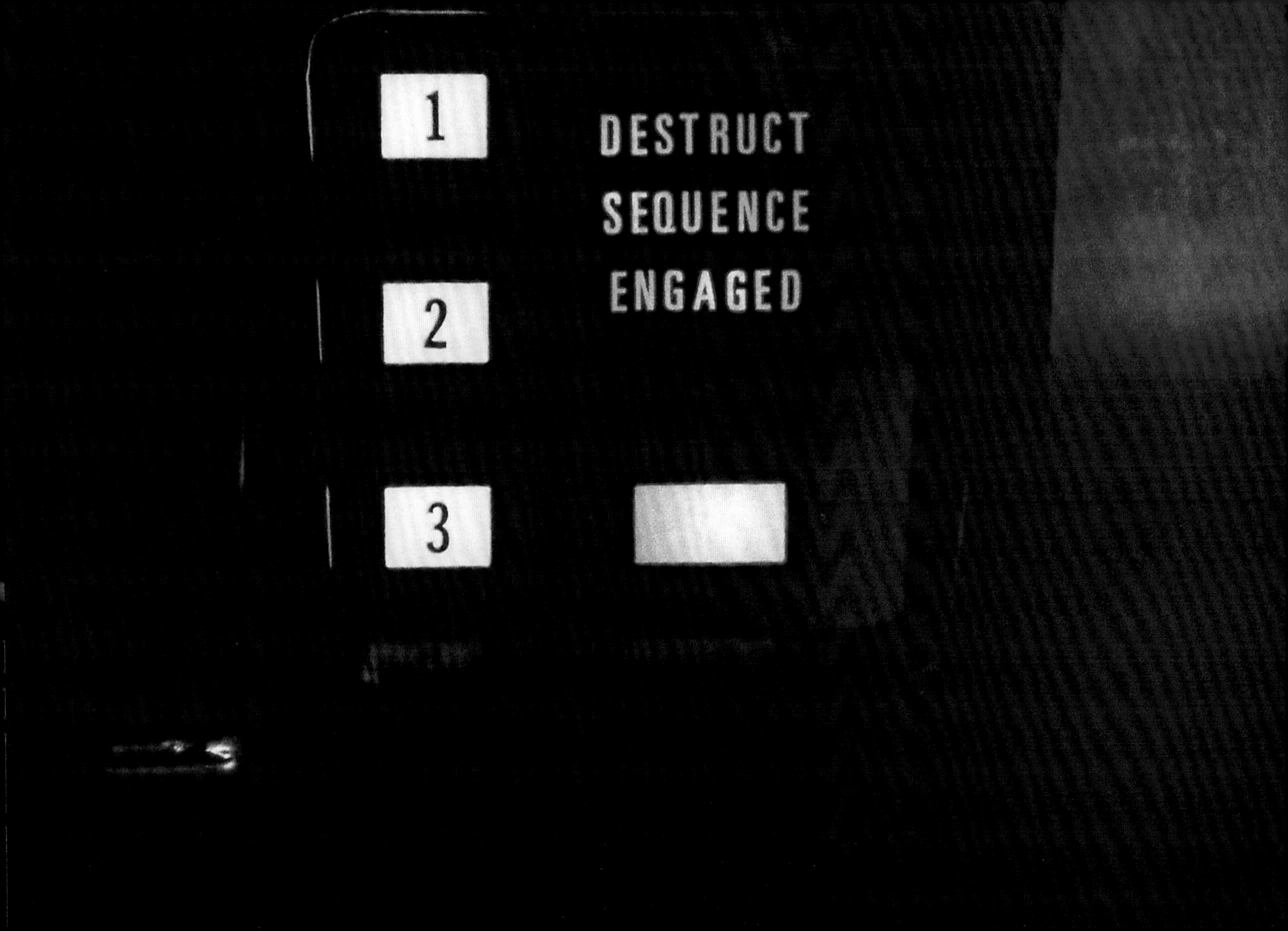
1
DESTRUCT
SEQUENCE
ENGAGED
2
3

WHOM GODS DESTROY

Marta: "He's my lover, and I have to kill him."
Spock: "She seems to have worked out an infallible method for assuming permanent male fidelity."

While delivering a promising new drug to Elba II, Kirk and Spock discover—a bit too late—that the inmates are running the asylum. The patient in charge is Garth of Izar, once a brilliant starship captain whose exploits were required reading at Starfleet Academy. Garth, Kirk learns, was rendered mad by a serious accident that left him badly injured; the well-meaning inhabitants of Antos IV helped him to repair his damaged body by teaching him cellular metamorphosis techniques. Once recovered, Garth learned how to use the same techniques to change his appearance at will. Now criminally insane, Garth plans to use the *Enterprise* to escape from Elba—if he can just get Kirk to reveal the code phrase that will convince Scotty that he is actually Kirk!

One suspects that Captain Kirk experienced a tiny (albeit indiscernible to viewers' eyes) moment of fear when he saw the chair that Garth was using to torture asylum administrator Cory—and, of course, him—in "Whom Gods Destroy"; it's the same nasty chair, slightly modified by the show's prop department, that Dr. Tristan Adams used to torture Kirk in "Dagger of the Mind."

Of course, the audience, too, may have suffered a collective tweak of déjà vu, because "Whom Gods Destroy" may be the *Star Trek* poster child for recycling efforts: props, costumes, and even film footage from previous episodes show up. Garth's garb originated as Commissioner Ferris's threads in the first-season episode "The *Galileo* Seven." Garth's furry-collared robe was worn first by Anton Karidian in "The Conscience of the King." The environmental suits that Garth's crazy henchmen wear while dragging Marta outside to die are the same suits created for the *Enterprise* crew earlier in the season (for "The Tholian Web"). And the film footage of the *Enterprise* firing phaser blasts at Elba II's force field originated as a sequence in "Who Mourns for Adonais?" when the *Enterprise* fires phaser blasts at Apollo's Greek temple.

Well, at least they get an A+ for "going green" way ahead of their time!

321

Visitors checking out the star-embedded sidewalks of Hollywood will find a particularly noteworthy one in front of the historic Hollywood Roosevelt Hotel, near Grauman's Chinese Theatre. Few actors within the pantheon of celebrities honored on the "Walk of Fame" are more deserving than Keye Luke, who portrayed Governor Donald Cory in "Whom Gods Destroy." The actor, who was born in China and raised in Seattle, Washington, began his career as a mural artist; among his many works are murals on the walls of Grauman's. But Luke soon laid down his brushes, trading them for greasepaint and dozens of appearances on the big screen. For several decades, Luke was the go-to actor for productions that actually cast Asians *as* Asian characters. His breakthrough role early on was as Charlie Chan's "Number One Son" in the 1930s *Charlie Chan* mysteries (which featured, most notably, Swedish actor Warner Oland as the first incarnation of the Chinese detective); he would eventually play Chan himself, in the 1972 animated series *The Amazing Chan and the Chan Clan*. Over the years, the prolific actor appeared—often in recurring roles—in more than two hundred movie and television titles, from Kato in the 1940s *Green Hornet* films to appearances in television's long-running series *M*A*S*H*. After playing Cory in *Star Trek*, Luke moved on to his seminal role as Master Po on television's *Kung Fu*, and he continued to act until his death, at the age of eighty-six, in 1991.

322

THE MARK OF GIDEON

"We must acknowledge, once and for all, that the purpose of diplomacy is to prolong a crisis."
—Spock

The United Federation of Planets has been trying to recruit Gideon—supposedly a virtual paradise—as a member world for some time, with no success. Now the planet's ruling council has agreed to the presence of a Federation delegation of one: the captain of the *Enterprise*. Kirk beams down to the specified coordinates, but finds that he is still on the *Enterprise*, which is unaccountably unpopulated—except for a beautiful young girl named Odona. In the meantime, Gideon's council reports that Kirk never arrived and refuses to allow Spock to mount a search party to look for the captain. On Kirk's *Enterprise*, Odona claims to be ignorant of how she herself arrived on the ship, but Kirk suspects that something insidious is going on.

323

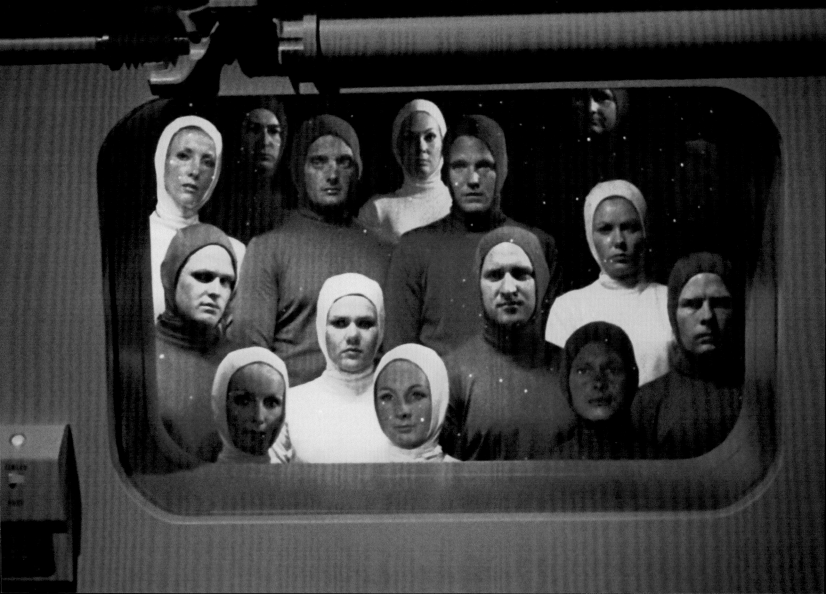

The subject of overpopulation has been a hot topic since Earth's population topped 1 billion people in the nineteenth century. Intellectuals of the day noted that humanity might eventually outstrip the planet's resources. By the beginning of the twentieth century, the world's population had jumped to 1.6 billion—and after that, it began to look as if those intellectuals had been right to be concerned. By mid-century, the population had increased by another billion, thanks in part to compulsory vaccination in many regions and improvements in medicine and sanitation. In the second half of the twentieth century, things really began to look scary, as the populations in Asia, Latin America, and Africa *each* jumped by more than 100 percent. As a result, the population was a whopping *6 billion* as humanity entered the new millennium. Clearly, a subject of such importance would draw the attention of writers of speculative fiction—and therein came the story idea for "The Mark of Gideon."

Perhaps it's not a coincidence that the story for this episode was cowritten by the actor who played Cyrano Jones in "The Trouble with Tribbles." That episode featured a creature that *defined* overpopulation! However, unlike the cheerfully mercenary character he played in "Tribbles," Stanley Adams (who died in 1977) is said to have been a man deeply concerned with the problems of overpopulation. During the filming of "Tribbles," Adams reportedly had some casual conversations with Gene Roddenberry, suggesting that *Star Trek* do a story reflecting that subject matter. "The Mark of Gideon" evidently was the result.

Hodin: *"We cannot deny the truth which shaped our evolution. We are incapable of destroying or interfering with the creation of that which we love so deeply—life, in every form, from fetus to developed being. It is against our tradition, against our very nature. We simply could not do it."*

Kirk: *"Yet you can kill a young girl."*

Hodin: *"My daughter freely chose to do what she is doing, as the people of Gideon are free to choose."*

The story outline for "The Mark of Gideon" is quite different from the final aired episode. Overpopulation is the crux of the dilemma for the people of Gideon, but the methodology by which Hodin chooses to deal with it is much more disturbing.

As with the televised episode, the "bait" that Hodin uses to attract the *Enterprise* is his world's apparent willingness to join the Federation. But rather than ask Kirk to beam down, Hodin and several of his aides beam aboard the ship—and then proceed to kidnap Kirk, Spock, McCoy, Scotty, and Chapel, who learn that they are to be the subject of experimentation. As in the episode, the Gideonites are "plagued" with their ability to regenerate all damaged bodily cells. They plan to use Kirk's crew as living blood banks in the hopes of introducing human ailments into Gideonites. Odona is not Hodin's daughter; she is simply a member of the populace, chosen as a test subject, and she does indeed fall ill—as does Hodin when McCoy manages to inject him with tainted blood. The *Enterprise* crew escapes when the guards learn that Hodin and other members of his council had never planned to expose themselves to harm; they were counting on the deaths of the common people to leave their exclusive group free to enjoy immortality in a much less crowded world.

Hodin is a more sympathetic person in the aired episode, and he seems to love his daughter. But there are obvious solutions to Gideon's problems that Hodin never considers.

One solution would have been for the inhabitants to forsake the lovely "germ-free" atmosphere of Gideon and travel to other worlds. Yes, apparently it's pretty there, but if you can't see the proverbial "forest for the trees" with all those people, what good is it?

The other was the solution that everyone at home was thinking, and that Kirk brings up: "Let your people learn about the devices to safely prevent conception. The Federation will provide anything you need."

Hodin's response is that his people believe that life is sacred. Yet, in following his rationale a bit further, Kirk (and the viewers) realize that what Hodin really is advocating is a policy of self-euthanasia for his people, which doesn't seem to support a philosophy based on a deep regard for the sacredness of life.

But all Kirk (and the viewers) could do was leave orbit and hope for a happier outcome the following week.

325

THE LIGHTS OF ZETAR

"When a man of Scotty's years falls in love, the loneliness of his life is suddenly revealed. His heart once throbbed to the sound of the ship's engines; now, all he can see is the woman."
–Kirk

As the *Enterprise* delivers science specialist Mira Romaine to Memory Alpha, the Federation's central library facility, Chief Engineer Scott falls in love with the pretty lieutenant—and the feeling is mutual, giving rise to hopes for a bright future. But a strange energy storm suddenly strikes the library's planetoid location, killing all of the residents and somehow endowing Mira with eerie precognitive abilities that allow her to predict where the storm will strike next: the *Enterprise*! Soon Mira seems to be in communication with the entities that make up the energy storm, the collective life force of the last survivors of the dead planet Zetar. The entities are searching for a host body they can inhabit, and, much to Scotty's dismay, Mira's psychological attributes make her the best candidate.

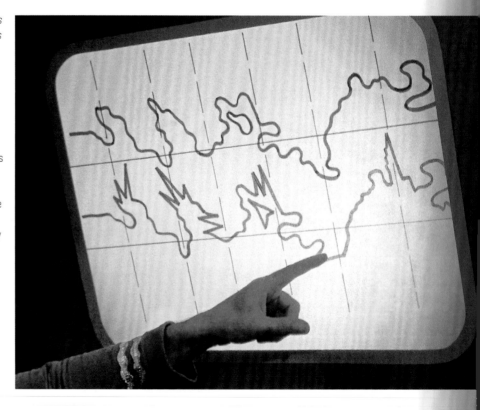

326

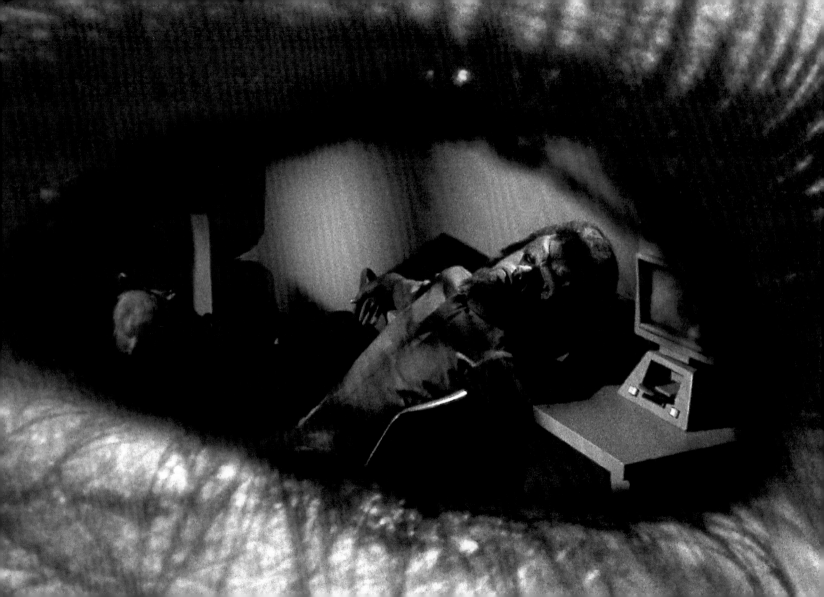

326

"Well, this is an Enterprise *first. Doctor McCoy, Mister Spock, and Engineer Scott are all in complete agreement. Can I stand the strain?"*
—Kirk

A large percentage of the television viewing public remembers Shari Lewis as a perky, ponytailed female ventriloquist, generally seen in the company of an adorable sock puppet named Lamb Chop. A smaller percentage is aware that Lewis and her husband, book publisher Jeremy Tarcher, wrote the *Star Trek* episode "The Lights of Zetar." Lewis was a devout fan of the series, so selling a script to the show was one-half of a dream come true for her. Unfortunately, the other half of her dream—to be cast as Mira, the character she'd placed at the center of the story—didn't come to pass; the role went to actress Jan Shutan. It may have been Lewis's closeness to Mira's story that blinded her to what many fans consider the episode's primary flaw. The story centers on an outsider—a character who isn't a regular *Enterprise* crew member—and it's *her* life that's in jeopardy, not one of the "big three" (Kirk, Spock, or McCoy). But alas, the audience, unlike lovelorn Scotty, had no emotional investment in Mira's outcome.

327

Even though Scotty often handled the transporter controls himself, the odds are that the first thing most people saw when they beamed aboard the *Enterprise* was the smiling face of Mr. Kyle. Which is not to say that Kyle never managed to leave the transporter room; throughout the starship's five-year mission, he saw service in many parts of the ship, including turns on the bridge as a relief helmsman and science station operator. But Kyle seemed most at home manning the transporter. Little is known about the crewman's background, although he seemed to be a nice guy; he did, after all, offer a bowl of chicken soup to a confused security guard in "Tomorrow Is Yesterday."

Played by British-born actor John Winston, Mr. Kyle was the only non-American crewman viewers met whose non-American accent (Yorkshire, in his case) was authentic. He would eventually appear in eleven episodes, three in season one, seven in season two, and one in season three, ranking him behind only Nurse Chapel as the recurring minor character with dialogue who had the most appearances. (Actor Billy Blackburn's navigator actually appeared in sixty-one episodes, but he never had a line of dialogue.)

"The Lights of Zetar" was Winston's final appearance on the original series. Although Kyle would appear in six episodes of *Star Trek: The Animated Series*, the character was voiced by James Doohan. But Winston would return to the *Star Trek* fold one last time, to reprise Kyle in *Star Trek II: The Wrath of Khan*.

THE CLOUD MINDERS

Droxine: "I have never before met a Vulcan, sir."
Spock: "Nor I a work of art, madam."

A deadly botanical plague has hit the planet of Merak II, and only one thing can stop it: zenite, a rare mineral substance found on the planet Ardana. But when the *Enterprise* arrives to pick up the desperately needed shipment, Kirk discovers that he's arrived at an inopportune time. The planet's Troglyte population, which mines Ardana's valuable zenite while the rest of the populace lives a life of intellectual repose in the floating city of Stratos, has begun to chafe under the burden of inequity. The upper-class Stratos dwellers, in turn, feel that the Troglytes are naturally inferior, and ungrateful to boot. While Kirk has sympathy for the underdog Troglytes, what he really needs is the promised shipment of zenite—and the Troglytes are unwilling to provide that without concessions from the folks above.

The design of Stratos, Ardana's beautiful city in the clouds, was based on one of Matt Jefferies's graceful renderings. The resulting model was built from lightweight extruded polystyrene foam, carved with hacksaw and X-Acto blades, and stuck together with common white glue. Clumps of cotton were wrapped around the bottom of the city to suggest clouds, and then the entire structure was hung from the ceiling against a screen conveying Ardana's brightly hued sky. The physical effect was later polished with the addition of a matte painting of clouds, which replaced the rather unrealistic cotton wadding.

Assuming you had a "transport card" allowing you to travel up to the city, the view you would see from the balcony was, in reality, a high-altitude photo of a dry river basin in Saudi Arabia. U.S. astronaut Ed White shot the image in 1965 while engaged in EVA (extravehicular activity) far above Earth. The maneuver—the first-ever American space walk—took place during the *Gemini IV* space mission.

"This troubled planet is a place of the most violent contrasts. Those who receive the rewards are totally separated from those who shoulder the burdens. It is not a wise leadership."
—Spock

A remastered version of the floating city by the artists at CBS Digital, as interpreted by *Star Trek* authors Michael and Denise Okuda:

The magnificent castle in the sky was a home worthy of Ardana's greatest artists, scientists, and scholars. Here among the clouds, they were free to pursue their studies, unfettered by mundane, worldly concerns. But the jewel of Ardanan society concealed a dark secret. Few knew that those who had toiled so long to build the glittering acropolis were unfairly denied its benefits. Even fewer knew of the shocking barbarism that brutalized the lives of those workers. It was an injustice that would soon rock Ardanan society to its very roots. And in the process, a vital mission of mercy would be placed in jeopardy, endangering the life of every living thing on the planet Merak II.

331

THE WAY TO EDEN

Spock: "One."
Sevrin: "We are One."
Spock: "One is the beginning."
Adam: "Are you One, Herbert?"
Spock: "I am not Herbert."
Adam: "He is not Herbert. We reach."

After the *Enterprise* apprehends the crew of a stolen space cruiser, Kirk learns that one of them is the young son of the Catuallan ambassador to the Federation. Because the Federation and Catualla are currently engaged in a crucial phase of treaty negotiations, Kirk has no choice but to treat the free-spirited transgressors with kid gloves as the *Enterprise* travels toward a starbase where the captain can drop them off. The idealistic group is led by Dr. Sevrin, a brilliant engineer who claims to be looking for the mythical planet of Eden, and although Spock admires Sevrin and supports some of his theories, he comes to believe that the man is quite mad. Kirk has Sevrin placed in protective confinement, but his followers—who have, with Spock's

assistance, located their potential "Eden" within Romulan territory— plot to free Sevrin and steal a shuttle. Meanwhile, Sevrin comes up with a plan to prevent the *Enterprise* crew from following them.

332

"The Way to Eden" was extensively revised after D. C. Fontana delivered her original draft for the episode to the producers. Initially titled "Joanna," the story Fontana had in mind would have introduced viewers to McCoy's estranged daughter, Joanna, suggested in the writers' guide but never seen. In Fontana's original concept, the younger female McCoy is one of the "space hippies" whom the *Enterprise* picks up. McCoy isn't at all happy to see her; Joanna's been telling him that she was studying to be a nurse, and here she is, traveling around with Dr. Sevrin and his strange tribe! To make matters worse, Kirk and Joanna get along, shall we say, rather well—talk about a father's worst nightmare. The rest of the story follows "Eden's" basic lines: Sevrin is searching for "Nirvana" (rather than Eden), and he's determined to get there, with or without Kirk's assistance. Joanna helps the tribe to gain control of the ship. The planet they find isn't literally poisonous, but it isn't livable either, and Kirk manages to get them to come back to the *Enterprise*. McCoy and Joanna eventually have a rapprochement similar to that of Chekov and Irina in the filmed episode.

All of which, with the usual fine-tuning, was likely to have turned out better than "The Way to Eden." But after turning in the draft, Fontana was told by the producer that McCoy was not old enough to have a twenty-one-year-old daughter, because he was Kirk's "contemporary." Fontana was incensed that the new guard didn't care enough about the series to sit down and read the show's existing writers' guide. Clearly, they didn't get it—and they didn't care.

"So I decided to wash my hands of it and move on to other things," says Fontana. "I wrote a lot of westerns after that, and the nice thing was that other producers seemed to respect what we did on *Star Trek*. They didn't think of it as a science fiction show. To them, it was a good show about characters and situations."

But while Fontana was gone, the episode moved forward, substituting Chekov's former classmate/love interest "Irina Galliulin" for Joanna. At Fontana's request, her name was dropped from the credits and replaced with the pseudonym she would also use on "That Which Survives": Michael Richards.

Kirk: "What makes you so sympathetic toward them?"
Spock: "It is not sympathy so much as curiosity, Captain. A wish to understand. They regard themselves as aliens in their own worlds, a condition with which I am somewhat familiar."

If there was a "generation gap" between baby boomers and their parents during the 1960s, there was a bigger one between the boomers and the MBAs in Hollywood's executive suites, who never got a handle on how to bring to the screen the colorful and vibrant idealism of that era's youth movement. More often than not, the end result was something like "The Way to Eden," colorful in garments if not in personality, with "space hippies" providing idealistic clichés more embarrassing than profound. All of which served to make Spock's interest in Sevrin's flowery group seem more than a little out of character. That the erudite, buttoned-down Vulcan was willing to jam with them in the rec area was peculiar enough, but his effortless facility with the pseudo hippie-speak used by the tribe brings to mind the sincere "Oh stewardess, I speak jive" scene in the movie *Airplane!*—spoken by the actress who had played fictional small-town homemaker June Cleaver in *Leave It to Beaver*.

Spock's interest in the search for Eden—as mythical a location as they come—is equally difficult to comprehend. Isn't this the sort of "pursuit of undomesticated aquatic fowl" that Spock would find illogical? Well, yes, but one got the sense that there was an underlying reason for Spock's fascination with the subject. And sure enough, exactly twenty years later, when *Star Trek V: The Final Frontier* appeared on the big screen, it suddenly made sense. There is a black sheep in Spock's family: his older half brother Sybok, who left home to pursue his visions of the mythical planet Sha Ka Ree, from which, according to Vulcan legend, creation sprang.

In other words, Eden.

Ah! It was in the blood all along!

REQUIEM FOR METHUSELAH

As an outbreak of deadly Rigelian fever spreads through the *Enterprise*, Kirk, Spock, and McCoy beam down to the planet Holberg 917G in search of ryetalyn, the disease's only known cure. Holberg has only two occupants: a reclusive man named Flint, and Rayna, his beautiful young ward. Flint is openly hostile, but he agrees to provide Kirk with the ryetalyn after Rayna expresses an interest in meeting the landing party. As the ryetalyn is being processed, Spock is surprised by Flint's astounding art collection, which contains original pieces by Leonardo da Vinci; meanwhile, Kirk takes an interest in Rayna. But the landing party begins to suspect that Flint is delaying delivery of the precious drug, and that his hospitality disguises an ulterior motive.

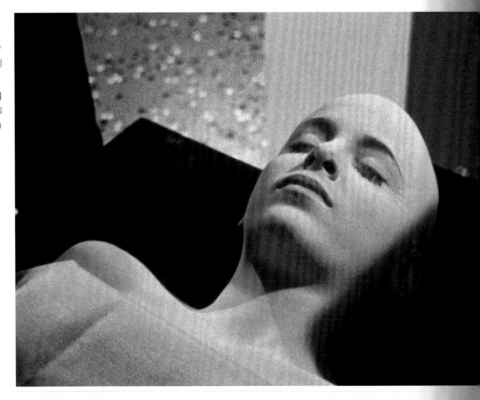

"Captain, something else which is rather extraordinary. This waltz I just played is by Johannes Brahms. . . . It is written in manuscript. In original manuscript, in Brahms's own hand, which I recognize. It is totally unknown, definitely the work of Brahms, and yet unknown."
—Spock

"Flint," as he refers to himself in "Requiem for Methuselah," was born some six thousand years ago in Earth's Mesopotamian region. Kirk, McCoy, and Spock are startled to discover that Flint not only *knew* some of the greatest minds in history, he *was* one . . . or actually, several, including Leonardo, Solomon, Alexander the Great, Lazarus, Methuselah, and even the mythical Merlin. Spock seems particularly taken by Flint's recent "Brahmsian" compositions—so taken that he sits down and plays a waltz on a convenient piano.

Credited with creating the Brahmsian paraphrase for the episode was Ivan Ditmars, a composer, orchestra leader, and musical director who worked in radio and television from the 1940s through the early 1980s. One of Ditmars's longest musical gigs was on the popular TV game show *Let's Make a Deal*. Like many shows of the era, the music on *Deal* was live, and it was Ditmars's job to come in each day and score the melodies that would be performed on the air. At showtime, he would play piano and organ while conducting three other musicians. He was with the game show from its debut in 1963 through 1976, when the production moved from Los Angeles to Las Vegas and switched to prerecorded music.

336

The original version of Flint's castle was a reuse of the beautiful matte painting created by Albert Whitlock for "The Cage." For *Star Trek*'s remastered episodes, the artists at CBS Digital reinterpreted a number of such "visual reruns" to give each episode a unique identity.

And to accompany it, one last literary portrait, as provided by Michael and Denise Okuda:

> *Weary of the human experience, the immortal man finally fled his homeworld, seeking solitude on a distant planet. In splendid isolation on Holberg 917G, Flint would never again suffer the insanities of Earth society; the petty jealousies, the endless trivialities, and the horrors of war. He spent years constructing his personal fortress. Ironically inspired by Earth's Renaissance architecture, Flint designed his castle to provide for his every need and to facilitate his every intellectual pursuit. Equally important, it would protect him from meddlesome intruders and curiosity-seekers. Yet when it was finished, Flint found to his great surprise that his life was still lacking. The man who had lived a thousand lifetimes discovered he still needed a woman's love.*

337

# 337

"I feel sorrier for you than I do for him, because you'll never know the things that love can drive a man to. The ecstasies. The miseries. The broken rules. The desperate chances, the glorious failures, the glorious victories. All of these things you'll never know simply because the word 'love' isn't written into your book."
—McCoy

Doctor McCoy often needles Mister Spock about his lack of emotions, a criticism the Vulcan usually ignores. In the closing scene of "Requiem for Methuselah," after McCoy lectures Spock about his inability to comprehend love, he remarks, almost as an aside, that he wishes the grieving Kirk could forget about the lovely android Rayna.

After McCoy departs, Spock approaches the slumbering captain, places his fingers at Kirk's temple, and murmurs just one word: "Forget." Fans immediately understand two things: that Spock has just implanted a subconscious instruction, telling Kirk to "forget" the pain of loving and losing Rayna; and also that Spock understands at least one kind of love—brotherly love.

It's an intriguing moment, one that neatly parallels Spock's meld with McCoy at the end of *Star Trek II: The Wrath of Khan*, when he instructs the doctor to "remember." It is only in the subsequent film, *Star Trek III: The Search for Spock*, that viewers learn Spock has placed his own *katra*—or living spirit—into his friend McCoy's subconscious for safekeeping.

Yet, as touching as these scenes are, there's something slightly "off" about both moments. Is it ethical for Spock to impose his *katra* on the doctor *without asking*? Similarly, is it right for Spock to manipulate Kirk's memories in order to ease his best friend's pain? One suspects that Kirk would say no, given that, as he later insists in the film *Star Trek V: The Final Frontier*, "I need my pain."

Ironically, both acts serve to prove one thing: Spock is definitely capable of comprehending—and falling subject to—"the broken rules" and "the desperate chances" of love.

338

THE SAVAGE CURTAIN

"Despite the seeming contradictions, all is as it appears to be. I am Abraham Lincoln."
—*Abraham Lincoln*

As the *Enterprise* surveys the planet Excalbia, someone or something on that planet also is scanning the *Enterprise*. Not long after, an extremely lifelike manifestation of Abraham Lincoln appears in space, asking to be beamed aboard. This facsimile of the former president has been sent by the inhabitants of Excalbia with an invitation to visit the planet. There, Kirk, Spock, and "Lincoln" encounter a rocklike creature that wishes to learn about human concepts of "good" and "evil." The *Enterprise* duo—plus the ersatz Lincoln and a facsimile of Surak, the father of Vulcan philosophy—representing good, are pitted against the likenesses of Genghis Khan, the Klingon Kahless, criminal scientist Zora, and Colonel Green, the despotic leader of a genocidal war. And if Kirk and Spock choose not to participate, the Excalbian tells them, the *Enterprise* will be destroyed.

Abraham Lincoln: "What a charming Negress. Oh, forgive me, my dear. I know in my time some used that term as a description of property." Uhura: "But why should I object to that term, sir? In our century, we've learned not to fear words."

Gene Roddenberry, it has been reported, held great admiration for President Abraham Lincoln, and his words and actions during the creation of *Star Trek* testify to that fact. While president, Lincoln wrote the Emancipation Proclamation, the document that freed the slaves in the South, and Roddenberry adhered to the philosophy behind it. From the start, Roddenberry steadfastly insisted that his starship's command crew include persons of all races, unlike the standard Caucasian monopoly that populated the majority of 1960s television shows. The producer also confirmed his belief, in the simplest of terms, when he created the Vulcan philosophy of IDIC, "Infinite Diversity in Infinite Combinations."

So it is only fitting that the single script Roddenberry contributed to *Star Trek*'s final season would include Abraham Lincoln interacting with the characters he himself had created. Unfortunately, the story seems a bit unrealistic, given that Lincoln, the great orator, is forced into hand-to-hand combat while the more powerful weapon of his words remains sheathed.

As the series geared down, Roddenberry and Majel Barrett made plans for their future together by starting a company that would distribute *Star Trek* memorabilia. The name Roddenberry chose for the company: Lincoln Enterprises. The uniting of those two words—one the name of his hero, the other a variant on the name of his starship—reveals how much each meant to the producer.

Prior to his introduction in "The Savage Curtain," the character
"Surak of Vulcan" had never been mentioned on *Star Trek*. Spock
introduces him to Kirk here as "the greatest of all who ever lived on
our planet . . . the father of all we became." Surak then shows himself to be a man of peace, which costs him, or at least this facsimile of him, his life. But he proved to be such an intriguing character
that mentions of him and his philosophy would remain popular topics
of discussion among fans for decades—even though the great man
himself would not appear on the screen again for thirty-five years.
The "Father of Vulcan" showed up at last—albeit as a *katra*-inspired
vision within the mind of Captain Jonathan Archer—during the final
season of the series *Star Trek: Enterprise*.

   The Klingon character of Kahless—whose "image" also appeared
in "The Savage Curtain"—turned out to be a similarly illusory character. His reappearance twenty-four years later, however, would find him
a changed man, no longer the "bad guy" of "Curtain" but a far more
honorable Klingon of the type that populated the kinder, gentler universe of *Star Trek: The Next Generation*. This Kahless, it would be revealed, founded the mighty Klingon Empire and wrote the laws that
unite its warriors. However, he was no more the real thing than the
Kahless that Kirk encountered on Excalbia. It turns out that the *TNG*
representation of Kahless was a clone of the real warrior.

341

ALL OUR YESTERDAYS

"I am behaving disgracefully. I have eaten animal flesh, and I've enjoyed it. What is wrong with me?"
—Spock

The star Beta Niobe is about to go nova; when it does, Sarpeidon, the only planet in the Beta Niobe system, will be destroyed. The planet is known to be the home of an advanced human civilization, yet when the *Enterprise* arrives, sensors show no sign of its inhabitants. Kirk, Spock, and McCoy beam to the surface and find it deserted—except for a librarian named Atoz, who explains that he has used the atavachron, an artificial time portal, to send the residents into various eras of their own distant past. Invited by Mr. Atoz to use the atavachron to examine the different historical eras, the *Enterprise* trio inadvertently passes through the portal into Sarpeidon's past: Kirk to an era equivalent to Earth's seventeenth century, where strangers like him were regarded with suspicion, and Spock and McCoy into the planet's deadly ice age. Kirk's attempts to find his way back to the library lead the locals to believe he's a witch, and he's thrown in jail. In the meantime, thousands of years earlier, Spock carries a frostbitten

McCoy to a cave inhabited by a beautiful exile named Zarabeth. She explains that they cannot go back to their own time, because the atavachron automatically alters their cellular structure when they pass through the portal. If they attempt to return, they'll die.

342

342

"Are you trying to kill me, Spock? Is that what you really want? Think. What are you feeling? Rage? Jealousy? Have you ever had those feelings before?"
—McCoy

When Spock and McCoy are tossed five thousand years into the past, Spock displays passionate emotions and violent mood swings. The two men eventually come to the conclusion that the Vulcan is reverting to a "warlike barbarian," just like his ancestors of that early era. But what of McCoy? He's in the same situation, and yet he doesn't seem to be reverting at all; he's still the same grouchy humanitarian that *Star Trek*'s viewers had grown to know and love.

Perhaps it's because humans, as opposed to Vulcans, have pretty much *always* been barbarians (at least, that's how Kirk explains *his* behavior in "A Taste of Armageddon"). Oh, they've had a few achievements scattered here and there between wars and more personal acts of violence. They built great monuments (often using slave labor), domesticated wild horses (which they used to conquer their neighbors), developed agriculture (and plundered the food stocks of other nations). In other words, it was pretty much business as usual for McCoy—which may be why there was such a big contrast between him and his favorite Vulcan, whose culture changed far more drastically over the millennia.

"All Our Yesterdays" throws *Star Trek*'s top trio into jeopardy with a story line that includes time travel, separation, isolation, injury, and even personality disruption, all standard plot devices used throughout the series. And yet, the episode stands out for a specific reason: It's a love story in which Mister Spock gets the girl.

Spock fell in love once before, in "This Side of Paradise," but only because he was under the influence of microscopic spores. This time he's not under the influence of anything artificial—particularly not the restrictive emotional restraints that Vulcans have so carefully adopted over the millennia. Freed from those shackles, Spock's inner personality emerges, giving him the freedom to kiss, to hold, to fall in love. Seeing the Vulcan behave so "humanly," and watching Leonard Nimoy shake the cobwebs off what had become by this time a set-in-stone type of performance, is a distinct pleasure.

Strangely, it's the usually overemotional McCoy who is the most levelheaded leg of this arctic ménage, and he makes it clear that he just doesn't trust the beautiful Zarabeth. "She would do anything to prevent that life of loneliness," he tells Spock. "She would lie. She would cheat. She would even murder me, the captain, the entire crew of the *Enterprise* to keep you here with her!"

In the end, of course, as in many great romantic dramas (think: "The City on the Edge of Forever"), Spock is destined to lose Zarabeth. In fact, that his love would be short-lived was predicted in the title, derived from Shakespeare's line from *Macbeth*, "And all our yesterdays have lighted fools the way to dusty death. Out, out, brief candle!"

A happier fate awaited Mariette Hartley, the talented actress who played Zarabeth. Although she performed in several films, Hartley spent most of her career in television, and audiences of a certain age likely will recall her as the teasing costar with James Garner in the extremely popular Polaroid commercials that the pair made in the late 1970s. The chemistry between the two was so engaging that millions of Americans became convinced they were actually husband and wife (they weren't). To fans of all things related to *Star Trek*, however, Hartley was equally memorable as the mutant Lyra-a in *Genesis II*, a two-hour made-for-TV movie written and produced by Gene Roddenberry in 1973. *Genesis II* was one of several science fiction pilots that Roddenberry created post-*Star Trek*. None, however, made it to series. Hartley's character in *Genesis II* was a denizen of the twenty-second century who possessed a dual circulatory system, with two hearts . . . and two navels—alleged to be Roddenberry's revenge against the years of being told by NBC's Standards and Practices department to hide *Star Trek* actresses' navels (including Hartley's as Zarabeth).

In addition to her acting career, Hartley actively dedicates her energies to the field of suicide prevention.

The files in Mr. Atoz's library appear to be early versions of CDs or DVDs—shiny discs that, when inserted into a machine, display the recorded information encoded onto them. The similar appearance makes it fun to speculate whether these props from "All Our Yesterdays" may have influenced the CD's inventors. The speculation, however, proves unfounded.

The man behind the real discs was American physicist, inventor, and music lover James T. Russell, who was irked by the inevitable scratches that threatened his collection of vinyl records. Russell hoped to find a sturdier medium for storing music, and his employer, Battelle Memorial Institute, supported his search for a digital solution. Russell soon realized that representing the binary 0 and 1 with tiny "bits" of dark and light would allow a laser device to read sounds (or any information) without damaging the source. By making the binary code extremely compact, he managed to fit large amounts of digital data—music—onto a "compact disc." Russell started his research in 1965, well before "All Our Yesterdays" aired on March 14, 1969, although his digital-to-optical recording and playback system was not patented until 1970.

TURNABOUT INTRUDER

The *Enterprise* receives a distress call from the planet Camus II, where a group of scientists who were exploring the ruins of a dead civilization is reported to be dying of radiation exposure. The expedition leader is a woman named Janice Lester, an old flame of Kirk's from his days at Starfleet Academy. Lester has come to despise the captain because he was able to achieve what she never could: command of a starship. When Kirk and McCoy beam down, they learn that most of Lester's party already has passed away, and Lester herself seems to be on the verge of death. But Kirk learns too late that Lester apparently has faked her illness—and killed her own staff—to lure Kirk into a trap. She's discovered an alien device on Camus II that is capable of swapping minds between two individuals. Before Kirk knows what's happening, she's incapacitated him and transferred her mind to Kirk's body and his to hers. At long last, she will be captain of the *Enterprise*! But in order to hang on to this hard-won victory, she must take care of one final detail: kill Kirk.

"Your world of starship captains doesn't admit women. It isn't fair."
—Janice Lester

Considering how forward-thinking the producers of *Star Trek* were, it seems ironic that the final episode of the series—indeed, one in which Gene Roddenberry received story credit—had at its core the premise that women were not fit to command starships. This from a man whose original template for *Star Trek* ("The Cage") placed a female first officer on the bridge of the *Enterprise*, suggesting that Starfleet considered a woman capable of commanding a starship—at least when the captain wasn't around.

Avid followers of the show did not want to accept Lester at her word when she lamented that females were excluded from Kirk's "world of starship captains." Surely she was just referring to Kirk, saying, in effect, "I couldn't be a permanent part of your life because you're a captain and you have no room in your life for a significant other." But that's a weak argument considering Kirk's response to Lester's original statement: "No, it isn't (fair). And you punished and tortured me because of it."

Kirk supports the truth of Lester's statement, although it seems he doesn't necessarily support Starfleet's stand. Roddenberry himself was in a similar position. The powers that be at NBC had decreed that he couldn't put a woman in command, and he'd yielded in that battle. It's conceivable that he was addressing that conflict as a parting shot: It isn't Kirk (or him) who's sexist, it's Kirk's superiors (read: the network).

Years later, however, when questioned about Lester's statement, Roddenberry admitted that the line was simply sexist. He made up for it in *Star Trek: The Next Generation*, establishing a number of female captains and even female admirals within Starfleet. Roddenberry's successors took things even further, contradicting *The Original Series* with the character of Starfleet Captain Erika Hernandez in *Star Trek: Enterprise*—which takes place a hundred years before Kirk's time.

As *Star Trek* finales go, "Turnabout Intruder" doesn't seem to measure up to the "last acts" later offered by the producers of subsequent *Star Trek* series: *Star Trek: The Next Generation*, *Star Trek: Deep Space Nine*, *Star Trek: Voyager*, and *Star Trek: Enterprise*. To be fair, however, those series had advance notice that they would be ending their respective runs, which gave their producers time to plan for a finale that would be jam-packed with action, suspense, danger, and a guaranteed lump-in-the-throat finish. When "Turnabout Intruder" went into production, cast and crew were hoping against hope to hear that there would be a fourth season for the show. Alas, the show's death knell was sounded not long after the episode wrapped. Despite the absence of a heroic send-off, everyone involved in the episode gave 100 percent, especially William Shatner, who came down with a bad case of the flu during filming.

The behind-the-scenes crew had given the script the joking title "Captain Kirk, Space Queen"; it was up to Shatner to *avoid* camping up his performance to the point where the episode was no longer *Star Trek*. That couldn't have been easy for a man who loves to make others laugh; anyone who's spent time with the actor knows how much he enjoys playing or telling a joke. While there indeed was on-set clowning associated with the episode, when the cameras rolled, all signs of a campy drag queen disappeared, and William Shatner disappeared into Captain Kirk—or rather, Captain Kirk as possessed by a half-crazed, power-mad female. Shatner's performance—altering the tone of his voice, his mannerisms, the range of his facial expressions, even the way he stood—revealed his early theatrical training and made the episode memorable in its own unique way.

"Her life could have been as rich as any woman's, if only. If only."
—Kirk

When Kirk starts to behave erratically in "Turnabout Intruder," McCoy insists that the captain report to sickbay for a thorough examination. The exam doesn't establish anything about Kirk's increasingly bizarre actions, but it does provide an ironic visual symmetry to the series. The first episode of *Star Trek* to be filmed following the two pilots, "The Corbomite Maneuver," was also the first to feature DeForest Kelley as Doctor McCoy. During a scene in which McCoy gives a bare-chested Kirk a stress test on what appears to be an upside-down stair-climber, viewers got their first taste of McCoy's gruff but instantly likable personality and his stubborn belief that a doctor's responsibility to his patient trumps that of a chief medical officer to his captain.

Flash-forward to the very last episode of *Star Trek*, and viewers find the two men poised in the same positions, performing the same activities, but the mood is much darker. There's none of the humorous interplay viewers saw before. It's emblematic of the change of tone in the series itself during its third season, nowhere so apparent as in this episode, which has absolutely none of *Star Trek*'s trademark light moments. No funny verbal sparring between McCoy and Spock. No humorous comment from Kirk to the bridge crew as the ship heads for its next destination. The episode—and the series—ends as McCoy escorts the insane Janice Lester, now back in her own body, down a corridor, and Kirk, Spock, and Scotty enter a turbolift, presumably heading back to work. Kirk expresses regret, and a bit of guilt, over Lester's breakdown. Spock says something mildly reassuring. Scotty says nothing.

And the door closes.

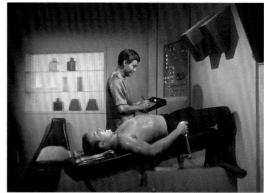

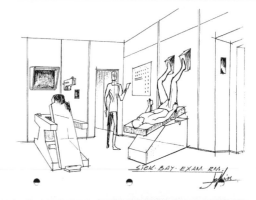

SICK·BAY·EXAM·RM·1

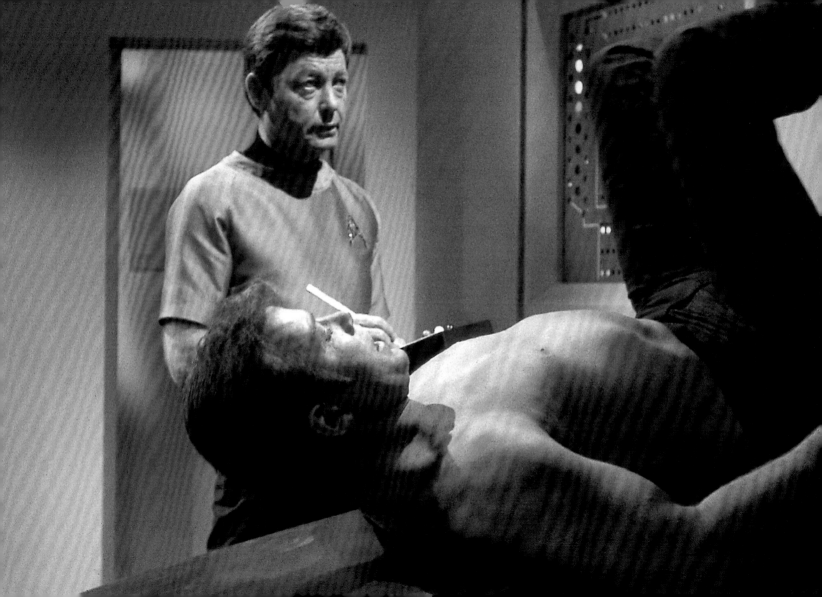

During *Star Trek*'s prime-time run on network television, licensing deals for series-based toys were scarce, most likely because *Star Trek* was considered adult (as in grown-up) entertainment. Initial *Star Trek* tie-ins included the highly collectible black-and-white Leaf trading cards and an adventure board game from Ideal. Model maker AMT, sensing a classic in the making, leaped into the fray early on, creating reproductions of the *Enterprise*, other *Star Trek*–related spacecraft, and even a much-prized model of Mister Spock blasting a presumably non-sentient, three-headed alien serpent.

Forty-plus years later, the AMT originals are considered retro chic, and licensed reproductions created from the models' original tooling recently have hit the marketplace in vintage-style packaging that uses the spectacularly kitschy old artwork.

It was only after *Star Trek* caught fire in syndication during the 1970s that children—and toy makers—really took a shine to Kirk and company. In their haste to take advantage of the burgeoning marketplace for all things *Trek*, however, some manufacturers seemed all too eager to slap the show's logo onto products they were already making for other franchises. They may have assumed, not altogether incorrectly, that a child may not really care if it made sense for *Star Trek* crew members to possess a utility belt (well, it made more sense than the ones that were merchandised for the Hulk and Mickey Mouse). Or if it seemed appropriate for Captain Kirk to become a "Sky Diving Parachutist."

On the other hand, AHI (Arzak-Hamway International), manufacturer of the parachuting toys, simply may have been ahead of its time—several decades ahead, in fact: In a scene that was cut from the general release of the 1994 film *Star Trek Generations*, *Star Trek* fans would learn that Captain Kirk is a big fan of orbital skydiving.

For most of the 1970s, the Mego Corporation led the pack in the manufacture of *Star Trek* toys. The company made a whole line of *Star Trek* branded products, including a tricorder, communicator set, command console, telescreen console, super phaser target game, and even a working calculator, dubbed "the Trekulator." But the product line perhaps is best remembered for introducing the first-ever *Star Trek* action figures, which appealed both to children *and* to the teenagers and young adults who had been fans of the series since day one. They would set the standard for action figure collectibles in the decades to come.

Mego's first set of eight-inch-tall plastic figures—Kirk, Spock, McCoy, Scotty, and a nameless Klingon—was released in 1974. Fans were impressed with the likenesses of the tiny crew members, which came with their own phasers and communicators (Spock and McCoy also carried tricorders). Uhura followed later that year, and subsequently, eight *Star Trek* aliens.

The likenesses on the alien series of figures were hit or miss. The Andorian, the Romulan, and even the figure representing a native of Cheron (from "Let That Be Your Last Battlefield") were quite good. The rest, however, missed the mark by a light-year. According to www.megomuseum.com, a Web site dedicated to the commemoration of all things Mego, the Gorn was "the only figure in Mego's entire eight-inch arsenal that is assembled completely from recycled parts." His

head came from the Lizard, a character in Mego's Marvel roster of characters, while his body was that of a Soldier Ape, derived from its *Planet of the Apes* line. To add insult to injury, he was garbed in the same duds as Mego's *Star Trek* Klingon figure. Mego fared no better with its figures from "The Cage"/"The Menagerie": The Keeper figure looks less like the diminutive inhabitant of Talos IV who held Captain Pike captive than a truly creepy version of Balok from "The Corbomite Maneuver." "Talos," on the other hand, while apparently a Talosian just like the Keeper, has proportions that hew closer to his television counterpart, but for some reason he's wearing a garish clown suit. Strangest of all was "the Neptunian," the only figure in the line that *never* appeared in an episode of *Star Trek*.

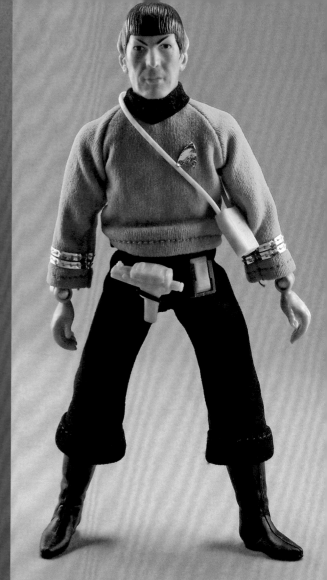

"Materialize us aboard at once, Mister Spock! Giant trees are trying to germinate us!"
—Kirk, Gold Key's Star Trek no. 1, "Planet of No Return"

Fondly remembered by some, scoffed at by others, Gold Key's lengthy run of *Star Trek* comic books (sixty-one issues published between 1967 and 1979) is surpassed only by the longevity of the *Star Trek* franchise at DC Comics through the 1980s and 1990s. However, Gold Key—part of Western Publishing—bears the distinction of being the very first publisher to present the adventures of Kirk and company in graphic form. And the fact that Gold Key began its run while new episodes of the television series were still airing earns the comic book series additional points from collectors. Although the plot twists and tech details sometimes drifted far afield from what viewers familiar with *Star Trek* might have expected, the comics were never boring, and on occasion, some stories were genuinely thought-provoking.

The first nine issues of the Gold Key comic series were published with photo covers; after that, each issue sported a well-executed painted cover. Maybe the characters didn't quite look like the actors who played them—the artists weren't always familiar with the source material—but in those days, buyers couldn't get more bang for their buck (actually, just fifteen cents each for most of the early issues)!

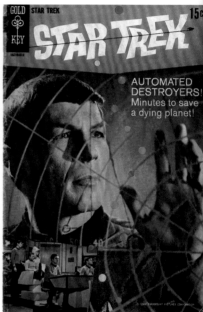

Publishing has long been an important category for branded *Star Trek* merchandise. Licensed books and comics first appeared in the marketplace during *The Original Series'* second season and have continued for more than forty years. In many ways, publishing can be considered a lifeline for *Star Trek* fans, keeping them interested in the adventures of their favorite characters even when no new *Star Trek* television show or movie is on their screens.

The Making of Star Trek, published in 1968, was the first recorded history of the series and one of the first books of its kind. The author was Stephen E. Poe (writing as Stephen E. Whitfield), an employee of AMT who was so smitten by early film clips of the brand-new NBC series that he not only negotiated a deal for AMT to manufacture *Star Trek* models, but also snared a commitment from Desilu and Gene Roddenberry that allowed him to write a behind-the-scenes look at the show.

The first *Star Trek* novel, *Mission to Horatius*, also came out in 1968. Published by Whitman Books, whose parent company, Western Publishing, also produced the Gold Key *Star Trek* comic books, this hardcover was targeted at young readers. The first novel intended for an older audience was *Spock Must Die!*, published in 1970 by Bantam Books. It was written by respected science fiction author James Blish, who earlier had adapted all of *Star Trek*'s episodes into short stories for twelve volumes of Bantam compilations. During the period

before *Star Trek: The Motion Picture* debuted, Bantam filled the literary pipeline with a dozen "Fotonovels" (adaptations of *Star Trek* episodes generously illustrated with photos from those shows), thirteen original novels, and two short story anthologies (*Star Trek: The New Voyages*). The anthologies bear a footnote in history primarily because the contents were written by fans who were, for the first time, being paid to write about subject matter they adored. Many had been filling the pages of fanzines for years; now some of them would "go pro" and become familiar names to the book-buying public.

Also published during this era were two loving portraits of *Star Trek* fandom: *The Making of the Trek Conventions* (by Joan Winston) and *Star Trek Lives!* (by Winston, Jacqueline Lichtenberg, and Sondra Marshak); Ballantine's adaptations of *Star Trek: The Animated Series* episodes (all written by Alan Dean Foster, who would go on to write the story for the first *Star Trek* film); and the *Star Trek Concordance*, an indispensable encyclopedic compilation of story lines, characters, aliens, ships, planets, and technology of *The Original Series*. Written by Bjo Trimble with the assistance of Dorothy Jones Heydt, the book was adapted from a fan publication that Bjo and Dorothy had been distributing for several years and featured pen-and-ink sketches rendered by avid followers of the show, including Greg Bear, Greg Jein, George Barr, and Alicia Austin, all of whom soon would become respected professionals in the fantasy and science fiction genres.

Since the late 1930s, readers of science fiction literature have gathered at conventions to discuss their favorite books and authors. Early in *Star Trek*'s genesis, Gene Roddenberry recognized that such events were fertile ground in which to plant seeds of interest in his series, and he attended several of them.

But by the early 1970s, with episodes syndicated in 170 television markets and the show's popularity exploding, *Star Trek* had worn out its welcome with hard-core science fiction fans. The "purists" at conventions openly began to frown upon the "interlopers" among them who wanted to talk *Trek* instead of literature. Thus, in 1971, New York fans Elyse Pines and Devra Langsam broached the idea of holding their own convention, a gathering where they could discuss *Star Trek* "with no one to sneer," recalls Langsam.

The pair contacted Joan Winston, another fan of the series. Winston worked in television; she had visited the *Star Trek* set while the show was in production and had met Gene Roddenberry. Soon the trio and several like-minded friends assembled a "convention committee." They picked a date (January 21-23, 1972) and a location (the Statler Hilton Hotel in Manhattan). Ticket prices were set at $2.50 in advance, $3.50 at the door.

Hoping to find speakers for the "little" event, Pines called writer Isaac Asimov, and Winston contacted Gene Roddenberry, who confirmed that he would come, along with his wife, Majel Barrett-Roddenberry, and *Star Trek* writer D. C. Fontana. Roddenberry promised to bring a copy of the never-before-seen first pilot, "The Cage," along with a blooper reel of outtakes from the series. Paramount Pictures offered to send 16mm copies of episodes to be screened. And NASA arranged for its touring lunar module exhibit to make an appearance.

Meanwhile, a steady stream of letters flowed in, requesting tickets. "We had a post office box," Langsam recalls, "and one day we went to pick up the mail and there were only a few envelopes in the box. I thought, 'Oh rats.' But as we turned around to leave, the guy working behind the counter shouted, 'Oh, no, no! Don't leave! You're the *Star Trek*! Wait a minute!' And he dragged out two full mail bags!"

On Friday, January 21, more than two hundred people were standing in line *six hours* before the doors were scheduled to open. By Sunday afternoon, the committee had sold upwards of three thousand tickets. At that point, à la Woodstock, they allowed everyone without a ticket to enter free of charge. The fans in attendance were friendly and cooperative and, more importantly, highly appreciative of everyone's efforts. But according to the late Joan Winston, no one seemed more affected by the impact of the event than Gene Roddenberry. "Gene looked stunned," Winston said. "He kept mumbling, 'I just don't believe it. All these great people coming here to honor *Star Trek*.'"

With a year to recuperate and the (extremely enthusiastic) encouragement of fans who wanted to repeat the 1972 experience, the con committee for the first *Star Trek* convention set plans for the second one into motion. The date: February 16–19, 1973; the place: New York's Commodore Hotel, a larger venue than the Statler Hilton, mandated by an anticipated attendance in excess of five thousand. The final tally for the convention was, in fact, sixty-two hundred. Guests included actors Leonard Nimoy, James Doohan, George Takei, and Mark Lenard (the calm eye of the human hurricane in the smaller image at right); *Star Trek* writers D. C. Fontana and David Gerrold; science fiction writers Hal Clement and Isaac Asimov; and an amazing full-scale re-creation of the *Enterprise* bridge, built by fans Mike McMaster and Art Brumaghim of Poughkeepsie, New York. Once again, the gathering was an unqualified success, thus guaranteeing that *Star Trek* conventions both large and small would continue to be held *somewhere* across the United States (and in numerous nations around the globe) every single year well into the next millennium.

Among the convention pioneers pictured on the bridge facsimile are members of the 1973 con committee, including Devra Langsam (top row, far left), Joyce Yasner (top row, center), Elyse Pines (center, with hand on James Doohan's shoulder), and Joan Winston (bottom row, left); also guests Hal Clement (top row, second from left), George Takei (top row, third from right),David Gerrold (middle row, far left), D. C. Fontana (middle row, in turtleneck), and Doohan (in the captain's chair).

Virtually every *Star Trek* convention has a costume competition. Fans take the challenge of creating a *Star Trek* costume very seriously, whether it's a highly detailed "salt vampire" reproduction or some unique vision of an unexplored aspect of the *Star Trek* universe. The results are as one might expect. Some are truly dazzling, suggesting that the designer should think seriously about taking up costuming as a career. Others are downright silly.

Star Trek's William Theiss (at center in the top image at far right) was a frequent guest at many of the early New York conventions. The highlight of his appearances was a fashion show of actual costumes from *The Original Series* and, occasionally, garments that he'd designed for other productions, such as the television movie *Genesis II*, which was written and produced by Gene Roddenberry. The models were typically members of the con committee or convention volunteers whose bodies best conformed to the dimensions of the actresses for whom the costumes originally were fitted. Included in the images at right are original costumes for "Elaan of Troyius" (at Theiss's immediate left); *Genesis II*'s Lyra-a (at Theiss's immediate right); "Wink of an Eye"'s Deela; "Is There in Truth No Beauty"'s Miranda Jones; "The *Enterprise* Incident"'s Romulan commander; and "Who Mourns for Adonais"'s Carolyn Palamas. The women reportedly bore the potentially embarrassing sartorial imposition with Starfleet-caliber courage and tongue-in-cheek pluck. Joyce Yasner,

the committee member chosen to model Carolyn's diaphanous Grecian gown, notes, "Overall the experience was a hoot, but honestly, what I remember best about that pink thing was the strategically placed double-sided tape that kept it from falling off!"

During President Gerald R. Ford's administration, NASA's Space Shuttle Program became a reality. The first shuttle scheduled to be built, designated OV-101 (for "Orbiter Vehicle"), was never meant to travel into space; it would be a prototype, equipped specifically for ground and low-altitude flight testing.

While the OV-101 was under construction, NASA Administrator James Fletcher referred to the vehicle as "*Constitution*," knowing that it would be ready for service in 1976, the nation's bicentennial. But that was before Fletcher became aware of Bjo Trimble's thoughts on the subject.

Like many *Star Trek* fans, Trimble and her husband, John, were major space fans, and they were eager to draw attention to the space program. "We thought the name *Enterprise* would catch the public's imagination," she explained. Drawing on the experience that the couple had acquired from their "Save *Star Trek*" letter-writing campaign, the Trimbles sent mimeographed instructions on how to run a mail campaign to twenty-three thousand fans, recommending that each person forward a copy to ten friends. The targeted address for the letters: the White House. Several months later, President Ford and Administrator Fletcher announced that the first shuttle would be renamed *Enterprise*.

On September 17, 1976, the *Enterprise* made its public debut when it was rolled out of the Rockwell plant in California. Among the special guests in attendance at the event: Gene Roddenberry, Leonard Nimoy, DeForest Kelley, James Doohan, George Takei, Nichelle Nichols, and Walter Koenig. As the ceremony started, the U.S. Air Force Band struck up Alexander Courage's *Star Trek* theme. Reportedly, there wasn't a dry eye in the gathered crowd.

As a test vehicle, the *Enterprise* flew several flights while mounted on the back of a modified 747, as well as five free flights, each launched from that 747; it landed four times on a dry lake bed and once on the concrete runway at Edwards Air Force Base in California. The pilot of the initial free flight was astronaut Fred Haise, making him the first captain of the space shuttle *Enterprise*.

In 1983 and 1984, the shuttle was taken "on the road," to air shows in France, Germany, Italy, England, Canada, and the World's Fair in New Orleans. Recruited once again for tests, the ship resided at Vandenberg Air Force Base in California and, later, the Kennedy Space Center in Florida. Then, on November 18, 1985, the *Enterprise* joined a fleet of other historic aircraft at the National Air and Space Museum. It now permanently sits on display in the Steven F. Udvar-Hazy Center, adjacent to Dulles International Airport, outside Washington, D.C.

During the filming of *Star Trek V: The Final Frontier*, critics began to suggest, for the first time, that perhaps the crew of the *Starship Enterprise* was growing a bit long in the tooth for their exploits in space. Even some members of the crew—one of whom had lived and died and lived again on-screen—seemed more cognizant of their own mortality, which may have prompted this recollection from actor Leonard Nimoy:

"In the early sixties, I was working on a job at MGM, and it was a lunch break. I was walking down the main street there, and I saw two guys, obviously doing a western, dressed in cowboy outfits, walking side by side, keeping stride. As they got a little closer, I began to hear their spurs, clink, clink, clink, coming down the street. When they got closer and I got a better look, I saw they were pretty well along in years—these were not kids—a couple of big old cowboys. And then I realized that it was Randolph Scott and Joel McCrea walking side by side. I got chills! They were working on Sam Peckinpah's picture *Ride the High Country*, a wonderful film that deals with a couple of old-time cowboys coming to the end of the line. And here they were, a couple of old-time cowboy actors coming to the end of *their* line.

"Now, every once in a while, when Bill and De and I are walking down the street on the lot, I'll see people looking at us, and I get that image in my head. And I wonder if people think about us—'Here they are, the old guys, walking down the street.'"

When Paramount Pictures donated the *U.S.S. Enterprise* studio model to the Smithsonian Institution's National Air and Space Museum in the early 1970s, it was merely a prop from a canceled three-season television series. No one envisioned the five additional series, the eleven feature films, all of the subsequent *Enterprise*s (for example, *Star Trek: The Next Generation*'s *Enterprise*-D), or *Star Trek*'s ever-expanding worldwide fan culture. The first conventions had only just been held—no one knew that the fervor would last, or that the birth of a genuine phenomenon had taken place.

Nor was the National Air and Space Museum what people recognize today. The Smithsonian acquired the *Enterprise* model for a "Life in the Universe" exhibit installed in the Arts and Industries Building (the museum's home before opening its flagship building on the National Mall in 1976).

The model arrived dirty, in pieces, trailing wires, and packed into the crates where it had spent the last five years. The images at right show the model during the restoration process. After museum staff reassembled it, the *Enterprise*'s history at the Smithsonian—and its path to recognition as a popular culture icon—began.

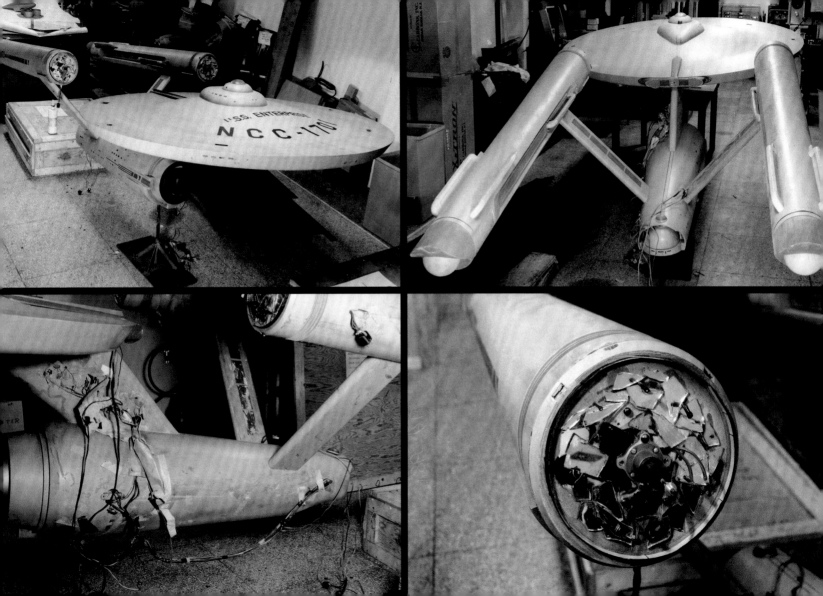

This is what it looks like inside one of the most famous fictional spaceships in history.

By 1999, the eleven-foot-long model of the *U.S.S. Enterprise* used in the original *Star Trek* television series had been displayed by the Smithsonian Institution's National Air and Space Museum for twenty-five years. Visitors and curators alike expressed concern about the model, which had not been built for exhibition. In particular, museum staff wondered about the stress factors created by permanently hanging a model that had been built to sit on a stand. They needed to look inside.

Before installing the *Enterprise* in a new case in the refurbished gift shop of the museum's National Mall building, curators took the model to Maryland QC Laboratories to be X-rayed. The results confirmed that using a stand was the best way to permanently display the starship. This composite view shows the engineering or secondary hull, including a question-mark-shaped eyebolt that supported a hanging point.

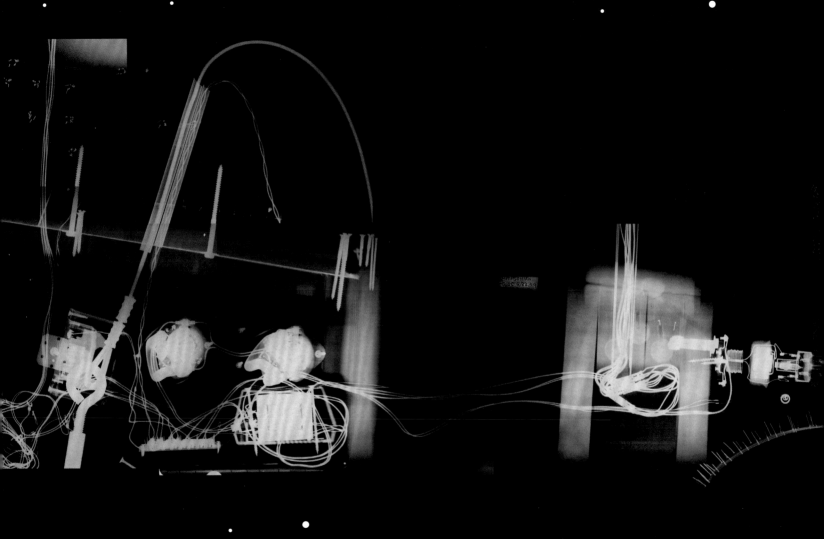

This is the actual eleven-foot-long model of the *Starship Enterprise* that was used during *Star Trek*'s original three-year run. When the show debuted, it was thought of as a kind of "space opera"—an action-adventure show set in space, but nothing more profound than that. But somewhere along the way, viewers became aware that there was more to the series than ray guns, miniskirts, and creatures in costumes that had zippers running down the back. The show's attention to current events and social issues of the day—subtly addressed in the scripts and also by virtue of an on-screen racially integrated cast of both males and females—cemented the series' place in television history and made the *Enterprise* a popular culture icon.

Since the Smithsonian Institution's National Air and Space Museum received the model from Paramount Pictures in 1974, the *Enterprise* has undergone several restorations. Installed in its current position on March 21, 2000, it now rests upon two stanchions specially built to hold it. The case protects the ship, while also presenting the model at eye level so that the serious (or the merely curious) fan can study it closely. Alongside the ship rests the model's original stand, still carrying traces of the blue chalk used to make it disappear in front of the blue screen.

THE U.S.S. ENTERPRISE

NCC-1701

MODELS

362

Two years before *Star Trek* hit the airwaves, William Shatner and Leonard Nimoy appeared together in "The Project Strigas Affair," an episode of *The Man from U.N.C.L.E.* Little did they know at the time that their identities soon would become so intertwined within the public consciousness that the mention of one inevitably would raise thoughts of the other. In addition to appearing together in *Star Trek*, on television as well as in motion pictures, they often have been paired on projects as diverse as *T. J. Hooker* and commercials for Priceline.com.

In one Priceline commercial, Nimoy humorously reveals that the sponsor is catering more to him than to Shatner, the commercial campaign's official spokesperson. The ad took full advantage of Shatner's famous willingness to be the butt of the joke and his readiness to laugh at his public persona. Over the years, the actor's self-assertive sense of humor came to define his career, and even translated into the personality of his Emmy Award–winning character, attorney Denny Crane, of both *The Practice* and *Boston Legal*. In addition, Shatner has written numerous fiction and nonfiction books; offscreen, he raises champion American Saddlebred horses on his ranch in Kentucky.

Leonard Nimoy continues performing on stage (*Equus*, *Vincent*), screen (*Invasion of the Body Snatchers*), and television (*Mission: Impossible*, *Fringe*). After directing the feature films *Star Trek III: The Search for Spock* and *Star Trek IV: The Voyage Home*, he directed the hit comedy *3 Men and a Baby*, which ranked as the highest-grossing box office hit of 1987. Nimoy has published two autobiographies, numerous books of poetry, and several critically acclaimed collections of black-and-white photography. In 2008, the newly renovated Griffith Observatory in Los Angeles dedicated the Leonard Nimoy Event Horizon Theater, a two-hundred-seat multimedia venue for educational programs and activities. On the other side of the country, Symphony Space in New York renamed the historic Thalia Theater the Leonard Nimoy Thalia Theater in recognition of the actor's philanthropic contribution to its renovation. Nimoy recently reprised the role of Spock in the 2009 theatrical relaunch of the franchise, titled, fittingly, *Star Trek*.

363

Following *Star Trek*'s cancellation, Gene Roddenberry continued to work in the entertainment industry. Over the next few years, he created several extended pilots that aired as television movies, including *Genesis II* (1973), *The Questor Tapes* (1974), *Planet Earth* (1974), and *Spectre* (1977). None of the pilots generated high enough ratings to be green-lit as a series. An animated *Star Trek* series featuring the vocal talents of many of the show's regulars debuted in 1973 and ran for two seasons. Although critically acclaimed, *The Animated Series* only served to whet fans' appetites for *Star Trek*'s return to live action.

During this period, the fan community, encouraged by Roddenberry's appearances at *Star Trek* conventions across the country, was abuzz with rumors about just such a return. Paramount Pictures actually began preproduction on a *Star Trek* television revival, to be called *Star Trek: Phase II*. The series, set to air in 1978, would have taken place during Kirk's second five-year mission aboard the *Enterprise*. But plans for the series were scuttled when *Star Wars* ushered in an era of science fiction mega-movies. Paramount executives, noting the change in the public's viewing habits, shifted their efforts to producing a *Star Trek* movie.

The result was *Star Trek: The Motion Picture* (1979), which demonstrated to the studio that fans who'd previously watched *Star Trek* on television for free would spend money to see it on the big screen. Although the studio continued to make *Star Trek* films, Roddenberry's involvement with them diminished after *The Motion Picture*. By 1987, however, Paramount realized that it could continue its successful movie franchise *and* support a new *Star Trek* TV series. Once again, Roddenberry was invited to create and produce a new series for the medium he loved best. The result—*Star Trek: The Next Generation*—ran for seven seasons, producing 178 hours of extremely popular television. Sadly, Roddenberry passed away during season five, leaving the cast and crew to explore the Final Frontier without him.

Majel Barrett-Roddenberry became the torchbearer for her husband's creative efforts, serving as executive producer and performer in two series based on his concepts: *Gene Roddenberry's Earth: Final Conflict* and *Gene Roddenberry's Andromeda*. The latter series, which starred actor Kevin Sorbo, was particularly successful and ran for five seasons.

In 1997, a capsule containing a portion of Eugene Wesley Roddenberry's ashes was carried above Earth onboard the Pegasus XL rocket; as planned, the rocket disintegrated, dispersing the producer's ashes high in the atmosphere. Following Majel Barrett-Roddenberry's death in 2008, the couple's son, Eugene Roddenberry Jr., announced that her ashes, along with the remainder of his father's ashes, would be launched into deep space in 2012.

Over the years, *Star Trek*'s characters and their heroic adventures have inspired future scientists, astronauts, politicians, physicians, and educators—humans of all races and nationalities—to strive toward an upbeat future of possibilities. A future in which all of mankind's ills could be healed, and where technology worked for the good of everyone. In short, a future where a United Federation of Planets might be possible, with hundreds of different cultures working together toward galactic cooperation.

Whether or not the actual future develops like the fictitious one that Gene Roddenberry created, *Star Trek* does seem to be influencing its course.

At his personal appearances, DeForest Kelley was fond of sharing letters he'd received from doctors around the world telling him that they'd gone to medical school because of Bones McCoy.

During *Star Trek*'s first season, as Nichelle Nichols states in her autobiography, *Beyond Uhura*, she had the opportunity to meet Dr. Martin Luther King, who told her that he was a big fan of the series and felt the character of Uhura was a role model for black children and young women across the country.

Following *Star Trek*'s cancellation, Nichols worked closely with NASA on a special project to recruit minority and female personnel for the space agency. One of those recruits, former NASA astronaut Mae Jemison, has cited Uhura as her inspiration for wanting to enter the space program.

A number of *Star Trek* actors—most recently George Takei—have been invited to speak on various topics at NASA's Goddard Space Flight Center.

In 2009, the official poster promoting the International Space Station's Expedition 21 featured that crew's three American astronauts and three Russian cosmonauts dressed in *Star Trek: The Next Generation* uniforms.

While the personnel of NASA don't exactly shout from the rooftops about their affinity with *Star Trek*, it's fair to say that a sizable percentage of persons who chose a career within the space program have watched at least one of the *Star Trek* series on a regular basis. Entering the words "Star Trek" into the search section of www.nasa.gov will net several dozen items about *Star Trek*'s connection with the agency.

It certainly *seems* as if the dream *Star Trek* inspired has obtained liftoff!

365

"Space . . . the final frontier. These are the voyages of the Starship Enterprise. Its five-year mission: To explore strange new worlds . . . to seek out new life and new civilizations . . . to boldly go where no man has gone before."
—the Star Trek "preamble," as spoken by Captain James T. Kirk

366

ACKNOWLEDGMENTS

We wish to express our heartfelt gratitude to the gracious people who lent their time, their talents, and their memories to this project.

For answering myriad questions at any and all hours, for pitching in and helping out when we were floundering, for being the most honorable keepers of the flame a television show/franchise/cultural phenomenon could ever deserve: Michael and Denise Okuda.

For the amazing images you provided, thank you to: Michelle Andonian and Emily Wallace; Mike Carano; John Farley for his photo of Vasquez Rocks; Gerald Gurian at startrekpropauthority.com; Brian Heiler at megomuseum.com and plaidstallions.com; Beth Jacques at mptv images; Richard L. Jefferies; Ray Pelosi of Graphic Imaging Technology Inc.; Ken Regan/Camera 5; Robbie Robinson; Joe Sena; Angelique Trouvere and Jeff Maynard; Richard G. Van Treuren; Cathy Elkies and Kate Brambilla at Christie's; Curt McAloney, David Tilotta, and Dave Rohlf at startrekhistory.com; and especially our beacon of light at CBS Consumer Products, guiding our way through the studio's archive of Star Trek imagery, the one and only Marian Cordry. We couldn't have done it without you, Marian.

For the interviews, images, and assistance you gave, thank you to: D. C. Fontana; Trish Graboske, Margaret Weitenkamp, Eric Long, and Mark Avino at the Smithsonian Institution; Bruce Hyde; Joyce Kogut; Devra Langsam; Tanya Lemani; and Joyce Yasner.

For the fanzines upon which you lavished so much attention so long ago, we send our appreciation to: Lori Chapek-Carleton and Gordon Carleton; Sherna Comerford (and once again Devra Langsam); Connie Faddis; and Sharon Ferraro and Paula Smith.

We owe unbounded attribution to authors of previous Star Trek tomes, whose great works provided enlightenment when we needed it most: Alan Asherman; James Blish; Jeff Bond; Myrna Culbreath; Tim Gaskill and the other good folks formerly at StarTrek.com; David Gerrold; Richard L. Jefferies (again!); Robert H. Justman; DeForest Kelley; Jaqueline Lichtenburg; Sondra Marshak; Nichelle Nichols; Michael Okuda and Denise Okuda; Stephen Whitfield Poe; Judith and Garfield Reeves-Stevens; Herbert F. Solow and Yvonne Fern Solow; George Takei; Bjo Trimble; Joan Marie Verba; and Joan Winston.

At CBS Consumer Products, we wish to thank John Van Citters and Risa Kessler. And at CBS Digital: Max Gabl, Niel Wray, and David LaFountaine.

To those fan-driven Star Trek sites across the Web universe, keeping the flame alive for generations past and generations to come, thank you.

At Abrams, we wish to thank our fearless, persistent, and ever-patient editor, Eric Klopfer, as well as copy editor Richard Slovak and, of course, Charles Kochman.

And a special thank-you for your friendship and assistance: Margaret Clark; Dan Curry; Dean Devlin; Jeff Erdmann; Brian Fies; Joyce Fitzpatrick at Los Angeles County Parks; and finally, while at the same time first and foremost, Gene Roddenberry.

Editor: Eric Klopfer
Project Manager: Charles Kochman
Photo Archivist: Marian Cordry
Designers: Seth Labenz and Roy Rub of Topos Graphics
Design Manager: Neil Egan
Production Managers: Jules Thomson and Ankur Ghosh

Library of Congress Cataloging-in-Publication Data
Block, Paula M.
  Star Trek : the original series 365 / Paula M. Block with Terry J. Erdmann.
    p. cm.
  ISBN 978-0-8109-9172-9
  1. Star Trek television programs--Miscellanea. I. Erdmann, Terry J. II.
  Title. III. Title: Star Trek three hundred sixty-five.
PN1992.8.S74B55 2010
791.45'75--dc22

                2010003284

All images provided by CBS Studios Inc., with the exception of the following:

Paula M. Block: Spreads 84, 151 (right-hand page, at right), 152 (right-hand page, at right), 153, 228 (right-hand page, at right), 301 (left-hand page), 349 (left-hand page), 353
Mike Carano: Spread 286
Christie's, Inc.: Spreads 69, 211, 281 (left-hand page), 297 (right-hand page, at left)
John Farley: Spread 105
Getty Images: CBS Photo Archive: Spread 228 (right-hand page, at left)
GAB Archive: Spread 22 (right-hand page, at left)
Hulton Archive: Spread 21 (right-hand page, at right)
Gerald Gurian: Spreads 10, 17, 18, 21 (right-hand page, at left), 23, 24 (right-hand page, at right), 30, 40, 75 (right-hand page, at left), 94, 143 (right-hand page, at left), 264, 275 (right-hand page, at right)
Michelle Andonian: Spreads 11, 26, 27, 29, 210 (right-hand page). [Props courtesy of Gerald Gurian]
Brian Heiler: Megomuseum.com: Spread 351 (except right-hand page at left, center)
Plaidstallions.com: Spread 350
Bruce Hyde: Spread 55
Richard L. Jefferies: Spreads 43 (right-hand page), 102 (right-hand page), 191 (right-hand page, at left), 275 (right-hand page, at left), 314
Devra Langsam: Spreads 4 (left-hand page), 5, 59, 77, 90 (left-hand page), 91, 93 (left-hand page), 150, 168 (left-hand page), 180, 189 (left-hand page), 201 (left-hand page), 218, 224 (left-hand page), 228 (left-hand

page), 232, 233 (left-hand page), 252, 255 (right-hand page), 258, 262, 290 (right-hand page), 308 (left-hand page), 325 (left-hand page), 355
Tanya Lemani: Spread 181 (right-hand page)
Curt McAloney, David Tilotta, and Dave Rohlf / Startrekhistory.com: Spreads 8 (right-hand page, at right), 31, 221 (right-hand page), 248, 254, 265 (right-hand page), 271, 272, 273 (left-hand page), 319 (left-hand page), 329 (left-hand page)
mptv: © 1978 Bruce McBroom / mptvimages.com: Spread 204 ; © 1978 Gene Trindl / mptvimages.com: Spreads 173, 152 (right-hand page, at left), 217 (right-hand page, at left), 292 (right-hand page, at left), 292 (right-hand page, at right), 301 (right-hand page) ; © 1978 Ken Whitmore / mptvimages.com: Spreads 151 (right-hand page, at left), 362 (right-hand page, at left), 362 (right-hand page, at right)
NASA: Spread 357
Michael and Denise Okuda: Spreads 123, 133 (left-hand page), 307 (left-hand page)
Ray Pelosi / Graphic Imaging Technology, Inc.: Spread 352
Bob Plant / Round 2: Spread 349 (right-hand page)
Stephen Edward Poe: Spreads 114, 263
Regan Pictures, Inc.: © Ken Regan: Spreads 238, 354
Joe Sena: Spread 351 (right-hand page at left, center)
Smithsonian National Air and Space Museum: Spreads 359, 360
Mark Avino: Spreads 158, 270 (right-hand page), 361
Eric Long: Front-cover image
Angelique Trouvere and Jeff Maynard: Spread 356 (left-hand page [all], and right-hand page, at right)
Richard G. Van Treuren: Spread 143 (right-hand page, at right), 172, 234
Joyce Yasner: Spread 356 (right-hand page, at left)

Published in 2010 by Abrams, an imprint of ABRAMS. All rights reserved. No portion of this book may be reproduced, stored in a retrieval system, or transmitted in any form or by any means, mechanical, electronic, photocopying, recording, or otherwise, without written permission from the publisher.

Printed and bound in China
10 9 8 7 6 5 4

Abrams books are available at special discounts when purchased in quantity for premiums and promotions as well as fundraising or educational use. Special editions can also be created to specification. For details, contact specialmarkets@abramsbooks.com or the address below.

THE ART OF BOOKS SINCE 1949

115 West 18th Street
New York, NY 10011
www.abramsbooks.com